A Fool's Gold

A Novel of
Suspense and Romance

Rae Richen

A Fool's Gold
A Novel of Suspense and Romance
by Rae Richen

Published in the United States of America by

Back Beat Publications
an imprint of Lloyd Court Press
3034 N.E. 32nd Avenue
Portland, Oregon, 97212
www.lloydcourtpress.org
Cover design by Diana Kolsky
Book Design by S.R. Williams
Paper 978-1-943640-10-2
E-book 978-1-943640-11-9

Library Page

Publisher's Cataloging-In-Publication Data
(Prepared by The Donohue Group, Inc.)

Names: Richen, Rae, author.
Title: A Fool's Gold: [a novel of Suspense and Romance] /
Rae Richen.
Description: Portland, Oregon: Back Beat Publications, an
imprint of Lloyd Court Press, [2020] | Subtitle from
copyright page.
Identifiers: ISBN 9781943640102 (paperback) | ISBN
9781943640119 (ebook)
Subjects: LCSH: Women mining engineers--United States--
History--19th century--Fiction. | Anthracite coal mines and
mining--Colorado--Crested Butte--History--19th century--
Fiction. | Murder--Investigation--Colorado--Crested Butte--
History--19th century--Fiction. | LCGFT: Romance fiction,
American. | Thrillers (Fiction)
Classification: LCC PS3618.I34 F66 2020 (print) | LCC
PS3618.I34 (ebook) | DDC 813/.6--dc23

Dedication

James N. Frey, Mitch Luckett, Bonnie Bean Graham, Eric
Witchey, Barb and Woody Spriggs, Dick and Gretchen
Williams, all of whom were helpful in the development of
this story and in the research for its details.

CHAPTER ONE

March 1878
Schuylkill County, Pennsylvania

Caroline Trewartha walked with care so the guards couldn't guess at the hardware she carried into the courthouse under her dress. Edging around the crowd of reporters and onlookers she entered the side door. In the echoing marble hall, a sign informed her that seats for spectators were filled on the main floor. She would have to climb to the balcony.

"Tarnation," she muttered. Steeling herself, Caroline grabbed the polished maple rail and lifted the front gathers of her traveling dress. She forced her splinted left leg to rise.

"Don't look up," she told herself. "Just go." Concentrating, she took each stair one motion at a time. The foot-worn risers seemed determined to make her high-buttoned boots slip. Pain from her broken ribs made her breath catch. To take her mind off the shocking stabs, she pretended to climb a mountain in search of ore – a vein of iron, or copper.

At last she arrived at the upper level. Caroline adjusted the metal body brace under her dark blouse. She pushed open the paneled oak door and stood a dizzying height above the courtroom floor.

The trial had not yet begun. On the main floor, people jockeyed for the best view. She recognized three mine owners sitting together near the jury box as if to intimidate the jurymen.

Last December, one mine owner, Mr. Rodden, had argued violently with her father over the unsafe shoring timbers in

1

Rodden's huge mines. She knew that the other two owners, Jeb Horner and Lot Beinem, were equally careless of safety on their properties.

She suspected these three were the real cause of the January attack that had killed two friends and almost taken her father's life. These three skinflints would be delighted if a union organizer like Gryf Williams became the scapegoat for their attempts to wipe out a pesky safety-conscious engineer.

Behind the mine owners, a blue-suited phalanx of bodyguards and enforcers sprawled over one whole spectator's bench. One of these men reared his head back and glared briefly at the man in the balcony's front row.

Her father calmly sat near the balcony rail. His coat lay on the chair next to him. Reacting not to the man below, but to the squeaky hinge on the heavy door, he turned to see who had entered the balcony. His lined face frowned, then scowled, but he jumped up and came to her.

"Carrie, what are you doing out of the hospital?"

"I had to see the accused, if only for your sake." She did not tell him part of her leg bracing included a gun, brought in case anyone attacked him after the trial. She would be keeping an eye on those who celebrated the inevitable outcome. Someone had tried to kill her father and herself. She hoped that person would give himself away in that moment of triumph.

Her father had tried to keep the truth from her, but she knew he'd received several threats since the night of the murder attempt. When he thought her asleep at the hospital, she had found notes, written in a scrawled and probably disguised hand. They'd been wadded and hidden in his jacket pocket. One read: "Witness for Williams and next time your daughter dies with you."

Thus, she had to be at this trial. Defy the bully and protect Papa.

Her father offered his arm, which she accepted gratefully. No rail graced the high balcony steps. He guided her into the seat where his long wool coat still rested on the chair back. Caroline sat on that warm fabric, stiff and prim – the only pose possible given the temporary metal stiffening she wore since the mine accident that had nearly killed her.

She watched the prisoner enter the courtroom – Gryffyth Williams, union organizer, miner and doomed man. He held his head proudly. His long body moved with a grace she did not often see in stoop-shouldered and overworked miners. When he arrived at the defendants' dock, he shook hands with his lawyer.

Caroline believed his lawyer must be a brave man, or perhaps crazy. Since the fear and the hangings of last year, no lawyer in his right mind willingly defended a miner and union man in Schuylkill County, Pennsylvania.

The dark-haired prisoner glanced at a short man in the first row behind the rail – a man her father had described as Gryf Williams' brother. The brothers raised their chins, as if signaling each other to keep strong.

Their gesture might appear the same, but all resemblance ended there. Mr. Williams's long limbs, dark coloring, and dark eyes, seemed almost elegant, except that his curling hair already escaping its morning wash and combing. His shorter brother was barrel-chested, with stick-straight hair that thick pomade couldn't keep plastered down.

Her eyes took in the crowd: big men, sturdy women, several youngsters with coal-blackened nails and slicked back hair – whole mining families dressed in their Sunday clothes.

"Papa, who are all those people?" she whispered.

"His friends. His family. Being here, they risk never again working in these mines."

3

Gryffyth Williams' own gaze drew her attention further back in the courtroom. There stood a more polished man. Under his finely woven suit coat, the man wore a weskit of brocade silk. His wavy blond hair shone in the light from the nearby window. He had the long-legged ease of a man who has always fit his clothes and always known his high place in society. The man raised his right palm in greeting to Mr. Williams, who nodded and then sat next to his lawyer.

Caroline leaned toward her father. "Who is the man toward the back?"

"That's Alexander Kemp, an Englishman, but a friend of the Williams brothers from early days in Wales. He has sold his horse farm to pay Mr. Williams' defense."

Caroline glanced at him again. A friend indeed, to put so much at risk for a condemned man.

** **

The jury would condemn him. Gryf Williams saw it in their grim faces as they filed into the courtroom. Twenty-seven good years to end on the gallows – exactly as his brutal father had often predicted. Gryf stood rigid, unable to hear anything for the pounding in his ears. He knew the beating of his blood signaled fear – the fear his friend James Roarity had talked about last year.

Since last June, many nights had brought Gryf nightmares about the last moments of James Roarity, hanged in the Pottsville prison yard for belonging to the Molly Maguires, a secret miners' organization. The trials of Roarity and thirteen other men had left Pennsylvania communities fearful of all union activity. And because of Pennsylvania's fear, Gryf, and those who stood with him, were in danger.

Gryf's attention riveted on the slow march of the jurors to their places in the box. Resigned to the sentence he would receive, Gryf thought of everything he must tell his brother, Samuel. He prayed

4

there would be one chance to talk to Samuel in the few days before the law took his life. Samuel and their friend, Alex, must listen to him at last.

As soon as Gryf had found the bodies in the alley near the bordello, he'd known that being first on the scene would be used against him. After making certain Carl Trewartha had been safely taken to the hospital, Gryf had tried to get Sam and Alex to leave town.

Yet, even when he'd been arrested, his foolish older brother refused to abandon him. And Alex had spent all he owned in Gryf's defense.

But the smell of conspiracy tainted this trial – two lying witnesses, including the bawd who'd followed him out of the brothel and then pretended to faint at the sight of murdered men. Throughout the trial, only one honest man came forth – Carl John Trewartha. Trewartha's courageous testimony had probably been made at the cost of his career as a geologist and mining engineer.

The jurymen did not look at him, but Gryf stared at the foreman, determined to force one person to acknowledge the truth. Sweat ran down the foreman's face and into his starched collar. He glanced at Gryf, and then his gaze held for a moment.

Gryf raised his chin to show the foreman he condemned an honest man of a heinous crime.

The judge entered the courtroom. All rose to their feet. At the bailiff's command, everyone in the courtroom sat. The judge asked for the jury's verdict. The foreman's gaze dropped from Gryf's. He lifted a piece of paper and read in a halting voice.

"Of the charge of attempting to murder Carl John Trewartha on January 10th, 1878, we find the defendant, Gryffyth Williams, not guilty."

Silence filled the courtroom. *Not guilty?*

Not guilty! Gryf's body went cold. They'd believed Trewartha after all. But Trewartha had testified only about what happened to himself. Since he'd been the first one shot, he could not claim to have seen the others go down. The jury would believe the deputy and the whore about the other murders. Gryf stiffened his spine, ready for the worst. The foreman raised the paper a second time.

"Of the charge of the murder of Alman Friedmann on January 10th, 1878, we find the defendant, Gryffyth Williams, not guilty."

Gryf's legs shook. He gripped the table. It would be the next charge, then. They would get him on the last one. The scoundrels would not have bribed the witnesses and left the jury untouched. Willing steel into his bones, he held himself upright, ready for the blow. The foreman stared only at his paper as once more he read.

"Of the charge of the murder of George Pankhurst on January 10th, 1878, we find the defendant, Gryffyth Williams, not guilty."

Gryf stared at the man in disbelief. Behind Gryf, the courtroom doors swung open as reporters rushed out.

**

Caroline stared at the jury foreman in disbelief.

"Thank God," her father shouted over the noise of the celebration. "Justice at last!"

Caroline winced as her father's hug pulled her dislocated shoulder. He became aware of the brace ramrodding her back.

"Sorry Darlin'. It's just so incredible that we've won."

We? she thought.

"Papa, if Mr. Williams didn't try to kill you, the killer is still out there."

Her father's grin of triumph slackened, but only for a second. "You're right, Sweetheart. However, your Papa is celebrating this incredible moment. Later, I'll tackle that other question."

When he turned back to the noise and jubilation on the courtroom floor, she followed his gaze. The handsome Mr. Kemp appeared to be speechless in the back row. At the prisoner's table, Gryf Williams hugged his lawyer.

The moment, indeed, seemed incredible, Caroline thought. Given the power of mine owners and the fear of the community, this could only happen if Williams knew something that the mine owners wanted kept secret. This year, 'Not guilty' verdicts in Schuylkill County were never about justice. They were about who held the high cards in a game of poker.

She wanted to know what cards Gryf Williams and his friends held that had forced the mine owners to fold. No doubt about it. Williams probably knew who tried to kill her father. She would have to force Williams to lay down his cards so she would know how to protect Papa.

**

Someone pounded Gryf on the back, his lawyer hugged him, others shouted, but Gryf could not take his eyes off the foreman. Even as the judge gaveled for silence and brought an end to the proceedings, the jury foreman stood in the box, staring at Gryf, the scrap of paper still in his hand. He leaned toward Gryf. His every muscle asked, "Did we do right?"

Gryf brought his right hand to his heart. "I promise you," he whispered.

"Damned right you're not guilty," shouted Amos Jawarski from the assembly behind Gryf. "That Carl Trewartha fella even said so – said it was never you that night."

The foreman nodded at Gryf, then sat down hard on the jurymen's bench. Within a blink, all of life lay in front of him. One last time, the judge brought down the gavel in the midst of chaos. Dazed, Gryf stared around the courtroom, watching the reaction of his friends. These people had believed in him thoroughly.

The mine owners and their ruffians filed out, faces tight, fists in pockets.

At his elbow, Gryf's short, red-faced lawyer whooped their triumph. Amos danced in the center aisle, though the security guard pulled at his elbow. In the row behind the defendant's table, Gryf's older brother, Samuel, held tight to his wife, Susan, and cried on her shoulder. Beyond Samuel, four rows of miners and their wives grinned, shouted, prayed and hugged each other. Big Olaf rocked back and forth, moaning, "Thank you, Jesus."

In the back row sat Alex Kemp, his long, patrician face as white as winter. *My God*, Gryf thought. *Alex is in greater shock than I am.*

"Ho, Alex!" Gryf caught his attention. Alex shoved unruly blond waves off his forehead, rallied, and gave Gryf the sign of triumph from their childhood – two arms flexed overhead.

Gryf grinned. He ran jerky fingers through his own wild hair and tried to take a deep breath of his new life. As he gulped in sweet air, he searched the courtroom for the other man he hoped to see – the one witness the police and the mine owners could never subvert or discredit – the geologist, Carl John Trewartha.

"Isaac," Gryf said to his lawyer. His voice cracked. He cleared his throat and yelled over the din of the mad courtroom. "Isaac, I want to meet him."

Isaac stopped polishing his glasses and stared up at Gryf with glistening eyes. "Trewartha? Not a good idea."

"He saved my life."

"You meet with him, and the mine-owning bloodsuckers will ruin his life. Leave it be, Gryf. He knows how you feel."

Gryf leaned down toward his stalwart friend and caught his eye. "There's one big problem here, Isaac."

"I know," Isaac said, wiping at his red face to rid it of tears. "Somebody killed Friedmann and Pankhurst."

"And that person is still free. Get Trewartha to guard himself."

8

Isaac stuffed his linen into his vest pocket and nodded at Gryf. "I'll do my best, but he's hard to find these days."

"Hiding out?"

"No. His daughter's been in a mining accident. He's mostly with her, under guard at the hospital."

"His daughter?" Through Gryf's mind there flashed a picture of a little girl under heavy rubble. His heart couldn't compass the idea. "A child?"

Isaac shook his head. "A young woman, twenty-four years or so. Nearly dead when they found her."

"God help the man." Gryf whispered. "What can I do?"

"Stay out of his life." Isaac punctuated his meaning by putting the wire frames of his glasses over his ears with a rhythmic snap.

Samuel's voice interrupted. "Trewartha's upstairs."

The three of them glanced up. At the balcony rail stood a tall, white-haired man of middle years. He gazed down upon Gryf without smiling, but with such intensity that Gryf knew Trewartha sent a message of congratulations, and of fatherly advice. The man's courage alone made Gryf want to be a better human being. The fatherly advice would be taken. No more brothels for him.

Next to Trewartha stood a pale young woman with thick auburn hair. Her dark eyes held steady upon him with the same depth of feeling as the man. But her eyes flashed a message of disbelief, and a question he couldn't quite read.

"His daughter," Isaac said. Gryf could plainly see the resemblance in face and courage. He had a quick impression of dark, shining dress fabric and shoulders covered by what must be her father's outsized black wool coat, the fabric a frame for her firm chin, delicate lips and emerald eyes beneath expressive, reproachful brows.

"*Prydferth*," Gryf whispered. "A beauty." Her belligerent stance mimicked her father's attitude, but her glare of accusation did not.

9

She squared her shoulders as if to say, *"I will find the truth in spite of you."*

That motion of her shoulders made Gryf's glance flick over her body, a lithe and enticing roundness. In response to his obvious assessment, the young woman jerked the lapels of her father's black coat across her bosom. Heat invaded Gryf's cheeks. He'd been caught in a fine, life-filled act – wanting a woman. He must consecrate this moment.

"What is she?" he whispered.

"A mining engineer," Isaac said.

Isaac's answer jerked Gryf from sylphic dreams.

"She?" he blustered. "Works in the mines?"

Isaac nodded. "But after her accident, I doubt her father will allow her to continue working. The accident meant to discourage him from witnessing for you."

Gryf's fingers tightened on the table edge. "Isaac, warn them."

"They know."

Gryf bowed toward Trewartha and his daughter. *A woman engineer?* He wondered. *Women in mines are bad luck. And after such an accident . . .*

Miss Trewartha thrust her small chin at him, a gesture so like his own he had to work not to smile. Her father waved his hat at Gryf, took his daughter's arm and helped her up the balcony steps. Only then did Gryf noticed her limp.

His sudden angry thoughts were interrupted by Isaac's voice. "If I were the two of them, I would be headed for Canada."

Gryf turned to his lawyer. "My great friend, I've put them and you in danger."

Isaac waved away the problem. "Don't worry. I leave for Denver tonight."

Gryf smiled, relieved. "You took a pick to every crack in their case and widened it until gold poured out."

10

"I had the pick," Isaac said, "Carl Trewartha had the dynamite. The jury had courage."

Alex joined them, pointing toward the jury box. "Their lives in Pennsylvania are finished."

Gryf glanced at the back of the jury foreman. The man hesitated before the courtroom door. He lifted his head and plunged out into a howling crowd. The jurymen would suffer indeed for this day.

Gryf put a hand on Alex's shoulder. "Thank you for sticking by me."

Alex's wide smile came slowly, "I plan to stick until we're done."

"Isaac Brown," Gryf said, "at last you can meet Alex Kemp."

"Ah, our under-cover, investigative bank roll."

As Isaac and Alex talked, Gryf pulled Samuel's head into the crook of his shoulder. "I'm free, Sam. Good God, I'm alive."

Samuel's arms awkwardly encircled Gryf's waist. Gryf laughed down into his brother's hair, "Little Big Brother," he whispered, "we've got to be out from here."

Sam straightened. "Where'll we go?"

"Colorado. I've a grand feeling about those mountains."

Samuel cinched his belt a notch tighter, the gesture he'd always used before they went into battle together. "We will climb out of this, Gryffyth."

Gryf swallowed around the tightness in his throat. "'rydyn, we will. You and Alex keep track of the fellows for me. When I find a mine we can all work, I'll telegraph."

Alex Kemp's lanky frame leaned against the table. "A mine and some range land, please."

Gryf chuckled. "I don't understand ye, boyo. Ye stand to inherit all the grazing land you might ever want in North Wales."

Alex studied his fingernails. "That land comes with sheep, not cattle. No Gryf and no Sam – a dull life."

"My God," whispered Sam, gazing around the emptying courtroom. "Could we now manage to be a bit duller?"

The reality of this great day hit Gryf at last. He stared at the jury box. "I promise, Sam. From now to forever, I'll be as boring as ever man can be."

He glanced up at the balcony in time to see Carl Trewartha, now wearing his own black coat. Next to him, the slender young woman in an iridescent purple gown exited into the upper hall. After her, the oak door swung shut with a bang.

CHAPTER TWO

June 1880
Two years later

Caroline Trewartha felt heat rise in her neck. She raised her voice to be heard over the echoing din of trains and people. "Mr. Jordan," she said to the ticket seller, "both my ticket and your schedule advertise two trains daily from Denver west to Isabeau. The next is scheduled to leave in one hour. It says noon, sir. Noon."

"Can't believe everythin' w'at you read, Miss." Mr. Jordan shuffled his papers and glanced at those behind her in line. "You'll 'ave to wait 'till tomorrow morning."

She felt like a petulant child, not a twenty-six-year-old woman. Far behind her a man in the ticket line called. "Move on, lady."

"With her looks," whispered another, "she'll get her way."

Caroline yanked her shawl about her shoulders and across her blouse. She swished her tartan taffeta skirts to take up as much space as possible. In her most commanding voice – her best imitation of a Blue Mountain mine manager, she addressed the ticket seller.

"Mr. Jordan, I will speak to your superior, at once."

Jordan spat off to his left. "My superior is 'avin' a bit o' supper," he said. "You'll 'ave to step aside and await 'is arrival."

Caroline tugged on her mother's paisley shawl. "Mr. Jordan, I am the Western States Representative of Allied Mines."

"That mean something to me?"

Caroline realized with chagrin that she had been about to act like a man – to use title and position in order to force compliance from her adversary. She could no longer pass for a young gentleman.

13

That useful pretense hadn't been possible since her eighteenth year, her last at the university.

Petty fools like Mr. Jordan hated to have women flaunt power. Nowadays, she had to try the method she'd watched Aunt Agatha employ over and over – help the man imagine having greater authority for himself. She hated it, but she could do it.

She stepped closer and spoke softly. "My responsibilities, Mr. Jordan, give me the chance to help further your career with the Union Pacific."

Mr. Jordan leaned toward her. "I don't make the schedule, Miss. I only work here."

"You sell tickets now. Soon you might be supervisor of the entire rail yard."

He tilted his head to one side. "How can that be?"

"You have an opportunity, Mr. Jordan," she said, "In weeks, Allied will be shipping whole trainloads of coal as well as silver and gold. If Denver becomes less convenient, we may use another rail yard. Pueblo, for instance, is nearer to our source."

Mr. Jordan's fine red mustache twitched. His lips tightened. "I can't change the train schedule."

"But you may have the foresight to show my company, and me, the advantage of renewing our shipping and storage contract with Denver."

"Miss. That noon train is a freight."

"Search your records," she said with the lilting voice Aunt Agatha used. "You will recall that freight may be accompanied by an agent. On your short list of agents is myself, C. J. Trewartha."

Mr. Jordan glanced at the papers in front of him. His face scrunched with surprise. "But ma'am, the other agents are . . ."

"Men," she finished. "Now please call a porter to carry my crate and valise to the loading dock."

Caroline raised an expectant eyebrow. The fellow scowled, but at last he barked out, "Porter!" and he punched her ticket for the noon train.

**

Half an hour later, several porters had wrestled her crate of tools onto a freight car headed to Isabeau. Caroline had telegraphed ahead for the stationmaster to hire a buckboard, draft horses and a drover for the last ten miles up the mountain to the mines. As soon as the head porter put a padlock on the freight-car door and walked off with her generous tip, Caroline glanced about, looking for the hired security man her father had sent – perhaps a Pinkerton Man – to make sure she traveled safely.

Hiring protection for each other had been the one thing they'd agreed on. She had asked several union friends of hers to follow and protect her father as he checked out their lead to Radford Mines.

She looked over the crowded train station, believing she would be able to pick out her father's man. So far, however, she'd seen no one she thought hovered too near, or followed her too anxiously.

For a moment, she thought she saw a gold waistcoat flash through the crowd, but couldn't see any more of the wearer than the brown brimmed hat on the head of a tall man.

That posture of his seems familiar, she thought. Perhaps he's father's hired guard.

"Telegram for Tree-wartha!" a young boy with very curly hair held the telegram aloft and gazed out over the passengers and freight.

Caroline glanced around to see if anyone watched for the person who would pick up the telegram. The brown brimmed hat had disappeared. No one else seemed to pay the least attention to the boy, so she approached him.

"I am C.J. Trewartha," she said.

15

The smile in his grimy face brightened. "Yeah? That's great. I thought maybe you was already gone." He handed her the slip of flimsy paper, and waited. "Any answer, ma'am?"

She opened the folded message. "Stay Colorado all costs. Action picks up in brotherly love. Join you when mining for truth pays off. Signed C.J. T."

Carl John Trewartha. Her father had sent this telegram from Philadelphia – the city of brotherly love – the city where murder and hangings were daily fare. She prayed her union friends watched his back as he searched for those who threatened them. Now more than ever, she wished he were here.

But she was on a trail of her own. Just this morning she had picked up a letter from Hume, the owner of Allied Mines.

Miss Trewartha,

Proceed to small town in mountains called By-Gum. Mine owned by a cooperative led by a man named Gryffyth Williams. Watch yourself. This man once accused of murder in Pennsylvania. Got off free by a fluke. Now owes Allied large sums within the next few months. We count on you to help them make enough for these payments. Contract in accompanying package.

Amazing information! At last, her chance to find Williams and learn what he knew about the man who tried to kill her father. She still believed Williams held the key to the whole nasty set-up back in Schuylkill.

Gryffyth Williams, owner of the mine where she would soon be expected as engineer and consultant. What luck. Neither she nor her father had been able to find out where he had gone.

"Ma'am?" the telegram boy looked at her through his mess of curls and said. "Was you going to reply?"

She folded the message from her father, gave the boy a tip and said, "No reply, as yet."

16

The boy took her offered coin, bit it without a second thought, and then said. "There's a telegraph office up in Isabeau, if'n you change your mind."

**

The train ride to Isabeau included harrowing views of deep valleys and sudden cliffs such as never appeared in the worn mountains of Pennsylvania, or even in most of the territory in Wyoming where Allied Mines worked.

At the small station in Isabeau, it cost her a great deal of money and a crew of seven to get her crate of tools from the train onto a wagon. The movers spent much time yelling contradictory orders to each other, in the fashion of self-important men.

After that exasperating episode, Caroline, her crate and one old miner endured a three-hour jolt along a narrow wagon road up another two thousand feet. She grew ever more grateful that she'd been able to dispense with the body brace and the leg splint before making this trip. "A very fine recovery," her doctor had announced. "But I do hope you will stay out of mines."

She had not told him of her plan to travel and work in Wyoming and now to Colorado.

Caroline gripped her seat on the buckboard as the unwieldy wagon rose above the timberline. The drover, Duncan, urged his team ever upward on the trail. On the other bench, across the wagon and beyond her big crate, sat a grumpy little man who pulled his hat over his face and slept through the worst jostling. She dismissed the idea that he might be her father's hired protection. Perhaps, she reasoned, that secretive person followed her trail hidden from view behind boulders.

Caroline studied the mountainside for signs of him and grew awed by the spring beauty of high mountains. On her right, a massive butte hovered above a sparkling alpine valley. In the lowland, fresh grasses, alpine thistles and the soft leaves of Black-eyed Susan poked out of the long-frozen ground. Caroline breathed in the fragrance of new green.

She could taste the excitement of good, hard work, the hunt for ore, finding clues in the folds of land, and in the vegetation. She ached to be responsible again for the careful construction that allowed men and equipment to operate safely hundreds of feet below the surface of the earth.

But she knew that her first job here would be to find out how Gryffyth Williams might have a connection to the murders. The man knew something. Why else had he been there exactly when hell came down on her father and his friends? What hold did he have over the jury, or what did he know that cowed the mine owners?

**

From under dark brows, Gryf Williams studied the buttressing ridges that rose to the butte above his mine. Birds chittered, Chipmunks tisked. Despite continued snow in the mountains above him, his valley awoke to spring. He'd come out of Mine Number One to repair the loose boards in the floor of his office shed, but as he strode toward the tool shed, Gryf listened carefully, hoping to hear more than chipmunks.

The familiar creaking of Duncan's wagon would be welcome. He desperately wanted Duncan and his big horses to haul the parts for the mine elevator around that last bend in the muddy road from Isabeau.

Gryf grabbed up nails, a hammer and scrap lumber, thinking. *Maybe Duncan'll have C.J. Trewartha, the new consultant, from Allied Mines in tow as well.*

For months, ever since the trial, he'd wanted to meet C. J. Trewartha. He wanted to show the man that Gryf Williams was worthy of the risk he'd taken to tell the truth. Now, the investor, Allied Mines, had hired the very man.

Without warning, birds ceased their noise. Gryf stopped walking. He glanced at the mountains. A marmot shrieked. Gryf felt tremors beneath his boots. An explosion rumbled across the mountains. He dropped his tools and whipped toward the west. He saw no plume, no rock-fall, no outward sign of a detonation. But what he'd heard could not be mistaken. Dynamite. Only a deeply buried charge could produce that muffled boom. And Gryf knew none of his men had set the charge.

Ach-y-fi! Sabotage!

Moments later, a second, thunderous blast sounded from the opposite direction. Gryf heard an avalanche of boulders crashing deep in the northeastern tributary valley.

A high, piping voice called. "Mister Williams, hey, Mister . . ."

Skinny, ten-year-old Jimmy Freya scampered between the legs of burros and the wheels of carts, as he charged out of the low haulage tunnel. Jimmy had little regard for flying hooves and switching tails. Gryf put out an arm for him to run into. Jimmy Freya had no brakes.

"What's fashing ye, bachgyn?" he asked, absorbing the boy's momentum with a backward step.

"Ol' Amos said come 'ee quick, sir. Water's pourin' through – Olaf's trapped."

Gryf signaled 'stop' to the boy's breathless report. "Get the boyos and the burros out of the haulage tunnel. Haul 'em out and stay out, you hear?"

Jimmy's back stiffened with pride. "Aye, Mister Williams." He flashed away on his commission.

Grabbing his leather gloves, Gryf chose the faster route, straight down the shaft instead of through the long tunnel. He dashed around the steam-powered furnace and ran to the temporary shed at the shaft entry. He shouted, "Amos, I'm coming down. Get the men out."

19

Of habit, he checked the pulley at the top of the shed. Grabbing the doubled rope, he wrapped it diagonally across his body and around his hip. He gripped the rope both above and behind, stepped into the wide bucket and lowered himself into the long dark hole.

With controlled speed, he sank into the guts of the mountain, away from sunlight and wind, down into dank darkness, playing the rope out so fast it burned his gloved palms. His nostrils dilated, sucking in acrid traces of burning leather, hardy ferns, ancient rock. His arms and hands worked automatically.

Every miner on his crew let a buddy crank him down, like a water bucket being lowered into a well. Gryf never counted on another man for his safety. He arrived at the bottom of the shaft in record time. Slogging through eight inches of water and around the escaping miners, Gryf heard the sound of sucking from only one of his two drainage pumps. The other pump had stopped entirely.

The wall lamp threw grotesque shadows on the main crosscut and illumined the crests of choppy waves. Near the lamp stood the entrance to the first coal room that followed the seam west into the mountain.

"Amos?" he called.

"Mess back here."

Gryf ducked his head and stepped into the room. Water poured from overhead. A slab of granite roof cracked, widening even as he looked at it.

"I want you out," he said to Amos.

"Olaf's back there. Water to his neck. Can't swim, the dumb Norskie."

Gryf glanced at Amos' who'd never put a toe in the Dyfi Creek.

"Olaf," Gryf shouted while shucking his thick boots. In the dark, he could barely see Olaf's white-blond shock of hair.

"Boss. Not long. Oh Lord Jesus . . ."

20

"Coming!" Gryf shouted. "Keep your arms movin', my man."
He thrust his boots at Amos and waded into the lake that now filled
the excavated room. He yelled, "Make sure the boys and burros are
out. We'll be right behind you."

"The roof," Amos protested.

Gryf didn't even glance up. Within steps, he was forced to swim.
As he approached the big man, fear stiffened Olaf's face into a
mask.

"Turn on your back," Gryf shouted, but Olaf's meaty hands
clamped on Gryf's shoulder. He climbed on Gryf – an island for a
drowning rat.

Gryf dove toward the bottom. Kicking away from Olaf's terror,
he circled Olaf's boots and came up behind him, grabbing his neck
and shoulders with one arm. For the moment he had the Norseman
stunned. Gryf's powerful legs kicked. His free arm pulled them
forward. Water rained down from the widening crack, pelting them
both.

He smelled oil before he saw the light. Amos's stubby body
stood, silhouetted at the edge of the lake where he held the lamp
high. Gryf kept his eye trained on that welcome vision as he
struggled toward the shallow end. Water sheeted in from above.
Gryf's muscles cramped with fatigue. His hand on Olaf's overall
strap felt like a claw. His mind focused on breathing. His spirit
concentrated on Amos and the light.

Olaf lunged up out of the water like a mad man. Gryf felt
Amos's pant leg brush his arm and realized they were in shallow
water at last. Amos took a stiff swing at Olaf's jaw – the quickest
way to control his crazy fear.

A loud crack followed the blow. For a moment, Gryf thought
Olaf's face had broken under the power of Amos' fist. A wall of
water slammed down on all three of them. The lamp drowned.

The roof.

21

"Get him out from here," Gryf shouted. He pushed himself up on his knees and grabbed Olaf's right arm as Amos grabbed the left. Hauling the big man's body, he and Amos slogged toward the main crosscut, turning right toward the burro tunnel. As they dragged up the long tunnel, they heard another thunderous crack followed immediately by the rumble and splash of boulders hitting the water.

Coal dust and water rushed at them. They stumbled out into the light of day followed by a blast of fist-sized rocks. Other men took Olaf's body from them. Water swirled, pulling at their legs.

Amos and Gryf fell on their faces at the feet of the burros. Gryf dragged in air. Nearby, Olaf sputtered and coughed. Gryf's heart thanked the good God for Olaf's life.

Jimmy Freya's boyish shout pleaded. "Get that burro away. Gonna kick Mr. Williams in the head."

"Yup," rasped Amos. "Gryf's rock head might lame that poor beastie."

Gryf winced. His head did feel like rock, but he caught the old man's eye and whispered, "Amos, before the flood, you hear those explosions?"

"Yup. Two. One west. One northeast. Down deep. And an avalanche. Set a-purpose, ye think?"

"Aye," Gryf said. He tried to get up, but his shoulders were limp lettuce.

"Bastards," said Amos. "Let's get Cordell, Mac and four other guys," he said. "We'll flush them out, wherever they are."

Olaf rolled over, hoisting his powerful shoulders up off the wet ground. "I come too."

"Rudy?" Gryf asked.

"Stop frettin', Gryf," said Amos. "Rudy Sperl's gone into Isabeau about them tools, and they ain't nobody else in Mines Two or Three today."

Gryf closed his eyes, grateful for Amos who understood his fear for the men. Gryf again attempted to rise.

Olaf stood. Once more he seemed himself – an enormous and immovable boulder. He reached down and lifted Gryf Williams as if he were a child, set him on his feet and mumbled, "Hope I didn't hurt you, Boss."

"*Nag.* Not hurt. Just winded."

Olaf gazed at his feet. "I kin find the explosions."

"Thanks, my man," Gryf said, recognizing Olaf's embarrassment.

Young Jimmy edged away from the men. Gryf didn't want boys searching for saboteurs.

"Jimmy, Keir, Joey, Sammy," Gryf said, "We've a big job to do, boyos."

"Aw, sir," Jimmy Freya slumped.

"Uncle Gryf!" whined the two smallest boys. "We wanna find the dyno-miters."

Gryf leaned down face to face with his eight-year-old nephews. "I need you gentlemen with me," he said. Joey pouted behind his straight black bangs. Sammy shook his long bangs out of his eyes and said. "What we get to do, eh?"

"Get to drain the mine and build a lake."

Sammy puffed out his chest. "Kin I skip school?"

"Not on your gazeesus, Sam. This work is after school only. Now let's hop to it. You know Miss Ellen would miss you."

Sammy brightened. "Oes, I make her laugh."

Gryf patted Sammy's head as he looked up over the steep valleys above By-Gum, thinking, Evil has caught us again.

Amos barked orders at Jimmy, who barked them in turn at his crew of boys. All four boys picked up sturdy shovels and marched after old Amos. At that moment, Gryf heard the squeal of Duncan's delivery wagon, and the snort of giant horses laboring up the switchbacks toward the high valley.

Jimmy ran for the overlook, waving his arms at the road below. "Hey-yah," he shouted, then reported, "Duncan's about two hours below, and he's got the shoring beams." He raced back toward them, yelling, "Dunc's got Rudy, and a ee-nor-muss box, and a dressed-up passenger."

"Great!" Gryf moaned, "I'll bet the dressed-up one is Carl Trewartha. And I wanted to impress him! Worst timing possible."

"No sir," shouted Jimmy. "That other 'un – she's nothin' but a woman."

"A woman? Must be one of Alex's. . ." Gryf stopped himself. Four youngsters gazed up at him. "Thank goodness, boyos," he hollered. "We've another week to get ready for Allied's inspector. Now let's to work here, eh."

CHAPTER THREE

Two hours after the little boy had shouted at them, Caroline's unwieldy chariot finally topped the last rise in the long, serpentine road. Duncan halted his team at the crest of their climb.

Before them lay a long and wide valley with fields of wheat beginning to poke green out of the winter snow. To the right, the steep sweep of a butte interrupted what seemed to be a view of two or three small valleys, separated from each other by a low but steep ridge. She guessed those valleys led northward, up toward the taller mountains of the Rockies.

Over the sides of the nearby butte, snow melt created waterfalls, ending in a stream that fed the fields and ran down into the bigger valley.

A man on a russet brown horse wheeled out of a side path toward the wagon. Leaning down from the height of his gelding, he smiled. "Welcome to By-Gum, Miss Trewartha."

Under the dust of his ride, she caught a glimpse of gold waistcoat and his brown jacket. The man from the Denver train station, she realized, so maybe her father's hired guard after all.

He swept off his brown-brimmed hat, revealing the golden hair she remembered from the trial in Schuylkill County Court. Mr. Williams' good friend.

"Miss Trewartha, I am Alexander Kemp. We've been awaiting your arrival." He gestured far down the sweep of snow and green, where she could see the darkening outline of a few small cabins. "The town is yonder," he said. "And a quarter mile to the south of the town is Mac Freya's farm. Mrs. Freya will be expecting you."

25

"Thank you, sir," she said, hoping she had just the right level of appreciation. Her hand checked the buttons on her jacket. Certainly, he might be a good man, but his interested gaze contained warmth she did not wish to contemplate. Besides, she really did not expect to need guarding in this little town.

Plus, she wished to work as long as the light lasted and didn't need an escort to Mrs. Freya's home.

"Miss Trewartha," he said, leaning close, "I hope I will see you again before you have to leave our mines."

She stiffened. "I expect to be here for some time."

"Very nice for us." Alex touched his forehead as if he were tipping his hat. "If you'll excuse me, I'll be off to my ranch." His blue eyes held her gaze a moment. Then Kemp nodded at the old man across the wagon. "Good day, Sperl. And you, Duncan."

As Kemp rode off up the side path, the older man glanced at Caroline, slouched into his seat and gave a snort.

"Mr. Sperl," she said, "are you always given to noisy displays of misanthropy?"

He wiped his nose with his sleeve. "I'm allergic to flummery and poppy-cock."

Not sure what she'd done to deserve this assessment, Caroline turned her face away from Sperl and studied the valley.

The lack of activity in the area disappointed her. There were few of the large buildings a fully operational mine would require – only one granite enclosed engine house, such as she expected to see over the mine shafts. And that one looked hardly adequate to hold a furnace for steam power, a winding engine, or a Boulton and Watts pump.

Duncan urged his tired team down into the valley. Caroline's concern grew with each turn of the wagon wheels. Closer to the town, she saw what appeared to be a blacksmith and carpenter's shop. Surrounding it at precarious angles, lay the debris of several

26

dismantled wheels, conveyor cars, the hulls of three miner's elevators and an assortment of rusted metal parts, all leaning upon each other for support.

As they neared the valley floor, Duncan hauled on the reins of his team. The wagon slowed.

"Ma'am?" said Mr. Sperl. She ignored him.

"Miss Treewart," he persisted. "You asked to be let off at the entry-shaft to the By-Gum Mine. This here's it."

"This?" Caroline looked around in dismay. Duncan had pulled the wagon to a stop next to the worst slop yard she'd ever seen.

"Ay-yup," Duncan said, pushing his grimy cap off his forehead and winking with a twitch at Mr. Sperl. "That over there – that's the shaft house."

Certain that he attempted to fool her, Caroline's gaze followed the line of his crooked finger to a little roof perched on four spindly poles next to the small engine house. The pole construction wouldn't keep rain out of the mineshaft, much less the twenty feet of snow they normally saw in a winter up here. Beyond the so-called shaft house stood several little . . . little donkeys she guessed they were . . .fifteen of them with their heads hanging between their shoulders, their thick hides twitching to keep flies at bay. She heard no sound of machinery and no sign of a working human being.

"I 'spec you want your big crate dropped here, too," Duncan said as he climbed down.

Caroline found the wits to say, "My good man, you don't 'drop' explosives, and certainly not here. From the looks of this yard, a fire started here would have gases enough to keep it fueled for days."

" 'Splosives! Damn, you never said nothin' 'bout 'splosives when we was loadin' this thing." Duncan glared up at her from the logs he unloaded off the sides of the wagon.

"There are valuable machines in there as well. They were my major concern at that time. It's just that you mentioned dropping the crate."

"Where do you want it *laid down*?" Duncan asked.

The old man, Sperl, slouched again, pulling his hat down over his bright blue eyes. His mouth twitched most peculiarly.

"Where?" pushed Duncan.

"I'm staying with the Freya family," Caroline said. "Set it upon their porch, I suppose."

"Porch indeed," mocked Sperl from under his hat. "Might as well suggest the parlor – why not the parlor?"

"Or where-ever Mrs. Freya would like it," Caroline said, glaring at both men. "And please tell Mrs. Freya I had to stop and get the work going."

"What makes you think the work ain't goin'?" Sperl asked.

"Do you see work?" Caroline gestured at a landscape devoid of workers.

Sperl snorted, tipped his hat up for a look and then said, "Missy, you gotta stop jumpin' at conclusions. If you been here any length of time, you'd know the By-Gum Mines is always at work, but the work can't always be seen."

Caroline ignored this stupid declaration. She talked to Mr. Duncan. "Would you tell Mrs. Freya I'll be over at dark. I'm sure one of the men can tell me how to find her home."

"Ask Jimmy Freya," offered Sperl. "He be one of the bucket boys in the mine. Little 'un. Never stops moving – can't miss him."

"Thank you," Caroline said. She climbed from the wagon, straightened her gabardine traveling skirt and gathered her frayed nerves before embarking across the murky field toward the wobbly looking shaft house.

She thought, *Caroline, you have seen worse than this. You've seen mines with no latrines. You have seen mines with slag heaps*

28

ready to collapse on the nearest home. You have seen any number of places where the miners know nothing of safe building practices. You can take charge and put even the By-Gum Mines in order.

And then another thought occurred to her. *Did my father cite a mine run by Gryffyth Williams for safety infractions? Was he asking the state of Pennsylvania to close down a dangerous mine?*

Her father, however, had been adamant that Gryffyth Williams had no reason to want him dead. "Gryf Williams is a good miner and a good leader," her father said.

Well, father, you can't tell that by looking at the slop he's created in this valley.

By the time Duncan stacked several framing timbers at the side of the road, she had almost convinced herself she could tackle even this situation and still learn about Gryf Williams' connection to the attempt on her father.

With barely a tip of the hat, Duncan climbed back up and snapped the reins. The wagon pulled down the road. The purple haze of afternoon sky hovered over the small town. Far above the houses, soft shadows and vivid orange light wrapped the butte.

Nearby, however, the stench gagged. Caroline pinched her nose with distaste and held up her skirts to avoid having them in too much contact with the filth. She kept a careful eye on her path, trying to pick the route of least gunk between the road and the supposed shaft house.

As if conjured by the mine, a man appeared ten feet from her. He stood tall and covered from head to toe in coal dust. Caroline's back shivered dark fear. She stiffened, telling herself his apparent magical arrival could be merely the result of her inattentive fatigue.

She looked more closely, but couldn't make herself move toward him. Coal had collected in his curly black hair, in his ash-colored beard and on every inch of his work clothes. He was far and away

29

the dirtiest man she'd ever seen, and at the mines she'd seen some
dirty ones.

The man stood with one leg straight under him, the other out to
the side as if it were a bracing beam for his long body. It occurred to
her that it required a very strong beam to keep such a tall, broad-
shouldered tower standing upright.

He glared down at her. Caroline felt thankful for one small thing.
His gaze did not rest on her jacket-bodice. Instead, he looked at her
shoes.

"Pardon me, lady," the man said, "You're standing in shit."

Caroline closed her mouth and stood as tall as possible. "I see the
substance, sir," she replied, lifting her square-toed boot to glare at
the muck. "What choice have you left me? There is mule dropping
in every part of this yard. Have none of you gentlemen ever thought
of shoveling?"

"They are burros, ma'am."

"Burro droppings then. How about shovels?"

"We're in a bit of an emergency since two hours ago," he said,
"explosion, cave-in, near drowning, all the usual. The drainage ditch
for the burro yard has overflowed. I thought I'd have a few days to
get it cleared away before Alexander brought any of his fine ladies
up to admire our work."

Caroline ignored the miner's sarcasm and the way his eyes
narrowed as he studied her boots and unladylike divided skirt. "This
mess," she waved at the entire area, "this mess is not only
aesthetically disgusting, it is sanitary disaster."

The tall miner pushed at his hair and raised one dust-covered
eyebrow. "Ahhh! 'I see the Substance, Sir'," he mimicked.
"Aesthetically disgusting, sanitary disaster . . .Let me guess," he
said, pressing his fingertips to his forehead as if he were a diviner,
"Yes! I have it. You bought the fancy new edition of Mr. Webster's
dictionary and studied it all the way up from Denver, eh?"

Suddenly, Caroline understood.

"Let me guess," she shot back. "You are Gryffyth Williams, known in the front office of Allied Mines as "The Mouth.""

The man's second eyebrow shot up in surprise, giving Caroline a moment's satisfaction. Then, he stepped closer to her, close enough that she could see the glint of humor in his dark gray eyes, even so close that she became aware of the smile lines radiating from those eyes – lines so deep, they had collected an extra sprinkling of coal dust. He looked a humorous, dark, devil of a man.

He studied her own eyes for a moment, making Caroline very stiff with discomfort. Suddenly, he swept an imaginary silk top hat from his head and made a deep bow, then stepped even closer, towering over her.

"Actually, my name is Gryffyth ap Rhodri ap Withliam, but those in the front office at Allied Mines can only pronounce simple things, such as the names of body parts. The Mouth for instance."

He ran his hand softly, almost meditatively over his lips, his teasing dark eyes watching her face, which she knew had turned white. To control her irrational fear, she interrupted him. "Where is your vent shaft?"

His hand dropped to his belt buckle, "My what?"

"I said 'Would you show me your shaft?' I'd like to get to work."

"To work?" he sputtered. "Right here?"

Pointing at the mucky ground, she cried, "Here? Right here?" Caroline straightened to her full five feet and four inches, gasping in astonishment. "Don't tell me even the ventilation shaft is covered in burro droppings?"

"The ventilation shaft? . . .the vent. . ." His thumb jerked toward a neat little building. Hidden beyond the last burro, Caroline had not seen the small shed until that moment. Its sturdy solidity surprised her.

31

"That's more like it," she said. "Of course we'll have to build a taller chimney."

"Ach!" His grey eyes opened wide as if at last he truly saw her. "And exactly who are ye, now?"

"I'm Trewartha, erstwhile editor of *The Transactions of the American Institute of Mining Engineers.*"

"Trewartha! Ye'r jesting me." He stared hard, then straightened, "You're a friend of Alexander's . . . Right? He asked you to pull a joke on me, neh?"

"You're expecting me. I sent a letter by Friday's post."

"You are Trewartha?"

"I am. And, since a week ago, I'm Allied Mines' regional consulting engineer for Colorado, Wyoming and . . ."

"I was looking for Carl Trewartha, Allied's letter said, 'C. J. Trewartha'."

"Caroline Jane."

"Oh!" He eyed her shrewdly. "Yes. That Trewartha. Daughter of Carl."

"I am The Trewartha. The only one you get."

"Damn!" he muttered. Then glancing at her, he said. "They send me rusty machinery and the daughter. Just what I need when I've nearly lost a good man in a cave-in."

"I heard those two explosions," she said, ignoring his insulting attitude – an all too common happening when she first arrived at a mine. "Allied sent me to help you with such problems," she said.

"Oh, certainly," he said.

"Mr. Williams, I truly am an engineer," she explained calmly. "Last year I worked in McFadden, Wyoming. They were barely making ends meet when I arrived. Now they are paying off debts and enjoying a handsome profit. I believe I helped make that change."

At that moment she could tell he decided to give her a hearing. He took a deep breath and asked, "You wrote the C. J. Trewartha essays in *The Transactions*?"

"I did."

"The editorial about unions took guts."

"It earned me the boot." The dratted tears rose again. She looked away to hide them.

He blinked, then laughed. "I'm not surprised. Hank Weller is a pompous ass. . .I mean. . ."

"Burro," she finished for him, and strode off toward the compact ventilation house.

"Asinine Donkey," he supplied.

Glancing over her shoulder, she came back with, "Thunder-headed Mule."

"Boetian Onager," he said firmly.

Caroline stared open mouthed at this filthy man with the appalling sense of humor. Her mind worked overtime to remind her what animal an onager might be. Boetian lay beyond her ken. There seemed to be more to this man than first she'd thought.

"Now who's at the Websters?" she asked.

He raised his shoulders in a gesture of false humility. "My edition is Antique, Ancient, Archaic..."

She held up a hand to stop him. "And insufficiently Abridged."

"We Welsh love words," he apologized.

"Could we move this conversation to a less odoriferous location?"

"Odoriferous," he savored the sound. "Good word."

"Perhaps," she said, "we could use the little creek to flush this field, Mr. Williams."

He was curt. "Miss, I'll clean this mess when it's more important than what I'm working on at the moment. Just before you arrived, I returned from searching for the buzzards that caused this disaster."

She raised her eyebrows.

He answered, "No luck. They've disappeared, it seems."

"And now?"

"Now, I've come back to fix my second pump so the boyos can quit and go home."

"I'll not stop you, Sir Mouth." Caroline headed off through the resting burros and toward the neatly made ventilation shed beyond them. Instead of going off to fix his pump, Gryf Williams' long legs brought him parallel to her in two steps. He asked, "Why did Allied send a female engineer, a writer and an administrator who has never worked underground?"

Caroline stomped one boot, spraying the local mud over his lower pant leg. She'd been patient enough, she thought. Time to squash his questioning. "How would you know where I've worked? I was in my first cave-in at age nine. It took twelve hours for the rescue crew to find us. The canary already flopped, unconscious when they broke through."

Gryf raised both hands, "All right. Whatever you say . . .." He stared at her with evident disbelief. Lowering his hands slowly, he shook his head. Abruptly, he too headed for the shed that protected the ventilation shaft.

Caroline stared after his thunder-headed self. So he had problems: he hired careless miners; he left muck in the mule yard; he had more machines broken than working; he didn't believe she knew mines – he deserved his problems.

She slogged after him, muttering angrily, "In the next millennium, they are going to discover a very large, unexplained gaseous deposit at this location; I hope you are part of it."

CHAPTER FOUR

Gryf reminded himself that he liked this woman's father. "I'll show you the vent shaft," he said, "but I need to repair my second pump in the main crosscut."

"I can help you with that," she claimed, "But first, I should see your set-up so I can recommend improvements and devise a production schedule."

"Oh, of course." He watched her face and saw she didn't recognize sarcasm.

"First the ventilation system," she said, "then your pump." She marched on toward the ventilation shed.

"Whatever Madam wishes," he grumbled, as he watched her back.

"I've brought a pretty good pump we can use," she said over her shoulder.

Gryf rolled his eyes at her All-Knowing Ladyship, and wondered how Carl Trewartha managed her. Her single-minded pursuit of her interests must have been a shock to her father.

As she strode ahead of him, Gryf watched the sun's rays glint off the red and gold strands in Miss Trewartha's dark brown hair. He was mighty disappointed not to meet Carl, but he had to admit that, up close, Carl's daughter looked even better than twenty feet above him. She was a visual treat – a small package of energy and dynamite temperament wrapped in a milk smooth complexion he'd bet had never seen coal dust.

He surprised himself, not having recognized her right off, but until she began with the mining talk, he never really looked at her. And the months since seeing her in the balcony after the trial had been full. He'd ceased dreaming about Carl Trewartha's daughter almost as soon as he found By-Gum valley; he'd worked hard and slept too soundly for dreams.

The fringe of her paisley shawl danced against her hips as she walked in front of him. Her shawl and her jacket bodice of black velveteen and wool had been drawn tightly across an eye-catching roundness of bosom. Since her hand had crept up numerous times to check the jacket buttons, Gryf realized she hoped the bodice concealed her shape, but he'd worked hard to keep his gaze from straying in the direction of the soft, light-catching texture which covered her feminine attributes. Back in Schuylkill County, he'd seen what that kind of glance did to her.

Caroline Trewartha's discomfort with her womanliness made Gryf feel oddly protective – a feeling he didn't like exercising. Equally intriguing was her mine expertise and that proved easier to think about. Her essay for *The Transactions* on anthracite had enlightened his whole crew. Of course, at the time they assumed they were reading the work of Carl Trewartha. His men believed women in a mine were bad luck, Saint Barbara excepted of course. Gryf was certain Rudy Sperl would be first to object to her presence.

There would be trouble.

She stopped so fast Gryf almost ran into her. He narrowly kept himself from catching her about the waist.

"Sorry," he murmured before he realized she remained unaware of the near mishap.

"Good," he heard her say. "Good and wide. How deep?" Her voice was a broken, muffled warmth.

As he turned, Gryf saw she'd stepped into the small protective shack and gazed down into the deep ventilation shaft. "Damnation," Gryf said to his conscience. "Why am I letting her interfere with my time?" He knew the answer to that – at least the part he willingly admitted to himself. Caroline Trewartha had become his responsibility. He couldn't let her wander around and get hurt. So, he retraced his steps and squeezed into the narrow doorway. She leaned on the protective rail he'd built around the updraft chimney and above the big steam-powered exhaust fan.

"How deep is the shaft?" she repeated. The whirring action of the fan broke her low voice into a thousand sunny echoes.

Gryf forced himself not to show his annoyance that she arrived on this disastrous day. "This meets our main crosscut, one hundred seventy feet below us. We're drilling south into the first coal room. Of course, that new room is filling with water and rock at the moment, so calling it a mine is moot."

"Water?"

"You did hear the explosions as you came up the last few miles of roadway?"

Her head cocked to one side, as if listening. "Of course. Didn't I say so? Underground – two blasts."

Now we're on the same earth, Gryf thought. He glanced at the nape of her neck as she bent over the fan housing. A dark curl, shot with red lights escaped her chignon and caressed her throat. He dragged his attention back to the fan.

"Don't you lock up your dynamite?" She glanced up at him, and became suddenly aware of how close he stood.

He saw her face stiffen. *I'll be damned if I'll step back.*

"Of course it's locked," he said. "That shed is locked and guarded twenty-four hours a day."

"Guarded this day?"

When she's scared, this dame gets pushy, he thought. But he said, "Jesse Polgren – very reliable."

"Where is Mr. Polgren?"

He saw her eyelid twitch with her fear. "Polgren's working with the men to figure out what the hell . . . what happened." Gryf

37

figured she had one more minute, then he would leave her and her insolent questions.

"What's the source?" Her voice tightened with distress.

I'll not treat her any differently than I'd treat her father.

"Mr. Williams, what is the source of all that water?"

He stared at her pallid face. The rail they were both leaning on transmitted the trembling of her legs.

My God, she's afraid of me.

Slowly, he leaned his back on the doorjamb and rolled his body away from her. "We don't know yet where the water is coming from. Last fall I hiked all over the cirque, measuring, mapping. I found no creek or spring that would account for the volume coming in the mine today."

He moved outside the shack, pointing at the circle of pristine peaks and dark cliffs surrounding the By-Gum mining valley. "I know of only one source for that much water," he said, "the falls and Dyfi Creek that runs next to our town. Yet, the creek has not changed one drip."

As she joined him outside, Gryf could hear her breathe, deliberately making herself calmer in his presence. She seemed such a contradiction: a bossy, self-confident engineer masking a frightened woman.

What made her this way?

"Well, let's not dilly-dally here," she said, moving past him, around the rock chimney of the engine house and toward the spindle-legged mine shaft shed.

"Where are you going?" he called as he closed the vent-shed door.

"Down to fix your second pump," she called. "Grab a wrench and a sledge-hammer."

"Be damned," he muttered. He hefted his tool chest out of the nearby tool shed and followed her one more time.

**

As she arrived at the shaft house, Caroline gazed down at the most primitive hoist she'd ever seen and told herself this kind of temporary construction no doubt accounted for the troubles this man found in making his mine work adequately.

"Are you afraid?" Mr. Williams deep voice was tinged with contempt.

Caroline jerked in a deep breath. "Afraid of what?" She forced her voice to sound firm.

"Afraid to descend into the pit of darkness . . ." Gryf intoned dramatically. "Afraid of the mine."

"Mr. Williams, I have been in mines several times as deep as this," She raised her hands, grabbing the sides of an imagined ladder. "I've climbed down long runs of ladders, sir. I have ridden up and down on chains. I've balanced on the rods of Cornish pump engines. This is a picnic. Haul …up … your … lift."

As she finished imitating the motion needed to balance on huge, moving rods, she saw Mr. Williams suppress a smirk. Then, he raised one eyebrow and ducked ahead of her under the rickety roof of the makeshift shed. He worked the rope around his hand.

As he pulled, he commented. "We hoped to have a steam operated miner's cage ready for your visit. However, your company insists on sending us rusty tools with major parts missing."

Caroline asked, "Why would Allied Mines be sending you tools?"

"They are as much a part of our contract as you," he said.

"Tools are nowhere mentioned in the contract."

"Best read it again, Miss." He pulled down one side of his mobile mouth as he hauled a wide coal bucket up to the level of the three-foot rock wall that encircled the mineshaft. He turned toward her, as if to gauge her reaction.

Caroline still tried to figure out how he read the offer of any tools into the contract she had in her valise. The fact that he offered her a ride on a pot-metal coal bucket became merely one more obnoxious event in an entirely obnoxious day. At a mine under construction, she had expected at least a horse-operated whim. A bucket and pulley system was unbelievable.

This Gryffyth Williams character clearly intended to get a reaction, so she refused to give it to him. Instead, she hoisted her skirt enough to lift her nether limb over the edge of the shaft wall. She planted her muddy boot squarely in the bucket. Reaching for the rope, she glanced up to check the strength of the rope and the pulley mechanism, then braced herself to haul hard on the rope until she had her balance and could begin to let herself down into the shaft.

**

For a moment, Gryf feared that she would succeed in wresting the rope away from him and plunge to the bottom. He leaned back, pulling hard with one arm while he reached out to steady her in the bucket with the other. His big hand wrapped around most of her waist before he saw her look of anger.

"Let go of me," she hissed.

"I'd have to clean up the mess at the bottom."

"I can do this, Mr. . . . "

"No gloves. . ." he started.

"No need. Let go of me and the rope."

He stared at her, incredulous. *The woman believes she can do it,* he thought. *Let her,* he decided and almost released his grip on the rope. *I can't let her fall.* He gripped again and then another thought assailed him. *I nearly let go and the rope didn't budge.*

Slowly, he loosed his fingers. The bucket stayed near the top of the well. Her grip seemed tight on the rope, her knuckles white.

With one hand, she wrapped the rope behind her exactly the way he did when he distributed some of the work from his arms to his rear end. He'd never give the back of her skirt much of a chance for survival, but she knew how to do this. Keeping his gloved hands near the rope, he looked down at her defiant expression.

"This'll hurt your hands," he said.

"I'm tougher than I look."

"There's a lantern at the head of the coal room. You won't be in darkness."

Her face flushed. She looked away from him. "I'll be all right," she whispered. She loosed the slack in the hand behind her and began to descend. Glancing up at him one last time, she unwittingly let him see how thin was her veneer of bravery. Her dark green eyes became big ovals of fear, but her mouth set in a determined line and her chin jutted toward him just before she disappeared.

Gryf willed his hands to keep from grabbing the rope. He hovered near, counting the inches as they played out in front of him, waiting for that moment when her white hands and small fingers no longer could hold. An eternity later, the rope stopped. He listened. Her boots swished through the water on the floor of the crosscut.

"My Lord." Her whisper rose out of the shaft. "It really is anthracite."

Gryf broke into a smile. He clenched two fists in a gesture of victory, raised his hands over his head and knocked his knuckles on the underside of the shed roof. Licking his grazed fingers, he thought, *Gonna rebuild this puny shed into a real winding house, soon as Allied sends parts for those wretched hoists.*

A second thought intruded on the first. *She did it. By-Gum, she did it.* He leaned over the short wall.

"May I come down, Miss Trewartha?"

Her answer sounded from farther down the drift. "I see where your water is coming from."

41

"You stay out of that room," he hollered.

"No need to yell at me. I'm perfectly safe."

"I'm coming down," he yelled and hauled the bucket up in record time.

As he dropped into the main crosscut, he saw that Miss Trewartha stood next to his ancient water pump. She held the lantern away from her looking as mythic as Lady Liberty had on the day he arrived in New York harbor.

"You're safe," he said, taking the lantern from her and studying her by its light.

"Of course, I am," she responded.

All his concern returned to annoyance. "Oh, aye," he mocked. "Never worry about the invincible Miss Trewartha."

"That's right."

He checked her expression. She had made this last statement straight-faced, with no idea he spoofed her – just went right on to her next request.

"May I have your sledge-hammer?" she asked.

Perplexed, he fished out and handed her a ball peen hammer which was the biggest he had in his toolbox.

She studied it, hefting it from hand to hand. "That'll do it," she said.

"Do what?"

She swung it up and then let its weight fall striking the governor at the top of his reciprocating steam pump. His recalcitrant machine kachunked once, hissed twice and then began pumping water out of the rubble of the coal room.

Gryf stared at her. He tried to close his mouth, but he was too amazed. She handed him the hammer and then noticed his astonishment.

"Stuck valve," she explained.

"I was going to clean the thing."

"That would have worked," she agreed, "but it would take longer. The water's getting ahead of you."

As if she hadn't done anything remarkable, she took one of the other lanterns from its wall hook and paced the murky cavern. She studied the black, hard rock, holding the lantern high above her, then low, following some particularly interesting substratum.

While he recovered from her swift fix of his pump, he also enjoyed her graceful motions. In spite of the long skirt and the puffed sleeves on her jacket, he could see her small body was beautifully proportioned – a nice length of leg, a slender back. He thought about that moment at the top of the shaft when she'd been imitating how she balanced on the Cornish pump rods. His chest had near burst with suppressed laughter. He didn't want her thinking he made fun of her, but he surely did enjoy the way her body moved when she grew angry.

Here at the bottom of the mineshaft, he watched her with pleasure. Using a little hammer and a small tool, both brought out of her pocket, she chipped at the wall. The pieces that broke off were smooth and curved. "Good," she said. "Conchoidal fractures."

He smiled. She used the same process he did – reassuring herself that this was truly anthracite. When she bent, staring at the wall, her back maintained its ramrod straightness. It amazed him she didn't topple to the fore, being cantilevered so far over her center of gravity. He did appreciate the lovely profile view her intent curiosity afforded him. Much good his interest would ever do him with a woman so afraid of men, but the aesthetic experience was worth something.

When Caroline straightened and turned around, she appeared to have softened. "The rock strata down here – a reverse fault," she said, "so the west side of the seam is a good fifteen feet higher than the east, right?"

Gryf nodded. "Here that's true. So . . .?"

43

"So, instead of taking the seam head on, in the usual pillar and room method, we cut our drift next to the western or higher side and use the long-wall technique. We can cut a drainage adit, letting the water drain into your boys' ditch from the lower back side of the seam."

No long-walling," he declared, feeling the heat of memory well up inside him. "It takes out too much of the structure of the mountain."

"Not if you dig and support the whole drift and then take the coal from the farthest end first, back-filling as you work your way out."

He snorted, "I suppose they taught you that back-fill is just as stable as original rock."

"I know how to back-fill so the stability is greater than before."

"It's ugly. It's unstable. It's dangerous.

"You haven't even tried it, . . ."

"Not since it caused a cave-in out in Nepal. Village swallowed up while I watched. Fifteen deaths." Gryf could never erase from his mind the image of his friend, Jaron, vanishing into the depths.

She remained silent. After a moment she said gently, "We've developed new techniques, new strutting systems . . . "

He rallied from the demons of his past. "New techniques may work better, but they won't do us much good. This coal seam is tilted like this only for the next mile to the south. Then it won't drain east because you've got an up-thrust of magma shoving the east side up."

"How do you know that?"

"I listened to it," he said.

"Mr. Williams, don't patronize me."

He raised one eyebrow in surprise. "Don't tell me you've never used sound to find what you want?"

"To find the cat at night, maybe."

"Seismic mapping," he prompted. "Surely you've seen it done."

44

"Oh, this should be good." Her voice dripped sarcasm. "Do explain it to me."

Gryf felt annoyed enough to consider telling her some phantasm, but then realized he'd have to work with her and might as well educate her.

"I first saw this technique in the Alsace-Lorraine, that's in . . . "

"It's in Germany at the moment," she supplied. "They won the most recent war with the French."

"Huh," he grunted begrudging thanks. "We were tracing a seam that started in the Saar Valley. This fellow drove an iron pike into the ground. Every time he whacked on that pike with his hammer, he'd whisper, counting the seconds off while his buddy kept his ear to the ground. His buddy would hold up a finger as soon as he heard the returning echo of the rock below. Then they'd mark on their map the depth of the various types of rock they heard."

Miss Trewartha had turned narrowed eyes toward him. He knew she didn't even believe the straight story. Still, he went on. *Might as well get the truth out on the table the first time, he thought. Later we can embroider a bit . . .*"

"Over the years," he went on, "I've seen the same idea with various tools. I use dynamite, myself. You get echoes from deeper in the earth."

Caroline shook her head and sighed. "You know, Mr. Williams, I too have read Jules Verne."

"This is not a writer's fantasy."

"I'm sure Mr. Verne claims his fantasies could come true."

"I'll show you how it's done," he snarled. "If you've the nerve."

Her bright eyes sent shafts of lightning at him. "I have had some doozers pulled on me, Mr. Williams. I'd love to meet a gentleman – a man who didn't set out right away to prove a woman ignorant."

"I'm telling you the truth. In Alsace we found. . ."

"In Alsace you found the giant grape and you drank deep."

"Ha!" he barked, watching her anger rise. It pleased him, body and soul, to see the rose flush her cheeks, her chin jut at him as it had when she descended in that wee bucket, her shoulders pulled back and her breath came in deep gulps. She was magnificent – short, but extraordinary – an elfin mountain queen.

Suddenly, she seemed to realize what he watched. He had never seen anger turn so quickly to hurt. Her brilliance faded, a misting over of liveliness and confidence. He barely had a chance to glimpse it before she turned her back on him, marching to the burro tunnel. Carrying the lantern, she waded through the deepest puddle just at the bottom of the rise. The youngsters stopped bailing to pull off their dirty caps to her. Gryf watched Amos, the old cad, doff his more slowly and used it to wipe coal dust off his grizzled face.

In a dignified tone, she asked, "Which of you gentlemen is Jim Freya?"

"I be that 'un, ma'am," Jimmy's head bowed slightly.

"I hope you will show me how to find your home, Jim. Your mother's expecting me."

"Ye be Trewartha's wife? Mum dinna know he come wi' a wife, ma'am. That room she's got ready be hardly big enow. Won't be able to turn yersel' about."

"Don't worry, Jim. I am Trewartha, by myself."

"Trewartha himself? herself?" In the lantern light, Jimmy colored up bright red.

"Her very self," Miss Trewartha said. "Now how do I arrive at your mother's doorstep? I don't want her to worry about me."

Gryf watched Jimmy bob another bow at Miss Caroline Trewartha and then cast a worried glance at Amos. Deciding it was time for the boys to be getting home, Gryf stepped into their midst, stooping low to get his tall frame in the tunnel.

46

"You boys have done yeoman's work. A bit extra in your pay for this. Back here tomorrow after school to decide the fate of this soggy bottom."

Jimmy's eyes opened wide as he stared at Gryf. "Ye'll not be closin' the By-Gum surely, sir?"

"I'll be figurin' how to make her safe."

"And we can't be just movin' off to one side or t'other?"

Gryf glanced at Caroline who barely hid a triumphant grin. Without knowing it, Jimmy was describing long-walling.

"We'll see," Gryf said, "Somethin'll come up. Now it's gettin' on toward dark, so you'd best get Miss Trewartha to your mam, eh."

"Aye, sir." Jimmy bobbed his head at Caroline again and then started off at a dash, getting out about twenty yards before he realized that his lady was using a more dignified speed. The other boys dispersed, laughing and wrestling with each other, but clearly being careful not to splash the lady. Their antics were carried on with an eye to outshining each other in strength and speed – and all for the lady they pretended to ignore.

Gryf smiled at their wildness when Amos's gruff voice interrupted his thoughts.

"Amazing," said Amos, "what a beauty can make boys do, ain't it?"

Gryf chuckled. He elbowed Amos. "I noticed you mopping your face when she came near. Thinking about sparking her?"

"Not this old codger. Not when I have to get in line behind a book-reading swell like yerself – you and possibly one other tall, curly-haired charmer. I heard you spatting with her – cats in heat, I told myself."

Gryf glared at the unflinching old man, then stared up the tunnel into the pink gauze of a mountain sunset. In the light, a dark silhouette strode purposefully across the muck she had so vociferously denounced. With every step, she swayed – an inadvertent, unmistakably feminine motion. But she hated muck, and she hated being female. He knew it with every woman loving bone in his body.

He snorted. "She's not going to be here long enough for the courtin' line to form. So, don't fash yourself about it, Amos."

When Gryf could no longer see Miss Trewartha, he noticed that Amos was watching him and grinning.

"Rev up that old pump in there," Gryf grumbled. "Got to keep up with the incoming water until we find the source."

CHAPTER FIVE

"And I told that wagon master, 'Duncan', says I, 'you're naught but a jokester.'" Jimmy Freya's mother twitched her skirts as she ushered Caroline up outside stairs to a room above a beautiful and large barn.

"I says, Duncan you know there's no lady engineers. This can't be our Trewartha. So, you can imagine how my hand flew to my mouth when our own Jimmy bolts in here saying Trewartha were a lady. And right handsome, Jimmy says. And he got that right, I must say."

The flow of words barely halted as Deirdre Freya turned assessing eyes on Caroline, who was still wiping ripe smell from boots onto a boot brush at the bottom of the stairs.

"Now don't you worry none about that stuff. Jimmy's little brother'll clean them off for you. Imagine, you comin' all this way just to lend our Gryf a hand. And don't he need a hand now after them explosions and that cave-in this afternoon? And Gryf nearly killed rescuing our bull, Olaf, from the flood down there."

"A bull in a mine?" Caroline asked, but she might as well have been whispering. Dierdre talked on while unlocking a water-warped door at the top of the stairs.

"Mary in heaven, the Lord was with them. Like to of caved in on their very heads and then where would we be, I ask you, without our Gryf. In hell, I tell you, and the Sweet Jesus knew it. Lookin' down, he was. Hand of God held up that roof until they got Olaf out."

Deirdre gestured Caroline into the upper room. "Isn't much, I'm thinkin', but what could I do on such short notice . . ."

As soon as Caroline stepped inside, her nostrils were assailed by the sweet smell of hay and the acrid odor of wet cows. Lowing animals, directly below this room.

Deirdre went on. "It's a sign. A sure sign. This mountain will only be messed with so much, I say. We got enough to live on last year, didn't we? And send some tidy profit to the investors' company. Now this isn't a room I'd offer a lady. More Irish lace and some candle-wicking for a lady's room, but you have to admit I didn't expect a lady, now did I?"

As she listened to the blur of her hostess' monologue, Caroline stole glances around the tiny room. Its one window was covered with bleached cotton curtains. On the bed lay a patchwork cover of denim work-shirt fabrics, quilted in hen's track and feather stitch with blue and yellow embroidery floss – fluffy and warm, and very masculine. A cracked porcelain wash basin and pitcher perched on the small table. Above the table hung a walnut-framed mirror. The silver backing had peeled, leaving dark spots in the glass. Its reflection of Mrs. Freya's broad back was a jigsaw puzzle of cracked lines and calico dress fabric with major pieces missing.

"This is a wonderful room, Mrs. Freya."

To Caroline's surprise, the woman blushed furiously. "Oh well – for a man. But I didn't know, you see. A lady alone, no chaperone... I could move my Jimmy out here instead."

"Oh no, Mrs. Freya. I like the quiet. I lived by myself in Baltimore and in Philadelphia."

This was not strictly true. However, Caroline was delighted to be alone and far away from the watchful eyes of her grandfather's family – especially to escape from the frivolity of women talk – fashion, beauty, men, sermons on what she should do to attract them. She had plans to write articles and submit them under a pseudonym *to The Transactions* or *Mining Press* or to any organ of communication that would pay her for them. She would be independent of any male-run mining company as soon as she could.

Deirdre fussed with the curtains, saying, "That little wood stove in the corner will take the chill off bedtime and risin' time until you can get to our kitchen for breakfast."

"What time is breakfast?"

"What's the matter with me? Ye've had no supper, I'll own. Supper in an hour and a half. Duncan put your suitcase on the floor over here. Your crate's in the barn below. You need anything from it tonight? That mouthy Duncan says it's full of explosives, but I put no belief in the sayings of a Scot."

"But Mrs. Freya, there are mining tools in the crate, including blasting caps and some wicking. It's not dangerous. I've packed it very carefully."

"You mean he was telling true? Well now, don't that beat all? Twice in one trip, too. Well, dear, you get freshened up and I'll ring the bell when supper is ready – an hour or so. Get a bit of colcannon inside of you, we will – such a mite of a thing. Put some thickness on you to ward off the chill, that's what we'll be doin' over the summer. Have to make it through winter some way up here, and without a man to keep you . . . "

Caroline's felt her face flame. Deirdre must have seen her involuntary recoil.

"Well now, I've gone and blathered long enough. I must be gettin' that wee boy of mine to heat up the kitchen wood stove. At least he remembered to fire up this one. Probably been out playin' with the dogs again when I told him to bring in the wood.

You know, my Jimmy was born on the passage over from Ireland during the great hurricane of 1868. Jimmy come out kicking, punching, and rolling with the ship and he ain't never stopped moving since. No end of charmin' he is, and no end of toil."

51

Mrs. Freya had edged herself toward the door and, not finding the right chord on which to end her symphony, she merely stepped out and descended the stairs, still talking as Caroline waved from the landing at the top.

"The endless Gaelic essay," Caroline whispered, smiling to herself. She watched Deirdre sail back to the farmhouse. Over the farmhouse roof, Caroline could see the village tucked into the west side of the valley, near the creek. About twenty tightly built log cabins faced each other across a wide plank street. Each cabin sported some small variation in roofline or porch, and each had a well in front and a privy behind the cabin.

At the far end of the row of houses, a small general store stood opposite what appeared to be a church or school on the other. It was a clean, well-planned little town. Caroline was impressed.

And she was giddy with delight at this isolated room. "I wonder if Deirdre sews as fast and as constant as she talks," Caroline whirled inside and closed the door. "I don't care how noisy she is, Deirdre Freya created this lovely room."

She stared into the mirror, but did not see herself, for her mind had taken her beyond the mirror and into her fears. She saw the image of a long-legged imp with curling dark hair and coal-black lines about his eyes.

"Mr. Williams, you will prove to be a noodle-noggin," she whispered. "Any man who signs a contract as Gryffyth ap Rhodri ap Withliam is an excessive and immoderate man." She shuddered with the implications of that fact. "Allied has made a foolish investment. I will soon be out of a job. I'll have to hop in that awkward wagon and ride behind those rump-ugly draft horses all the way back to Isabeau."

Sighing, she closed her eyes and recalled her first cooling view of the alpine valley. "What a shame," she said. And then, she forced herself to be practical again.

She poured water from the pitcher into the bowl to wash her face. In the mirror, she saw her hair had gone wild again, so she decided to undress and start from scratch. This would be her first supper with the Freya's and their other boarders. She wanted to be fresh and ready.

She turned her back on the mirror and began unbuttoning her jacket bodice. Watching her fingers work, Caroline's mind pictured the way Gryf Williams had looked at her when she'd gotten so angry down in the mine. His coal hard eyes had gone all soft for a moment and she knew he wasn't listening to her logic any longer.

She knew what he was thinking, and she hated it. Why did men find this attraction in roundness? Why not squareness or triangleness; weren't those shapes just as classical? Didn't art and architecture exploit those other shapes to the great benefit and enjoyment of humankind?

Caroline slipped out of her split skirt, carefully laying it across the chair to preserve what was left of it from wrinkles. *That mud will have to be washed*, she thought. And then her mind went on arguing with an imaginary Gryf Williams while she untied the ribbons on her chemise.

See there? she glanced at her skirt. Triangular sections for a split pants-skirt, practical, walkable and every bit as attractive as round. Certainly, less fabric to trip over or to pick up road dirt.

She stepped out of her pantaloons and began untying her corset. This chore was a little difficult, since some fool had designed it to tie in the back. As she struggled with it, she argued more forcibly.

I wouldn't have to wear stupid pieces of self-imprisonment like this, if I weren't so blasted round. I would be able to breathe all day long – at this point she dropped the hated garment on the floor and stretched her arms above her head in relief. She stopped berating her invisible companion and inhaled deeply. Naked, warmed by the glowing wood stove, she was the very picture of all she wished Gryf

Williams would not notice. Relaxed at last, her body took on sensuous grace. She pirouetted toward the wash basin. Never looking at her reflection, she washed her limbs and dried her body with languorous motions. She unpinned and brushed out her thick, dark hair. Static electrified the air as the tresses floated down her back. In the small light from the stove, her body was a sinewy length of creamy glow – her legs, her arms, her throat and torso the ultimate argument for round as the most classical of shapes.

Clean and very tired of wearing the mask of strength, Caroline pulled back the patchwork quilt, discovered soft cotton sheets beckoning her. She never even thought about opening her valise to find her flannel nightgown. Instead, she slipped into the bed and sank quickly into a dream of water and of a bull being rescued by a dark devil from the pit of the earth.

**

In the kitchen of Freya's boarding house, Gryf Williams stood with his back to the room. One shiny boot rested on a chair rung. His scrubbed fingertips drummed the windowsill. His coal-soft eyes stared at the pale glow of the window in the upper level of the barn. Behind Gryf, unheeded, Dierdre Freya clattered pots and blathered about how wrong it was of her to make the new engineer sleep all by herself in that man's room so far away from help.

Gryf had stopped breathing when the woman's silhouette appeared on the window curtain. She'd been reaching behind her, awkwardly. Some garment fell away from her body. For a brief erotic moment, she lifted her arms over-head and danced for him. It had been half an hour since her dance took her away from the curtain, yet he was still gathering his wits and calming his body.

"Damned fool," he repeated over and over. "Damned fool."

54

Even to him it was not clear which of them he was deriding. He knew where to take this physical need. There was a big house down in Sapinero where any man would be more than welcomed.

But, ironically, it was this woman's father he had promised to shun such a place.

What he didn't know how to take care of was this anger. Women never had the power to infuriate him. They had given him pleasure with their bodies or they intrigued him with their wit, but they never owned enough of him to make him feel.

"She wants to take over the damned mine," he muttered. "I won't have any long-walling! Too cramped. Not enough air."

Heck! He thought, there's more than her bossiness that bothers me. For one thing, she isn't her father. I wanted this chance to thank Carl Trewartha. Her being here cheated me of that.

All his attempts to explain his anger, seemed wide of the mark. He leaned his head against the glass of Deirdre's fine kitchen window. Why? he asked. Why does she hover in my head after one meeting?

Hell, he admitted to himself, there's lust at the foundation of this monumental aggravation. I met Caroline Trewartha four hours ago. We argued the whole time we were together. In spite of her voluptuous silhouette, I already know she will never grace any man's bed – certainly not mine. And that fact is going to drive me nuts.

"Ah, here's Olaf, now," sang Dierdre. "Thought you might be eating at Ellen's tonight, Olaf. Come in the kitchen first. Duck your head under that door and just slide on in here. Sure an' I've laid aside some tidbits to hold your great appetite until supper is ready. Don't be shy, you great bull. It'll keep yourself upright for a few minutes, now won't it, Gryf?

"Gryf hasn't touched a one of those little prilochs, and tasty they are too. I expect Gryf be frettin' about the dynamite. No sense lettin' the brain languish from over-use and want of food, now is there. Where's that Jimmy got to now? Jimmy? Jimmy?"

Dierdre sailed out of the room as Gryf pulled himself away from the window. He was sure Olaf wanted to disappear on down the road toward some other mine – no doubt mortified by what had happened between them in the flooding cave. But Gryf and the By-Gum needed Olaf now more than ever.

Olaf glanced briefly at Gryf, then lowered his head and shuffled backward toward the dining room where the other men were talking.

"Olaf," Gryf said casually, reaching for a small pastry, "What have you found?"

Olaf shook his head. "Combed everywhere in the cirque. Can't find explosion sites. No dynamite missing from our stores, Boss, but a lot of rock came down the northwestern vale. Some near hit the town."

"What's Jesse Polgren say?"

"I 'spect Jesse's with some of the men up the ridge."

"But he was guarding the shed today."

"He wasn't there when we got there, Boss. Doors locked. No sign of tampering. Jesse'd already gone with the others."

Gryf jerked to attention. "He left the dynamite shed?"

Olaf lifted his big shoulders, "Guess so, Boss. But Philpot is guarding it now." Olaf's gaze fell on the pastries, but he backed toward the door again.

Halting Olaf with his upraised hand, Gryf said, "Man, I'm gonna need your help."

That stopped Olaf's embarrassed retreat. Gryf went on quickly.

"I'll be wanting to put you in charge of the third mine. I'll concentrate on solving those damned explosions, and I need you, Amos and Rudy to work the rest of our mines. We've got to find and dam up the source of that water in Number One and get all the mines in full operation."

"But Boss," Olaf still didn't look up, "Number Three is Rudy's baby."

"Was. Now he's agreed to work Number Two full time. Amos is set to help me hire new miners. We'll be getting the three mines all up to full capacity. I realize now that we should have put more into Two and Three before this. Have to be sure of a decent haul during the short summer. What say ye, my friend?"

For a moment, Olaf could only nod. After a silence, he said, "I'll do my best, Boss."

"That'll be a help to all of us," Gryf said holding out the plate toward Olaf. "These things are pretty good."

Olaf reddened, but he grasped three prilochs in one fist. A second long-fingered hand reached around Olaf and took one pastry off the plate.

"Alex," Gryf smiled. "What did you find out in Denver?"

Alexander Kemp's look was grim. "I found that Allied has sent no replacement parts at all. They didn't answer my telegram, so I rode out to see Isaac Brown. He says Terry Branahan has been ousted as President of Allied Mines."

"Good God! Ousted by whom?"

"Hume. The new guy's name is Morton Hume."

Before Gryf could ask anything more, the parlor door opened. The whisper of taffeta made the hairs stand up on the back of his neck.

Too soon. I'm not ready, Gryf thought. He glowered at his pocket watch and realized that for the last fifty minutes he'd been trying to beat down his reaction to one sense-stirring image on a window curtain. Now he tried to sort out the image of Caroline being hired by some dirt-pockets named Morton Hume. An inexplicable fear for her grabbed at his chest. He couldn't explain why, after all the women he'd known . . .

He snorted at himself. *You're loony, Gryf Williams. The painted nude over the bar down in Isabeau is warmer than this Trewartha woman.*

CHAPTER SIX

Caroline was acutely aware that among the men who turned when she entered the front door were Alexander Kemp and Gryf Williams. They stood in the kitchen doorway at the far end of a long room. She should have guessed Mr. Williams would be a boarder. It was her kind of luck.

Mr. Kemp's elegant clothes had been replaced by a more workaday plaid shirt and butternut-dyed pants. His blue eyes brightened as he spotted Caroline. His welcoming smile warmed her. She had gone out of her way to reject his attention when she first met him, yet he seemed happy to see her. She regretted her earlier attitude. It was pleasant to have at least one person glad you existed.

In contrast, Gryf Williams' stern face offered no welcome. The difference between the two men was emphasized by the fact that they were both tall and with a tendency toward wild curls, though Kemp's were always under control. There, the similarity ended. Kemp's blond hair, blue eyes and tanned face offered a memory of warm sunshine. The darker skin, gray eyes and black hair of Mr. Williams recalled a fearsome, moonless night.

On this night, Mr. Williams was scrubbed cleaner than one could have thought possible. She guessed he'd taken to the creek to get rid of all that coal dust.

As he faced her from across the room, he planted his feet wide apart and squared off almost as if preparing for a fight. His deep-set eyes offered only cold assessment.

Discomfited, she glared at him. She dared not glance down to see if her gray dinner dress was badly travel-wrinkled. Besides, she was not here at the By-Gum to look fashionable, so why should she care? Still, she touched her row of buttons, merely to check them, stood as straight as she could and hoped proud carriage would overcome crinkled fabric in her first meeting with these people.

"Gentlemen, meet our new engineer," announced Deirdre, pulling Caroline into the dining room. "Miss Trewartha, this is my husband Mac Freya."

"Right glad to meet you, Miss," said Mac. His round face seemed a match for his wife's warmth, and his quiet voice a foil for her volubility.

Next, Deirdre pulled on the gray shirtsleeve of a huge man. "Come on out, Olaf," Deirdre insisted. The poor fellow peered from beneath a white-blond shock of hair. His glance flicked up to greet her and then back to his bootlaces. "Miss Trewartha," chirped Deirdre, "this is our Olaf Fedje."

Olaf backed away as fast as he could.

"Oh, don't mind him," fluttered Deirdre. "Olaf'll be talkin' yer ears red by next week."

Pulling Caroline down the line of men, Deirdre introduced her to Amos Jawarski.

Caroline held her hand out to the man who'd been working with the boys in the burro's tunnel. "We met at the mine."

Amos stopped himself from using his sleeve to wipe his face. "Pleased, Miss Trewartha," he mumbled.

In quick succession, Deirdre introduced skinny Dalton Zerben of North Carolina, then Cornell Ivisson from Schuylkill, Pennsylvania, and Duncan, the wagon drover, and finally, Rudolph Sperl, the wizened Swiss miner of red cheeks and bright blue eyes who had ridden with her in the wagon from Isabeau.

"I've had the pleasure," he said, "of watching Miss Trewartha in action. Most enlightening." Rudy Sperl's eyes sparked with challenge as he bowed an imitation of civility.

Caroline rankled, but she held her tongue and merely extended her hand in greeting.

Oblivious of any tension, Deirdre guided her toward the men who clustered near the kitchen door.

Caroline glanced up, struck by how Mr. Kemp, Olaf and Mr. Williams loomed over everyone else. Duncan was a large man, but not tall.

"I believe you met Mr. Alex Kemp on your way up here," Deirdre said.

"It's nice to see you again, Mr. Kemp," Caroline said.

"My pleasure, Miss Trewartha. I've been telling Gryf here about our meeting on the road."

Deirdre twisted her toward Alex's dark companion. "And, of course you've met our Gryf," Deirdre cooed.

Caroline took his extended hand, staring at its amazing lack of coal. "Good evening, Mr. Williams," she said, but her mind was imagining him scrubbing his hands with a pig bristle brush. He held her hand long enough for her to grow uncomfortable. She jerked her attention all the way up to his face. There, surrounded by immaculate whiskers, was a very expressive mouth, upper lip peaked, full lower lip pulled down at one corner, holding back laughter. She dared not look him in the eye as she pulled her hand away.

He transferred his abandoned hand to her elbow and smoothly steered her toward the dining table. "All right if I show Miss Trewartha to her place, Dierdre?"

Dierdre, never hearing more than the obvious meaning, made shooing motions with her big hands. "Sit. Sit," she said. "We shan't be waiting for the Reverend and Marvelle Wright this evening, though the Lord knows we should offer thanks for their good work among us."

Caroline tried to turn away from Gryf to speak again to Amos, but Gryf practically levered her into a tall-backed chair, saying softly. "Miss Trewartha, would you do me the honor of sitting next to me, this evening?"

"I could hardly do otherwise," she whispered, "since you have possession of my elbow – the rest being, unhappily, attached."

"I would like some opportunity to discuss your brief tour of our mine."

She bridled at his broad hint that she leave soon. "The brevity of my stay depends entirely on the satisfactory outcome of our work together."

"I'm sure we can plan a good few days."

Furious, Caroline, glancing in the general direction of Gryf's beard, smiled a false, tight smile. Though she nodded toward each gentleman as he sat down in his place near or across from her, her soft words were definitely directed at Gryf.

"I need to see all three mines tomorrow," she began. "Then we must come to some conclusions about the source of all that water in mine Number One. Subsequently, we will be able to order the materials needed to deal with the problem, meanwhile continuing to develop mines Two and Three – don't you think we could give these mines names instead of numbers?"

Caroline rattled on as fast as she could, pleased that she'd learned a thing or two from Deirdre about frustrating others who wish to control the conversation. She smiled sweetly whenever Mr. Williams tried to shovel a word in here or there, but she *kept* talking.

"By the time the railroad begins coming up here," she continued, "it would be easier to attract workers if each mine had a catchy and memorable name – perhaps the Greek Gods, or" (she glanced down the table toward Deirdre) "or Irish mythic heroes or . . . well I'm sure Allied Mines can come up with something appropriate."

"You mistake, my dear Miss Trewartha." There was a steel edge to his voice when he finally succeeded in interrupting her.

"Oh?"

"The last word in the name By-Gum is a possessive pronoun."

"You mean the By-Gum Yours? Presently it is yours, I understand. But the contract you signed with Allied doesn't give you much chance to keep it. Were you drinking that night? You've nothing to show for all the money Allied loaned you. That spindly winding house? You should have a coal washer, track for your haulage carts, an endless rope winding engine and a miner's cage in your most productive mine. The vent shaft and fan housing, now that was well designed, I grant you, but you clearly need help making use of your up-front money, and less seat of the pants . . .."

"Let us thank the Lord for our Blessings," Deirdre piped up from the far end of the table. "Mac, dear, would you lead us in saying grace?"

Caroline halted her whispers and innocently bowed her head over folded hands. She was quite pleased that next to her, Gryf seethed.

Then Mac's soft but distinct voice said, "May we all join hands in fellowship."

Gryf took Rudy's gnarled hand on his right and then slowly extended his left hand toward Caroline, out of sight of the others, below the level of the table. On her left, Jimmy's small hand reached out and merely took hers, but on the right, Gryf's hand was asking her to come halfway. She knew everyone's eyes must be on her, waiting for her to make this simple gesture. Why couldn't she do it? Why?

In desperation, she turned a glazed and, she hoped, a distracting smile toward Jimmy and dropped her right hand into her lap. Mac bowed his head and began praying, "Now that our circle is complete, Lord . . .."

Warm fingers closed over her fist, resting there, not moving, not insisting on acknowledgement – just being there until Mac's prayer concluded.

"Amen," the company said. Gryf's fingers gave a slight pressure on her hand and then returned to his fork.

During the rest of dinner, Gryf conversed with Rudy Sperl, and Gryf's friend Alex. He and Rudy compared mining techniques they had seen. Gryf, and his frequently mentioned brother Sam, seemed to have seen most of the mines in the vast British Empire before they came to the United States.

Cornell looked down the table and said, "Olaf, I witnessed a miracle."

Olaf glanced up from his study of the plate, "A miracle?" he asked.

"Ellen sliding down the snow on our big hill riding on two slabs of wood."

Olaf colored and stared at the plate again. "Yah," he whispered. "She learn mighty fast."

Cornell smiled. "I think she likes the teacher."

Olaf now studied his fingers. His face reddened.

Everyone at the table laughed. So, Caroline guessed she should meet this Ellen.

And as she studied Cornell Ivisson, she realized she'd seen him before. The jury foreman in Schuylkill County. Maybe she had already found the reason for Gryf's acquittal.

As Gryf and Rudy exchanged stories, Caroline wondered where Mr. Williams' brother was now, and why the two of them had left their home near Aber-Dyfi, Wales, but no one even referred to that time in Mr. Williams' life.

Mr. Kemp finally shed some light on their life back home. He was answering Mr. Ivisson, the gentleman from Pennsylvania. Ivisson asked Kemp if he intended to remain at By-Gum next winter.

"Certainly. Winter is milder in Northern Wales," Kemp said, "but life at Sunderland Manor has gone dull." Kemp leaned over to aim his next remark down the table toward Gryf. "It was never the same after your family left."

Mr. Williams smiled tightly, "The hunting's more difficult, I'll wager."

This cryptic remark caused Mr. Kemp to blush. A sudden silence fell around the table, and then a rush of small conversations. Next to Caroline, Mr. Williams stared at the crockery for a moment before visibly shaking off tension. He turned toward her.

Sensing his need for diverting conversation, Caroline asked, "Do your parents still live in Wales then, Mr. Williams?"

"They are dead," he said softly. "Of grief and venom."

She was stunned by his tone of deep torment. His dark, gray eyes held hers a long moment before he asked, "And your parents?"

Caroline heard her fork drop onto her plate. She had not been able to talk about her mother for all these years. All too clearly, she understood his point. "I'm sorry, Mr. Williams," she said.

His gaze flicked down to where her fork lay and then back up to her face, "I'm sorry as well, Miss Trewartha. I have great admiration for the work of your father, which I saw in Pennsylvania."

"My father is still doing admirable work, sir."

Mr. Williams' hand touched her forearm a moment and then retreated, "I'm glad to hear it."

During their brief companionable silence, Caroline realized all the other conversations about the table had stopped. In the lull, she heard Rudy say, "Don't know what kind of school is giving away engineer's degrees now."

Caroline's face heated, but she kept her gaze on her plate. To her relief, Amos answered Rudy.

"Her university near Philly makes them students work hard to earn their way."

The conversation surged again, covering Rudy's reply. Mac Freya said, "Gryf, we've gotta sound the hills. Find the source of the water that's invading Number One."

Next to Caroline, Gryf shifted in his chair to glance at her. "Sound the hills, Mac?" he asked innocently.

"Sure. An underground spring should be easy to find."

"Indeed," said Mr. Ivisson, "No doubt it's trapped between two layers of granite up to the point where the explosion busted through."

"Granite," Amos brightened, "It'll be real easy to hear echoes from that."

Suddenly, Caroline knew. They'd all been talking about her earlier argument with Gryf. Seismic mapping – wasn't that name he made up for it?

For the first time Duncan spoke, "Wasn't you mapping rock with a hammer and a long spike when I hauled up the first dynamite?"

Inside, Caroline groaned. Now they would give her the Big Lie and expect her to swallow it whole. Certain that Gryf's eye winked at Amos, she took a deep breath and waited for the worst.

Amos hunched over, both his elbows on Deirdre's linen tablecloth. "That's right, Duncan," said Amos. "Gryf's been known to use just about anything to get a sounding out of them rocks," he explained as Deirdre and every man and child and at the table leaned forward, apparently eager for whatever balderdash Amos planned to tell them.

"Normally," Amos drawled, "when we search for ore on the east coast, Gryf just has me hack down a big ol' pine. I kin drop one of them things so's it thunks downright next to whar Gryf is sprawled on the ground. Then I counts seconds and he holds up fingers accordin' to the kind of echo he hears. You know, one if 'metamorphic', two if 'conglomenate' and three if the echo is that mush sound what comes out of ol' vegetation, like coal. He's got the ears of a regular musician."

Next to Caroline, Jimmy smothered a giggle in a napkin. Amos eyed him balefully. "What's so funny, Jimmy boy?"

The child choked on laughter, "Nothin', Mr. Amos."

"Well then," Amos' face cracked a brief smile as he continued, "Pine thumping is fine fer the east, but it don't work everywhere. One year, Gryf and me was up in Montana territory, searching for gold and copper. In the high Montana mountains, the trees cain't get big. Don't make much thunder when you fell 'em. Gryf was reduced to all kinds of lesser stratagems, like dynamite and such. On this one swelterin' afternoon, we was ridin' around in what he thought was prime copper territory. We heard this mighty rumble. It was gettin' closer and closer and I started in to know that we was in the way of a herd of buffalo.

'Let's high-tail it.' I shout to Gryf.

" 'High-tail it?' says he, 'and give up this golden opportunity? Not on your life.'

"Right then and there he flops down off his horse, gives its rump a smack and throws himself on the ground. Wall, I'm not about to leave my buddy alone in the path of a herd like that. So, I smacks off my own glue factory and I straddles Gryf's body. I yanks off my hat and begin countin' and wavin' like you never saw.

"It must 'ov been the color of that hat – a plug-ugly mustard yaller – come from the hide of a old pack horse we once had to eat just to git ourselves out of a fix, but that there's a different story.

"Anyway, I waved that ugly hat and that herd split right around us. Left us mebbe a foot of breathin' space on either side 'fore they closed in again at the far end of Gryf's big feet. Not a one of them cows tripped on Gryf's boots, and that's a fact."

There were hoots of laughter around the table.

"Yup," said Amos, getting his audience back. "That was a fact. Thank God them buffaloes is graceful. For twenty minutes, I'm there wavin' my arms till they 'bout like to come off. After the first ten minutes, my throat was so full of dust and my nose was so stopped up by the rancid smell of old cow hairs that I couldn't count no more.

"Finally, the last decrepit bull rumbles past us. My arms 'ov been in the air so long they are stuck up there, but I can bend just enough to see Gryf crawling out from under a pile o' Montana dust. He wobbles to his feet and cranks my arms down before he tells me the results of his soundin'.

" 'Amos', says he, 'now that was a thing worth doin', cause not three hundred feet below us I definitely heard the lovely ting of copper.'

"Then, he goes and scratches some itch he's got inside his shirt and pulls out this mean lookin' snake what tooken refuge in there from the herd.

"'Amos,' says Gryf, holdin' that spittin' critter behind the jaws, 'In honor of this beautiful big ol' snake, I believe we should call this mine The Anaconda'."

Amidst general groaning, Caroline started to rise, angry at being the butt of their joke, but Gryf put his hand on her arm and held her down for a moment. She glared at him hotly, but his hand remained, barely warming her sleeve beneath the table. She was as angry as she ever remembered being.

In the hubbub of laughter, Gryf leaned over and whispered, "Caroline, no one except Amos knew about our argument in the mine. And he knew only because he overheard it. I said nothing. The men are laughing at his tale, not at you."

A gust of pent-up anger whooshed out of her. Relief and a strange warmth spread through her as she bowed her head and looked at those long fingers gently holding her arm.

Across from them, the Pennsylvanian, Cornell Ivisson, leaned over to look at Amos. "Aw, Amos, I can't be believing that story."

"Not believe me, Cornell?"

"Naw. There've been no Anaconda snakes in Montana for at least two thousand years."

In spite of herself, Caroline laughed and subsided into her chair. Gryf smiled at her and removed his hand.

Suddenly enjoying the men's laughter immensely, she realized that if Gryf and Amos had been teasing her, their style was good. The best thing for it was to join in the mood.

A few moments later, Alex Kemp rose, thanking Deirdre for including him at her table. He excused himself early for the long return to his ranch.

Caroline was pleased when he spoke to her.

"Miss Trewartha, when this rough lot gets to joking around, please remember that a gentleman lives nearby and is plenty willing to rescue you from their humor."

"I appreciate your offer, sir. I believe we will be quite too busy for joking around."

A sudden silence greeted this statement. Then Jimmy Freya said, "But Miss Trewartha, seems like we get more done when we laugh."

The table full of hooligans guffawed at this. Alex grinned, raising his eyebrows and shrugging his shoulders. "You see," he laughed, "they are a difficult bunch at the best."

"Aw, go on with ye, Alex," said Amos. "Ye'll have Miss Engineer scared of a pack of softies."

"Two miles to the north," offered Mr. Kemp. "When they wear you out, send little Keir here. He'll bring me to your rescue."

As Kemp was hooted out the door, Jimmy's brother Keir called across the table, "Papa, can I ride Sheba to rescue Miss Engine?"

"I thank you very much," Caroline said to Keir.

Rudy snorted, "Boy, yer a bit young to be mounting fat mares."

"That's enough, Rudy." Gryf's voice cut through the few embarrassed laughs.

"I meant Sheba," Rudy protested.

Caroline sat very still, her eyes on the child, who seemed puzzled by Gryf's angry tone. She could not look anywhere else at that moment. She had been called many things by miners who wanted to be rid of her, but somehow, 'fat mare' hurt more than most.

"Keir, my boy," said Mac Freya, gently. "It's time you help your mother in the kitchen."

The child protested but stood up, giving Caroline an excuse to leave as well. As she rose, Caroline turned to Gryf. He watched her too carefully, as if he knew how badly she wanted to escape them. To keep him from guessing more, she spoke with firm and businesslike tones.

"Mr. Williams, I've been meaning to tell you that I've rebuilt a reciprocating steam pump similar to yours. It's in a crate in Freya's barn. Feel free to use it in the flooded mine."

Gryf's dark eyes widened, startled, hopeful. He half rose out of his chair, then sank back into it, laughing. "That's a good one, Miss Trewartha. I admit you had me going there for a moment."

Caroline began to protest her earnestness, then caught herself. No harm letting him think she, too, could tell tall tales. She gave him merely a small smile before she followed Keir to the kitchen. Though Caroline offered help, Deirdre shooed her out the door, saying, "You'll need catchin' up on your sleep. I 'spec you and our

Gryf will be traipsing around these mountains studying up on the mines and all."

After Caroline left, Gryf chuckled. "She got me in one sentence. Rebuilt a steam pump – that's a good one." Everyone guffawed at that – except Gryf caught Duncan and Rudy winking at each other for some strange reason, as if it were they, and not Caroline, who had pulled a fast one on him.

Caroline reopened the front door, stepped in and glanced at Gryf. "Mr. Williams," she said quietly, "Senior Manuel Lauriggue and his son are out here. They say that from their sheep-grazing meadow they saw one of your men buried by a sudden rockslide. They brought you his horse and his cap."

Gryf bolted for the door. "Manuel . . .? Juan Jesus . . . ?"

CHAPTER SEVEN

Caroline held her Davy lamp high as Gryf lifted Jesse Polgren's battered body from the unstable slope. Manuel Lauriggue leaned heavily on the thick spar of pine with which he and Olaf had levered the last boulder from the site. His son, Juan Jesus, removed his wool cap and crossed himself.

Earlier in the afternoon, Manuel and his son had spotted Polgren yelling, and running across the talus slope. They'd heard a sharp crack followed by a low boom. From their high vantage point in an alpine meadow, they saw the far mountainside lift itself into the air, hover for agonizing seconds, then drop tons of rock swiftly down, burying Jesse.

The Lauriggues left their flock, racing down one side of the ravine and up the other to attempt a rescue. Unable to dig Jesse out by themselves, they climbed down to By-Gum in search of Gryf, leaving all that was theirs to God's shepherding. Even tonight, Caroline could hear occasional bleating from their flock on the high meadow opposite this slope.

Gryf carried Jesse down the boulder-strewn slope. A circle of miners' lamps lit the pallor of the dead man's face. Each man, silenced after hours of frenzied digging, stepped forward, touching some part of Jesse's arms or shoulders as Gryf moved down the rockslide toward the valley town.

Outside their circle, Caroline bowed her head, not wanting to intrude on the miners' last gesture of affection and apology to their comrade. With one hand, she clutched Jesse's cap and the reins of his silent bay. Low to the ground, her other hand held her safety lamp. As Gryf strode past her carrying his cold burden, she glanced at the dead man's hands. His immaculate fingernails were drained of all color. Caroline lifted her lamp to light Gryf's pathway. Jesse's head lolled against Gryf's shoulder. In the lamplight, the back of his head shone with a circle of deep blue and magenta wetness.

Manuel, Juan Jesus and the others followed Gryf down the ravine to the valley. Caroline urged the bay to follow her, but Rudy Sperl stepped into her path, cutting her off from the trail down to By-Gum. "Mighty convenient this happening just as you was arriving."

"I don't wish such a death for any man."

"Gonna make it easier though, now ain't it? Can't make our quarterly payments, Allied steps in and owns the whole shootin' match."

"I want you to succeed."

"Oh, I believe you. Question is, do you want us to succeed as Allied Mines or as By-Gum Mines? You got a interest in the one. I got venture capital in the other."

Rudy Sperl turned and stomped on down the ravine. Behind Caroline, a sepulchral voice murmured, "Stay away, bitch." She jumped with fright. Five shadowy men surrounded her. They were miners she thought, but none held a lamp. In the circle of light from her Davy lamp, she felt as if a spotlight had been turned on her. Terror chilled her whole body, but she knew she must not let these men see her fear.

"I arrived after this explosion. I heard it happen as Mr. Sperl and I came up the mountain trail."

"You coulda sent the sneaking dynamiters ahead of you," said the same deep voice.

"Sperl says you want to hurry things," said a man to her left. "Build shoddy and get out quick."

"You wantin' to use long-walling," insisted another.

Caroline could no longer tell which of the men was speaking. In the darkness, they seemed to be moving around. She was wary of their repositioning, unsure what they planned to do. She decided to use Mr. Williams' leadership to make them think carefully about their next move.

"Mr. Williams and I are in the discussion stage," she said. "He will have the final say about what techniques we use."

There was an audible backing away from her. These men didn't want to answer to Mr. Williams for her safety. However, they were not about to give up threatening.

"We got money in this and we don't aim to lose it."

"Allied's investment grows only if yours grows," she said.

"Talk all you want," said the deep-voiced man. "Parade your little body in and out of Williams' and Kemp's beds. But stay out of the mines."

As if on a signal, they moved off down the trail. Left alone, Caroline began to shake. She tried to steady her hand enough to hold up her lamp and identify them. She saw the red-brown shirt and dirty tail of hair at the back of the tallest man, the one she assumed had that deep cemetery voice. Not one of them looked back at her.

Her arm could no longer hold the lamp. She let it droop at her side while nausea washed over her. Cold shivering forced her to kneel between Jesse Polgren's horse and the lamp. In the darkness she relived her mother's death. She was ten years old, in the cellar with Aunt Agatha's hand clamped over her mouth, Grandfather O'Donnell cowering in the potato bin. Above them, the sound of her mother in the farmhouse kitchen, screaming as renegade soldiers surrounded her. Chairs scattered, a heavy pan crashed to the floor. Off in the distance, the incessant rumble of guns near the market town of Gettysburg.

Moments later, her mother's screams had ceased. As Aunt Agatha held her immobile, Caroline vowed never again to be without power. She would be the one making decisions, when to defend the farm, when to shoot those who threatened. She promised herself to be the man Grandfather thought he was.

And then the cellar door opened.

Here in the wilderness, she was no more a man than Aunt Agatha – fearful, cowardly, shaking in every part of her self. Still without power. Still making decisions through a man and hiding behind his name. Damn the Gryf Williams of the world – the ones who held power because they were big and because they were men.

And thank God his name had made the monsters leave her alone.

Polgren's bay nuzzled her into action. Caroline leaned against the bay's warm nose and then rose bringing the lamp up with her. She turned the lever down, killing the light. She had no wish to announce her movements. She reached up to the saddle, thinking to ride the horse in case any of the men lay in wait for her along the way. Her hand knocked against a rifle in a saddle holster.

Jesse had a gun. Why didn't he use it? Why was he off the bay, running and yelling? Was he trying to save someone else from a disaster he saw would happen?

She glanced up toward the looming shadow of the ridge. From here, Jesse could have seen who started the avalanche.

The bay's nervous prancing convinced her to stop questioning and get moving. The lamp was almost cool as she swung up into the saddle, but she held it away from her to keep it from singeing the bay's mane. With the tied reins looped around the pommel, Caroline let the horse have his head. She kept her free hand near the rifle butt all the way back to town.

**

Gryf carried the body home to Jesse's wife. Caroline arrived as Gryf came to Polgren's cabin. She saw that the women of the town had gathered with food and linen. Dismounting, she stood at the back of the crowd, holding the bay's reins. The procession of miners hovered uncertainly in the yard. Glancing about, Caroline could see no sign of the man with the queue of hair, either in the crowd or behind her.

Mrs. Polgren stepped off the porch, touched her husband's head, took his hand in hers, held it to her cheek and then tried to place it over his chest. It slumped down, dangling beside Gryf's leg as it had all the way down the ravine.

"I'm sorry, Marie" Gryf said. "I don't know how it happened."

For the first time, Marie looked at Gryf and then around at the men and Caroline. "You must all be exhausted. Please bring him inside. Ellen would you help me with the children?"

"Of course," said a tall, quiet woman who stood near the cabin door. Caroline remembered the mention of Ellen at dinner. One of the men had teased Olaf about her. Ellen opened the door to the cabin making way for Gryf. Directly inside stood a ten-year-old boy, his eyes sleepy, his hair in spikes. "What's Daddy doin', Mamma?"

"Mr. Williams has brought him home, Matt," Marie said.

"What's that lady doin' with our Sukie?"

Marie glanced at Caroline far at the back of the gathered crowd. Caroline answered the boy. "I brought your bay home."

A silence followed, during which no one seemed to know what to say. Matt gazed at his father's body in Gryf's arms, and at the bay. Then in a strained but dignified tone, he said, "I thank you all for helping my Daddy. I will rub down Sukie, Mamma."

Marie nodded at him.

Ellen said, "Matt, if you'll tell me what to do, I'll help you."

"Thank you, teacher," the boy said. "The saddle is kinda big."

As Matt stepped off the porch, the crowd parted. Caroline handed him the reins and his father's hat. He gazed at the hat. Then, without looking up again, he said, "Thank you ma'am." and stepped unsteadily toward the horse shed at the back of the property.

The woman named Ellen, touched Caroline's arm. "Thank you, Miss Trewartha."

Caroline, numb with grief for the child, merely nodded. She watched the young boy reel toward the shelter of the shed. Once he and his teacher were inside it, Caroline heard him sob, "Oh teacher..."

**

An hour later, unable to sleep, Caroline slumped against the porch rail outside her barn room. She listened to the sound of a carpenter sawing and hammering, somewhere off in the town. She watched the light in Marie Polgren's cabin.

Caroline knew that as an outsider in the community she should leave the gathered mourners alone. She'd come to her room, but she could not sleep while another woman readied her loved one for burial. She had seen it too often, knew every change of emotion. Marie, like the miner's wives for generations before her, would alternately weep and berate her husband for getting himself killed. She would try to rid his body of evidence of its last trauma, straighten his broken limbs, attempt to scrub away deep bruises. She would comb his hair, remembering its feel between her fingers as they made love and created children who would now be without a father.

If only the dynamite hadn't been so available. If only Gryf had kept better track of who intended to use it on that day. Jesse Polgren's death was tragic, and unnecessary.

It was her responsibility to find out why it happened. She must take a better look at the evidence. She had to figure out what they were trying to accomplish. Caroline descended the steps from her barn loft. She listened for the sound of stealthy boots, knowing the men who had surrounded her in the ravine might still be out.

She had been the unwanted engineer once in Kentucky. She decided then that she couldn't live her life locked inside safe buildings. Those who didn't want her were less belligerent if she went about the same as every other miner.

She carried a knife in her boot and forced herself to be out if there was reason to be out. Daylight or darkness, it didn't matter. It was always dark when she ventured into mines.

Beyond the town, even through the darkness she could see crystal water shimmering down from the hanging snowy valley. The sound of splashing drew her on a path around the town and to the base of the falls at the creek. Caroline tried to recall the name Gryf used for this creek. A Welsh word she thought, but she hadn't caught the sound of it. She had a depressing feeling that she wasn't going to get much chance to know this valley better.

**

As Caroline Trewartha walked past the Freya's house, a tall shadow moved behind her from the aspen grove toward the barn. For a long moment, the figure hovered between the barn and her path, then moved decisively toward the barn.

**

Gryf tossed another pebble into Dyfi Creek. He tried to muster up towering rage, but felt only an abyss of sadness. His whole body ached, wrung out from digging and then from building Jesse's coffin. But he couldn't sleep until he had the answer to what

78

happened. He studied the creek bed, and beyond it, the rocky avalanche which had killed Jesse. His death was no accident. Jesse of all people knew the explosive rules – he'd insisted on those rules as a condition for joining the By-Gum Venture Company. Impossible that he caused this disaster. The scene Manuel and Juan Jesus had described kept returning to Gryf's mind – Jesse at the bottom of the talus slope, running and yelling.

Did Jesse realize at the last moment what was going on? Who was he yelling at?

Gryf heard a boot scrape on the rocky shore of the creek. In the darkness, he withdrew into the camouflage of scrubby cottonwoods.

Come back to see if you've left any evidence, have ye?

He tensed for the unknown. It would be a stranger, that much he was sure of. In this remote valley he knew everyone. And, except for the Wrights and a few ranching or sheep-herding families like Manuel's, every inhabitant in the region had been invited here by his company. Gryf crouched low.

Revealed by the light background of the rushing creek, Miss Trewartha stepped gingerly along the bank, lifting her skirts clear of the water. Gryf hesitated.

Doesn't she know it's dangerous here. A mad-man has blown up the mountainside.

A second, unwelcome train of thought forced itself to his attention.

Is she as flawed as all the other tools Allied has sent me? Is she here to meet someone – an accomplice here before her arrival?

He worked to maintain his grip on suspicion. However, merely watching her move put his logical mind on hold. Gryf knew from experience that following his instinctive responses to a woman was the same as courting danger. Still, tender memories of Caroline played across his thoughts: her barely disguised fear as she lowered herself into his mine; her nymph's silhouette dancing on the curtains of the barn-loft window. His inner conflict intensified as he tried to replace those endearing images with reasoned thought.

Heat rose in his body as he watched her raise a foot to remove one boot – an awkward process, made difficult, he imagined, by bone stays in her undergarments. Gryf's mind flickered on an imagined hero's task, freeing the maiden. His fantasy was fed by the play of light from the water onto her dark-stockinged limb.

Limb, be deviled, Gryf thought. That is plainly a beautiful ankle and calf.

Plain speaking did not cool his blood. When she dropped her left shoe, wiggled her freed toes over the edge of the river and proceeded to remove the stocking, Gryf clamped down on a moan. He had to act now, lest she intended to undress completely and bathe, as he had done only hours ago.

"I thought you had already retired, Miss Trewartha."

She whirled toward his voice, feet apart, arms up, fists clenched. From one fist, her stocking dangled, marring her warrior image.

Gryf sauntered from his cottonwood lair. "Goodness," he said, "I never believed myself so formidable as all that."

"Why were you hiding in the underbrush?" she gasped.

"Were you hoping to keep your meeting a secret?"

"Meeting?"

"Quite the theatrical display of innocence, Miss. Dramatic, but not convincing."

She dismissed his assessment with a stagey wave, "Oh la, sir. Who would expect such elevated taste from so *miner* a critic?"

"Oh, a pun. A small touch of bardic blood after all." Baiting her took his mind off Jesse for a moment. "Who were you waiting for?" he asked.

She made the lovely motion of exasperation he'd been working for – turned partially away from him, raised her chin, glanced over her shoulder and said. "You'll never know now, Blunderfoot."

Those magnificent eyes! he thought.

"I confess," she announced, "my co-conspirator faded into the forest at the first thump of your boot." She stuffed her stocking into her skirt pocket and stalked away, saying, "I may as well be gone, myself."

Within five steps she hopped to an abrupt halt. "Ow!" She bent over her bare foot.

"Step on a thorn?" he asked, retrieving her forgotten boot.

She studied the bottom of her foot. "Not sure." She wobbled.

Gryf reached out to steady her, his hand on her forearm. She jerked away, lost her balance and fell to a sudden seat on a boulder. "For want of a shoe," she whispered dejectedly. Wrapping her arms around her knees, she leaned her forehead onto her fists.

"Did you cut your foot?" He knelt in front of her.

"No." Her voice was muffled by her arms.

"Shouldn't we check?"

"I . . . I couldn't sleep. Even though I don't know her, I keep thinking, now Marie Polgren is crying, now angry, now caring for him and whispering goodbye."

Gryf tasted the bitter truth. "Yes," he whispered. "Marie sent me away, saying she wanted to cuss at and lay Jesse out alone."

Even in the little reflective light Gryf could see Caroline's eyes refocused beyond his shoulder. "What would Mr. Polgren gain by doing that?" she asked.

He glanced over his shoulder at the rock-fall, "What would anyone be trying to do up there?"

In silence, Caroline studied the terrain near them for long moments. "As Duncan drove me up here, we passed hundreds of trickling waterfalls. I noticed you'd diverted many of them into small pipes beneath the wagon trail."

"I worked with the local ranchers to do that. It gave us a stable transport road."

81

She nodded without looking directly at him. "However, " she said, "up here in the valley, I saw that the source of most of those small trickles is the snowfield on the north cliff above the By-Gum Valley. . .the cliff which is interrupted by this half-mile ravine."

"Yes," he agreed, "both sides of the ravine, all those small creeks drip down that cliff."

"And then, off to the west a bit," Caroline waved an arm, "is the boom of the bigger falls.

"The one that directly feeds Dyfi Creek," he said.

"Dyfi. Your home."

"Once," he heard the bitterness in his own voice. Diverting the conversation, he asked, "What are you leading up to with all these musings on our geography?"

Caroline was slow in answering. And her reply seemed evasive. "Who stands to gain if you could no longer work these mines?"

"Certainly not Jesse Polgren, if that's what you're hinting."

"Who would gain?"

"Jesse's hands were clean. He'd not dug nor drilled a hole to insert the dynamite stick. Furthermore, he was hit in the back of the head by a small rock – a pebble imbedded from directly behind him, traveling at a very high speed. That is what killed him. He'd nay a chance."

"Rock from the explosion," Caroline stated.

Gryf shook his head. "As Jesse ran, the explosion was above, not behind him. Jesse Polgren was shot in the back of the head. The sharp crack Manuel heard."

"Shot?"

"The pebble has rifling scratches. It was meant to look like the result of the explosion."

The revelation stunned Caroline. "But that's murder!"

"Aye."

"Who would want to . . . "

"*Nag y* . . . I mean, I don't know."

A long silence hung between them. Gryf watched the creek toss itself joyfully over the rocky bed, as if Jesse's death was of no concern to eternity.

As much to fill the void as to convey meaning, Gryf said, "Always, Jesse insisted on safe procedures. Always."

"Mr. Williams, has it occurred to you that with only a little more force, this explosion could have damned all of these creeks, large and small."

Gryf stared at Caroline. She was right. The bed of the *Dyfi* was only a little lower than the valley floor. Mere inches kept these rivulets and the creek from making a lake of this whole valley. He'd been so busy trying to figure why Jesse was killed that he hadn't understood the destruction Jesse'd been trying to stop.

"Also," Caroline said, "While the shed was unguarded, the dynamite could have been contaminated."

Gryf was so stunned by the thought of what Jesse might have seen that he was barely listening to her.

"Mr. Williams," she insisted, "We should check for moisture. Supposing someone sabotaged your shed after Jesse died and before John Philpot began guarding?"

He stood abruptly. "You have a point. Let's take a look."

Miss Trewartha hastily fished out her stocking, wiped her foot and donned the sock and boot. Through a fog of whirling possibilities, Gryf's mind registered the suppleness of her fingers as, in her haste to avoid lace hooks, she wound leather boot strings around her ankle. He reached out, offering her a hand up, but she pushed off the forest floor with one hand and rose under the power of her own native grace.

The sun rose on his mountains.

**

As Gryf and Caroline neared the dynamite shed and Freya's house, shrieks arose from the barn.

"The horses!" Gryf shouted.

Caroline lifted her skirts and ran, trailing Gryf by only a few steps. They rounded the corner and nearly hit the swinging barn door. Gryf grabbed her shoulders, hauling her up against his side as he dodged the open door and ducked into the barn. In the darkness, Caroline saw sparks of light flash as one of the horses stomped the latch on his stall door.

"Sol's gone crazy," Gryf muttered. "Stay back." He dropped Caroline into the straw which spilled out of the second horse stall.

"Sol! Down!" he yelled. "Sol!" The big roan rose one last time, then lowered his hooves and shoved his head over the stall door, neighed once and then stopped.

In the sudden silence, Caroline heard another sound – the quick writhing of a body in pain. The sound came from the stall next to her. She climbed onto the stall door. In the small light of dawn, she could see the outline of a horse on the floor.

"Gryf. Over here," she called as she unlatched the stall door and stepped inside. She dropped onto the floor near the horse's head and found a rope twisted with vicious tightness around the muzzle. The horse couldn't breathe. Caroline sought the end of the rope but couldn't find it. At that moment, several bodies seemed to enter the barn, but she was aware only of the death throes of the horse.

Pulling her knife from her boot, she called, "She's strangling!"

Lantern light flooded the stall. The rope end appeared, tangled under the last wrap. The suffering horse threw her head about, taking the end away from Caroline's grasp. Caroline straddled the mare's neck, holding her down while she cut the knot end. She shoved the rope end out of the last wrap. The mare's neck lifted

Caroline off the floor, but Caroline hung on, leaning over the mare's face and working with all the speed she had to unwind the rope from the muzzle. Behind her, the mare's legs thrashed, crashing against the stall. The mare's eyes rolled until only the whites showed.

Caroline felt the hovering shadow of Gryf Williams. She worked frantically to undo the last of the winding. His hands took the lengths of the rope from her as she paid them out. The mare snorted violently as the rope came off. Her head whipped up. Someone lifted Caroline by the waist and yanked her from the stall just before the mare rolled over.

"My Sheba," shouted Mac Freya, backing away from the stall as the mare dashed out into the barn yard. "She nearly suffocated."

Caroline scrabbled at the arm that wrapped around her. "Put me down."

"Ach, then stand," Gryf ordered, setting her on her feet. She whipped around to face him, her fists raised. He jumped back startled at her belligerence. "Ah *llances,* ye had me that frightened when ye crawled in there with her. Sheba's a big mare, weighs several times yer small self."

She breathed, "Thank you," and collapsed against Sheba's door.

Mac turned from examining Sol's stall door. "That Sol was almost out of here. Look what his hooves did to that hasp."

"He was trying to save her," said Gryf.

"Who would do that to her?" Caroline asked.

Gryf shook his head. "I've no idea. But I'll wager Sol and Sheba both know who it was."

Mac hung the lantern on a hook and began cleaning out Sheba's stall, which she'd fouled in her fear. "Whoever did this," he said, "He'd best not show his face near that pair of horses again."

Gryf straightened suddenly. "It has to do with the dynamite. I've got to check on John Philpot."

CHAPTER EIGHT

Caroline turned from counting sticks of dynamite in Jesse Polgren's neatly arranged shed. The tallies were perfect. The dynamite dry.

Gryf, stood outside, holding the shed door wide open. "Jesse's marks here on the door," he said. "The number of dynamite plugs still in storage . . . all in agreement."

Behind him the guard, John Philpot, nodded. "Jesse don't never let dynamite out of his sight," said John, " 'less he knows where it's agoin'."

"What about intruders?" she asked.

Gryf glanced at her quickly, then stared hard at Jesse's tally marks as he spoke. "Our people watch the traffic up from Isabeau carefully."

Feeling very much the intruder herself, Caroline glanced from the shed to the road not fifty yards away. "The guards would hear even the night traffic?"

"Aye, they do," Gryf said.

"The dynamite had to come from *somewhere,* Mr. Williams."

From behind the two men, a powerful nasal voice answered, "My thought, exactly."

John Philpot and Gryf whipped around. Caroline peered out of the shed door. There stood a tall, stiff woman of about thirty years. Next to her, babbling and bobbing, hovered a short round man. Both were dressed in a threadbare black worsted relieved at collars and cuffs by yellowed linen.

The man pointed his stubby forefinger at Caroline, saying, "I understand you sneaked explosive materials up here with you, Miss Trewartha."

The man continuously ducked his body to one side as if to deflect the strong feelings his words aroused. "Have your stores of dynamite been checked?" he asked.

Anger at his accusation swept over her. She strode out of the shed to confront the roly-poly fellow. He bobbed and wove, changing directions with every phrase, but when the woman nudged him, he stopped mid-word, like a mechano-man whose spring had been cut. The stiff woman aimed a brief, tight smile at Gryf, while offering the fingers of one slim hand, as if in welcome to Caroline.

"I am Marvelle Wright," she crooned. Without waiting for a handshake, Marvelle Wright removed her fingers from Caroline's vicinity. "My husband, the Right Reverend Mr. Garland Wright, is overset by what has happened while we were not here at our post. We were making such good headway for the Lord among the heathen in the high parklands, weren't we, Garland dear? I'm sure you can account for all your explosives, now isn't that correct, Miss Trewartha?"

Caroline started to reply, but had no chance since, Mrs. Wright leaned toward Gryf and simpered, "Mr. Williams, we want to offer our condolences on Mr. Polgren's death. We know what store you set by his skill and his apparent honesty."

Next to her, Caroline felt Gryf freeze. When he spoke, each syllable was carefully enunciated, his voice brittle. "What do you mean "apparent" honesty, Mrs. Wright?"

Only a moment of surprise gave away the woman's discomfort. She adjusted quickly, re-adopting a tone of caring goodness. "'Apparent'," she said, "in that Jesse Polgren ordinarily used his skill for its God-given purposes. Yet, if he chose, he could put his knowledge to work for the devil. Why even Mr. Nobel, who discovered the dynamite, felt a soul-scarring guilt for having unleashed that power. Or so I've heard. We may never know what tempted poor Jesse to blow up the side of the draw, flooding the mines."

Caroline's mouth tasted the excessive sweetness of coal tar crystals. She wanted to spit. She didn't know Jesse Polgren, but she knew innuendo. "Mrs. Wright," Caroline blurted, "Mr. Polgren may have acted carelessly, but there is certainly no evidence of malicious intent, which is more than one might say for . . ."

"Carelessly!" Gryf bellowed. "How could you say that? You know nothing about him."

Caroline felt unfairly attacked, "What would you call it," she rounded on Gryf, "when the man was killed in such an avalanche?"

"Damned suspicious!"

Reverend Wright's high nasal voice piped in, "Exactly. And where are your explosives, Miss Trewartha?"

"My explosives were with me at the time."

Mr. Wright's bobbing halted. Leaning into his pudgy face, Caroline said, "You and Mrs. Wright hint that either Mr. Polgren or I have acted without honor. Produce proof. My crate has not been opened since it left Wyoming. It's been locked in the Freya's barn since Duncan delivered it there for me yesterday."

Caroline froze. She was wrong. The whole tableau in the barn with the horses played across her memory. She stared at Mr. Williams. He shook his head. He was right. The fewer people who knew about the attack on Sheba, the more chance they had of discovering the attacker. But now she worried about her crate.

Mr. Wright's bobbing became more dizzying. His hands clasped and unclasped in rhythm with his agitated motion. At the same time, Marvelle Wright's entire body, though absolutely motionless, seemed to have stretched up to its greatest possible height. Mrs. Wright's frost-blue eyes flared, her pale lips opened slightly.

Caroline braced for a storm from the woman, but Mrs. Wright merely said, "Come, Mr. Wright. We have done our duty here. We have other recourse." She reached out, guiding Mr. Wright away by his elbow while she bowed stiffly toward Gryf.

Caroline was sure her mouth was open, but her utter disbelief kept her from closing it. Moments later, as the Wrights disappeared toward town, she regained speech. "Do you think they know?" she asked, "about Sheba's attacker, I mean."

"I've no idea. But, right now, you and I are going to check that damned crate." He grabbed her hand and pulled her at breakneck speed toward the barn. It took Gryf very little effort to break the hasp on Mac's puny replacement lock. Once inside Mac's barn, they walked all around the crate, finding where a crowbar had been used to pull at the nails. The effort had failed, possibly because the two of them had raced toward the barn at Solomon's frantic call and the thief had to escape quickly – leaving the barn door swinging into them as they approached it.

Once they had checked the crate, Gryf left Caroline to guard the barn while he hurried to the blacksmiths' shop and rustled up a better lock and a door bar. They worked together to attach the bar inside of the door frame. They gave Mac a key to the new lock and showed him how to lever up the door bar from the outside using a rope and pulley system whose trigger end Caroline had hidden well away from the door.

Mac returned to working with his son, Keir, on turning over a vegetable garden for Deirdre. Gryf and Caroline stood outside the barn, a companionable silence enveloping them as they rested from a good hour's work. Both stared at the dynamite shed, some three hundred yards away.

Then Caroline moved her shoulders to loosen their tension, and she walked toward the mine buildings. "Why was Mrs. Wright so vehement in attacking me and Jesse Polgren?" she asked.

Gryf slapped his gloves into his palm as he strode beside her. "Marvelle Wright is merely over-zealous in protecting her congregation from danger."

"And I am danger?"

"You are the unknown. An outsider. A woman who builds mines. For Marvelle, that is danger."

"And Jesse Polgren? Why did she imply that he might be dishonest?"

Gryf voice sounded a note of intense emotion, tightly controlled. "Jesse performed magic – blew up things, very precisely. To Marvelle and Garland, he was a sorcerer. To me . . ."

Caroline's throat tightened with sadness for Gryf. In losing Jesse Polgren yesterday, he'd lost an admired and trusted friend, and was blindly casting about for an explanation that coincided with his image of that friend. Embarrassed to witness his struggle, she moved her attention to the surrounding mountainside. They neared the dynamite shed again. Gazing upward, she realized for the first time that from where she stood, she could see the top of the slope that had buried Jesse. She experienced the flash of several images from last night – Manuel's story of watching Polgren run across the talus slope, the men digging frantically, Polgren's body at the bottom of the blasted slope.

"He could see from the shed," Caroline said, pointing upward. "He saw who was setting the dynamite."

Gryf studied the sharp slope above them, then his attention turned toward the small town, then to the main mine shaft. "Why run beneath the dynamiters?" he asked.

"To save someone else," she suggested. "To warn them of danger. Maybe he thought they were making an honest mistake."

Gryf's thick, dark eyebrows drew toward each other. His long-fingered hands grabbed onto the straps of his overalls. He made an about-face. Without seeming to notice if she followed, Gryf strode up hill past the granite-solid engine house and the puny entry shed. He worked his way across the burro's field past the vent fan housing to the shed that worked as the office of the By-Gum Mine.

**

Caroline leaned on the doorjamb of Gryf's office shed as he searched through his rolls of maps. "Ah." He yanked one out and spread it on his wobbly table. "Come see this," he waved her into the room – the first time he'd acknowledged her presence since he began rethinking Jesse's death.

Caroline left the office door wide open. She stepped over discarded papers and Gryf's big work gloves that lay scattered in his wake. Halting well away from Gryf and three feet from the table, yet still near the door.

"Here we are." He rocked slightly away, giving her a good view of the map. He pointed at the lowest contour on the map. "Here," his finger moved up the steep contour lines, "the cliff to the north, the snowy upper valley and the falls. Here the dynamite shed, far from the town. Beyond this, the short *cwm*, or ravine. Here, on the west side of the ravine we found Jesse."

Caroline stared at the map. Even from this distance she could see clear Spencerian cursive marking ranches in the valley and grassy parklands to the north. One of the biggest ranches had the name *Kemp* penciled across it.

She asked, "Are any of the ranchers or sheepherders angry about the mining operations?"

"No. We're on friendly terms. And the mines aren't on grazing land."

"But the dynamite – maybe that . . ."

"Aye. It bothered the sheep and cattle at first, but Manuel Lauriggue says they are so used to it, they seem to eat more when

92

we blast. Ye've seen it yerself. Manuel's little gobblers were up there munching while the mountain fell away across the cwm."

She needled him gently. "Are you trying to tell me all creatures love mining – even Manuel's sheep?"

Gryf relaxed his tight shoulders and he smiled at her over his shoulder. "Aye, the sheep, the dogs . . ."

"The burros," she added.

"Definitely the burros," he chuckled.

Caroline wanted to hold that moment, his soft smile, the warm sensation in her chest when he enjoyed something. But his smile faded, and the moment disappeared. He gazed beyond her, a despair in his darkening eyes.

"However, someone hates me," he whispered. "I'm too blind to see why or who." Gryf turned back to his map. "And I can't figure where he placed the charges to flood the mine."

He gestured her to draw closer to the map. Though she too needed to know where the explosion had occurred, her feet seemed unwilling to leave the spot of sunshine near the doorway. For the first time in years Caroline hated this reaction she had to closeness with other human beings. The best she could do was to lean toward Gryf's desk to peer at the contours of the valley.

"Look here, Miss Trewartha. This whole area was once ocean, I figure. Eons of dead plant matter under pressure, then folded up and shoved about by time and earth's own motion. The granite roof of the By-Gum is an intrusive sill – a horizontal intrusion of volcanic rock."

Gryf continued to explain as if elementary geologic terms were beyond her intelligence. Caroline laughed inwardly, yet she listened indulgently as he wound up his lecture. "The granite sill," he said, "cooled above the plant matter, the anthracite seam. The volume of water required to break it would be far greater than any of the possible sources I've found.

"See these creek beds?" Gryf shifted a little, again inviting Caroline to come closer. Anxious to find the cause of the flood, she finally forgot herself, stepped next to him and leaned over the map.

He pointed at several thin lines lacing across each other as they ran down from the butte toward the town. "These creeks will be swollen with melt-off at this time of year. Yet, they could never throw that much water down this hill that fast."

"Is there a glacial lake?" Caroline asked.

"Yes, a moraine lake." Gryf pointed. "Up here at the head of the next two buttressing ridges above the butte." On the map, Caroline saw an alpine lake perched above the valley, trapped behind a thick dam of rocky debris left by a receding glacier.

"It's huge," she whispered.

"That lake could do some damage if released," Gryf said, "but Cornell Ivisson rode past it yesterday. Still brim full and intact."

Caroline's finger traced the contours from the lake back toward the By-Gum and realized that its waters, if able to flow, would never flood the mine without first burying the town. She returned to study the area under which the coal seam was located.

Gryf followed her interest and then ran his finger up the slow rising ridge. "Within this long, gentle slope is the anthracite seam, a layer of sandstone lies beneath it. Above the coal, sits our intrusive granite sill. And the layer above the granite is shale."

He tapped at a sharp incline, marked by close contour lines. "At this point, hundreds of years ago, subsequent folding of the layers separated or broke that granite sill from the rest of itself about a half mile behind Mine Number Three."

"So," Caroline mused, "Since shale is impervious to water, the water had to have an underground source, normally trapped above the shale somewhere uphill. The explosion allowed the water sudden access to the space between the shale and the granite. The spring or source of the water has to be somewhere between this break in the granite sill above Mine Three and down here at Mine Number One."

She glanced up at him and saw his eyebrows raised high, in surprise. She finished her thought quickly. "Otherwise, the water couldn't have followed this granite path into the mine."

Gryf straightened away from the table and faced her. Caroline found herself staring at his overall buttons, aware at last of the confined space and the expansive man between herself and the doorway. She tried to breathe.

"I've been patronizing you, Miss Trewartha. I apologize."

Caroline cast a glance up toward his mouth, checking for his sardonic, lopsided grin. She met with an unexpected softness in his gaze and no twitch of humor in his lip. Confronted by her stupid fear and his polite regard, she lost her bearings.

"I . . . Mr. Williams. . ."

"And now, you wish to bolt out of here."

Paralysis gripped her.

"Breathe," he commanded.

She could not.

"Get angry, then," he ordered her.

Her throat would not swallow. She was aware that Gryf grasped her shoulders and shook her briefly. "At least order me around," he said loudly, leaning down to glare directly into her face.

Caroline wasn't even aware she'd raised her boot until her foot came down sharply on his instep and her ankle gave out. His eyes widened before they closed in pain. He leaned more heavily on her shoulders and let out a growl.

A shadow darkened the office doorway. Amos' voice cut across Caroline's befogged mind. "What are ya doin' to 'er?"

She tried to stand on both feet. Instead, she hopped because of the pain in her ankle. Gryf, still leaning on her shoulders, hopped because of the pain in his foot. Next to her, Amos hopped about,

95

probably, she thought hazily, trying to figure out why the two of them were hopping.

"Un-hand her, Gryf," Amos shouted. "Ya know she's afeared of ya."

Gryf moaned. He leaned against his spindle-legged map table. It scooted away from his weight, dropping papers and map rolls around their feet. To stay upright, he renewed his grip on Caroline's shoulders. Yet somehow Caroline was no longer afraid of him. The grimace on his face, their trio dance in the small office with flying papers – the whole situation suddenly revealed itself to her as ridiculous. Relieved of her nightmare panic, Caroline doubled over in mirth, sniffing and laughing until she was breathless.

"It's all right," she gasped, trying in vain to stifle herself. "Mr. Jawarski, It's . . . It's. . .Ohhh! It's . . .!"

"Not funny," hissed Gryf. "Tried to jab me with her boot, she did." He attempted to push himself away from leaning on her. Thrown farther off balance, Caroline careened into the table which gave way completely.

"Oh!" she cried.

"Bloody damn!" Gryf grunted as they collapsed together onto the floor.

Surrounded by the clatter of falling objects, aware of the loose boards beneath her and the trembling office walls, Caroline covered her head with her arms. She fully expected the whole shed to tumble around them. Moments passed in heavy silence. The shed stood. Caroline glanced out of her circled arms. Gryf was glaring at Amos and rubbing his instep.

"What do you want, Jawarski?" Gryf blared.

"Marie sent me. Wants you to do the honors at Jesse's service. Won't have that Wright fellow."

After a long silence, Gryf asked, "You find the coffin?"

Caroline remembered last night's rhythmic sawing.

"Looks purty," said Amos. "All planed and with them beveled finishes around the lid – Marie is grateful to ya."

"She ready?"

"About to drop, if ya wanna know. But she ain't gonna quit till he's safe on his way to heaven, so ya best come."

Gryf glanced at Caroline, as if he were assessing something about her. "Amos," he said, "Miss Trewartha and I have one thing to deal with. Then we'll be right along. It'll be just a minute. Would you mind gathering everyone together at Marie's?"

"I'll do that." Amos said. "Jesse's crew is set to carry him to the cemetery."

Amos' attention shifted to Caroline, checking her well-being as she sat amidst the paper mess on the floor. She straightened her back, smiled at him and said, "I'm quite safe, Mr. Jawarski."

"Well, all right, ma'am." He touched his head and backed out the shed door.

Gryf waited for Amos' footsteps to recede. Caroline, certain Gryf was about to let her have a lecture, busied herself with unpinning, straightening and retwisting her coil of hair. It seemed to her a vain effort to become a little respectable before Mr. Polgren's funeral. She raised her arms, pinning her hair firmly to the back of her head. Beside her, she heard Gryf drag in a deep breath. She checked her pins once more and glanced at him. "Well?" she asked.

Slowly, while staring at her hair, Gryf let out his breath. "Well," he began, glancing quickly away from her to the corners of the office. "Well, is Amos correct?"

"About us needing to hurry?"

"No damn it. Are you afraid of me?"

She felt the color leave her face. She stared at his crag-like visage with its lines of care. It crossed her mind that this man had been through hell in the last twenty-four hours, yet he worried about her. His dark gaze probed her expression for a hint of her answer.

"Are you afraid?" he asked more gently.

At first, she was able only to shake her head. Finally, she said, "Not of you."

"Of men," he supplied.

She bit her lip and dropped her gaze to her lap.

"How could you become a mining engineer and be afraid of men?"

Without thought she blurted out, "They weren't miners. . ."

"Oh God, "he whispered, "Someone hurt you."

"I try. . ."

Gryf reached out, touching her hand briefly. "I know you try. You stand your ground. You win your arguments. You work, you learn, you fight. You are intrepid. But when you are trapped, you can't breathe."

Caroline swallowed back a sob and glanced up defiantly. His eyes understood too much. Her tears welled. She tried to swipe them away. Gryf reached into his coveralls, clear into the pocket of his inner shirt and pulled out an immaculate white handkerchief. Her surprise must have shown. "Got it out clean for dinner last night," he explained.

She smiled, and sniffed, and took the linen. "We should be going," she said rising from the floor. He followed her up. Without looking at each other, both tested their injuries and found they could walk without grimacing. They glanced at each other and Caroline felt herself blush with remorse for having hurt him. She hastened toward the office door, but Gryf's hand on her sleeve detained her.

"Consider if you will, Miss Trewartha. This fear you try to fight off, must you continue to try alone?"

Caroline was totally baffled by his question.

"You've a need to wipe right here," he said, pointing at the end of her nose. "A little dust from our fall. And swipe at the back of your skirt a bit before we're off."

CHAPTER NINE

Standing in the sparse shade of an alder, Gryf waited. The townspeople arranged themselves on either side of the shallow grave. He saw that Caroline hung back, behind the other women. On the far side of the grave, young Matt Polgren stood between his mother and his best friend, Jimmy Freya. Both ten-year-old boys stared straight ahead. Matt's younger sister and his tow-headed brother wrapped their arms around their mother's waist. Marie, weary from her last hours with Jesse's body, held onto the young ones.

The women of the town were gathered around Marie, aware that her grief could one day be their own. Next to Matt and the Freya family stood the widow, Ellen Robertson, whose ranching husband had died only eighteen months ago.

Marvelle Wright nudged her rotund husband away from the female mining engineer, and ever closer to the grave. The poor man winced with fear of the hole. Miss Trewartha recognized the slight and seemed to shrink within herself.

Gratefully, Gryf watched his sister-in-law, Susan, and Ellen Robertson pull Miss Trewartha into the circle of women. As he watched her shy response to the women, an insistent tattoo played in his brain.

They weren't miners. They weren't miners.

Mentally, Gryf shook off his concern for her, and forced his whole attention to Jesse. He stared at the coffin. Every saw-cut and strike of the hammer had been part of a conversation with Jesse's spirit. Now, those thoughts returned to help him talk to Jesse's friends and family. He opened his ancient copy of the Testament.

The congregation became silent, every one of them staring intently at the worn brown leather of his Bible.

"Let's listen to the promises of Jesus interpreted by Paul in one of his letters," said Gryf in a conversational tone.

"Behold I shew you a mystery; We shall not all sleep, but we shall all be changed, in a moment, in the twinkling of an eye, at the last trumpet."

"Today we mourn a fine man," Gryf said, "and when that trumpet sounds for him, we ask God to take good care of our friend, Jesse Polgren." Little Matt's gaze moved to Gryf's face. From that moment, Gryf spoke for Matt and Marie alone.

"Jesse Polgren chose a difficult and demanding craft," said Gryf. "He perfected his skill. I do not believe Jesse died of an accident. I believe he died trying to stop a disaster.

"We can discuss why I believe this at some other time, but now, we are here to honor Jesse's memory. One way we can honor him is to thank God for the way Jesse taught us the safest mining practices. We'll think and work as you want us to do, Jesse.

"We also remember how he enjoyed life with his family. He looked forward each evening to your meal together, to helping you learn to read and do sums and then play games. Matt, as the eldest, you have many memories of Dad. You can help your little brother and sister remember him. Try to grow as he would want. Be honest. Be curious, learn, and play, and take care of each other the way your dad and your mother showed you.

"Marie, we all want you to be at home here for as long as you choose to remain. Staying in By-Gum without Jesse may sometimes seem very hard. We hope our friendship will help you in those times."

Gryf gazed at the pine coffin. His fingers ached to hold his plane once more, to smooth a bit of roughness he'd missed last night in the poor lamplight.

"Now, Jesse, I'm talking to you," Gryf said quietly, "Rest easy, there with God. You helped build a solid home up here in By-Gum. You invested in shares in our venture, and we pledge to make those investments grow. Marie and your children will continue to be cared for by your foresight."

As Gryf drew toward a closing, he noticed Garland Wright open his mouth, bob to one side and start to fling his arms upward. Forestalling the man's urge to pontificate, Gryf said simply. "Now, let us all bow in silent prayer and thank Jesse's spirit for what he gave to us while he was alive."

Wright's arms fell limply at his side. He glared at Gryf before bowing his head. Moments later, Mac Freya began to sing "Rock of Ages" in his clear tenor voice. By the second phrase, all had joined him, singing in harmonies that Gryf had not heard since he and his brother, Samuel, left the Methodist Church in Caerdydd, heading out to the mines of South Africa.

As the hymn closed, Marie and her children approached the grave, dropping small white blossoms of daisy-like Fever-few onto its simple lid. Gryf prayed, "We thank you God, for our friend, Jesse Polgren. May he rest in your care."

Across Jesse's coffin from Gryf, the widow Ellen Robertson slipped an arm around Marie Polgren and announced to all. "We women have laid on a dinner to honor Jesse's memory. You're all invited to the school room to share your memories of Jesse with each other and with his family."

Gryf was relieved to have Mrs. Robertson guide Marie and the children away before the burial was completed. He was also glad to see the speed with which Deirdre Freya reached out to gather in Miss Trewartha, saying, "Today even mining engineers are needed in the kitchen."

Miss Trewartha reddened, smiled briefly and allowed herself to become part of the town. Gryf told himself he was grateful to have

101

the woman nowhere near his sore foot. He picked up a shovel. Each scrape of shovel on soil sounded a call to arms.

Why attack Sheba in the barn last night?

Why murder Jesse?

What bastards hurt Caroline Trewartha?

**

Ten minutes later, Rudy and Samuel approached Gryf.

"Mac Freya thinks you ought to come see somethin' in his barn," Rudy said.

Gryf nodded, still watching the shadow of the alder decorate the sandy soil that now covered Jesse's grave. He didn't want to see what Mac found. He dreaded the possibilities.

"I wanted to be through with this," Gryf said.

"I know," said Samuel. He took Gryf's shovel and leaned it against the tree. "Whoever it is, they've found us again."

Gryf straightened his shoulders and gazed at his short, dark brother, "So what's Mac got, Big Brother?"

They found Mac on the threshing floor, just beyond Sheba's stall. He stood over the chest-high wooden box. Its top was askew. The nails had been completely pried out, and the wood around the holes destroyed.

"The crate wasn't broken up like this when Duncan and I put it in here," Mac said.

Rudy crowded up toward the crate. "How'd anybody know this was here? She must have told them."

Sam shook his head. "It's a big crate, Rudy. She couldn't have exactly hid it on the way up the mountain."

Rudy reached out to pet the nearby mare, but Sheba shied from his hand. "Damn," Rudy spat. "I think whoever it was, Sheba put up

102

a noisy stink about them being in here, and they tried to silence her."

Gryf broke into their speculation, "Miss Trewartha and I checked this crate an hour ago. Someone had tried to pry it open, but they hadn't succeeded. It wasn't like this when we fixed your lock, Mac."

"You mean somebody was in here during the funeral?" Samuel asked.

"After you showed me the changed locks, I just left you both here," Mac said. "Surely you shut the lock when you left."

"Maybe they were hiding in here while we work," Gryf said. As soon as he spoke, he remembered it was Caroline who closed the hasp. Gryf touched the twisted wood around the nail holes. "Let's have Miss Trewartha up here to tell us what they took."

**

"This'll just take a few minutes, ma'am," Samuel said, so Caroline left Deirdre and hurried toward Freya's barn. Once inside, she took a moment to adjust to the darkness, then she saw what had happened – the nails of her crate were pried out and discarded, the lid shoved askew on her crate.

"During the funeral?" she asked, reaching for the lid.

"Kinda looks that way," Mac said.

Gryf helped her lift the lid. "We need to know what's missing," he said.

"I locked the door," she whispered, but his solemn eyes didn't blink. Hurt at his withdrawal, and afraid of what she would discover, Caroline pulled out packing material. But her Watt's steam governor gleamed beneath the excelsior. The lightness of relief made her smile at Gryf. "My little pump sir."

He tilted his head to one side, narrowing his right eye in an attempt at disbelief, then he couldn't help himself. He looked in, glanced up at Sam and then chuckled. "Well stuff me with feathers! Wonder what that reciprocating arm is doing down there?"

She pulled out more packaging cloths to show him the motor. Then a fear grabbed her. She leveraged herself up onto the side of the crate to reach the bottom.

"My blasting caps!" She hoisted herself toward the other end of the crate. Pushing aside the tools and other wrappings, her pulse hammered in her throat. "The . . . sticks and the wicking," she said.

Gryf straightened. "How many were there?"

She plowed under the other tools once more, reaching as far as she could with both hands, praying to turn them up.

Just a silly mistake, she thought, they were there all along, but under the picks.

"How many, Miss?" Rudy's voice was harsh.

She stopped and stared at him. "Ten. They were in this box when we rode up here. The box was solid. It was nailed tight."

Rudy said, "You were mighty secretive about the dynamite when it was loaded. No one would of guessed there was anything but tools in here."

Caroline nodded, "One doesn't advertise dynamite." A fearsome thought came to her. "What if one of the little boys finds those sticks?"

"You were in Wyoming when you packed it?" Gryf asked.

"Yes. Yes. I was finishing that job near McFadden, but the dynamite was stolen here. It might be lying around somewhere the boys play."

But Gryf seemed deaf to her worries. "Did they see you pack the dynamite in Wyoming?"

Caroline's frustration showed in her clipped answer. "Four gentlemen helped me lift the main body of the pump into the box, but I packed the rest afterward. I suppose they could have guessed I packed my dynamite, since I didn't leave it behind."

104

"Miss Trewartha," Gryf said slowly, as if calculating how best to ask his next question. "How did you hear about this job?"

"Mr. Hume at Allied told me to come here."

"Hume used my name?"

As soon as he asked this, she was aware of the group rearranging itself around her. Sam stepped close to his brother. Rudy and Mac moved to either side of her. Tension filled the barn – tension she didn't understand. She answered carefully, not sure what they were listening for.

"Mr. Hume didn't say who I was to meet, nor what the job was to be. He just telegraphed saying I was to come to Denver and pick up a letter from him at the post, so no one in Wyoming knew I was to meet you. Hume wasn't specific about the job until the letter."

"But your father has spoken of me." Gryf said.

"Of course, he did," Her spirits lifted at the mention of her father.

"Surely Carl Trewartha told you Gryffyth Williams was here," said Samuel.

Caroline searched for a memory of letters or conversations with her father. She shook her head. "Mr. Hume's letter in Denver told me. Not my father. My father and I have been on separate jobs ever since I graduated."

"Where were you in January, 1878?" asked Sam.

Mr. Williams leaned forward as if extremely interested in her answer. "Kentucky. I was at the Carr Mines. I'd been there since autumn of 1877."

My weeks in the hospital there are none of their business, she thought.

"And you didn't read the newspapers?" Samuel asked.

"Sure, I did, whenever I got them. What news?"

Gryf snorted, probably disgusted with anyone who didn't seek out the dailies at every turn of the sun. She'd hated newspapers ever

105

since she was ten years old – had enough of reading about war and killing, and of being a part of them.

"Samuel," Gryf said. "She knew about the trial. She was there."

She realized finally what Samuel meant. "Of course! I was at your trial. I came to protect my father from the mine owners. He believed you were innocent. I didn't know you, but I knew if he testified for you, he was as good as dead."

Gryf looked at her. "We need to talk about the day of the trial, but not now."

Gryf pushed himself away from the box, obviously calling an abrupt end to this interview. He slid the lid back onto the box and began hammering new nails into the crate, saying, "We must get to the schoolhouse and Jesse's wake or Marie will be hurt. You go on down, Miss Trewartha. We'll close up here."

"What about my dynamite. What about the children? How are we going to find it?"

His hammer poised over a nail as he spoke, "I'll warn their fathers. Then we'll figure out who wishes to destroy us." He spoke then to Mac, as if she were already gone, "Mac, we need to check that new padlock, have you the key?"

As Caroline slipped toward the door, Marvelle Wright and her husband, Garland pushed past her going in. "Mr. Williams," said Marvelle. "We insist on knowing what you have discovered."

Garland Wright strode toward the horse stalls as he waved his arm. Pointing at Caroline, he stopped in front of the roan, Sol. "This young lady has bewitched you, Mr. Williams. She came here dressed in male garb, swiveling her indecent body before you in the manner of a snake . . ."

Caroline shrank back to the shadow of the barn door, feeling as if she had been stripped. Her body went cold.

"Attention!" yelled Gryf, his face dark with anger.

At Gryf's command, the roan, Sol, reached his long neck over the stall door and clamped his teeth into Mr. Wright's shoulder. The man gasped as the horse pulled him upright and back against the stall door.

Marvelle shrieked, "That vicious horse! Whip him!" She yanked down a pitchfork from the barn wall.

Gryf quickly took both Marvelle's skinny arms in one hand and removed the weapon with the other. "Mr. Wright is perfectly safe," he said firmly, "as long as he stands still."

Caroline, amazed by the speed of his action, stood rooted near the door. Gryf addressed Garland Wright.

"As a minister of the Good News, I expect more from you, Mr. Wright. Did Jesus judge as you do? Did he search for ways to slander others? Not according to what I read of him."

Pinned to the door by the horse's firm jaw, the man sputtered and sweated. "But look at how she dresses! And she does a man's job."

"She does a good job and that is what counts."

Gryf's tone warmed Caroline, made her feel whole and decent again. It was the first she knew that he approved, even minimally of her presence.

Gryf turned toward her as she hovered at the barn door. "Go on to the school, Miss Trewartha."

He dismissed her so abruptly, and so soon after seeming to champion her right to work, that Caroline was totally unsure of his attitude. She pulled herself together with difficulty. In as dignified a manner as she could, she strode from the barn and blazed a path down to the town and straight to the kitchen door of the schoolhouse.

CHAPTER TEN

Except for the hovering malevolence of Marvelle Wright, Caroline felt safe hidden away in the kitchen. Each dish she washed whistled its question as her fingers rubbed against the glaze.

Who took my dynamite? Why?

The dishes squeaked their soapy rhythm as Caroline's mind inserted other disturbing thoughts. Marvelle whispers. "It's her." Garland whines. "It's her. It's her."

Caroline heard Marvelle passing the story of the opened crate among the women. Yet Caroline could not respond. Marie Polgren had a right to an evening without rancor. Instead of thinking about Marvelle, Caroline tried to dig out a memory of her father talking about Gryf Williams.

Samuel had asked her about 1878 – the year she'd nearly been killed by a cave-in at the Carr Mines. She'd been down there by herself in the brief break between shifts, checking the timbering process. January 19th – a date she'd never forget.

And while in the hospital, she'd realized that her accident had to be related to her father's near death and his testimony for a man named Williams.

As recently as yesterday, she had thought Mr. Williams must know who tried to kill her father, but today she was certain he was as in the dark as anyone.

She'd been in By-Gum less than forty-eight hours, yet already she thought of him as Gryf, not as 'Mr. Williams'. At the funeral, she'd been proud of his simple, helpful eulogy. She chided herself for feeling any kind of pride in him. The truth was, she barely knew him.

And she cringed to remember how much Gryf Williams guessed about her. One question from him and she had blurted out her fears. And then in the barn, his gaze had been cool, assessing. He thought she knew more than she said about the dynamite theft. She didn't know how to prove her innocence or how to find the missing sticks.

Geology – that was her skill. She could find the source of his flood. Then he would trust her, and they could get this mine on the road to success.

First, she must make sure the children were safe. She waited until she and Ellen Robertson were the only women in the kitchen.

"Mrs. Robertson," she said to the tall schoolteacher. "During Mr. Polgren's funeral, dynamite was stolen from the crate of tools which I brought up here yesterday. Would you help me tell the mothers so their children will be careful?"

"Oh, my goodness. Of course."

Within minutes, Ellen rounded up the mothers who listened attentively as Caroline, her hands still wet from the dish pans, explained how Freya's barn and her crate had been broken into. She didn't mention Sheba's near death. Only one person knew and might give themselves away by mentioning the horses.

She finished her simple explanation, saying, "I'm afraid the thief may have dropped some of the dynamite. Nitroglycerin, the main ingredient, can blow up from the heat of the sun, or if kicked, thrown or stomped on. Please warn the children not to touch any. Get me or Mr. Williams if they find anything that looks like a dynamite stick, or like a strange shape."

A silence followed her speech. Caroline's head throbbed. She was sure they thought her careless and negligent. She would be sent packing, a failure. She had taken a risk in telling them, but she could have done nothing else.

Then, Marie Polgren reached out and took Caroline's wet hand. "Thank you for telling us, Miss Trewartha. We want no more tragedy here."

Through her blurring headache, Caroline smiled at Marie. "I hope we find the dynamite soon," she said.

"Whoever took it," said Deirdre Freya, "we'd best be finding out who they are and what they plan. Up to no good. No good at all."

Marvelle pushed her way to the front. "How can you take the words of this woman for the truth?" she asked. "She's come up here dressed unnatural and doing men's work. She works for a company that wants to own your mines. She could have cohorts who came up here before her. It could have been them that blown up the ravine."

Ellen said, "Marvelle, how do you know her company wants to own the mines?"

Marvelle became red in the face, "Ellen Robertson, you are an innocent in the ways of business. They loaned the mines all that money so's you couldn't pay it back and they'd have to foreclose on the loan."

Another woman said, "Why did we have to borrow money? I thought our coal was valuable. It's been bringing in a good price, isn't it?"

Marie said, "Our coal is valuable, Sarah. Jesse explained that to get at it, we must have machinery so we can dig deeper, safer, and pay the company back soon."

Another spoke up, "Miss Trewartha, I am Nan Philpot. My husband says your company has been sending us machinery that's broken or is missing parts. Why is that?"

Caroline was puzzled, "I have seen the machinery lying near the blacksmith's and carpenters' shops. Did some of that come from Allied Mines?"

"Every piece," said Nan Philpot.

"I came here from a job in Wyoming and haven't yet talked to the Allied officers in Philadelphia, but you can be sure I will ask them to explain."

"Best ask them to cough up the missing parts," said Nan, hotly.

Ellen stepped up next to Caroline. "I commend Miss Trewartha for her concern and honesty on behalf of our children."

"I'll say!" chimed in Deirdre. "Other troubles can be worked out on another day."

Marvelle Wright said, "Miss Trewartha was forced to tell you because she knew that I knew."

Ellen stared at Marvelle. Marie stared at Caroline.

Caroline said, "Mrs. Wright, you are remarkably alert. I hope you were also able to see who broke into the barn."

"No," Marvelle stammered. "How do we know it wasn't you?"

"Let's believe the best about others, Marvelle," Nan suggested. "I'm willing to believe the best about you."

"As well we should," said Deirdre. "Thanks, Caroline. We'll tell our children about the missing dynamite sticks."

Relieved, Caroline turned back to the dishes in the sink, breathed deeply and tried to calm her wretched headache. She was helped in this process by Nan's adroit introduction of humor into the women's kitchen talk. Over the next hour, Caroline listened to funny stories about other mining towns where their husbands had worked together. They told about Jesse meeting Marie, which poignant story led to telling of the unhappy romance of Rudy Sperl who once had a crush on an older woman. She couldn't abide dirt. Rudy's plight brought out Deirdre's description of how easy it was to locate her husband, Mac, by following his trail of carbon footprints.

Each woman's story led to another until late in the evening. Nan Philpot told how she and her husband met Amos Jawarski in a gold rush town called Rome, Nevada. On the boardwalk in front of the

111

Last Swill Saloon, Amos performed a pantomimed wrestling match with The Demon Drink. According to Nan, for his highly entertaining performance, Amos earned enough gold nuggets to buy a round for everyone both in the bar and on the street.

As Nan's story finished to appreciative laughter, Marvelle Wright whipped off her apron and slapped it onto the sideboard. "Really Nan," she said, "You are condoning drunkenness."

"Naw, Marvelle," Nan shook her head in mock severity, "I'm condoning the arts. Amos Jawarski can be real fine theater. Besides, Amos bought us all a round of Sarsaparilla with ginger water."

Incensed, Marvelle stalked off into the larger room. With heads shaking in amusement, the chuckling women began to disperse.

At the soapy sink, Caroline could be useful and never have to enter the larger room where Marvelle might confront her, or where Mr. Williams might ask questions. Through the doorway, she'd seen him watching her, no doubt wondering what to believe about her dynamite.

Marie glanced at her from her seat at the kitchen table. "Miss Trewartha, thanks for bringing Jesse's horse home last night."

Caroline, warmed by the woman's friendly tone, answered. "I hope caring for the mare will help Matt get through these times."

Marie's eyes filled with tears. "I expect we'll all have to work at something mighty hard to get through."

Throat tight, recognizing Marie's unusual courage, Caroline offered, "I've got a strong back, Marie. There's something you need help with, you let me know."

"I will," Marie brought her apron to her eyes. "I will."

Alex Kemp ducked under the short doorway and brought a stack of platters to set on the sideboard. She held her breath, hoping he'd come to bid Marie good night.

"Evening, Miss Trewartha." He put a hand on the sink counter next to hers.

She moved her hand to the nearest dirty dish. "Mr. Kemp," she said brightly, hoping he never sensed how uneasy it made her to be in this small room with him. "I thought you'd be off to that ranch by now. It's getting late."

"I'm going to spend the night at Gryf's and ride out in the morning. Please, call me Alex."

She decided that a little teasing might make him treat her with less gravity. "Actually sir, I'd rather call you 'Forward'.

He laughed, but removed his hand. "Better forward than 'Backward'.

"Or," said Caroline as if considering, "there's 'Presumptuous'."

"I'm presumptuous for liking you?"

Ellen Robertson came through the doorway carrying an armful of dirty dishes. "Alex," Ellen said, "grab a few of these."

At the sound of his Christian name from Ellen, Mr. Kemp flashed an impish grin at Caroline and helped Ellen with the dishes. As Ellen began noisily sorting crockery, Mr. Kemp leaned close to Caroline.

"Can you say Alex now?"

"Alexander," she said stiffly. "Alexander the Persistent."

"You're a tough one." His disarming dimple creased his right cheek. He grabbed a fudge cake and sauntered out of the kitchen.

Ellen leaned over and whispered, "Stay tough, Miss Trewartha. Alexander Kemp needs to be thwarted, once in a while, just to keep him within sight of humble."

Caroline was startled into laughter. Ellen put a companionable arm around her shoulder, saying, "He has the most beautiful smile, though, doesn't he?"

"Brilliant," agreed Caroline, "but too serious around me, I'm thinking."

"Certainly has taken a shine to you," Ellen said. "You play reluctant. That'll keep him after you. Won't it, Marie?"

113

Marie Polgren smiled and gave her the circled thumb and forefinger – the sign of the perfect score, saying, "Nice work, Caroline. Alex deserves a bit of reluctance every now and then. That way, you could win him and all his land between here and Kentucky."

"But I don't . . ."

"That's the tone," laughed Ellen.

Caroline gave up explaining and pretended she was as clever as they thought. She put her finger to her cheek, curtsied and pantomimed a 'Coy Miss'.

Mr. Williams chose that moment to enter her sanctuary. She jumped back to washing dishes, as Ellen and Marie laughed behind their hands. Gryf bumped his head into the low door lintel. Rubbing his forehead, he glanced up at the women.

"That's a lesson to me," he joked. "Never let a short fella build the door frames, eh?"

Caroline concentrated all her attention on the fork before her. She heard his easy banter with Nan. Then he turned to Ellen.

"I see that Olaf has been teaching you to ski again."

Ellen smiled. "He's a fine teacher, Gryf."

Gryf shook his head. "He tells me those boards are going to be all the rage one day."

She laughed. "He really believes that, too. You should try it."

Gryf chuckled and shook his head. "I've got enough trouble just walking without tripping over my own boots."

After his exchange of pleasantries with Ellen, Mr. Williams sat at the small worktable to Caroline's left, where Marie Polgren was shelling peas and wiping her eyes. Quietly, he urged Marie to call on him about Jesse's investment in the company.

Glancing around, Caroline realized the other women had left the room. She dried her hands on her apron, preparing to leave Gryf and

Marie. As she approached the doorway to the main schoolroom, Olaf Fedje met her. Eli Polgren lay asleep in his arms.

" 'Scuse me, Miss Trewartha," Olaf ducked his head toward her. She backed away, leaning on the kitchen's outside exit.

This door, she thought, will make an excellent escape route.

Olaf glanced into the kitchen. "Mrs. Polgren?"

Marie stood. "My poor Eli needs his mother to tuck him in. Mr. Fedje, would you and Ellen walk me and my children home?"

Olaf smiled, and reddened. Marie shook hands with Gryf. "Mr. Williams, you made this afternoon's service very much better for my Matty than it might have been. Jesse was proud to be your friend."

"Thank you, Marie."

As Caroline slipped out the back door, she could hear Marie's black faille Sunday dress rustle as she walked into the schoolroom to get her Matty.

**

Caroline found Gryf following her out the back door.

"Good night Mr. Williams," she said as she turned toward Freya's barn.

"Miss Trewartha, we need to talk." His long-legged stride steered them toward his office shed. Caroline did not feel like dealing with his small office again.

"Mr. Williams," she said, hanging back so they could talk in the open. "I can't explain the loss of my dynamite."

"I need your help figuring out what is going on – Jesse's murdered, your crate tampered with . . ." He began walking again, toward his office. Caroline followed, just long enough to state her position.

"I can't help. You don't trust me," she said.

115

He turned to wait for her. "Someone besides Duncan and Rudy knew you carried dynamite."

She caught up and fell into step. "I practically slept on that crate all the way from McFadden, Wyoming."

Gryf appeared to watch his boots move forward. "There had to be sometimes, Miss . . ."

Remembering some ugly out-houses, Caroline blushed. "Most every time, I could still see the wooden sides of the crate through the . . . through the gaps between dried planks."

Gryf cleared his throat and launched in a new direction. "If you remember a time, . . ."

"I will let you know." They'd arrived at his office. She did an about-face, striking out toward Freya's barn, but thinking again, she stopped.

"Mr. Williams," she said, "the contract that Mr. Hume sent me, it is extremely lop-sided in favor of Allied. I can't believe you would sign such a thing."

"You have a copy?"

"In my valise, I'll go get it."

Gryf shook his head. "Don't bother. Allied has not lived up to any part of the bargain I made with them." He waved at the junkyard surrounding the blacksmith's shop. "Everything Allied sent has been detoured through a fellow in Denver named Stemmins; the cream disappears before it gets out of his office."

"Exactly what has disappeared, Mr. Williams?"

"Fifteen thousand dollars. And key parts to most of the tools."

Apprehension shivered Caroline's skin. "You've written to Mr. Hume?"

"I've written, telegraphed, got no answer. Terry Branahan was president of Allied Mines when I signed. I don't how this Hume fellow ousted him."

"Show me your contract, Mr. Williams."

116

"Come," he said, pushing open the door to his office shed. "What a mess," he groaned. Caroline watched him light an oil lamp. She glanced at the litter they'd left on the floor this morning, remembering how vulnerable she'd felt when he saw straight through to her fear. He waved her in, but she stayed where she was.

Gryf shrugged and opened a locked safe. Out of it he yanked a folder which he brought to the front stoop with him. He sat on the doorsill, leaving room for her. She continued to stand.

"Here's the contract."

Caroline reached for it, but Gryf didn't seem to notice her hand. He leaned into the pool of lamplight and began reading aloud. "*In consideration of the machinery purchased by Allied Mines for By-Gum Mines (see list below) Allied Mines will be given shares equal to twenty-five percent of the company – the rest owned equally by the investing miners.*

"*In addition, Allied Mines agrees to loan $25,000 to By-Gum Mines. By-Gum Mines agrees to repay said loan in sixteen equal quarterly installments at two-and-one-half percent interest, compounded annually.*"

Gryf glanced up at Caroline, and added, "That means we owe about one thousand five hundred dollars every three months."

Caroline shook her head. "My copy of the contract says you have to pay off in four installments."

"Ridiculous!"

"Can we prove which is the true contract?"

"That's the point of Hume's never answering me, neh? Short of going to court, we can't make him do anything."

"Oh, powder!" she whispered.

"A helpful sentiment. We can't prove anything about this contract unless we can find Terry Branahan."

"He can't have gone far. What else does your copy say?" she asked.

"Aye then," He shuffled the pages. "Given what you believe is the repayment schedule," said Gryf curling his upper lip, "there follows this fine piece of bargaining. '*If said By-Gum Mines fails to meet its financial obligations to Allied any two payments in a row, the ownership of By-Gum land and mineral rights reverts to Allied Mines at the date of the second defaulted payment. This contract agreed to by Allied Mines and By-Gum Mines on this day October 15, 1879. etcetera and so forth.*'

"But how can you repay any of it? Your equipment is just a . . ." Caroline waved toward the jumble of broken parts.

"A fiasco of useless junk," Gryf said. "And that's why I asked Alex to find this Stemmins fellow and twist his mustache."

"So that's why Mr. Kemp met Duncan's wagon on the road up from Denver. You didn't ask him to meet me?"

Gryf looked surprised. "I expected your father. C.J. Trewartha. I didn't know that was you." Then he chuckled. "I'd say Alex finished his job, started back here, and then met you by accident. Or more likely, by design."

"By design? If you didn't know me, how could he have known who I was?"

Gryf grinned up at her, "Given how attractive you are, Miss Trewartha, I bet he saw you, decided to meet you and then discovered who you were."

"Oh." She said, staring hard at her own twisting fingers.

"Indeed 'Oh'," echoed Gryf. Then he held the contract up toward her "Here's the part you asked about. "It's signed Terry Branahan, *President and Chairman of the Board, Allied Mines.*"

She stared at it. "President and Chairman of the Board?"

He nodded. "Oddest thing is, Terry can sign papers with that mouthful of title and not even twitch his whiskers. Very good at bunkum, is Terry."

She glanced at the next signature. "*and Gryffyth Williams, Grand Digger of the By-Gum Moles*," she read. "Being your usual serious businessman, I see."

"I'm serious about making By-Gum the best mining company in Colorado."

Caroline slowly handed the papers back to Gryf. "Something is dreadfully wrong here," she said. "This is not the contract."

"*Oes.* It is."

"A simple telegram will straighten this misunderstanding."

He nodded, "It might, but the telegraph office is back down that road in Isabeau."

"I'll borrow a horse from Mac and Deirdre."

"Tomorrow is Saturday. Abel, the telegrapher goes off fishing or hunting. He'll open late Monday afternoon."

She took in one long breath. Letting it out very slowly, she adjusted to the realities of Isabeau telegraphy. She smacked her hands together and announced, "Tomorrow I must search for the source of this flood."

He bristled. "*You* must?"

"I came here to do a job," Caroline pointed out. "We have to reopen Number One as soon as possible."

"Miss Trewartha, you are out of line. We – you and I – are not a team. When By-Gum's Main Mine reopens, it will be because the company's miners, its adventure-investors, have decided it is safe."

"You have financial investors to satisfy, Mr. Williams. Allied Mines won't accept shilly-shallying."

Gryf stood, waving his copy of the contract in front of her. "As far as I'm concerned, this is our contract. You represent a company with dishonest intentions. Moreover, you're unable to account for explosives for which you were responsible. And there is more, Miss Trewartha, isn't there?"

"What more could there be?"

119

"You knew who Gryf Williams was before you accepted this opportunity. Did you decide the jury didn't do its job? Did you set out to have your own justice?"

Caroline felt she'd been moved to a different state while napping. "Mr. Williams, what are you yakketing about?"

"Oh, come now, Miss Trewartha. Don't play obtuse!"

"Why would I decide the jury was wrong?" At his guffaw she dropped his contract on the porch and stepped down saying, "I admit that your acquittal was such a miracle that I believed you held something over the mine owners. What did you know that made them back off from bribing the jury?"

He stood abruptly. "It can't possibly be that I am innocent, and the jury knew it?"

"Guilt and innocence meant nothing in Schuylkill County that year, or even this. What hold did you have over some key person?"

"You are beyond the pale, here, Miss."

"You leap at the first opportunity to discount my right to ask?"

"Your rights are not in question," he said, grabbing up the contract as he turned toward his office. "It is your character and the character of the company you represent."

"Well, I noticed that the foreman of the jury is now here in By-Gum."

"Cornell? The man was in danger. After the trial, Samuel found him beaten and took him into his home to recover. Cornell had to come up here with us for his safety."

"Are you trying to convince me you had no hold over the miners or the jury."

"According to Cornell, your father's courage gave the jury their courage. They believed him and made certain their families were gone from the town before the verdict was read."

"Are they all here with you?"

"Cornell, the Philpots and that's all. The others live in Lancaster County."

In Amish territory," Caroline said.

"Safer for everyone."

Silence hung between them. "Am I still suspect? or can I get back to work on these mines?" he asked.

"We can get back to work," she said.

"Oh? We?"

She put her hands on her hips, stretching up toward him for emphasis. "Mr. Williams, with or without you, I will take care of these mines."

Gryf towered over her. "You may accompany me to the other mines tomorrow," he offered. "You may not go off tearing into things that are not your business, and which might get you killed."

"I will see what must be seen, make a report to Allied and shake the dust of your town from my feet."

He leaned over, glaring at her, "Not even waiting for Monday at the telegraph office? Made up your mind about the validity of me and of my contract without any real evidence, have you?"

"Real Evidence?" Hot anger rushed to her face.

"On a flim-flam, you've decided I have disreputable aims."

He straightened abruptly. "I'll see you at five in the morning."

"Way too late."

**

As Caroline strode away, Gryf tried to cool the heat of his anger at . . . not at Miss Trewartha, but at some unknown. He was scared for his mine, his valley and most of all, for the safety of every man on his team. Hume had forged a sham contract and ousted Terry Branahan from the company he'd founded. Hume or someone he'd hired flooded the mine and murdered Jesse Polgren. They wanted this mine.

They wanted Gryf Williams to fail.

He'd survived a murder trial in Pennsylvania, walked away a lucky and a free man. He'd come up here to find peace. He had found this rare seam. He'd invited only those he trusted to share this new life. He'd borrowed from a man he trusted. And now his work was being destroyed.

For the first time, Gryf questioned the past. He allowed himself to think perhaps all those other times, those other disasters were not just hard luck following him around. Those were planned, just as this catastrophe was planned. Someone hated him with a passion, deep and abiding.

CHAPTER ELEVEN

While stalking toward Freya's barn in the still night air, Caroline questioned her reactions to Gryf. Did she learn to be so judgmental from Grandmother O'Donnell? All those years of fighting against the pompous woman, only to end up her mirror image?

She didn't really believe Gryf was responsible for any of this mess. The more she learned, the more she believed her company was responsible. As the representative of Allied Mines, she was responsible. She had to pull this situation back from the brink. By finding the truth about the contract, about this fellow Stemmins down in Denver, and most especially, about the explosions that killed Jesse and flooded the mine. From studying his maps, she had a good idea where to begin searching for the explosion site that was uphill on the west side of town.

She decided to leave early in the morning. That way, she wouldn't be held back by Gryf's worry over where a woman should be. When she discovered the source of his problem, he'd have to accept that she could make By-Gum work.

As she approached the darkened barn, Caroline remembered the imposing roan – the horse that had raised a ruckus and warned them of Sheba's danger last night. This morning, that same sharp roan had held the Reverend Garland "at attention" when he tried to accuse her. He was restive, she knew, even a bit wild-eyed, but as an eleven-year-old, in spite of Grandfather's protests, Caroline had ridden his great charger all around O'Donnell farm.

Intending to request the use of the horse, she followed the path around the barn toward the house. The kitchen door opened and out stepped a tall man. He was silhouetted against the light from inside, curly hair blowing in the gentle spring breeze, broad shoulders filling the doorway.

Caroline stopped.

How did Gryf Williams get here so fast?

The man in the doorway spoke to someone inside. His tones were in a low register, resonant – Gryf's voice, she thought, but then Caroline heard what the man said next.

"I'll tell Gryf when I see him. Thanks, Mac."

Of a sudden, the mirage of Gryf Williams dissolved itself into the reality of Alexander Kemp. Mr. Kemp lowered his head slightly, as if to watch his step on the Freya's back stairs. The golden flash of his wavy hair confirmed her foolish mistake. Caroline hesitated, unsure of what to do with Mr. Kemp's too serious interest. Still, she did have to ask him a question, so she stepped out of the shadow of the barn.

"Ah, Miss Trewartha," he bowed slightly.

"Good evening," she replied. "Sir, did you see Mr. Stemmins when you were in Denver?"

He raised his eyebrows in surprise, "I did see him, my lady."

It was clear that Mr. Kemp was glad to see her. For that she should be grateful; Gryf Williams seemed only worried or annoyed by her presence.

"What satisfaction did you get from Stemmins?" she asked.

Mr. Kemp glanced appreciatively at her hair and eyes, making her feel warm, even apprehensive.

"Mr. Stemmins?" she reminded him.

"All business tonight, eh?" He sighed. Then he shrugged as if accepting her boundaries. "This Stemmins fellow claims to have no idea what is happening to our tools. I checked his delivery yard and storage shed thoroughly. No parts and pieces. I checked his books – $25,000 arrived, was endorsed over to Gryf Williams and sent to By-Gum Mines via the train to Isabeau. Isabeau Bank, which by the way is that three by ten-foot hole in the wall next to the telegraph office and upstairs from the post office, has no record of the money. Thus, I have to conclude that both the money and the tools are being stolen between Denver and By-Gum, probably on the train or in Isabeau."

Inwardly, Caroline groaned. She was sure Gryf Williams would hear no suspicions of his friends, including Duncan who was sole deliverer of goods to By-Gum.

Aloud she said, "The difficulty will be discovering how and who. If you will excuse me, I must speak to Deirdre about borrowing a horse."

"Going riding?"

She didn't want him to think she would be sight-seeing. He might offer to accompany her. So, she explained quickly, "I'll be inspecting the damage of yesterday. Have to start early or I won't have time to get there."

"Such explorations would be safer with an escort," he began.

Caroline was afraid he would offer to meet her, so she lied a little. "You needn't worry, sir. Your friend, Mr. Williams has offered to accompany me."

"Ah. Well. Good evening then, Miss Trewartha." He reached out to shake her hand.

Caroline put her hand in his. He slowly lifted it to his lips. She tried to pull her hand back, but his thumb caressed her palm causing her hand to jump toward his mouth. His darkened blue gaze held hers. The smile creases about his eyes deepened as her fingertips contacted his lips. The warmth of his touch caused Caroline's breath to stop. Her skin became cold.

She clamped her mouth tight, grimly ordering, "Mr. Kemp, I need that hand. Now."

Kemp let out a startled 'Ha!'.

"My dear lady," he said, freeing her fingers, "I certainly wouldn't stop this fine hand from being useful."

"Kissing hands has no pragmatic application whatsoever," she said, rubbing her tickling palm against her skirt.

He chuckled. "You'd be amazed at the results it gets in some corners." He glanced at her hand as it scrubbed at her gabardine skirt. She stopped its motion, hoping he wouldn't realize how much he had bothered her.

"You'll excuse me," she said, marching up the stairs. "I must speak to Deirdre."

He followed, swinging the screen door open for her. "Deirdre is baking bread. She'll be delighted to see you." He grabbed the handle on the back door.

"Sir, I will speak to Deirdre alone."

"But of course." He bowed, turned gracefully and walked down the steps. Caroline peeked in Deirdre's kitchen to find her hostess covered in flour.

"Oh, my dear, are you still up?" Deirdre sang out. "It's going on eleven o' the clock. Close that screen, Caroline," she said. "Don't want moths in here while we bake, now do we?"

As she turned to close the screen, Caroline saw Alex walking toward town. She thought a hulking shadow-man paralleled Alex's path for a few steps. Remembering the threatening group who surrounded her last night, she stepped out and peered more closely at the shadow. Alex turned and waved at her, unaware of her concern for him. When he blew her a kiss, she had no doubt she'd been caught watching. Then he saw the shadow man as well.

"Duncan," he called toward the shadow, "do you still need help with that wagon axle?"

She hastily closed Deirdre's screen door, but she heard Alex's deep-voiced offer. "I'll meet you at the carpenter's barn."

126

Behind her Deirdre chortled. "Law he's a handsome man, in't he though?"

Caroline was sure the heat rushing up her throat must be visible across the room.

**

At one in the morning, Gryf tossed wood into the wood box. The wood box overflowed already, but he had to throw something. He'd rather be tossing punches at somebody's face, but no face presented itself.

Caroline Trewartha feared him. No surprise there. No surprise except how much it hurt his gut to realize it. She'd been hurt by someone – badly hurt. And his wasn't exactly a soothing face.

Plus, she believed he had bought his acquittal somehow. That took the glow off his miracle – his second chance at life.

The cabin door opened. Alex took a careful look around the doorjamb. "You about finished with this anger? I'd like to go to bed, if it's safe."

Gryf dropped the last split log into the box. "It's safe."

Alex stepped in, shaking off his wet coat and hanging it on a hook. "Sam warned me. He and Susan can hear you whapping about clear from next door. The twins claim Uncle Gryf is in his "bads.""

"God. What time is it?" Gryf sank onto the side of his bed.

"Late. Nearly one in the morning. I understand you're doing a tour of mines Two and Three tomorrow."

"I expect I'd better. I'd rather be wringing somebody's neck."

"Not Miss Trewartha's?"

Gryf shook his head. "Not her fault."

"Don't you think it a bit of a coincidence that Allied sent her?"

"She doesn't seem to know anything about our troubles with Allied."

127

"Come on, Gryf. They didn't send her here because of her expertise."

"She turned around their mines in Wyoming."

"So, she knows something about mines, but what does she believe about you and the attack on her father? You, a union organizer?"

"Not attacked by me."

"I know, but that had to be how it was talked about. And then acquitted when all was against you? What does she believe caused that miracle?"

At the word 'miracle' Gryf glanced at his friend. Had he been talking to Miss Tewartha?

Finally, he said, "She believes I held some secret that made the mine owners back off. But I also believe she wants to help, here. She wants to find the source of our water, wants to help me understand how this happened."

"You be careful, Gryf. She may be an extraordinary actress with revenge in her heart."

"I'll keep it in mind. But now, I need you to think with me. All these things that have happened to us – to me – I think they've got to be masterminded by one person. And that person has to have a powerful hate to keep after me all these years."

"All these things? All?"

Gryf nodded. "Oes."

"Jesus! You don't mean clear back to that time you and Sam were nearly drowned by that boatsman in the Dyfi?"

Gryf raised his head, staring at Alex. "God, I hadn't even thought that far back."

Alex glanced at the overflowing wood box and then at the potbellied stove before he spoke. "Gryf, some of the things, like in Nepal, those were plain accidents."

"No. Even in Nepal. I inspected the haulage track the day before. There'd have been no reason for that rake of cars to jump track except the brake broke and one two-foot section of the track went missing. I was supposed to be at the far end of that tunnel when it went. If Rudy hadn't yelled at me for advice, I'd be under that load of ore with those five men."

Alex bowed his head. After a moment he glanced up. "If you're right," he said, "and I don't concede yet that you are, what have you done to deserve it? For years someone's tried to murder you? I mean that's way beyond ... beyond reason."

"I've been dredging up stuff, trying to find the cause," Gryf said. "Women? – maybe one of them lied, was married. Other miners who died? – maybe a relative holds me responsible."

"This goes back to Wales?" Alex asked.

"It's why I left Wales."

"Have you thought to return home and see if you can figure it out?"

"I left nothing there I want. Mam and Da – that mean streak he had got worse. Ye'd not believe some of the things he said to her while she cared for him."

"Why did your mother stick?"

Gryf's surprise jolted him, "His wife, man. How could she just leave him, and him shot up and losing the use of his legs?"

Alex stared at Gryf, "Loyalty? You think she did it for loyalty?"

Gryf slumped back onto his bed. "Ye've got to know it had nothing to do with love, and that's a fact."

"Indeed. That I know for sure."

In the silence, Gryf pulled off his boot and dropped it on the floor. He recalled his father's long festering hatred. Rhodri, growing meaner and meaner toward his wife. And then one day, his father, games keeper to Alex's father, went out to help with the hunt. He was shot, no doubt by one of the guests, though none were accused.

129

As if to bury the deed, the great Earl of Gwydden, Lord Forest, Richard Kemp, packed Gryf, Sam and the rest of them off to the south of Wales. British Justice, Rhodri Williams had called it. After the shooting accident, Gryf's invalid father dripped venom toward his wife during every waking moment.

Why? There was so much in her to love?

Alex's voice cut into his harsh reverie. "I saw Miss Trewartha tonight."

"Huh," Gryf muttered, untying his other boot.

"Now that woman is a puzzle."

"Alex," said Gryf, "I'm too tired to discuss the perplexing Miss Trewartha." He'd already grown overwhelmed with acid memories of his parents, and of Jesse's death. He did not wish to air his conflicted emotions surrounding Caroline Trewartha.

"She's clearly quick of mind," said Alex.

"And tongue." Gryf yanked off his second boot.

"That too," Alex chuckled. "She told me kissing hands was not a pragmatic endeavor."

Gryf laughed. "Aye, quick-of-tongue, but long-of-word."

"And oh, what a beautiful body!"

Gryf dropped his boot, rolled into his down quilt and said, "That'll do, Alex. Go to sleep."

Long after Alex turned down the lamp, Gryf held himself silent, fighting images of Caroline; of her slender back and taut hips as she walked angrily away from him; of her dark green eyes round in fear when she descended into his mine; of her standing on tip-toe to lean over her crate, searching for missing blasting caps; and last, and hardest to fight, the image of her at the sink in the schoolhouse kitchen, scrubbing pans with such vigor he wished to be a sauce pot and have his enamel worn out.

CHAPTER TWELVE

At three in the morning, Caroline nailed her note on the door to Sheba's stall.

> *"Mrs. Freya,*
> *Thank you for the loan of Sheba. I've decided to leave earlier than we discussed. I believe I know where on the west flank of the mountains the first blast of dynamite blew, and hope to be there by noon so that I may return before sunset."*
> Caroline Trewartha

She touched her fluttering note one last time, then tied her hemp rope to the pack behind Sheba's saddle. For one last stalling tactic before taking off into the darkness, she inventoried her preparations – the saddlebag with the food and water, the rope, the lamp for the cave she expected to discover. In the pocket of her split skirt she fingered her extra cartridges. She stuffed her father's walnut grip Regulator Deluxe pistol into her belt, covered it with her shawl and tried to appear calm.

She could not forget the men who had surrounded her that night after they found Jesse's body. She knew that none of them except Rudy appeared at the funeral or at the wake. She would have recognized the voices, those memorable menacing voices. And, though she had only seen his back and his long-queued hair, she remembered well the tall leader of the group. Any one of them could have been in the barn while she and Gryf improved the security system.

On Gryf's maps there'd been a notation for a bunk house for unmarried miners. Perhaps some of the men lived there. Yet, it seemed unlikely that any of the company would miss a colleague's funeral. Perhaps they were not miners, but phantoms, sent to scare her off and then disappear back to Isabeau. Sent by whom? Why?

Caroline screwed her courage together, telling herself she made too much of a brief and ultimately harmless episode. The men had done nothing but talk. They were gone. Long ago she had promised herself never to let threats keep her from doing what she thought right for a mine. She would act as a man would act – as Grandfather O'Donnell should have acted – with courage to do what had to be done.

However, she wished she could have ventured into the night with a friend, someone who trusted her. Marie or Ellen would have accompanied her, if she'd asked. They would want, as fervently as she, to find the cause of the explosions that killed Marie's husband. But for the sake of those who loved them, she couldn't risk their lives on this trip.

Caroline felt certain she would discover the site of the explosion high on the mining ridge leading up behind the Butte that loomed over the town. She imagined finding the exact spot and then dropping that gem of information like a sharp pinecone right in the lap of the overbearing Gryf Williams.

Thus, bolstering her courage, Caroline grabbed Sheba's reins. After leading the mare into the night, she swung her leg over the saddle and turned Sheba's head away from the Freya's barn. They climbed toward the ridge behind the Butte. As Sheba plodded up the flank of the mountain, they left behind the small town and the cemetery with its fresh grave. They left behind the sheer cliff that marked the north eastern side of the valley, and the western ravine where the avalanche had killed Jesse.

The night air seeped into her boots and gloves. It wormed its way under her blue wool cape and burrowed under her mother's paisley shawl where she'd crossed it over her chest and tied it behind her. Above the low clop of Sheba's hooves, she listened to the sounds of night hunters.

In the far-off hills, a mountain lion squalled its anger. Sheba's ears twitched, but she plodded on. Moments later, a large wing flapped so close that its tip feathers touched Caroline's shoulder. With a cry, she jerked back. Sheba's flanks shivered. The shadow of a horned owl extended its talons and then rose, a squealing mouse in its grasp.

Breath whooshed out of Caroline. She hated fear. It revealed a woman's weakness. The mare snorted. Nodding her head against the bit, she plodded up the ridge. The saddle creaked and Sheba's hooves clotted over the snowy, rocky ground. Inhaling the familiar scent of cool, damp granite, Caroline leaned closer to the mare's ears. Surrounded by the heat that rose from Sheba's coat, she yanked her cape around her throat.

**

In the light of false dawn, the man Kidde, scratched his neck whiskers and then let his hand come to rest on the shelf of his belly. He rode boldly on the top of the ridge watching the back of the woman and the mare on the other side of the valley between ridges. Old man Stemmins and the manager at the ranch, had said to follow her all the way up. Stemmins wanted to know if she found the spot. But Kidde thought the idea laughable. He knew the cave lay too well hidden for any ever to see again. Following the woman promised to be a bore. He flicked the reins at the muzzle of his

133

gelding – a snap of the wrist that made a sharp sound. The gelding's wide-eye fear pleased him.

**

By sunrise, Caroline rode saddle weary. After a time, she slid to the ground and hiked through a layer of snow in front of Sheba to ease the ache in her thighs. With her attention on the terrain down both sides, she stored information about the plants and the earth. Large boulders lay in precarious balance along the ridge flanks. The rocky ridge-top lay bare of any vegetation except an occasional drift of moss or a clump of alpine lily. In the low spots on the backbone of the ridge, water collected and froze after a storm. Twisted mesquite or scrub pine grew in such places. Plants struggled each year for very little growth. But where water could collect, there grew the whips of aspen and the stout pine.

**

The sun had risen at last. Kidde dug his spurs into his gelding. The horse's flesh jumped with pain, but the horse did as Kidde's heavy hand directed. He headed down from the exposed ridge top so that he might not be so easily spotted. For several miles, Kidde rode along the eastern flank of the ridge, five hundred yards behind the woman. Tracking this woman proved no challenge. He grew disappointed with the game – disappointed and bored. But he would not be disappointed in the end. He knew just by watching the sway of her body as she walked.

She turned to glance over her shoulder. He froze up in the shadow of a boulder.

**

Caroline's heart stopped surging. She sensed a distant motion below and east of this ridge. When she turned, she caught a shadow of that motion by a large boulder. Her skin tightened with fear, or anger. Could the men from last night be following her?

To be safe, she clambered onto Sheba's back and urged the mare to the western side of the ridge, down a sheep trail and up onto the next ridge, riding out of sight, below the ridge spine. Above she saw that a wall of boulders had been stranded by a receding glacier. Enormous rocks spanned the narrow space between the upper reaches of the two ridges. A steep climb took her atop the boulder wall where she stood in awe at the lip of a lake. The wall was not more than a foot and a half thick and thirty feet from ridge to ridge at this point. Below her, the walls of the natural dam fell away for two hundred feet, the rubble of boulders deepening to fifty or more feet toward the bottom. On her left, heated air rose swiftly up the frightening precipice; on her right, bright and deep cerulean blue shone from the waters of a huge lake ringed with the last of winter's ice.

Fresh wind filled her lungs with the scent of glacial-clear water, sun-warmed rock and sand. She dismounted. Leading Sheba, Caroline clambered along the shore of the lake and up onto the slope. She looked back toward the Butte, knowing the town was at its base. From here, she enjoyed a clear view of the valley below. At the lake's edge, Aspen trees, low shrubs and marsh-marigolds poked their green leaves above drifts of snow.

A flutter of wings drew Caroline's attention to lower Aspen trees. Rocketing from a high rookery, a rust and black harrier alternately somersaulted and dove, caught a rising breeze and rose. Caroline smiled at his antics, certain they were not performed for the silent Bighorn Sheep, but for a shy and hidden lady love.

She kept a watch over her shoulder for her imagined follower, studying the terrain behind her. No one. She breathed clear, free air.

The sun rose. The day shone. She concluded it had become safe to head back to the other ridge and ride down, searching for the explosion site. The shadow had been a shadow.

**

Kidde waxed angry and frustrated. She grew too careful, too aware. She'd slipped away from him toward the west. He drove his lathered gelding up the ridge behind the Butte. He hated changing plans – it meant work. He drove hard toward the explosion site. He could sit out the hot afternoon in the cool shade of a pine plantation he'd discovered when he and Cal first came up here.

From the stand of pine and aspen, he figured to watch the cave opening and be there if she discovered it. If she came back this way, she'd pay for trying to outsmart him. With pleasure, he'd kill her, if she discovered it. If she passed it by, he felt free to do whatever he wanted with her.

**

Reluctantly, Caroline whispered farewell to the beauty and peace of the moraine lake. The mare picked her way carefully down the buttress ridge some two thousand feet above By-Gum. Caroline convinced herself she'd misjudged the movement behind her this morning. She'd over-reacted. She returned her attention to her job.

Poking up through the snow, a bedraggled plant caught her attention. She leaned forward slightly. Examining the torn branch of a mesquite, she searched for any other sign of disturbance and found none. This ridge built up shale over intrusive granite. Beneath the granite lay the seam of coal. And above the shale, she believed there had been an underground stream. The stream lay hidden within the structure of the mountain until the explosion broke through and sent water cascading from the impervious shale layer into the granite and coal layers, and down the mountain into the mine.

Glancing over the hump of the ridge, right to left and back again, she continued her search for any disturbance of the ground; shrubs askew, fresh trails of rolling rock, or a sign that rocks were lifted higher than usual above their pockets of surrounding topsoil.

She approached a new watershed that lay off to her right. There, two hundred feet below her, lay a lovely pine and aspen plantation covering nearly the whole of a small mountain valley. The two species grew together like rows of corn inter-planted with garlic. She guessed these might be the work of Manuel and his people – a noble and optimistic reaction to the devastation that mining could bring to their land. Her eyes widened as she realized these trees were healthy because their roots had access to water – until yesterday, they had been watered by an underground stream.

**

Within the drifts of snow in the pine and aspen forest, Kidde waited. He watched clouds building up in the mountains to the north. He'd impatiently followed the woman's progress returning down the ridge above his hiding place. The smart woman had gone above and ridden back down thinking she'd lost him. He could hardly wait to see her face when he caught her.

Damned if he'd wait much longer. He pulled his dark hat close over his eyebrows and hunkered among the trees. The woman stood directly above the dangerous place. As old man Stemmins had hoped, the ancient boulders served to cover the cave opening from sight. Not much of an opening anyway. Kidde knew he'd grown too big to get into it. That's why he'd left the little rat, Cal, inside.

Above him, the woman rode on. The breeze from the gathering storm blew her cape out behind her, revealing her figure. She treated a man to a fine sight. Soon he'd close the gap between them. Had to take care of her before this storm got to rolling. Already he could see the black undersides of a towering cloud. Way off to the north, sheets of sleeting rain turned gray as pot metal. Lightning jagged near the cliff above the By-Gum. The clouds moved over the plains, shoved up against the mountains, and spread north and west toward him. Kidde gathered his gelding's reins and waited for the woman to move.

**

Caroline stopped abruptly. Three pines once lived on the spot in front of her. Now two stood. The other lay ripped out of the ground by its roots. The roots of the dying tree twisted away from a shallow dip near the center of the ridge. Beyond its fallen and still-fresh roots waited a long drop into the interior of the ridge.

Caroline's heart thumped her excitement. This she'd been looking for. Beneath the knuckles of the root system, she could see a thin veneer of cracked sandstone, ready to break at the least shift in weight. Near the uprooted tree, stood a short, flat dike of granite. The rock poked its fresh face out of the ground. No moss grew in its crevices. The dynamite exploded here.

Not exactly here. But beneath, maybe one hundred to one hundred fifty feet below the fallen tree – a powerful explosion – powerful enough to toss the tree, turn a granite sill on end and shove it out of the overlying soil. And the explosion had left the sandstone fractured and unstable.

138

Somewhere down the side of the ridge there must be an entrance into the belly of the mountain, a cave big enough for a human to crawl into and lay the charge. She reached for the loops of rope, untied them from behind the saddle and climbed down from Sheba.

She puzzled over which side of the ridge she should search. Caroline took a quick guess and decided to walk over to the north-facing slope to get a look down that side that faced away from the town.

Tucking the rope loops into her belt, she walked Sheba around the thin and cracked sandstone and picked a careful path down the side of the ridge near which the tree dangled. Small animals seemed to have used this path, perhaps as they gather pine nuts for the winter.

For long minutes, she searched the hillside for any oddity that might show her the way. She found none. Above her, the hairy fingers of pine roots mocked her, pointing to an answer she couldn't recognize.

**

Kidde raged. She'd fuddled around on top of the ridge, and then suddenly disappeared down the far side. He swung into the saddle and spurred the already bleeding flanks of the gelding. Hard work to catch up with the stupid woman. And now, his skin prickled with the change in the air, the heavy, wet quiet before a storm. Farther north, the afternoon heat crowded clouds up against the range. He wanted her. And he planned not to be doing it in lightning.

**

"Whoa girl," Caroline crooned to Sheba. She led the mare down a narrow path twenty feet below the spine of the ridge. From here, Caroline could see the whole of the ridge flank for almost a mile in either direction, yet she saw no more clues that might lead her to a cave opening or an excavation. She'd narrowed the search to below the blasted pine, but finding the entrance would require a crew on both sides of the ridge. She would have to have help for this search.

It made sense now to return to By-Gum. She admitted disappointment at not finishing all by herself, yet it would be great to tell Gryf Williams exactly where the water came from and how the dynamiting had been done.

She glanced toward the sky and became aware of the storm. It stretched its dark clouds toward her ridge. Disgusted with herself for being too intent on the terrain. She knew that as the plains warmed, the mountains developed these daily lightning shows. She should have turned back at least an hour ago.

Reaching up, she hoisted herself to Sheba's saddle, but before she swung her leg over, a voice stopped her.

"Don't move."

Her back tightened. She turned her head. Thirty yards behind her stood a hulking man – a man she'd never seen before. He held a Yellowboy Winchester and aimed it at her.

"Get down or I shoot the horse."

Fear hit as if she had been jabbed in the chest. She wanted to lean upon Sheba for support, but she lowered herself from the stirrup and stepped away, forcing him to choose his target.

"Don't try nothin', Missy," the man said. "Won't do ya no good."

Caroline stared at the man's thick neck, the wiry hairs sticking out from under his cap.

She was ten years old again, frail and paralyzed with fear. "Won't do ya no good," the soldier had said that day.

The mare, Sheba, yanked her reins out of Caroline's paralyzed grip. She swung toward the horse. Sheba's eyes showed the whites around the iris. Backing down the slope, the mare never took her

140

gaze off the man. And suddenly Caroline knew. The terrified mare recognized this man.

The night in the barn! Poor Sheba.

Caroline's mind surged with rage. In one sweeping motion, she grabbed the walnut grip of her father's Regulator from beneath her shawl. She turned back shooting. Her first shot caught him in the shoulder. Her second hit his ear as he ducked.

His shot whizzed past her as he fell.

Caroline ran uphill. He grunted and came up firing where she'd been. She twisted and shot again. Rock spit near his head. His Winchester flamed, but she climbed. His shots zinged across the ground behind her. She charged to the right, then left, always uphill with a picture forming in her mind, a safe place, protection.

Behind her, she heard Sheba's squall of fear and the pounding of her hooves as she escaped downhill along the steep side of the ridge.

A shot whicked the high ground in front of Caroline, throwing rock chips against her arms. She leapt to the left and let off a fourth shot in his direction. He yowled as the bullet thunked into the ground near his belly. He must have reloaded. He lifted himself up to aim, but Caroline reached the crest of the ridge and rolled to the ground. His Winchester let off a crack. The bullet whistled over her head as she dropped. She crawled across the ridge top as fast as her arms and legs could move.

Never again. Her heart pounded a rhythmic incantation. *Never again. Never.*

The earth echoed his tread. Caroline rose just enough to run in a crouched position, charging toward the three pines.

"Aha!" he cried. Caroline didn't glance back. She leapt the exposed trunk of the fallen tree and scrambled to the far side of the two standing pines. A bullet whocked into the nearest pine. Caroline grabbed ammunition out of her skirt pocket and fell to the ground facing him. She refilled the chambers of her Regulator and waited as he ran toward her.

CHAPTER THIRTEEN

Seconds before the storm of sleet swept into the mountain tops, Gryf glimpsed a small woman walking the fat mare, Sheba. In that moment, she'd been miles above him, at least twenty minutes ride away. He had only seconds to target her location – where a narrow animal trail dropped down from a thicket of scrub pines toward the valley between the ridges. Then, thick, wet clouds rushed around him, obscuring his view of the ridge and her silhouette.

"Damned woman," he muttered. He could not remember ever being so afraid and so angry because of a woman. Deirdre showed him the note Caroline left – interpreting it liberally as an attempt to help save the mines.

But Deirdre didn't know she might still have those ten sticks of dynamite that appeared to be missing from Miss Trewartha's crate in the barn. And sure enough, she rode up on the ridge – the one key ridge in the mountains. What the hell did she plan to do to him?

Solomon twitched his ears. Solomon's ears were about as far as Gryf could see in the swirl of clouds, but he kept the roan headed up the flank of the ridge. In this cotton-thick fog, he would remain silent. She might run into him accidentally if she followed her original course down the west side of the ridge. He strained to hear the clop of Sheba's hooves.

Instead of her hooves, Gryf heard the wild shriek of a frightened horse. Shots from two different guns rang over the mountainside. Terrified, Gryf leaned over Sol's withers and urged the roan, "Go. Find them. Go."

Gryf's heart pounded as loudly as Sol's hooves. From that moment, his suspicions of her were as nothing. He found himself praying. He hadn't even prayed as he searched for Jesse; it had been all too clear they would find Jesse dead. He heard two more shots coming from the top of the ridge. His throat tightened. Fear dried his mouth.

For a brief moment, the heat of the sun hit his arms and neck. The sun shown on the upper reaches of the long ridge. A mile above, it shone on the two ancient pine trees. Into the clear sunshine ran Caroline Trewartha, fleeing a giant of a man.

The clouds closed. The sky blacked. A bolt of white split the air. Blinded, Gryf saw only jagged black and white, a replay of the moment of the lightning strike. Caroline, a frail silhouette against a white ground, her arms stretching jerkily out, her blue cape falling behind her under a trodding boot.

Then the freezing rain sheeted. Sol charged up the snowy trail. Gryf heard Sheba's hooves thundering toward him. She would pass on the right. He leaned far toward that side and reached out an arm, yelling "Whoa, Sheba. Whoa." The mare tried but couldn't slow herself by the time she passed Gryf.

"Damn it, woman," he exclaimed, either at Sheba or at Caroline. His heart swelled with fear. His knees urged Solomon up a steep incline. He glanced over his shoulder. Sheba shivered, sweating and wild-eyed, but she turned to follow her son. Rain and snow curtained down between them. Above, a rifle rang out.

**

Caroline waited. The man charged along the ridge top. His coat sleeve gaped. Blood dripped from his shoulder and his thigh. Wrath twisted his mouth. He aimed his Winchester at her head.

"Don't move, Missy. You're in my sights."

The wind swirled. The air grew heavy. Caroline's chest heaved with exertion and with anger. Beyond the man, a red horse appeared from the mist, his flanks and mouth bleeding. The gelding's battered condition confirmed her fears about the man who owned him. She held her Regulator steady and counted backwards from six waiting for him to step on the fractured shale.

But the man halted beyond the fallen pine. "Stand up. Carefully. Yellowboy can make a ugly hole."

Caroline whispered, "I'm standing."

She inhaled the pungent air of upturned earth. Pushing up onto her knees, she left the Regulator on the ground. She raised her hands. "What do you want?" she asked.

He smiled, a slow dark creasing of his lower face. "First off, I want that pistol."

"Yes sir," she said and backed away from it. "I won't touch it. You can have it."

He lowered the Winchester slightly, "Nope," he said. "Pick it up by the barrel and bring it to me."

Caroline's shoulders sagged.

"Get it now," he urged.

She bent and lifted her gun by its hot barrel. When she straightened up, she held it gingerly in front of her.

"Give it over," he said, folding his Winchester under his armpit and reaching toward her with his good arm.

Caroline limped forward. "My foot," she moaned.

"Damned slow, Bitch." He strode toward her, stepping into the dark earth of the root ball. The ground caved in around him, rushing toward the center of the root hole. His eyes bulged with surprise. He scrambled to keep up with the fall, but his feet slid deeper and deeper beneath the exposed roots. His Winchester disappeared through the earth. He screamed and grabbed for the largest root. The uprooted pine slid toward the hole. From the cavern deep within the ridge, they both heard the rifle hit solid rock and then fire itself.

As the shot echoed, soil and rocks rushed into the gaping hole. His grip slid down the slick pine root as his great weight pulled him toward the void.

He yelled, writhing, searching for something solid to grab hold of. Suddenly, his wide belly hung up on a long root a yard below the surface of the soil. Frantic, the man wrapped his good leg around the root and stretched out along its length, dangling half in and half out of the hole.

"Oh God. Oh God," he muttered.

"If you move, Mister," she said, "I'll stomp on this end of that root and send you on down."

"Ain't movin'. See, Missy?" he whimpered.

She hated that word, *Missy*. With it he became every man who had ever tried to pull anything on her. She unhitched the rope from her belt and pointed it toward him. "Don't say another word except to answer my questions."

She tied the rope around the sturdy mid-section of the fallen pine trunk and then tied the tail of it to one of the two standing trees. Now his pine could not completely fall into the void, but he would have to work hard to keep his grip on the roots.

"Now," she said, "pull that wounded arm up out of the dirt and unbutton your jacket."

The moment he opened his mouth to protest, she lifted her boot over the root. He clamped his jaw tight. With great effort, he dragged the arm up and reached to do as she said.

Every time the man moved, his bleeding gelding shied sideways, ducking his head. The man must have abused this animal for a long time. Sheba's reaction to him had been absolute terror.

She spoke with calm. "Give me the gun from your shoulder holster."

146

Moaning from pain, he did as she said. When she had the pistol. She turned it over. There on the back she read, "Simon Kidde. Well, Simon Kidde, you were in Freya's barn two nights ago."

"I don't know any Freya."

Using her boot, Caroline pushed one branch of the root system out of the ground. The tree slumped two inches into the hole.

His body jerked. "Yes!" he screamed. "Yes, I broke into that barn."

"Where did you take my dynamite?"

He watched her boot hover over another root. His gaze remained on that boot as he answered her. "I took it out to Stemmins."

Ah, she thought. Stemmins of Denver. "Where'd you meet Stemmins?"

"Out in the north valley. I met him at this shack. Five miles north of that herky mining town."

"You got paid for that little job?"

"Sure. Well, I will. I mean I get paid when we're done."

"Done? How will you know when you're done?"

"When Stemmins says."

"And you hope "done" is before you die and not after, isn't that right?"

Reluctantly, Kidde nodded.

"Stemmins told you to follow me."

"Just to see if – to see what you was doing."

"And to whom does Stemmins take this information and the dynamite?"

"He takes it . . ." Kidde's face changed. He appeared to look into the distance and see something more terrible than his inevitable fall. He barely stammered out "I . . . no! I . . . I don't know where he takes it."

Her sturdy boot pulled out the next major root. With a jerk, the tree fell more deeply into the void. Kidde's body slid further toward the vast cavern inside the ridge.

"Who does Stemmins report to?"

"He, oh Jesus! He talks to this slick fellow down in Denver, but I never seen him. They say he's got money in every state. He can arrange murders that happen miles from any place he's ever been – just pays for it."

"His name."

"God, Miss. I don't know his name. Get me out. Out. Out." Kidde's voice rose as his panic rose.

Caroline took one look at the roots. The sandy soil oozed away. It wouldn't last. And when the root let go of the earth, the pine would drop. Like his Winchester, Kidde would bounce on the boulders.

She couldn't leave any man to die that way.

"You tried to shoot me," she stated.

"I got no rifle."

"And if I haul you up here, then what?"

"You the one with the pistols, ma'am, and at least four shots."

"Three," she corrected. "At close range."

Caroline grabbed a rope from Kidde's saddle and tied one end to his pommel as the gelding whiffled its fear of the sleeting rain and crazy wind.

"Whoa, boy," Caroline crooned. "You're safe with me, safe with me, safe with me."

The horse calmed but Caroline feared to count on him. No predicting what this horse would do if the storm grew louder.

"Please, ma'am."

Caroline lay down in the mud. Leaning once more over the abyss, she dangled the end of the rope into the hand on his injured arm. "You have to put this through your belt and then hand it back to me," she said.

Grunting with pain, he shoved the frayed end into his belt. The belt nearly buried itself in the heft of his belly. He yanked on it. "Ahh!" he moaned as it came through and offered her the end again.

"Hold very still, Kidde." She whispered, taking back the rope. He held his breath. His good arm gripped the thick root so tightly that his knuckles were white. Around them both, the snowy rain poured down. The mud slipped, threatening to take them both into the hole. Caroline slithered back toward his gelding where she tied the second end to his pommel.

"Your horse know the command, "Back?" she asked.

"He damned well better," His voice shook. "Whupped it into him good."

Caroline hesitated, but at last she commanded the gelding, "Back."

The gelding plowed his forehooves into the rocky ground. His haunches tightened and he backed up.

"Agh," Kidde hollered. The belt and rope caught him hard, threatening to cut him deeply.

"Back, Back," Caroline urged, pushing the gelding's sturdy chest. "Good work, great work," she encouraged him.

Kidde's rotund body rolled and scraped up the side of the hole. His raw voice *Damned* and *By-Jesused* all the way until he lay panting at the ridge crest. Caroline soothed the sweating horse. Electric air fitzed about her, raising the hair on her arms, leaving acrid taste on her tongue and the smell of iron in the air.

"Lightning. I feel it," she said. "Get up."

Kidde's coughing and moaning stopped. Caroline raised her pistol. "Pull the rope from your belt," she ordered. "Get up and wrap the rope around your right arm." She already regretted the weakness in her that decided to save him. If she hoped to keep him under control, she had to immobilize his good arm. They had a long ride ahead of them.

Kidde crawled up onto his knees. He glanced up at her, his wiry hair matted across his massive forehead. She didn't like the tension in his shoulders.

"Wrap the rope around your arm," she repeated.

He pushed his bulk upright. She realized anew what a big man he was. Dread tightened across her shoulder blades. As Kidde stood, he ripped the rope from his belt, letting a four-foot length of it hang from his right hand. He swung the rope end in a circle in front of him.

The gelding, his hooves dancing on the wet earth, backed away from his master. His breath whistled out his long nostrils. Caroline backed with him. She raised the pistol.

"Do as I say, Kidde."

Kidde stepped toward her, swinging the rope.

Caroline aimed at Kidde's massive belly and pulled the trigger. The hammer thumped. Mud jambed her gun.

Kidde laughed as he lunged. He swung the rope at her head. The knot whapped her temple. Caroline ducked away from the horse, but the gelding's reins were still wrapped about her right palm. Kidde's rope end wrapped itself in the reins, pulling the gelding toward him. Kidde let go of the rope. He reared back, raising his rock-like fist to smash her face.

CHAPTER FOURTEEN

Gryf and Sol raced up hill, searching for the trail to the ridge top. Snow clung to the trail and water sheeted down the steep sides of the ridge, turning the animal trail into a slogging stream. As soon as Gryf realized what the stream did to the trail, he was out of Sol's saddle. Leaving the two horses in the trees, he scrabbled up the steep incline. This climb was safer done on foot, too steep for Sol or even the low-slung Sheba.

Lightning flashed. Thunder clapped. As he scrambled, Gryf smelled burning air and wet iron.

Snow and rain pelted him, beating down so he barely heard the whickered complaint of Sol and Sheba at the bottom of the ridge. Above, he heard the scream of a third horse and the crash of hooves.

"God, keep her from that mad horse," he prayed.

He grabbed for holds in the hillside. Rivulets flowed, dragging fist-sized rocks around and down. Mud and snow collected in each boot-step. His arms reached out for new purchase, swinging in uneven but relentless rhythm.

He listened as he climbed – her voice, a footstep, anything. *Show me some clue.*

Snow swarmed, a film of gray between him and the top of the ridge. Still, he could see the green and white flickers around him with each stroke of lightning. This deluge was more unyielding and brutal than most.

Slogging at a near vertical angle, he struggled upward, pushing, reaching until his arms ached and his thighs trembled with fighting snow, mud and sliding rock. He was numbed to any feeling beyond the need to find her . . . and the fear that he would find her dead.

151

**

Kidde's fist crashed into her left ear as Caroline raised her pistol. She jabbed the barrel at Kidde's Adam's apple. She saw but couldn't hear him gag. The gelding rose on his haunches, his flying mane and rippling shoulders back-lit by sheet lightning. Kidde's hands were at his own throat, his eyes rolling with the effort to breathe. At that moment, the gelding's hooves thudded onto Kidde's skull, driving the man to his knees.

The gelding reared once more. Caroline, nearly deaf from the blow to her ear, wrestled the reins. Pulling herself to the horse's side, she shouted "Down. Down."

Kidde's body fell face down in the mud, his head crushed.

A second sheet of lightning lit the uprooted pine and the body where it slumped over the edge of the cliff. The gelding snorted and jerked against Caroline's grip. She backed toward the east side of the ridge, pulling the horse after her. He trembled, breathing hard and fast. She rushed him toward lower ground, toward the valley of the pine and aspen forest.

The gelding resisted as she crooned him down.

"Good boy," she said, shivering with the aftermath of her own fear and pain. "Got to get you in the pines."

The wound in her forehead washed blood down her face. The gelding watched her, focusing on the sound of her voice. "You've been through enough. Enough. And I need you."

She did need the gelding's help, but more, she didn't want the poor animal to remain with the body. Talking the crazed horse down the steep ridge flank kept her warm, helped her concentrate on the next step, on the future. It kept her from collapsing into her own ugly memories.

152

**

Gryf's left hand reached up for the next purchase. His palm slapped down on a horizontal surface. His other hand tangled with pine needles. The unexpected placement of the tree disoriented him until he smelled the acrid fumes of burnt wood. The lightning must have split one of the pines. When last he saw her, Caroline was running near the pines.

Scrambling to the top of the ridge, he shoved the pine branches aside, searching for her body. The impenetrable snow made it impossible to see more than a foot and a half in front of him. It forced him down on his hands and knees under the remnants of the tree. Branches grabbed at his oilskin coat. Sharp pine needles poked at his neck and hands as he plowed through them, feeling for signs of Caroline. His hand landed upon a soft, wet warmth. He stared, dazed by the sight of mud-blackened fabric. At last, it registered in his mind as the once-blue wool cape. Gryf stood, heaving the weight of the pine tree off the fabric. Close to the cape he saw the white of a hand and then through the thick curtain of snow, he was able to see a black shirt and overalls, just enough so that he could make out the shape of a large man.

"Where is she?" Gryf fell on his knees next to the man, looking for any sign that Caroline lay nearby. The man's hand was large, callused, gripping a piece of sturdy brown fabric. Gryf recognized the weave in spite of the sodden darkness of the color – it was a torn piece from the edge of her split skirt. The man who held it – her pursuer – was dead, his head caved in above the right ear.

And beyond him, no sign of her.

"Caroline!" Gryf yelled into the deafening storm. "Caroline. It's me, Gryf Williams."

No response.

Still the snow and rain sheeted down, drumming upon the rocks and rattling in the creek beds. Gryf's instinct told him to go where he'd last seen her running – toward the standing pines. Instead, he forced himself to search the mud near the body. He groped about for the print of her small squared-toed boot.

Caroline was running, he reasoned. Only the impress of her toe would be left. Squared off. Small.

There. and there amidst snowy hoof prints.

He studied the faint indentations – difficult to spot because the snow filled them.

He ran his finger at the edges of one small semi-circle. *She pivoted here. And turned right.*

Gryf's right hand leaned briefly next to the body of the dead man. He felt a lump in the man's shirt, at breast pocket level. Ripping the shirt open, he found an empty gun holster. In the bottom of the holster lay two silver certificates worth $500.

Someone paid him to do this. Where are they?

Gryf stuffed those in his pocket, hoping for a signature that would give him a clue. He rose, pulling the dripping wool cape with him. He found two more faint footprints going in the same direction as the first. And in the same direction as the horse.

Following that line toward the eastern flank of the ridge, he stumbled around a rock outcrop, starting small avalanches of pebbles in his haste. The storm calmed. Gryf could now see the bottom of the hillside. He scanned the slope of run-off mud and rock, hoping to see some motion, some bit of color that would tell him where she was.

"Caroline," he called over the dulling roar of the storm. He watched for movement in his tree plantation, remembering that she might not want to be found, especially after the fright she had at the hands of the other man.

They weren't miners, she had said when he spoke of her obvious fears. *They weren't miners.*

154

She wouldn't remain up on the ridge top, facing the chance the man had survived the lightning strike and the crash of the tree.

But where would she go?

Back to By-Gum.

He clambered toward his valley of pine and aspen, then stalked down the gully between the trees and the run-off slope of the ridge. One mile below, sun now shone on the lower reaches of the mountainside. White topped clouds billowed far below. Gryf realized he was watching the creation of a new wave of thunderheads. If he hoped to find Caroline before that second storm hit, he had to work fast.

The soggy cape he trailed over his shoulder seemed an unnecessary weight, but it was all he had of her at this point. He walked and folded and squished water out of the wool as he moved along, keeping his attention on the ridge and on his trees. No telling what fear she conjured at this moment, what place she huddled, trying to hide from man and the elements. He knew what being close to a strike of lightning could do to the human mind.

Fry the living Bejeepers out of you, he thought. Take your reason.

Gryf yelled her name over and over. The clouds below him were building a towering rage, sweeping toward his mountains once more.

A noise behind him made Gryf turn abruptly toward the trees. There he was – a wild-eyed horse, tied to a sturdy pine, twenty feet inside the plantation. The animal watched him, silent, tense. Still there was no sign of her.

He closed his tired eyes, listening for her, willing her to show herself. When he opened his eyes, the sight of her boot print seemed to leap at him. It was so clear, and so near, he could hardly believe he'd not seen it before. Her square toe and sturdy round heel cut

155

sharply into the snow and mud not five feet away and slightly uphill from his present position.

She'd hidden the horse, then she'd walked on toward By-Gum, just as he was walking. Gryf stepped up to that part of the hillside where he'd seen her footprint. He followed the lighter half-boot marks which showed she'd begun running again. Not far in front of him two boulders lay next to each other. He skirted the rocks on their lower side.

The sun shone through between the old storm and the gathering clouds. In the bright light, the deep biting impress of her boot print appeared at the joint between the boulders. Beyond it, another print, also full, but this time turned toward the jumble of rock instead of aiming downhill.

This was the last of the footprints for as far as he could see. He faced the boulders, the direction of her print. Staring at the ground, he attempted to read what had happened here. A small whisper of dry grass rose from somewhere within the pile of rocks. A mere shuffle followed by a damped-down voiceless breath.

Gryf knelt at the print. There, below the lowest part of the rock, in the dry dirt protected by the overlap of two huge boulders, he found a scooting, slithering trail. Beneath the rock he saw what appeared to be a small animal den, the opening was almost invisible in the overhang. As he stared at it, he grew certain she was inside this tiny refuge.

He doubted his ability to crawl within, and for her sake, was sure such an action would not be a good idea. In the last half-hour, Caroline Trewartha had been attacked by a huge man, nearly killed by lightning and tumbled down a steep hillside with a crazy horse.

In the best of times, he thought, she doesn't take well to being near Gryf Williams in a small space.

Rolling himself off to one side of her exit, he whispered, "Miss Trewartha. It's me, Gryf Williams."

A rustle of fabric told him he had indeed found her.

"Don't you worry, my little engineer, I'm not coming in there. I know you had a fearsome time up top of this ridge. I can wait 'til you're ready to come out and go home. Sheba and Sol – that's my horse, you met him in Freya's barn – they're waiting for us. Other side of this ridge."

He stopped talking, and glanced out from under the rocks, studying the effects of wind in his pine trees. The big gelding jittered about in the trees. Gryf knew he and the poor horses were about to get bejeepered once more.

"Miss, don't have your back against the rock walls. Storm's about to come back for another round of lightning. Get in the middle of the space if you can."

He heard her move a little.

"Is there anything between you and the rock floor of that little burrow?" he asked.

Faintly, her answer came. "Yes."

"Good. That's very good. You sit tight."

"You're touching rock," she said.

He couldn't see her, but she must know somehow. "That's the truth," he answered. "It's a small space here."

Silence followed. He thought he could hear her heart pounding, her mind evaluating her choices. At last, just as the clouds rushed into his pine trees, she whispered, "I guess you must come in, Mr. Williams."

"I'll do that," he said, just as if she'd asked him to pass her the muffins at breakfast. "Here's your cape, a bit worse for being rained on." He shoved the cape through and was glad to catch a glimpse of her hands as she took it. Slender, graceful fingers, dirty nails. His engineer, all right.

Gryf poked his head inside. He tested the opening. She reached out and pushed his left shoulder upward, saying, "Come in sidewise. That's how I did it."

"Ah! Thanks to ye, Kind-heart." He heard himself slip into the talk he used with the women of his earlier days. He had to stop himself abrupt-like, trying to become very formal. "I appreciate your help Miss Trewartha."

"Shut up and get in here."

CHAPTER FIFTEEN

"Such a kind welcome she offers," Gryf muttered, crawling through the small opening. Outside, the wind kicked up and the sleet spattered. A flash of green light warned him to brace. The accompanying clap of thunder was so close he felt his hair curl tighter. He tucked and rolled a somersault into the small burrow.

"Stay down," Miss Trewartha whispered in a soft voice. "It's electric."

"You already had straw here," he said.

In the brief flicker of green lightning, he saw that mud streaked her face and caked her dress, her knees were drawn up tight against her chest. He had a moment's impression of Caroline in taut control, then her image was hidden by darkness.

"Someone was here before us," she said. "The person who blew up the ridge, he must have brought in this straw."

Gryf couldn't see her but listening to her voice told him she was desperately trying to maintain an even calm. She had to be soaked, freezing and frightened, but she didn't want him to know it.

"Miss Trewartha," he said, carefully shifting so he could face her but not touch her. "That blue cape of yours, being wool and all, it's bound to give some warmth."

"This is the place, you know," she said. "They did it in this cavern."

Her ominous tone warned him that what happened to her on top of the ridge had more than touched her mind. "Did it here, did they?" he asked. "And how did you come to find this out?"

"The dead pine. Blew through the whole layer of granite and fractured the sandstone."

"I'm not following yer thinkin' here, Miss Trewartha."

"They exploded the charges from back in here. Diverted the underground river that watered the pine and aspen forest."

The storm briefly lit the cavern. He saw she was holding two pistols. Lying very still, he considered his position. It seemed he'd rolled into the nest of a loony bird, her talking all kinds of craziness and just sitting there with two pistols across her knees. No doubt about it, he thought, that man up there had pushed her too far.

Gryf wanted to pull her to him, offer her shelter from evil. But anything he did would frighten her more.

And she might shoot him.

"His name was Kidde," she said. "Do you know anybody name of Kidde?"

"Who is Kidde?"

"The man I killed up there."

He saw the flash of low light on a gun barrel as she pointed upwards. Gryf held his breath. She didn't pull the trigger.

"I tried to save him," she whispered. "But he wouldn't be saved." Her breath whistled out of her as she crumpled. A long, awful silence followed and then a deep, ragged sob.

Gryf reached out an arm, found her wet shoulder and drew her shaking body toward him. "Come here, My Diligent Engineer. You've had enough."

She collapsed against his chest, shivering uncontrollably. Surprised, Gryf wrapped his arms about her. Outside their den, the sleet and rain splashed, and the wind whipped the trees.

"Put them damned pistols out of yer lap, girlo."

Through her cries, she laughed – a hiccupping, convulsive laugh. "I was cleaning mine," she said, and set both guns in front of her.

In the dark, Gryf reached out and made sure she'd pointed the barrels away from them. Then he took her fully in his arms, rubbing warmth into her back. Massaging her back brought Gryf in intimate contact with the stiff stays of her garments. His hand ran into her wet cape, which she still gripped in her left hand. He unfurled the wool garment and draped it over both of them, cursing himself for noticing how her breasts pressed softly into his chest.

"It's all right," he whispered. "When this storm passes, we'll go down to By-Gum, my brave one."

"Sheba?" she asked.

"Sheba and Sol, they're in the lee of this storm. And you did the right thing to tie up that gelding in the low land. The lightning will spend itself on the ridge tops and then have to gather up energy as it passes over the horses."

Gryf wasn't strictly certain this was true, but he'd played poker with the most suspicious of men and could bluff without hesitating. Caroline couldn't change Sheba's fate, so he convinced her not to worry.

He could feel her breathing slow. In the light of the next lightning strike, he found her forehead had been abraded, but she'd poulticed it with mud. He wiped the mud and blood from her cheekbone. As he touched her, her dark eyebrows pinched, her lids tightened and fretted as if she were watching a nightmare. A slash of wet hair hugged her temple. After the light glimmered out, he reached up to brush back the strand and pull the cape over her tresses.

He added the weight of his hand to the weight of the wool, stretching his fingers out among the strands of her hair and massaging her scalp. He was rewarded when her body ceased its small shakes and gave in to the lulling motion. The next flash of lightning showed her lids at rest, her injured brow smoothed in sleep.

Gryf turned slightly toward her, reveling in her trust, the beat of her heart against his, her warm breath on the base of his throat. His body swelled with pleasant awareness where her belly rested against

161

him. He let his hands continue to soothe and explore her hair. He held himself back from any other motion. Already, he knew her well enough to know that even as careful as he was trying to be, she might awaken frightened. He wanted to be able to look himself in the mirror when her large eyes accused him of being a wretch.

God, what a delicious body, he thought.

But Gryffyth Williams had never lain with a woman who hadn't offered herself. He wasn't about to start, no matter the lovely temptation. He wondered if that was why she was sent to his mine by the Allied Mines Company.

Was she an entrapment?

As he thought about this possibility, the receding storm occasionally illumined her face. Her beauty was remarkable, but so, he admitted, was her skill. She knew geology, and mining techniques; much as he'd resisted it, her idea for long-walling on the upper side of Number One had some merit. It might help with the drainage problem.

He heard the sleeting rain and soft snow outside slow and then stop. The shimmers of lightning were farther away. Thunder ceased. After a time, the sky cleared. The moon's light wriggled its way into their hole. Gryf sighed deeply.

"We must bury him," Miss Trewartha whispered.

Gryf jumped at the sound of her voice. "I thought you asleep."

As she sat up, she pushed the warm cape down onto his chest. "I'm sorry to have . . ." She turned away.

He saw that she was embarrassed. "Your trust is worth a great deal, Miss Trewartha," he said. He lay still, appreciating the glow of her profile, waiting for her to make the next move.

She glanced at him, then toward the back of the cave. "I don't suppose you brought any candles," she said, "or phosphorous sticks."

"In my coat. The buttoned pocket," said Gryf, laying his hand tentatively on her arm, an offer of support. She did not shake him off. "I'll get them out in a moment. But tell me why Sheba screamed so."

"I think Kidde is the one who strangled her," Caroline said. "His own gelding was frightened of him." She glanced at him, "Do you suppose Sheba ever belonged to Kidde?"

"Not a chance," said Gryf, "Sheba's lived with Freya's all her life. She gave birth to Solomon when we all worked together out in Pennsylvania."

Perhaps because of her recent terror, Miss Trewartha giggled, a tight, edgy laugh. "Sheba and her son, Solomon. Was that your idea?"

"Aye," Gryf smiled, glad she recognized his humor. The moon soon would rise too high to light their hole much longer, so he took one last study of her soft, loose tresses, and the contours of her throat and shoulder.

"And was it you who trained Sol to do that trick?" she asked.

Gryf frowned, trying to remember which trick she'd witnessed.

"Last night in Mac's barn."

"Oh, you mean holding Reverend Wright at 'Attention'."

She nodded.

"One afternoon, back in Pennsylvania, Mac and I were fooling around with a straw man – an effigy of the mine supervisor. The English miners planned to burn it for Guy Fawkes Day. I guess Sol got fed up with us tossing the dummy past his nose. He grabbed him by the shoulder with his big mouth and held him. We'd been having trouble with union busters sneaking into the miner's camp, so we decided to teach Sol to grab union busters and other intruders that way."

Miss Trewartha stared up at him, then down at her lap as she asked, "You really were a union man?"

"*Oes*, I was."

In the pale moonlight, he watched Miss Trewartha glance everywhere but at him: out of their rabbit hole; down at her hands. He squeezed her arm where his hand had lain all this time.

"Miss, you wrote a fine article for *The Transactions* on the right of miners to organize."

"I believe in that right," she said vehemently, then her voice softened with sorrow, "but I don't believe in the violence."

"Ah . . ." Gryf felt it coming. At last she would admit she believed he might have something to do with the attempt to murder her father in 1878.

"Those trials," she said, "the ones in 1878 revealed viciousness I'll never believe was necessary. If they wanted safety for themselves, how could miners kill others?"

"In 1878? You mean . . ."

"The murderers of Mr. Sanger, Uren and that young policeman, Yost."

Gryf was relieved. She wasn't talking about him and her father. But he was sad to recognize judgement in her voice. "Ye're thinkin' of the men hanged as 'Molly McGuires'."

She nodded. "Whether they'd joined the Molly McGuires or not, they were found guilty of those murders."

His voice was thick with barely controlled emotion, "Guilty in the Sunday newspapers, therefore guilty."

"There was evidence."

"Was there now? May I ask how ye learned that fer a fact?"

"The journalists . . ." her voice trailed off.

"And who owns the newspapers? Did ye think they had no interest in finding any union man guilty of conspiracy and murder?"

Miss Trewartha remained silent.

In a gentler voice, Gryf pressed his advantage. "Did ye think only union men were violent?"

164

"I was afraid for my father many times."

He waited. Still she didn't say anything about his trial. Could it be true that she didn't believe him guilty? He tested the topic.

"I admired your father even before his witness saved my life."

She said nothing, merely tilted her head, waiting.

He continued, "Carl Trewartha is respected. Honest. Faced down a violent mob once, so they told me. And equally he faced down mine owners who were fools."

Even in the soft darkness of the burrow, he could see her smile. "Oh yes. He did that." She glanced across at him, "and now it's my turn."

"And am I the fool yer planning to face down?" Gryf asked.

"Of course," she said in a light voice. "You know I'm right about the drainage in Number One."

Suddenly certain she did not believe him guilty, he let relief rush through him. Hume and Allied may have had underhanded reasons for sending her here, but she had no revenge in her heart. More elated than he'd been for months, he forced himself to discuss the mines.

"I know long walling could work," he said, "but we need better equipment. Otherwise yer idea would be risking the lives of my friends."

"And," she waved a shimmery soft hand through the blackness, "the fans, the pumps, steel wire hoisting rope, they're all on your contract list . . ., so you say."

"Aye," he agreed, "but, evidently, not on any train comin' up from Denver."

"When we do the long-walling," she continued, "we can adapt square-set timber supports for the tunnel – much stronger."

"Miss Engineer," Gryf whispered, his heart in his throat as he listened to her talk his kind of talk. He experienced a flash of knowledge as blinding as the lightning. She was precious to him, as

165

precious as any person he had ever known. In two swift days she'd filled his thoughts and his senses with the need of her.

"And back-fill as we work our way out . . ." she continued as if nothing was happening between them, only her plans and quotas were moving forward.

"Miss Trewartha," he whispered.

She stopped yammering. In the darkness he could see her head tilt again, her habitual way when listening.

"We both need sleep," he said. "We can plan in the morning on our way down the ridge."

"How about the candles?"

He rustled in his oversized pocket, brought out a leather packet, unfolded it and placed a miner's spider in her hand. "Want to find a place for this?" he asked.

He heard the rustle of her wet dress. She reached behind her and jabbed the sharp end of the candleholding spider into a fissure in the cavern wall. He heard its solid thump, then he struck a phosphorus stick against his rough pant leg. It flared, illuminating her startled eyes as she watched him hold the burning stick to the wick of a stubby candle. She reached for the candle, her slender fingers touching his as she took it.

Gryf worked to keep his face immobile, not reacting to her touch. She smiled, a tired, shivery smile and then she held the candle over the platform of the small candle spider, letting wax drip into the shelf so the candle would hold. He knew he was daft when the sight of her performing this simple task brought him so much pleasure. Her graceful gestures seemed to be a caress for him.

In the light of the small candle, he stretched out in the straw. She glanced at him, then studied her wool cape and the paisley shawl beneath it. After only a moment, she opened the cape, covered his chest with half of it and snuggled under the other half with her back to him.

He turned his head to look at her. Her back was rigid.

"Thank you, Miss Trewartha."

"You're quite welcome, Mr. Williams." She moved to resettle herself more comfortably in the thin layer of straw.

He smiled to himself, watching the motion of her hip, now softly outlined by the candlelight that gave her comfort from her night fears.

**

The candle guttered. Caroline raised her head. Sunlight illuminated the small cave. Morning, pink and fresh, had come. Caroline felt anything but fresh. Somehow in the night she had rolled into Mr. Williams. His hands were both tucked under his head, forming a pillow for his cheek, so the rolling had been entirely her fault.

Her hair was plastered to Mr. Williams's shirt. His shirt, and therefore probably her face, was far from clean. She decided to climb outside and wash her face with the snow from the grasses. As she peeled away from his chest, his hand touched her arm.

"Do ye hear that running water?" he whispered.

She held herself immobile, hearing the double-thump of his heart, and farther away, the strong gurgle of a brook. Sun lit the cave, but its low angle would not last long. Already the shadows were moving down, obscuring her view of the interior. Directly across from her, she noticed a peculiar, low archway opening to another space. Beyond that space was the sound of running water.

Her loose boot slipped off as she crawled toward the small archway. In too much hurry to retie it, she grabbed the boot and knelt at the opening. Around the edges she found the striations she now expected; this opening to the second chamber had been created with a diamond bit drill. The sun's shadow moved, warning her that

167

lighting into the second space was about to be gone until tomorrow morning. She hunched over, to see inside.

It was cut like a stope or low tunnel. Miners often cut a stope just tall enough so that there was sufficient space for a man to lie down and work. The prone miner cut away at the important mineral or seam, sending the material out to the main drift by conveyor belt.

Here, there was no conveyor belt. And even more oddly, she could see nothing worth mining. The entire space was granite, much marred by drilling and dynamite blasts, but containing no sign of gold, silver or lead. If her calculations were correct, this stope was many feet above Mr. Williams's seam of coal.

She moved to the far side of the drilled opening and peered into the right side of the room.

A screaming face glared out at her.

**

At her shriek of terror, Gryf scrambled to the opening, ready with her pistol.

"Watch out!" Caroline yelled. With unbelievable speed, she struck out with her right boot as if it were a weapon. "He'll kill you," she cried and struck again.

Gryf thrust her away from the opening so that the danger could not get at her. There, in the last of the morning sun, he saw what she had found. A man's body lay against the inner wall of the space. Gryf was sure even before he thrust his hand toward the man's throat that he'd find him dead. Not recently, but not long ago, either. Though the cave was cold and dry, they would have smelled decay if he'd been dead very many days.

"Did I kill him?" she whispered.

Gryf withdrew his hand from the cold skin. "I think ye've saved my worthless life, Brave-one." Gryf turned to her. "That buzzard'll never threaten me again."

She sighed and slumped against the wall. "You're all right."

"Aye. All right. And you. You can shriek with the Warlocks, I'm thinkin'."

She looked up at him, her hair a mess of pinned and unpinned locks. One amber hair comb threatened to drop from its perch. Her dark green eyes caught the last of the sun. She was, in that moment, his vision of home, of the forests, of Mount Snowdon, of the Dyfi River, of the new grass on the steep hillsides of Wales.

Gryf lowered his head toward her. She tensed. He caught himself, remembering. A kiss might break the spell they'd cast about them – the warm memory of caring for each other last night, the triumph of her saving his dusty self from certain destruction.

Gryf ducked his head and held her gently off from him. "I thank ye."

"He . . . he didn't really put up much of a fight, you know," she admitted.

"Yer war-cry must have paralyzed him."

"He was already dead, wasn't he?" It wasn't a question.

Gryf nodded. "It doesn't matter, that. Yer a courageous person, Miss Trewartha."

Her gaze held his. Then her solemn face broke into a brief grin. He knew the overwhelming power of a short glimpse of heaven.

It was she who broke the moment. "What killed him?"

Gryf sighed and then turned back to the ugliness of the world. "Could ye light a new candle, Miss Trewartha? I'm climbin' in there to find out."

"Yes. Let's." she said.

Gryf stopped short, glanced over his shoulder, frowning at her. She was already rummaging in the pile on the cave floor. He shrugged and started inching his way into the stope. In moments, Miss Trewartha handed him the spider with a lit candle. He studied the body a few moments, blew out the candle and handed it back to her. "Grab an arm and help me haul him out of here."

"Don't you want to know what killed him?"

"Rock. Back of the head."

"Like Mr. Polgren?"

"No. Jesse's rock was shot from a rifle. This fellow died from the explosion he created down here. Help me. I don't want to be in here any longer."

Without further questioning, Miss Trewartha reached for an arm. Gryf was grateful for her prompt action. He didn't like the looks of this place. This fool corpse had died because of his own sabotage. Yet he'd lived long enough to wreak havoc on the rock in here, making this a very dangerous place.

Together, they pulled the man through the small opening into the burrow. Gryf tossed their belongings out the opening. Then, with her climbing out first, they pulled the dead man into the light of a new day. Miss Trewartha knelt in the new snow by the body. Gryf saw that a brief examination convinced her he was correct in his assessment. The man had been hit at the base of the head with several blunt blows. At least two of them had caved in the back of his head. Another had severed his spinal column.

"He paid for his work," she said.

"Aye. Paid dearly."

CHAPTER SIXTEEN

"I'll retrieve our horses," Gryf said as she rose from checking the body. "Will ye be all right while I'm up there?"

"I'll guide you," she said. "Otherwise you'll fall in the hole."

Gryf stared at her.

"You still think I'm crazy." She thrust her chin up at him in that gesture of defiance he relished. "The dynamite blew a hole in the layer of granite. The explosion made a sinkhole under one of the three pine trees. When you found Kidde's body, you came close to falling in the hole yourself – a drop of at least one hundred feet, from the sound of it."

Gryf straightened in surprise, "From the sound of it?"

"His rifle fell," she explained. "I heard it bounce . . ." She glanced up. He heard the intake of breath that signaled sudden understanding. "Seismic mapping?"

"Aye," he chuckled. "You were using seismic mapping, though dropping rifles is an expensive form o' the technique."

"I'm coming up the ridge with you."

"No," he said as he wrapped her blue cape across her shoulders and hair. "I'll stay well away from that hole. You take care of that poor gelding in the trees."

Gryf gave her cape one more tug to cover her throat, silently thanking the manipulative men at Allied for sending him this darlin' girlo.

Miss Trewartha glanced at the entrance to the burrow and Gryf got a sick feeling in his stomach. "No," he said. "The roof in there is unstable. We were lucky to have last night in safety."

"I want to see how to stop the water." She looked up at him, her lips a stubborn pout.

"Please," he said, "take no more chances. We can solve the engineering problems on the information both of us gathered while in that stope."

"You weren't in there very long," she said. "You couldn't have taken in enough details."

Gryf felt his jaw muscles tighten, "Ye present me with a problem in logistics," he said.

"Which is. . .?"

"I've only two horses we can trust. So far, I've the two bodies. If there are three bodies when I return, which shall I leave up here to rot?"

Her stubborn look came. "I'll walk, thank you."

He leaned over her. "Stay out o' there or I'll be suin' ye for trespass."

"You're an overbearing, granite-headed, . . ."

Gryf pulled her to him and touched her lips with his for the briefest of moments.

"I am that," he said, realizing that she had come into that moment with surprising ease.

She tossed her head. The amber comb finally fell from her tangle of locks, but she didn't seem to notice it. "I'm going to get the gelding from the woods," she said with princess coolness.

"Do, please," Gryf mumbled to himself. As she strode into the pines after the horse, he reached down quickly, grabbed up the amber comb and stuffed it into his shirt pocket.

**

Where is that Gryffyth Williams? she fretted.

The truth was that she'd had too much time to think since she fed, wiped down the gelding and loaded the small man's body onto him. As she held the jittery horse's reins and sang to him, she thought. The more she thought, the more she was ashamed of herself for having actually cried on Gryf's chest.

How could it take him this long?

She'd promised herself never to show feminine weakness at the mines. She didn't know how she could ever recover from such a misstep. She'd have to be more distant, stronger. She'd have to forget how warm it felt to have his hands on her back, massaging her head and neck. She should never have let him get that close.

What has happened to him? Gone too long.

And she was shivering from having washed her face combed her hair with the new snow. She pulled the black and blue caped over her wet hair.

"Halloo," came the deep voice of Gryffyth Williams.

Caroline whipped about to face him. She forgot her resolutions, grinning at his dirty face and lanky form. His big roan and Sheba trudged together behind him. On Solomon's back she saw the flopping arms and legs of the man, Kidde.

Sheba nudged Gryf down hill toward Caroline.

"Whoa there ye sharp-hooved buzzard," he muttered. "Don't be hurrying me in the home-stretch."

"You're safe," she called.

"*Oes*. Quite safe." As he neared, he added, "These beasts surrounded me of a sudden. Like to've scared the stuffings out o' me."

His smile lit his face, turning his craggy, dusty countenance into a deeply etched work of beauty.

"Yer a fine sight," he said.

Reminding herself to maintain a cool distance, Caroline spoke sharply, "I was about to find my way down the mountain by myself."

"It's good to hear ye feelin' more yerself, Miss Trewartha."

"I am quite well, thank you," she retorted stiffly, petting the gelding's nose with vigor just to keep herself from reaching out to touch Gryf. She was determined to live up to her resolution.

**

Gryf was sore disappointed when she put her arm around the blasted gelding's slobbery muzzle. At first, she'd seemed very glad to see him. He relished the lilt in her voice when she called up to him. Yet as he approached, he saw that for some reason, her pleasure paled. He was bone weary and frustrated.

He was, however, relieved to discover she'd already hoisted the dynamiter's body onto the gelding. Gryf had had the devil of a time getting the bloated body of Kidde onto Sol's back. Then, he'd thought it prudent to cover Kidde's distorted face with the saddle blanket. He'd also wasted precious time calming Sol who didn't like the smell of dead humans.

So, tired and wet, he'd looked forward to greeting Caroline again. But she hugged the gelding instead of himself, and then grabbed up the hand of the small dead man.

"Did you see this odd ring he's wearing?" She thrust the hand toward him. "Have you seen this design?"

He felt the blood drain from his face. The ring was, in fact, too familiar. Gryf bore the imprint of its winged cat as a scar beneath his beard. "Ach y fi!" Gryf muttered, staring at it. This was the ring his father had worn as games keeper to Richard Kemp, Lord Forest, the Lord Gwydden.

Gryf took a deep breath and faced the probable truth. His father always claimed that the shooting which took his legs was no accident. Rhodri Williams believed that Lord Richard, Alex's father, intended to kill him. Gryf never wanted to accept these

174

accusations. But here was the insignia of Lord Richard Kemp. And it was on the hand of a man who had tried to destroy Gryf.

If Alex's father was somehow behind these catastrophe's, Alex would be devastated. Gryf had to spare him the grief of it.

"Gryf!" Caroline whispered as she dropped the hand. The ring glinted in the sunlight. "You know this man."

"No." He could not tear his gaze from it, but he could not tell her. This ring was his shame and his anger come back from the grave.

She stepped closer to him. "What does it mean?"

He steeled himself to lie. "You were the one who noticed it. Do you think it significant?"

"I wish I knew," she said gazing at him. "And I wish you would tell me."

He felt heat rise in him as he faced down her curiosity, asking, "Were either of these dead men on the train when you rode up to Isabeau?"

"I never saw this one before," she jerked her head toward the gelding's small load. "And you haven't let me have a look at the other one yet. I only saw him in the storm."

"Kidde's all bloated."

"If I don't take a look in daylight, I'll never know."

Gryf took a deep breath and whipped the horse blanket off the man's face.

She pulled the man's hair, lifting his crushed head and studying his face, which amazed Gryf since he barely had the stomach to glance at the man.

"I don't know him, either," she said.

Then she lifted the dead man's hands, one at a time.

"No sign of a ring."

"There's only one," he said.

At her sudden glance, he added camouflage to his bald statement. "Looks unique, don't you think?"

"Buncombe," Miss Trewartha said in utter disgust. She turned her back on Gryf and reined both the gelding and Sheba onto the trail, walking fast as if hoping to put the stench of death and Gryf behind her.

With regret, Gryf watched her ramrod back. She exuded disdain and the knowledge that he'd been dishonest. She had no more use for the safe refuge she'd needed in his arms last night. He wished he could tell her what the ring meant, but it meant too much. Beyond that, making this ring public knowledge would not be fair to Alex. Loyalty to their friendship had cost Alex much, first in Wales, then in Pennsylvania. Gryf could discuss this ring with no one but him.

222222

CHAPTER SEVENTEEN

Early the next morning, in his office, Caroline worked with Gryf to clarify the problems that digging and blasting the adit might give them. Gryf seemed pre-occupied. Twice he started a sentence that trailed off into silence. Then, he pushed himself with renewed vigor, as if trying to put something behind him.

"Gryf, what is worrying you?"

He straightened, tried to smile, but failed and said, "It's nothing. I'm just waiting for some information. Alex has gone into Isabeau for it." Immediately, he bent over the adit plans.

Caroline studied his bowed head. His hair, which was brushed when first she came in, had already sprung back into curls. The front strands wafted down onto his brow. Gryf's gaze seemed to be on the plans at the table, but she could tell by the taut lines near his mouth that his mind followed a path to some distant place.

Gryf must have sensed her scrutiny, for he looked up, catching her heart at the pain and worry she saw in his face. The black depths of his eyes studied her.

She bit her lip and then plunged in. "Can you tell me about it?"

For a moment, she thought he would let her help him. Then he dragged in a deep breath and dropped his hand to her plans. "No, Caroline. It's not mine to tell. Let's just solve the flooding problem and let Alex do what needs to be done."

"Then let's plan for the possibility that what we do turns very wrong," she said.

"What do you mean?"

"We need a safe place for the village to escape to if we have guessed wrong and our blasting is a mistake."

She stepped to his door and gazed up at the ridges behind the Butte. Gryf looked over the area with her.

She said, "That meadow above the town, the place where Olaf taught Ellen to ski, that's the place."

"I can't spare men to cut a trail up there," he said.

"Down here, the snow is nearly gone, now, and we've a whole town of women and children. I think we can handle it, if they know you think it's important."

He glanced at her and said, "Let's call a meeting at the school then."

**

After the meeting, Ellen and Deirdre took over the creation of a path up to the meadow, while the men worked to redirect the underground stream.

Under Gryf's direction, the men cobbled together sections of conduit pipe, loading each section onto Duncan's buckboard for its trip to the ridge. All morning, the sound of hammering and reshaping metal rang throughout the valley.

Ellen organized the children's help creating the escape route up the west facing slope of the skiing hill. They worked with an urgency caused by the short timetable Gryf and Caroline had set out for the drilling on the ridge.

In the alpine meadow across the valley from their hill, Manuel Lauriggues sheep grazed, but the whole sheep-herding family assisted the building project. Working with them were Marie Polgren, Sam's wife Susan and several other By-Gum women. Ellen and her school students had arrived together, each with a shovel or rake. To everyone's amazement, Marvelle Wright brought a shovel and joined in with a minimum of grumbling.

Two families built a shed to store emergency items. Others cleared space for tents. Ellen explained that they had all lived in tents when they worked at various mining sites, and most of them had kept the canvas for just this kind of need.

Jimmy Freya found a long chain in the pile of broken tools, so they decided to use it to create a way up to the tent village.

Manuel and Juan Jesus joined Marie, Ellen and Caroline, sweating over shovels and picks, digging ten holes in which they set the bottom half of eight-foot posts. Marvelle organized the children. Their line passed small rocks and larger stones up the slope for Manuel and Juan Jesus to use to stabilize the post holes. By late in the afternoon, the posts were packed so tight in the ground they couldn't be budged. These became the foundation of the handrail up to the meadow.

Manuel and Caroline bolted the large chain to the posts.

"Aye, Sammy," Manuel called. "You see, does this chain work?"

Gryf's nephew acted out a heroic effort to escape flooding. He pretended to wallow up to his neck in rushing water. Hand over hand he pulled himself up the chain, grunting and groaning most convincingly while the other children and mothers cheered him on. When he reached the top, everyone laughed, so Sammy tried it again. And so did the other children.

Caroline swiped sweat from her forehead and smiled at Marvelle. "The children liked working with you. And you had fun too."

Marvelle stared at Caroline, then she glanced quickly at the children. "Yes," she said. "Yes, I did."

"We've got lots more chances for fun tomorrow."

Marvelle laughed, a short tentative laugh. "I'll see you in the morning, Miss . . ."

"Caroline, please."

Marvelle smiled. "Caroline, what tools?"

"Do you have any wheels? We'll be hauling lots more rock."

"I shall search my church storage area."

**

Before the sun was up on the second morning, Caroline and Gryf worked with Amos and Rudy in the carpenter's shop. They coordinated the blasting schedule for the stream redirection. They planned a way for some of the stream to continue watering the pine and aspen forest.

As they talked, Caroline noticed a discomfort among the men.

"What aren't you telling me?" she asked.

The men glanced at each other. Amos shrugged. Rudy's jaw tightened. Gryf's lips pursed a moment before he answered her.

"Olaf has been missing since before you went up the ridge. Alex hopes to find him in Isabeau."

"Did he go off hiking with his skis?"

"His skis are still at his cabin," Amos said

"He's not up at the third mine?"

They shook their heads.

"Surely not in the cavern where we found the body?"

"Checked there," said Amos.

"Ellen?"

"She thinks he's at the mine. I don't want her to know there is anything to worry about." Gryf said.

Her heart thudded in her throat. "Kidde? Could Kidde have done something to him before he came after me?"

A light shone in Gryf's dark eyes for a moment. He appeared almost thankful that she'd asked the question. Then, the light flickered out and he shook his head. "We've searched the pine forest and any place else we think Kidde might have been."

Caroline remembered the man with the queue. "Gryf, after you went on down the mountain carrying Jesse's body, Rudy stopped to talk to me and then he left following you."

She carefully did not reveal that Rudy had been angry at her. "After Rudy left, there were five, maybe six men who surrounded me." She heard her voice start to go thin. Gryf stared at her. She cleared her throat and pushed on, reporting calmly, trying not to remember her terror. "I'm telling you because it's possible Olaf has met up with them, too. They wanted me to leave. They threatened. But they did nothing."

Gryf's forehead tightened. "Which men?"

"It was dark. I saw only their backs as they left me."

"Would you know them?"

"The tall man, the leader. He had dirty blond hair, long, tied in back."

Gryf shot a questioning glance at Rudy and Amos.

"Got nobody like that," said Rudy. "I thought they were part of our crowd, but it was dark. I didn't really look at the people who were there just before I left."

Caroline wondered if he told the truth, but she added, "I haven't seen any of them working with you since then."

Gryf's hand brushed over his eyes. "Miss Trewartha, I must insist that you not go out of the town without me. And don't go out at night."

"I don't take chances . . ."

"Caroline! Don't go out." Gryf reached toward her, pointing in the same gesture her grandfather used when he grew angry at her independence.

She backed away from him, saying, "Mr. Williams, don't yell at me. I will do what my job requires. And I will be careful."

In frustration, his hands hacked at the air, drawing a box as if to contain her there. "Caroline," his voice pleaded, "I'm not trying to prevent you from doing your job." He leaned across the carpenter's table toward her. "Just don't be out alone until I know what has happened to Olaf, and until I find this man."

She would give him as much as she dared. "I will take every necessary precaution."

"But you won't promise."

"I will not be out without protection," she said.

He studied her a long moment, then let out a long breath. "All right," he said. Behind him, Amos watched Gryf, but Rudy glared at her.

She folded her arms in front of her and said, "Now, gentlemen, could we get back to work?"

At that moment, Marvelle pushed open the door to the carpenters' shop. "Caroline?" she said. "I found one wheel."

"Ah, great," Caroline waved her in. "Let's build a wheelbarrow."

**

The women terraced steps into the hillside to make the climb easier. Marvelle and the children wheeled rocks to the site. A crew used the rock to shore up each step so it wouldn't wash away in a flood. As he carried one large rock up the hill, little Roderick chanted, "Watch me! I'm Sissy-fuss!"

Caroline asked Susan Williams, "Where did he get this word 'Sissy-fuss'?"

"His Uncle Gryf tells stories. Sisyphus rolls stones uphill."

"Yeah," Sammy said, "with steps he coulda finished the job easy."

Caroline laughed. In her imagination, she entertained a warm image – Gryf by the fireplace, sitting on the hearth and acting out stories for his nephews.

At noon, Caroline declared that all steps were sturdy and finished. A few moments later, below them in the valley, Gryf strode from the carpenters' shed. She stopped her work, staring at him. He waved to her, calling, "I'm going to the ridge. I'll be back before dark. We should be able to get into the underground stream tomorrow morning."

A few minutes later, she saw him ride out of Freya's barn on Solomon. A sense of emptiness surprised her as he disappeared over the first rise. Her inner hopes and wishes disturbed her. One night together in a cave shouldn't give him the right to monopolize her waking thoughts. After all, he had barely reacted to nearly kissing her. Nor had he even indicated that he remembered coming close and touching her lips. Yet the longer he treated her in a business-like manner, the more she thought about his warm hands.

Then she thought about the ring with its flying cat design. She remembered his horrified reaction and his secretiveness. Soon after their return, she'd noticed a change in him – his worry over Olaf's disappearance. He had plenty to think about besides a moment of closeness stolen with her.

She shook herself free of all but wisps of that memory as Ellen Robertson caught her sleeve.

"I think he'll be all right," Ellen said.

Carolyn glanced quickly at Ellen. How did she know?

Ellen smiled. "It doesn't show much, really," she said. "You keep it hidden better than I would."

**

While creating a landing platform at the top of the steps, Caroline taught six-year-old Hannah Polgren how to build the framing box. Sammy and Roderick scoffed at a girl doing boy's work.

Hannah put her hands on her small hips – hammer in one fist, nails in the other, as she shouted at them. "You boys don't know work from the wag end of a dog."

Caroline smiled to herself, remembering her own childhood encounters with such boys. However, she whispered to Hannah, "Our best work is the loudest argument for our skill."

True to his word, Gryf rode in an hour later from the ridge. He waved and went into the blacksmith's shop. A few minutes later, Caroline glanced down into the valley while Hannah nailed corner blocks in the platform frame. Below them, Alex Kemp rode into By-Gum on a quarter horse. He dismounted, tossed his reins around a post and entered the blacksmith's shop on the run. Caroline glanced at Ellen, who seemed to see no significance in Alex's arrival.

Caroline said, "Could you help Hannah with this board? I'll be right back."

Ellen took Caroline's hammer. "Go ahead," she said.

Leaping down the new steps, she hoped to find out what Alex knew about Olaf. Even before she reached the bottom, Gryf strode out of the blacksmith's shop. He turned for a moment to gaze at the activity on the meadow.

Caroline touched his shoulder.

"Oh!" he jerked toward her in surprise.

"Where is Olaf?" she asked.

"I . . . He . . . The sheriff says he's in big trouble. But, please, don't worry Ellen until I bring him home."

"Where?"

"Little town south of here. I've sent for Samuel. I'm leaving him in charge of the adit project. Alex can explain everything to you."

"You need some help with Olaf? Wouldn't Ellen . . .?"

"Caroline, the telegram says he was drinking and . . . and . . . "

She guessed, "and dancing?"

Gryf stared at her, then saw what she was really saying. "Yes 'dancing'."

"Go get him, then. Ellen still believes he's with the crew on the ridge."

"Good. I need you to finish what you've started here." He glanced up at the stone steps, the chain rail and the storage platform.

His eyes softened. When he looked back at her, he nodded. "It looks like a safe haven."

"Gryf."

"Don't worry. I'll be back soon."

**

Minutes later, Caroline watched Samuel ride into town as Gryf rode out toward Isabeau. She wished she knew what Olaf had done that all the mining plans were to be put on hold in order to rescue him. Drinking and womanizing didn't normally require rescue by the boss. Perhaps drink made him violent. Olaf violent could mean disaster.

That image was impossible to reconcile with the Olaf they all knew.

Above, Ellen worked in innocent unconcern.

Caroline balanced a small load of lumber against the bottom of the slope. She and Hannah were ready to climb up when they heard a high voice.

"Miss Trewartha! Miss!" Jimmy Freya ran at Caroline. She put out an arm to act as his brakes. When he'd stopped, Jimmy hauled on Caroline's arm to keep her from falling because of his weight and speed.

"Whew!" she said, "You're a locomotive on greased track."

His ears turned pink with embarrassment, and he glanced up the hill toward the women. They had all stopped digging and pounding long enough to see what news Jimmy brought.

"Sorry, Ma'am. Mr. Kemp wants you at Mr. Williams' office."

"He wants to help build?" called Ellen in a teasing tone.

"I don't think so, ma'am. He says he has a message from Mr. Williams for Miss Trewartha."

She had just spoken with Gryf before he left. Why would he leave Alex with a message instead of telling her himself?

"Hannah," Caroline said. "You take that bag of nails up top. I'll be right back."

"Can I hammer?" Hannah asked.

"Sure. Mrs. Robertson will help you."

In the carpenter's shed, she met Alex Kemp. He stood over a map that Gryf had shown her. When she came in, Alex smiled a welcome.

"Gryf's been called away," Alex said, "but there are a couple of things he wants us to do."

"Why couldn't Gryf tell me himself?"

Alex ducked his head and looked perplexed.

Caroline decided to relieve his embarrassment. "I know he's gone to get Olaf."

Alex coughed. "Gryf'll be back in a couple of days. Samuel's not going to blast clear into the underground stream until he returns."

"While we wait for him." Alex continued, "Gryf wants Samuel to get the adit ready, the pipes laid out and so forth. He wants you and me to go back down to Denver. I'm going to pay that man Stemmins a visit. With what you found out from Kidde before he died, I can put the screws – I mean I can force Stemmins to tell us what's going on."

"But Stemmins is dangerous," Caroline said. "And there is someone worse who directs Stemmins. Kidde was so frightened he wouldn't tell me the guy's name even when he thought I would drop him into that cavern."

Alex grimaced. "It won't be easy, I know. But I'll be prepared for both Stemmins and his boss – I believe I've met his boss before."

She could see Alex had no intention of elaborating on that statement. Alex straightened his shirt cuffs as he went on, paying careful attention to their alignment. Caroline watched this display of nervous embarrassment with concern while she listened to him.

186

"Gryf wants you to visit his lawyer, Isaac Brown," Alex said. "Mr. Brown negotiated that contract with Terry Branahan and should be able to explain the discrepancies between the two versions."

She was silent: disturbed to be putting off the action on the ridge, yet aware that while they waited, getting the answers about Stemmins and the contract would save valuable time. However, Alex's dealing with the murderer on his own worried her. Surprising herself, she admitted she'd become fond of Alex, though not as fond as he might wish. She must talk him out of taking on the suspect by himself.

"Alex," she said, "I think we should know more about this boss you think you know."

Alex cleared his throat. "Miss Trewartha, we, Gryf, Samuel and I, think we know who he is. That's as far as our suspicion needs to go right now. If it's him, I'm the one to handle him."

"But if you are correct, this man has killed Jesse Polgren."

"And there will be a reckoning," Alex assured her. "He won't get off."

"That's not what worries me. If you are correct, then this man is clever and vicious. I don't want you going in there by yourself."

"Miss," Alex said, in a quiet, firm voice. "Believe me. I know this man's capacity. I will be well-prepared."

She wanted to keep him from going at all. "Alexander Kemp," she said hotly. "Don't you know that Gryf Williams cares more about you than about having vengeance? You die and he will be devastated."

In an instant, Alex's face went ghost white. He stared, but not as if he were seeing her. He seemed to be seeing something with new clarity, and what he saw horrified him. "I must do this," he whispered. "It is too late to turn back."

She stepped toward him. "It is never too late. Take Samuel, Cornell, me. We can watch your back while you meet him."

"Miss Trewartha," Alex interrupted, "Gryf and Samuel appreciate what you've done for us – your ideas – all of them have helped us solve the mining problems. But this thing can only be done by me. If anyone else goes, it would only make it worse."

This secretiveness hemmed her in, angered her. "Go to Denver on your own, then," she said.

Alex shook his head. "You must help us solve the contract problems or the rest will be worth nothing."

Caroline felt inexplicable fear rising in her throat. She couldn't explain it to herself, certainly couldn't tell Samuel what bothered her about this idea of Alex and Gryf's. She wished Gryf had asked her to do this, not told Alex to convince her.

"I have to teach Hannah Polgren to build." She blurted without thinking.

Alex glanced at her. She almost believed she could see a smile tug at the corners of his mouth. Then he asked, "Do you suppose you might start for Denver in the morning, then?"

"I will have to consult with Hannah on that. I'll let you know."

CHAPTER EIGHTEEN

Reluctantly, Caroline rode with Alex Kemp into Isabeau. During the night, she'd convinced herself that her reservations and her anger, were partly caused by Gryf's not consulting her. His high-handed way no doubt resulted from his worry about Olaf. And surely she could overlook the slight and carry out the request. Nevertheless, she worried about Alex's meeting with Stemmins.

A letter, written by Samuel, lay in her valise. It introduced Miss Caroline Trewartha and explained what Gryf wanted to know. Samuel's letter might convince the man to talk to her about Gryf's company affairs. All she could do was try.

Once in Isabeau, Caroline picked up their train tickets to Denver while Alex stopped at the telegraph office to make an appointment for her with Isaac Brown, Gryf's lawyer.

Alex exited the small telegraph office and strode toward her on the short boardwalk of Isabeau's only street. A smile lit up his face and he tilted his head as if to study her.

"Ah, the lovely lady from Philadelphia," he teased as he met her. "Do you mind if I accompany you on this trip?"

"If you keep in mind this is a business trip."

He leaned over and whispered dramatically, "I promise to watch my own back."

Alex looked especially urbane, traveling in a tan shirt and a chocolate wool suit. His boots shone. The finishing touch to his elegance was a greatcoat of warm brown with fur at the collar and the cuffs. Caroline smiled when she saw him, thinking how easily he put on the mantle of success and power. He made good use of his dramatic presence. The porters and even the conductor scurried about, eager to handle their suitcases and find them the best of seats as they entered the train in Isabeau.

"Sir," Caroline said, once they were left alone in their seats, "is there anything these people would not do for you?"

He laughed. "It's just the suit. They never stop to think that I have to get dirty in order to earn the money that buys it."

Caroline smiled, but looked askance at his fur collared coat where it lay across his lap. "I could buy a dress as elegant as your suit and great-coat, but do you for a minute believe they would bow and scrape for me as they do to you?"

"Of course, they will," he said. "All they have to believe is that you have power and wealth."

"What if they believe I have wealth, but no power?"

He chuckled, "That is an impossibility. Wealth is power."

She stared at him. "Mr. Kemp, my O'Donnell grandfather indulged his daughters in their displays of wealth, but not in their pursuit of independent resources. The power was, and still is, his alone, though my aunts have all the wealth they might ever want."

"Yet you pursued independence. They might have done as you, if they wished to do so."

"Not so. You see, I cheated. Grandfather enrolled me in a lady's finishing school in Philadelphia. I found a way to divert my tuition to my own purposes. When grandfather found out I was attending the university instead, he yanked support of my education right out from under me. Luckily, I had saved enough dress money to pay for the last two terms."

Alex's eyes widened. He fell back against the leather seat, chuckling. "My dear, I've never before met an educated bunko artist."

"I learned the skill from my grandfather," she said in acid tones. "He married my grandmother's money. The rest of his life was one large confidence game – swindling the distaff side of any semblance of life other than serving himself."

Alex had stopped smiling. "You hate him so much?"

"He was a coward." Her voice choked as she remembered the day grandfather proved himself craven.

Alex leaned toward her, touching her gloved hand briefly. "Please do not judge all mankind by his example."

She stiffened, "I don't bother to judge. I make sure I do not have to rely on mankind for my safety."

Alex regarded her silently. Then he spoke gently. "Perhaps we should have some dinner."

**

During the train ride, Caroline fretted inwardly – afraid that Alex under-estimated the devious evil that Stemmins represented. Beyond that, she grew concerned that Gryf would be unable to get Olaf out of trouble. She worried that, during Gryf's absence, Samuel might be tempted to get at the underground stream from the cavern at the bottom of the ridge. The dangerously weakened geologic structure might collapse on him.

She knew Gryf would grieve deeply for any man, but most especially for his brother. Her own feelings about Gryf were a source of embarrassed amazement to her. Caring about him made her see the enterprise of the mine in a new way. It wasn't that she no longer cared about extracting the coal or making her reputation as an engineer. She wanted that very much. Now, however, she wanted to be sure it was done in the way that kept the By-Gum Valley beautiful and the people safe.

Yet she would soon arrive in Denver, miles away, with no news about the project on the ridge and no news about Gryf and Olaf. She'd shouldered the job of fact-finding when she didn't believe Gryf's lawyer would credit her with common sense or even the right to know about the contract. Furthermore, she accompanied a man prepared to face dangerous people with a quiet confidence she found unnerving.

"Alex," she said, as the train pulled into the Denver Station. "This man Stemmins is vicious. But it is the man behind Stemmins you have to watch out for."

Alex leaned toward her, "Miss Trewartha, did Kidde say anything at all about this other man? Describe where he'd met him, or suggest what his purpose might be?"

She thought over those few moments on the ridge. In her memory, the storm beat down again. The pine tree slid ever closer to the void beneath them. Kidde's fear again became visible to her.

She glanced at Alex Kemp. "I believe Kidde stole my dynamite from Freya's barn. He met Stemmins at a shack north of By-Gum to give it to him. All Kidde would admit about Stemmins' boss was that he'd heard this fellow was so rich he could arrange a murder to happen miles from any place he'd ever been – just by paying for the job."

"Had Kidde any idea of the man's name?"

Caroline shook her head. Her memory strayed again to that night. "God, Miss" Kidde had cried. "I don't know his name. Get me out. Out. Out." Kidde's voice rose as his panic rose.

"Miss Trewartha, are you all right?" Alex laid his hand on her gloved fingers. She glanced up into his blue-eyed concern. "You're shaking," he said. "Are you chilled?"

"I tried to save him, but he came after me and I had to . . ."

"You did what had to be done," Alex said, calmly. "Now think no more about it."

They strode from the Union Pacific Station, his hand nearly imperceptible at her elbow. Down the street, Alex steered her around a large construction site – the impressive façade of a brand-new railroad station. Across the roadway from the construction, a

192

line of black carriages waited to carry passengers. Alex haled a hackney carriage and then spoke to the cab driver for her.

"The lady wishes to visit the law offices of Isaac Brown. Ninth and Kalamath Streets, I believe it is."

"I think I know the place, sir," he said. "Near the corner. Upstairs of a fine house, i'n it?"

Alex handed her into the carriage, held her hand a moment and studied her with great intensity. "Will you be all right on your own?"

"Of course. It is you I worry about."

He smiled. "I'll find you at Isaac Brown's."

As the carriage drove off, Caroline glanced back to see Alex running toward a barn near the new railway station. She couldn't help remembering how a mere week ago she would have boxed Alex on the ear for presuming to speak for her to the carriage driver. How tame she had become. What had happened to her? Is this what came of caring about people?

Was it Alex? His small, quiet attentions?

Or that moment of closeness with Gryf? Truly she had to stop thinking about Gryf Williams! Why allow one man and his warmth distract her? The night in the cave meant nothing to him.

Settling back in the leather squabs of the carriage, Caroline deliberately concentrated on the contract and the questions she intended to ask Isaac Brown. She remembered that Gryf spoke highly of Mr. Brown, yet the discrepancies between the two contract versions meant the difference between possible success and inevitable doom for By-Gum. And Isaac Brown had been the lawyer who had negotiated the contract.

The dust and heat of raw Denver assailed her. People and animals seemed to be everywhere, moving in all directions without apparent order. As the carriage jolted along the road, Caroline noticed the corner of Ninth and Kalamath go by.

"Driver, haven't you passed the location of Mr. Brown's office?"

"No ma'am, I looked careful. I believe I remember it at Ninth and Lincoln, not Kalamath . . . a way down the road here. Your gentleman miss-remembered, I 'spect."

She gave better attention to her surroundings. The traffic became thick, and the carriage slowed to a stop on several occasions. It cost them another thirty minutes of dust-laden travel to arrive at Lincoln Street.

"Ere we be, Miss," said the driver.

She glanced out of the vis-a-vis seat and saw, with relief, a finger-sign pointing to the *Offices of Isaac Brown, legal advice, contracts, notary public.* A long run of sturdy steps climbed the outside of a fine home. In the back, at the top of the steps, was Brown's office door.

"That'll be fifty pence, if you please." prompted the driver.

Caroline handed him four bits and a picayune. The driver glanced at the coins. "What? Not gold dust, Miss? Yer got to be from the east, eh?"

She smiled. "Yes. New to Denver, sir."

Climbing down from such a height in a bell-shaped skirt felt awkward. After she had safely alighted, she fluffed her travel taffeta to be sure nothing caught up wrong.

I'm not wearing this piece of stupidity anymore, Caroline promised herself as the carriage drove off. It's bad enough to have to wear this tight jacket. I'd like to afford clothes with less stuffing and stiffening.

In truth, she admitted, she spent on drafting and mining tools what should have been spent at least once a year on repairing and replacing her wardrobe.

A high whinny caught her attention. In the alley behind the house, a nervous buckskin horse trotted forward a few steps. It halted, shaking its head from side to side as if seeking its negligent rider.

She peered more closely. On the animal's haunch she could make out a brand. Against the tan of his hairs she spotted a winged lion standing on its hind paws, offering to scratch any who might cross its path.

She thought this an odd emblem for a brand. Odd also that his rider had left him untethered and alone in the alleyway. But the buckskin should not be her concern, so she climbed to Mr. Brown's office, and discovered another reason for not wearing a horse-hair underskirt. It belled out too much for the width of the stairs.

Clearly, she thought as she squeezed the sides of her skirt, only men are invited up for legal advice. She heard a rip and twitched her crinoline from a loose nail, then raised her hand to knock on the tin-covered door which seemed to radiate all the afternoon's sun.

Its heat hurt her knuckles, but no one answered her knock. Caroline tried the brass doorknob and found it – extremely hot. Again, she tested the tin that covered the door. The metal seared her fingers. She smelled no smoke to account for the heat on the door. She remembered this kind of fire from the mines.

This is going to be a bad one.

She licked her burned fingers, turned, squishing her crinolines together, and raced down the stairs and around the house. She dashed up the front steps, rapped the brass knocker, calling, "Fire! Is anyone home? Please. You must get out."

A barefoot boy of about eleven loped along the street side. He halted abruptly. "What's the matter, Miss?"

The front door flung open. A matronly woman stood there, annoyance written all over her face as she wiped her floury hands on her apron.

"Fire, Ma'am," Caroline gasped. "In Mr. Brown's office."

The boy called, "I'll get him for you, Miss."

"No!" Caroline darted off the porch to stop him. He halted in the side yard, his dusty curls blowing around his face as he gazed up at the door. The metal door at the top of the stairs moaned against great pressure.

The woman stumbled after Caroline.

"Hey there, mister," shouted the lad, shading his eyes and looking toward the upper story. "Hey mister. Halt mister. Halt there."

From a window on the far end of the house, a tall man swung out, holding tightly to a length of rope. He wore a long, blue, cotton jacket. A ragged straw hat had been jammed down over his hair and most of his face. Caroline held her breath as he dropped to the alley. The buckskin whinnied in fright, dancing sideways to avoid being hit.

The man landed with catlike grace. He darted toward the buckskin, but the horse bolted and ran past Caroline, dragging his reins.

The man gave up on the buckskin, pivoted and charged off in the opposite direction. From the way he acted, Caroline believed he had set the fire. She knew the open window should have caused an explosion – unless Brown's office had been sealed from the rest of the house.

"Let's get 'im, fellas!" yelled the curly-headed street urchin to a group of arriving boys.

"Stop. He's dangerous," Caroline shouted. But the boys ran after him. The leader called back, "Danny start the fire bell." A very small boy peeled off from the crowd and ran to a neighboring house. The small child, Danny, whacked at a triangle-shaped piece of iron on the neighbor's back porch. Others up and down the street took up the signal from their porches, summoning the volunteer fire department.

The door to Brown's office creaked and groaned.

"My home," Mrs. Porter shrieked. "My beautiful home." She fingered her key chain in agitation. "He'll be dead." She whispered. "I told him. Warned him against these people."

The woman swung across the lawn and climbed the first stairs before Caroline caught up with her. The fire engine arrived as they pounded up the stairs. A volunteer fireman chased the women up the stairs. Caroline grabbed Mrs. Porter's arm. "Stand to one side, Mrs. Porter. The fire will explode out of there."

The landlady glared at her, "I beg your pardon?"

The firemen behind them laughed. "There in't no fire in there. In't no smoke."

Caroline deepened her voice, using the tone she'd heard men in authority use so often. "A ball of flame will blow out that door the moment it is opened."

Mrs. Porter's face went slack. "How . . .?"

"Believe me. Move," Caroline ordered. She had Mrs. Porter's full attention now. The woman waved a hand near the door. Her brows rose in surprise.

"Hot," she said. "Burning."

"Get away."

The landlady moved down the steps, her gaze riveted to Caroline's. The fireman had to back down with them.

A second fireman from below called up to them. "There's a fine fer a false alarm, Mizz Porter."

They were almost down the steps when the first fireman tried to pass them. Caroline stood between him and the door, saying, "Don't open that door. That fire has been starved of air. Air will bring it to life like a vicious monster."

He scoffed, "You got some imagination, lady." He lifted her by her upper arms and, in spite of her kicking at him, set her on the ground. She tried to catch up with him, but he took the steps two at a time and her crinoline caught again on the nail.

From below, another fireman yelled, "Tom. Don't do it. I heard about such fires."

The explosion blasted out, more powerful even than she had imagined. It sucked the door and the fireman into the room, then blew them out like small toys. Ripped from its hinges, the door slammed into the stair rail. The burning fireman, Caroline, the rail and the door flung off the steps and down into the alleyway behind the house. As Caroline fell, she had one absurd thought. I hope that buckskin didn't trot back for me to land on him.

**

"Her eyelids are blinkin'," exclaimed a boyish voice.

Off to her right, Caroline heard the muffled blowing of a nose, stifled weeping. "Would 'ave killed me, it would," sniffed Mrs. Porter. "But she says 'No! Get down the stairs. Don't be anywhere near the door.' She knew there was a bomb in there. She knew it."

Every bone in Caroline's body felt sundered from its sisters, every muscle and sinew shredded. She heard the commotion of fire-pump and horses, felt the edge of the spray mist over her. The explosion seemed to have brought out the whole neighborhood. Deciding whether to remain alive or call it quits, Caroline peeked out.

The face of the street urchin peeked back. She remembered that dirty face from an earlier time.

"See," he exclaimed. "She's comin' round." His smile disclosed gap teeth and a deep dimple in one cheek. Behind him Caroline could make out two other boys of his following. She also saw the florid face of a whiskered gentleman.

"Was Mr. Brown in there?" she asked.

"Yup," said the lad. "Part of him was cooked right there in 'is chair, he was."

The whiskered man pushed the boy out of her line of vision. "Don't you know when to keep quiet, lad?" he gruffed. "The lady has had fright enough."

Now she remembered. "You deliver telegrams."

"Yes'm. Brown fixed me that job," the boy said.

She saw tears well just before the boy straightened away from her.

Caroline pulled herself to a sitting position. She realized her skirts were a mess, her ankles revealed, and her dignity frayed. She adjusted her skirts, ignored her dignity and tried very hard to ignore her aching back. Still addressing the lad, she asked, "If not Mr. Brown, then who came out the window?"

"Dunno ma'am," the boy said. " 'e were right fast. Big fella, 'e was, but fast."

"What did his clothes look like?" asked another, familiar, voice. Caroline glanced up and found Alex Kemp hovering over her. He seemed not to notice her disarray. Instead, he concentrated his whole attention on the boy. "Did this ruffian wear anything you'd recognize again?"

"Oh yes, sir." The boy was proud to be paid attention. "This man, 'e wore a blue jacket – the kind w'ot you 'as to pull on over yer head-like. Me granda used to wear one. It 'as big pockets, you know, 'ere in front."

Mrs. Porter sobbed loudly, "My lovely house. What'd he have to do business with them for?"

"And this ruffian's face, lad?" asked Alex.

"Couldn't see 'is face at all, cause o' the hat."

The whiskered man now entered the conversation. Over the din of the pumper truck and the neighbors' bucket brigade he shouted, "Describe the hat, son."

"Squashed down, it were. Wide brim all 'round like this." He gestured, fluttering his hands low over his brow.

"What was the hat made of?" asked Caroline.

"Some kind of straw, I'm thinkin'." said the boy. "It had broken twiggy places at the edge of the brim."

Right, thought Caroline, glad her memory had not been affected by her fall.

"We chased him down the alley," said a younger, panting boy. Their young leader added, "Disappeared into the fire-pump engine barn, but 'e didn't never come out and no one was in there when we went in."

"Where's the buckskin?" she asked.

Mr. Kemp frowned down at her. "What buckskin?"

The whiskered man ignored the question. Instead, he asked the boys, "Can you show me which barn, soon as we're done here?"

All three boys nodded vigorously. One said, "We kin show you the rope where he swung out of the upstairs, too."

As the sheriff and Mr. Kemp followed the boys, Caroline took advantage of their preoccupation with the escape route. She rescued her paisley shawl from the dirt, then pulled herself up to a standing position. Luckily, she had landed on the softest part of her person – her horsehair crinolines. Stretching stiffly, she tested whether any bones were broken. Her sleeve was torn, and her arm scraped with gravel. Her head pulsated with pain. She attempted to swipe at her skirts with one hand, while holding her head with the other, but was distracted by her first real view of the fire's destruction.

The fireman lay where he'd landed on the alley, his inert body covered with a braided rag rug. She held her hand over her mouth, wanting to cry, but unable. "If only," she whispered. "If I'd been a man, he would have listened."

Above him, where the door had been, there was now a gaping hole with ragged boards and the ends of pieces of metal and lath jutting out. Caroline glanced down the alley and noted that the buckskin was indeed gone.

For the first time, she admitted to herself how frightened she'd been as she raced up the steps after the fireman. She knew she'd had no choice. Too few people had seen such fires.

From above, in what had been Mr. Brown's office, one sauntering volunteer fireman dropped smoldering and sodden papers out onto the side lawn. He retreated into the office, returned to the door hole and hurled out an armload of heavy dark fabric. Dark wool still sizzled from the meeting of heat and water. Sadness welled up in her as she stared at the pile of what had once been a man's life and work.

Hearing boot steps, Caroline smoothed her skirts and tried to appear composed. As he returned, the whiskered man shouted up at the fireman who had returned to the doorway with a third load from the office. "John, cut that out. You know better than to move evidence."

"Evidence?" said John, "Brown lit hisself afire with that cigar he's always chewing on."

"John, you move one more thing I'll unvolunteer you from the fire department."

The fireman shrugged but carried the pile back into the office. The whiskered man turned back to Alex and the boys. The lads gathered about the two men, gesturing and re-enacting the escape of the man who had jumped from the upper window. Alex Kemp asked a lot of the questions, trying again to get the boys to give a detailed description of the man.

"Like I said, he wore this blue fisher-jacket," said the leader of the urchins. "He was real tall, sir. Taller maybe even than you, and fast."

"A real scuttlin' cockroach he was," added Mrs. Porter.

Alex glanced at Caroline. She suspected she didn't cut an impressive figure covered with dirt and soot, but he stepped toward her, reaching out to brush a strand of hair from her forehead. "Are you better now, Miss Trewartha?"

"Much. I'm glad you arrived so quickly."

"Did you have a chance to learn anything from Isaac Brown?"

"This is the oddest situation, Alex. In order to create an oxygen starved fire, the room must be airtight."

"Yes," he nodded. "You saw the metal door. Isaac lined the walls with tin as well."

"Why would he have done that?"

"To make it fireproof. Isaac was afraid of arson."

Caroline bit her lower lip as the irony of the situation hit her. "Oh, the poor man." She murmured. "The poor man."

Men appeared with a stretcher and rolled the fireman's body onto it. The fire in the second floor appeared to be out. The line of gathered neighbors dwindled to separate knots of gossip.

The whiskered man finished talking to the boys and strode toward her. Caroline watched him hastily pin a star, somewhat cockeyed, on his jacket lapel. As he neared, she saw that the star proclaimed him a deputy sheriff.

"You truly all right, Miss?" he asked.

"A bit mussed up and rattled," she admitted, "but no permanent damage done."

"That's amazing, considering how far you were blown. What were you doing up there, Miss?"

Caroline hesitated to state her actual purpose. She didn't want to cast suspicion on the name of By-Gum Mines in the very town where they would sell most of their coal. She chose to be vague.

"I needed the assistance of a lawyer, sir. I knew of Mr. Brown and came to confer with him."

"You had an appointment?"

"Yes, sir. Mr. Kemp here telegraphed Mr. Brown from Isabeau yesterday."

The deputy glanced up a Kemp, then peered at her closely as he asked his next question. "How did you know about the fire, Miss?"

"I've seen explosions where a fire has been starved of oxygen. Considering what the boy tells me, that fire must have burned some time before it couldn't get anymore air."

"What did the lad say that tells you that?"

"Why that Mr. Brown was 'partially . . .partially cooked', as the boy said." It made her sick to think of the poor man's body being consumed.

But the deputy didn't seem squeamish about their discussion. "Why does the fact that he warn't all cooked tell you anything?" he asked.

Caroline gulped in fresh air, unhappily dragging in the smell of charcoal with it. Still, she had to finish what she'd started in this ugly survey of facts. "Mr. Brown had to have been killed some time ago," she said. "Then the fire started. It used up the oxygen before Mr. Brown was entirely . . .; Well then, the fire hunkered down like old embers in a campfire. It sat in the room, smoldering for an hour or two, waiting for air to be let in."

"You know a great deal, Miss."

"I've unfortunate acquaintance with these things," she admitted, "but I must admit the result of adding the air is even more powerful than I remembered."

"Blew her right off the landing," piped up the boy.

"You've seen explosions like that?" The whiskered deputy said in disbelief.

"Oh yes. It happens in the mines. For instance, the air-lock doors might close and leave a fire smoldering. It uses up the oxygen in the small space between doors. And then it waits. The next time one of the doors open, the fire receives air of a sudden and . . ." she fanned her hands out dramatically.

The sheriff's deputy was silent, studying her. After a few moments he said, "Miss, you're not going to tell me you're some kind of hill-billy miner."

"Mines *are* often in hill country. I'm a mining engineer."

The deputy sheriff actually snorted before he said soberly to Alex Kemp. "I need you to give me your address and the young lady's as well. Isaac Brown is a man of importance – was of importance. I expect the marshal will want to question you both."

CHAPTER NINETEEN

As they sat under a gaslight chandelier in the elegant hotel restaurant, Caroline toyed with her fork, drawing contour lines in the linen and arguing with Alex.

"I know the timing is off," she said, "but his death is too coincidental. It has to be connected to our visit."

He shook his head. "Brown has been central in several important cases in Colorado. Just last month he successfully defended a sheepherder accused of murdering a cattle man up near Littleton. Any number of people hold a grudge because of his skill. You are not responsible for this, Miss Trewartha."

"I feel it in my heart," she declared. "Our coming here triggered someone who needed to destroy Brown's records. That's exactly what Brown was afraid of, the reason he encased his office in metal."

But when Alex pressed her, she could not explain how anyone but Brown might have known they were on their way to Denver.

"The Denver telegraph office might be the source," she suggested. "Others might have read the message you sent to Brown."

"Tell you what I'll do," he said, "I'll return to the telegraph office and watch the manner in which telegrams are treated – the number of people who see them before they are sent off with the delivery boy."

"I'll follow the delivery boys," she suggested. "One of them might be in the pay of Stemmins."

He leaned toward her, his blue eyes piercing. "You will not. He stopped the end of her wandering fork with his pointer finger. "You will not be out on the streets and in danger. If you don't agree to this, I will be forced to give up investigating the telegraph office and watch over your safety."

Caroline stared at him.

"I mean it," he said. "You are too important to me to take a chance."

She settled back into her seat, studying his earnest face. "All right, Alex," she said. "I promise to stay away from the delivery boys."

He let out a relieved breath. "Thank you. I can't tell you how frightened I was when I saw you lying on the ground outside of that blasted office, today."

She ignored his warm glance and asked, "How can you follow the delivery boys? Your suit is a bit conspicuous for that."

He chuckled, gazing down at his vest. "It's not much for stealth is it?" He glanced up at her and Caroline was struck with how brilliant his smile could be. "I know a couple of fellows who worked for Isaac. I'll do telegraph office detail and hire them to follow the delivery boys."

"All right then," she said. "You've got everything covered. And I could certainly use a rest after being thrown off that stairwell."

He glanced at her, then sighed. "Yes, rest. I hope you're as well as you pretend to be."

Saying nothing, she folded her napkin, preparing to excuse herself to her room. She knew she'd disappointed Alex this evening. After the marshal questioned her, she had not fallen into Alex's embrace, shattered and crying as he seemed to expect. She had not even leaned on him, nor accepted the warmth of his suit jacket as they rode a carriage to the hotel. She could not give the kind of affection he hoped for. He'd have to realize that soon.

As he left her at her hotel room door, he said, "I'll report to you in the morning. In the meantime, sleep soundly." He bowed a stiff goodnight to her and left.

**

Caroline shivered as she opened the door from her room and peeked into the hall. Between gas lamps, large shadows cast into every doorway up and down the hall. The air smelled of cigars and whiskey.

Alex had left for the telegraph office half an hour ago. As she checked for people in the hall, she listened also for Alex's footsteps on the stairs. There was no telling how long his research might take. Tonight, she had important research of her own to do, and she wasn't going to do it with Alex Kemp expecting her to tumble into his arms at the least fright. She had to go back to Isaac Brown's and see if she could find anything that would help identify the monster who murdered him.

Some of Brown's records had escaped the fire. The fireman with a tidying streak had shown her that fact by dumping soggy papers onto the lawn – papers she had managed to plop into her bag when most everyone was off searching for the man in the blue fisherman's jacket.

She hoisted a canvas valise of necessary tools over her shoulders, straightened her gabardine skirt, pulled her cloak close about her throat and locked her door. Through a haze of gaslight, she followed the palm-frond pattern in the hall carpet to a door at the far end where she stepped onto the landing of a fire escape and breathed deeply of fresh air. Her fingers found the hole in the jamb where the door latch slid in to click shut. She stuffed a wad of paper in the hole and allowed the door to close. The latch was free. The door would open from the outside when she returned.

She stood on a landing above the alleyway. Trash cans settled askew at the backs of businesses. She adjusted her awareness, listening for footsteps or whispers that might announce danger.

When she was convinced that the alley was empty, she ran down the steps and headed for Mrs. Porter's on Lincoln Street.

**

Mrs. Porter's house looked uninhabited. Caroline hoped Mrs. Porter decided to sleep in a neighboring home after the trauma of the fire. Relieved of the worry about being overheard in her search, Caroline stared out over the dark area where she'd been thrown by the blast. Something had happened just as she regained consciousness – something that niggled at her memory. In the edges of her mind's eye, she saw a dark shape flying through the air – but just as she was about to identify the air-borne shadow, her attention had been interrupted by the deputy's voice yelling at the volunteer fireman. She had to let the image go and turn her mind to climbing the two-inch wide board, or stringer that represented the total remains of the stairs. To do it, she had to remove her boots and hide them in the shrubbery.

The stringer was nailed to the house siding. It had been the left side support of the original eighteen steps. A few of the rail posts on that side were still bolted to the two-by-ten stringer. She tied a rope around each post as she climbed, hoping the temporary handrail she created would be of help when she needed to climb down.

She grasped tightly to each post and used her toes like fingers in order to keep herself on the narrow board. Her long gabardine skirt tangled with her feet whenever she bent over. In exasperation, she hiked the front of the skirt into her belt and proceeded to the tenth step.

The odor of charred wood filled the air and invaded her lungs. As she glanced up toward the hole where the door once stood, it struck her again, how close she had come to becoming a part of the conflagration. If she hadn't had so much experience of mine disasters, she might have opened that door as the fireman had done.

208

Above the twelfth step, the upper posts had blown away with the door. She stretched up and grasped the jagged door jamb, fighting for finger and toe holds as if on a granite cliff.

She spider-walked her way up the last two steps and into the charred office. The stench of ash and burning flesh made her gasp, even though Mr. Brown's body had been taken to the morgue.

The end of her rope was just long enough for her to tie it to the leg of Brown's desk. Two legs and half of the heavy oak desk had burnt away. The other half lay collapsed on the scorched floor.

Caroline wrapped the hem of her dress over her face, tying it behind her head. In her pantaloons and stockings, she wasn't exactly ladylike, but the filtering effect of dress fabric made breathing possible.

She whipped off her cloak. On tiptoes, she hung her blue cape over the ragged ends of metal that outlined the door, to keep her light from being seen outside.

Pulling her bag from her shoulders, she set it on the floor and lifted her Davy lamp from its interior. Here was the real reason she was left with few clothes on this trip. It was difficult to pack tools like the rope and lamp for emergencies and have room left for a dress.

Striking a phosphorous stick, she lit the oil in the gauzy cylinder. The interior of the office became flickering shadows of empty bookcases and charred typewriter. All that was left of Brown's desk chair – the central post and four spans on casters – sat before the half-body of the desk. Blackened stacks of coalesced paper lay on every inch of the floor. The murderer had searched and emptied the file cabinets before setting the fire. Wooden files, their drawers opened, emptied, and seared black, stood against the walls.

Nothing seemed to have escaped the fire. Caroline couldn't imagine where the fireman found the wet but unburnt stack of paper that he threw to the ground yesterday. She held the lamp high, hoping other files had escaped, but every drawer was completely empty.

Disappointed, she leaned against the fourth wall to rest. The wall gave way. She nearly fell into a second room. She pushed the disguised door open most of the way, but it stopped, impeded by something heavy at the bottom. She pushed harder and stepped inside the next room.

Holding her lamp down, she saw what had stopped the door – a dark wool fabric, still sopping wet. This was what she'd been trying to recall – the fireman had thrown dark, wet wool into the yard this morning.

This hidden room was where the fireman had been as he removed wet objects. This undamaged room appeared to be a small linen storage and dressing room off the office. Opposite the door from the office stood a second door. When she peeked, she saw the second door led into the upstairs hall of the home.

Within the dressing closet, she opened a cupboard door and found a stack of blankets and bed linen. Pulling out a nearby drawer revealed table linens.

In the middle of the dressing room stood a large bucket of water. Staring at the bucket, Caroline realized that the murderer had searched Brown's office, then set the fire and escaped into this dressing room. Whether the water was here by plan or by luck, the murderer had soaked the fabric in the bucket and stuffed it against the door to prevent the fire from escaping Brown's office. He had known of Brown's metal encased office and arranged this water and wool device to perfect the air-tight seal.

He meant to create an explosion. He meant for Alex or me to be killed when we arrived.

Caroline shivered. "No," she whispered, "It is to do with some local case. Our appointment was a recent change – Brown barely fit us into his tight schedule."

She started to close the drawer of table linen, but felt an odd rustling give to the material underneath. Beneath the deep layers of linens, she found papers. The drawer was filled with neatly arranged files.

Setting the Davy lamp on the dressing table in front of the mirror, she was able to illumine most of the small room. Directly in front of her, she found a neat stack of recent letters – unopened and fresh, as if they had arrived only today. One letter was marred by much handling. Its return address was a London solicitor's office. Nothing here seemed to concern By-Gum or Gryf Williams.

She opened other drawers. Taking out old handkerchiefs and worn pillowcases under which she found files in such neat order that she was certain the murderer had known nothing about their existence. At first, she plied her fingers past each file, reading labels carefully. Then, realizing how long this would take her, she grabbed the one file that had the name "By-Gum" on it. Inside, she saw some of what she sought – deeds and claims registry documents for the valley and the ridge in which the seam was found. She dropped the file into her valise.

Next, she stooped to the drawer where the files were in the last portion of the alphabet. The title "Williams, Gryffyth Rhodri" gleamed at her from several slim files in a row.

His wild hair, dark eyes and teasing smile appeared in her memory. *"Actually, my name is Gryffyth ap Rhodri ap Withliam,"* he had said.

"God care for thee, Gryf," she whispered.

She quickly stuffed the 'Williams' files into her bag. At that moment, she heard a heavy door close in the house – the front door perhaps. Afraid that Mrs. Porter might have returned, Caroline grabbed the last of the files in the W through Z portion of the drawer, dumped them into her pack and with as little noise as possible, closed all the drawers. At the last moment, she picked up the pile of fresh letters and tossed them into her pack on top of the rest. Then she took one ragged napkin and wiped the floor hoping to obscure or obliterate her sooty footsteps.

The sound of boot steps on the main floor of the house warned her that this was not Mrs. Porter, but perhaps the deputy, the marshal, or even another thief.

A thief like myself, she thought as she doused the lamp and slipped back into the devastation of Isaac Brown's office, closing the dressing room door. She retrieved her cloak, took the hem of her skirt from her face and tucked it into her belt. Hoisting the warm lamp and the canvas bag onto her back, she tested the temporary rail she had created. The oak half-desk did not budge as she pulled on the rope. At the top of the skimpy steps, she hesitated, listening for the sounds inside the house.

The boots mounted the inner steps, climbed two stairs and halted, then deliberately continued up toward the second floor. Caroline ducked outside and swung to the wall. Using her rope rail, she climbed backwards down the narrow step-cut board. As she stepped onto the gravel at the bottom of the steps, she heard the booted intruder run down the inside stairs. Guessing that he had heard her descent, Caroline grabbed her boots from their bush, pivoted and ran toward the alley. She headed toward the back-porch stoop of the house two doors away where little Danny had first rung the alarm bell. She crouched within the walls surrounding the stoop. Someone searched the shrubbery around Mrs. Porter's house. She tried to catch a glimpse of him, but he returned to the office side of the house before she could see his shape. She was certain the intruder would find her rope and would know that the office had been searched. With haste, she put her boots back on and prepared to retreat to the hotel.

She slipped from the stoop and worked her way from house to house back toward the fire-engine barn. She peeked into the barn, spotted a guard, asleep on the seat of the pumper truck. She moved on silent feet into the barn just far enough to find what she sought, a window opening toward the house.

In the darkness, she watched Mrs. Porter's house long enough to be sure, by following his light, that the intruder was searching from room to room on the second floor. She took advantage of the opportunity to make a dash for the hotel.

A chapel bell sounded one o'clock in the morning as she skulked along dark alleys. She rounded the corner near the train station, one block from their hotel. The next alley was the one which held her fire escape. She glanced down the length of the alley, searching for sounds that might indicate unwanted inhabitants. No one whispered, snored or even seemed to breathe in the half block between her and the steps. She darted down the alley. Her skirt caught on the stave of a wooden trash barrel, sending it rolling. She dashed up the stairs. The barrel clattered after her, stopping at the bottom of the steps while she raced to the landing and grabbed at the door handle. To her relief, her door was still unlatched. Slipping inside, she heard a neighbor below holler "Teach you to mess with my trash. Come out with your hands up."

Caroline slipped her fingers outside between the door and the jamb and removed the small wad of paper in the latch hole. The door clicked softly shut.

When she was safely in her room, she lit the smallest oil lamp to help her clean up. She didn't want a lecture from Alex if he discovered she had been out in the night without his protection. She wouldn't tell him until she discovered something they could use to capture Brown's murderer. She glanced in the mirror and was startled by the gaunt, dirty face she saw there. She washed soot off her face and changed her clothes, folding her ash stained gabardine over the few thin files and the letters she had stolen from Mr. Brown's office. She emptied the rest of the oil from the Davy lamp

213

and wrapped it in its canvas storage bag before packing it into her valise. She wanted to read the files and letters, but she was too exhausted to make sense of anything she read, so she pulled out her flannel nightgown, hung her poor, worn tartan dress on the back of the door and closed her valise.

She caught herself searching under her bed for her rope, then remembered where she'd left it. Suddenly, her eyes filled with tears. She swiped at them, thinking how much she hated to be left with no rope – being unprepared for emergencies made her uncomfortable.

She was more than uncomfortable, she realized. She was on the edge of erupting. The enormity of Isaac Brown's death came through to her at last. Up until this moment, she had been able to hold off the devastation of his murder, and the death of the fireman. Now that she had seen something of Isaac Brown's meticulous personality in his files, the man seemed real to her, real and very important to Gryf.

She shuddered with rage, determined to find out who was hounding Gryf and killing everyone he cared about. Exhausted, she pounded the mattress with her fists, letting tears sting her eyes. Unspent sobs tightened her chest until she was unable to hold them back. She cried for Gryf and his friend until her state of shock sent her to deep sleep.

Hours later, a knock on her door roused Caroline. "Wake up, sleepy one," said Alex softly. "We've a train to catch in one hour."

Caroline jerked up, staring about her, almost unable to remember the excursion that had consumed all her energy the night before. She was a thief who had netted a few files – not even sure of the value of what she'd stolen. But she determined to discover the murderer who had killed Jesse, and now Isaac, and who perhaps hoped to murder Alex in the explosion.

"Did you find anything at the telegraph office?" she asked through the door.

214

"I did. Tell you about it in the train."

She hastened to the wash basin, slapping water on her face. "I'll be with you in ten minutes, Mr. Kemp," she called.

"Ten minutes. Ha!" He chuckled. "Never saw a woman able to get up and out in ten minutes."

"Start your watch," she ordered.

"I've hung a new dress for you on this side of the door. You've got thirty minutes, but that's the limit."

She heard him walk down the stairs toward the lobby. Unsure that she'd understood him, she opened the door a crack. Sure enough, there was a beautiful green-print dress hanging from the picture rail in the hall. She reached out and brought in the dress, afraid, until she held it up to her, that it would be too long for her short self.

She spent a good five seconds worrying over the propriety of accepting such a gift from a gentleman. Aunt Agatha would have the vapors if she knew. One glance at her torn and bedraggled tartan was enough to decide in favor of the green dress. It was thoughtful of him – and he must have asked that it be hemmed. She imagined him showing a seamstress just how short his lady-friend was – no higher than his shirt pockets, to the lady's great distress.

Caroline lay the lovely dress on the bed and glanced at herself in the mirror. Her eyes were puffy, her hair a nest for mice. Perhaps she should use the thirty minutes Alex offered. If she looked rested, he might think she'd enjoyed a good night's sleep. If he knew the truth, he'd have an attack of male authority and never again let her out of his sight.

Caroline grabbed her reticule and fished out her comb. She decided to be clean, presentable and ready for the train to By-Gum in fifteen minutes.

**

Caroline stared at her hands where they lay crossed over her valise. The valise lay on her lap, tempting her to open it and study its contents. Her finger toyed with the lock as she held herself steady against the bumping rhythm of their rail car and listened to Alex.

"At the Denver office, I sent a telegram to Abel, the telegrapher in Isabeau. I asked for immediate action. Here in Denver, the telegrapher was the only one who handled the out-going messages. In my outgoing message," Alex said, "I used a code that Able, the Isabeau telegrapher, would recognize, but few others. I asked Able to send a telegram to Stemmins, one to Brown and one to me at the hotel. Then I hung around waiting for a reply.

"When Brown's came in, four people in the office saw it before it went to the delivery boy. I'd already hired a friend of Brown's, Lon Moulton, to follow that delivery. After Stemmins' telegram arrived, those same four handled it before it went out. Dan Kyle followed that delivery. My telegram from Isabeau came in, went through the same four people and finally was delivered to my room at the hotel.

Later, I met Moulton and Kyle at the gaming room downstairs in the hotel and they reported what happened. Both messages were delivered to the proper address, but no one was at home at the house where Brown's office had been. The boy left it in a post box on the porch. After delivery, someone from the house took the telegram from the box and carried it to Stemmins."

"Someone came out of the house?" Caroline asked.

"That's what Moulton described. Came out dressed to go somewhere."

Caroline couldn't understand where that person had been when she was in Brown's office. Perhaps it was the person who searched the shrubbery after he heard her descend. "What time did you meet the men in the gaming room?"

Alex looked surprised by the question. "Time?" he asked, glancing at his pocket watch. "What does that have to do with it?"

"I'm just curious."

"Time has not much bearing on the fact that the message ended up at Stemmins'. If that is what happened to my message asking Brown for an appointment, it proves that Stemmins could have warned his boss and set off the murder of Brown after all. It's as you guessed, Caroline. Our visit was related to his death."

"But what time did you meet Kyle and Moulton last night?" she asked again.

He laughed. "You are persistent, even about barking up the wrong tree."

"Indulge me."

He put up his hands in surrender, as he calculated. "I suppose it was around one in the morning. Let's see," he hauled the watch from his vest pocket again. "I left you at about 9:30 p.m.. I sent the telegram around ten. I waited an hour and a half for the replies – that's eleven-thirty. They followed the messages – say another half hour to midnight. No one answers the knock at Mrs. Porter's. Maybe another ten to twenty minutes goes by and someone comes out, takes the message and Moulton follows him to Stemmins. Twelve thirty or one o'clock. So, Moulton is back at the hotel by one thirty."

Caroline tightened her grip on the valise. It was possible the deliverer was the same man who had been in the house just before she fled. She remembered hearing a bell tower chime one o'clock as she approached the alley. The man who had invaded Mrs. Porter's could have been at Stemmins with the telegram by then.

She wished she had gone closer to the house, tried to see who he was. But she'd been scared, she admitted. She hadn't done as thorough a job of investigating as she should have.

"You look even more beautiful than usual this morning," Alex said.

He took her by surprise. She glanced at the glass door of their seating compartment. People passed them in the outer hall of the passenger car, oblivious of his compliments. No one could have heard him, she realized, but she had to stop him paying this kind of attention to her. It couldn't lead to anything and it was wrong to let him think it might. "Mr. Kemp," she began.

"Back to Mr. Kemp, are we?"

She determined to see this through. "Mr. Kemp, I wear the green dress because the fire destroyed my taffeta. Though I appreciate your thoughtfulness, I wear it because I have no choice."

His blue eyes lit with humor. "You had no choice, but I did. And it looks as if I chose correctly. The green is almost as deep and compelling as the color of your eyes. And the little sparkle of rose in the print brings out the bloom in your complexion, the deep reds in your hair."

"Mr. Kemp, I do not want to hear this."

"Brace yourself. There is more. I admire you, Miss Trewartha – your courage, your intelligence and yes, even your beauty."

She sat as upright as she could, trying to appear more in control. "Sir, you will have to practice your nice talk on someone else. I don't do admirers."

He tilted his head to one side. "That's part of your charm. You don't want it. You try to deflect it. You never flirt. You work hard, study and think hard. And I'm hoping someday, you will fall hard."

"I'm more likely to drop you," she muttered.

He chuckled. "I already know this to be the truth. But I'm watching my back."

218

Caroline stood. "I will meet you in the dining car in twenty minutes, Mr. Kemp. I am buying your dinner this time."

She put the valise in front of her and strode to the door of their compartment. Every muscle in her back seemed about to seize up – a reaction to the battering it received when she was thrown from Brown's stairwell and then again, when she climbed the stair stringer last night.

He rose to pull the door to one side for her. "You could leave the valise. It will be safe here, and I can bring it with me to the dining car."

She pointed to it. "I must freshen up."

He leaned closer. "Goodness, your hair – after almost twenty-four hours, it still smells like charred wood."

She kept her hand from touching her hair. "It's cigar smoke from the gaming room," she claimed. "I won at Twenty-One. Poor at ten thirty in the evening. Wealthy by eleven o'clock, and no time to wash my hair before the morning train."

Alex stepped back. Then he burst into laughter. "I should have known you wouldn't go to bed. It's a good thing you didn't try to invade the Denver Club."

"Too far away. I promised you I wouldn't put myself at risk."

He smiled, "They've a higher quality of gentleman at the Denver Club, however."

"I suppose," she said as she swept out. "Does that mean that as they lose money, they smoke a higher quality cigar?"

She heard him still laughing as she crossed the double doors into the next car. Her valise was calling her. The previous night, she'd fallen asleep exhausted, and this morning there'd been no time to study the papers before they had to rush to the train. She must see if she had the original contract with Allied. Even more, she wanted to see if there was any hint that might point her toward the person or persons who stalked Gryf and his friends.

219

She stepped into the lady's room to find echoing marble floors, three sinks, three stalls, three ladies primping and other ladies coming in every moment for one reason or another. When she finally entered a stall, she sat down on the toilet lid, and began to open the valise. At that moment, the train whistle blared. The train swerved. The pull chain hanging from the water tank behind her knocked into her shoulder. Her valise scooted across her lap. Her miner's pick slid out of the valise and landed with a crack on the floor next to the toilet. She heard a gasp from every lady in the room. She reached down and retrieved it, glad it hadn't been a file of stolen papers that fell out. She shut and locked her valise, gave up on the papers until she reached the privacy of her room in By-Gum. Then, she merely took care of female business. By the time she left the room, she had endured stares from every lady in the train. She ignored them, propping her valise between her feet while she straightened her hair in its knot at the back of her neck.

At the dining car, Alex stood as she entered. He looked as if he intended to be attentive and careful with her. Warily, she sat down, putting her valise against the outside wall of the dining car. She rested one hand near the coolness of the window on their mountainous world.

He carried on banal conversation about the timetable for their trip, about how he must have left his fur-collared coat in the hotel gaming room, about the lovely mare he owned that would be a perfect fit for her – shining red-brown coat and high spirits. She ignored the way his conversation inched closer and closer to inviting her to his ranch. She grew certain that Alex merely pretended not to know she was holding herself aloof.

However, after the waiter took their order, Alex put his hand close to hers, leaned over and confided, "I understand from dining-car gossip that there is a lady in the rest room who carries an axe of some sort in her luggage. Isn't that taking independence a step too far?"

She glanced out at the rushing scenery, the snowy massifs, the pink and gray bluffs and the hurtling creek next to the train tracks. "Too far? I suppose it depends on just how persistent the admirer is, don't you?"

"You don't need anything as blunt as an axe."

"No?"

"Not at all," he said, his fingers brushing hers. "You've a rapier wit."

She picked up her menu and gave him an icy stare. "Order," she said.

CHAPTER TWENTY

Gryf sat on his office porch stairs at By-Gum Mines, his head in his hands. He couldn't get the images Alex had given him out of his mind: Caroline blown from the second-floor steps; Isaac Brown burnt in his chair, sacrificed by someone who hated Gryf. Like Jesse. Like so many other friends in other mining towns over the last ten years.

Next to Gryf, Alex leaned over, his elbow on his thigh. Gryf could feel his concern without even looking up. Tension hovered in Alex's normally robust voice. "I told the marshal I'd help him sift through the evidence," Alex said. "I may be able to find any notes Isaac had about the contract."

Gryf shook his head. "She might have been killed. You might have been killed. Why the devil did you let her go off on this hare-brained expedition?"

Alex looked startled. "Actually, she was worried about me going to see Stemmins. We suspected he was dangerous. We had no idea there was danger at Isaac's."

"How did they know you were coming?"

Alex frowned before he answered. "I checked out a theory Miss Trewartha proposed," Alex said. "It appears that telegrams to Denver are delivered to people other than the intended recipient. So, it appears, my wire message from Isabeau telling Isaac we were coming to Denver could have reached Stemmins as well. Stemmins could have hired someone to murder Isaac and start that fire even before we arrived at the train station."

Gryf saw gaping holes in their security. "Alex," he said. "What happened between you and Stemmins?"

222

Alex's laugh was full of sadness. "When I first came through the door, Stemmins called me "My Lord" and the sweat poured off of him. I must look like him now, Gryf."

The sound of raw pain in Alex's voice made Gryf study him with concern. "Alex," he whispered, but Alex lifted his shoulders as if hoisting a burden and continued his story.

"Stemmins ended our brief visit quaking in his boots. Forked over another three thousand and the major missing part to the miner's elevator. Duncan's bringing the part up on his next trip. I expect to have the rest out of Stemmins over time."

Gryf bristled, "We're not going to let Stemmins have more time."

"We can't prove his involvement in Isaac's murder. But in the process of getting your tools and money out of him, we will find enough evidence to put nails in his coffin."

Gryf glanced up at Alex, the friend who left Wales in order to be with him and to thwart his own father when Lord Forest turned against Gryf's family. And now it was Alex who promised to help him uncover Brown's murderer – Alex who had followed the reckless Caroline to Denver and brought her home safe and sound. "I hope you know I appreciate your help," Gryf said.

"Hell, you better," Alex said. "And you better succeed with these damned mines. I've a vested interest in having a town up here that needs my wheat and my beef."

A great rock seemed to sit in Gryf's chest because of Isaac's death. In this grim situation, it wasn't clear what his next move should be. He had to be sure no one else got hurt because of him.

Alex said softly, "I checked out one other factor while I was at the telegraph. I cabled home. The next morning, before we boarded the train, I had an answer. Lord Forest is in the United States and has been for many months."

Gryf bowed his head. "I'm sorry, Alex. I've no idea what drives him."

"Perhaps he hopes to discredit you – makes it look like you were a bad apple all along and not worthy of my friendship. He seems vindicated. I return home. All is forgotten."

"If . . . He can't be in his right mind."

"No."

Samuel stepped out of the blacksmith's shed. Seeing Gryf and Alex, he waved and called, "I didn't know you two had returned."

Watching him run toward them, Gryf's throat closed with sudden love for his brother and his family. Joey and Sammy trusted their Uncle Gryf. He must keep them safe from harm.

"Gryf, did you find Olaf?" Samuel asked.

Gryf shook his head. "He was here when I got back. The sheriff in Sapinero had never heard of this tavern brawl and has no idea who sent that telegram."

"The hell you say!"

Gryf said, "I was decoyed out of town for some reason, Big Brother, and I think it had to do with what's happened in Denver."

"What's Olaf's excuse?" Alex asked.

Gryf shook his head. "He's got no need for an excuse. I got back here, and Olaf was out eating breakfast at Ellen Robertson's."

"Breakfast?" Alex and Samuel glanced at each other and began to laugh.

Gryf put up his hands to stop them. "Not what you think. He's rebuilding her barn. Before that he was in Gunnison, buying lumber and hardware – a surprise for her."

"Yeah, sure," said Samuel.

"Whatever he's doing at Ellen's is better than drinking and brawling," muttered Alex.

Gryf didn't want to gossip about Olaf. He wanted to make his town safe and get back to mining. "Sam," he said, "I thought you'd be up on the ridge."

"We've been putting together more pipe. Blasting that adit into the ridge is tough, but we're close."

Wanting to reassure himself that at least Samuel was solid and safe, Gryf felt the need to touch his brother, but he didn't want to embarrass Sam, so he punched him lightly on the shoulder, then let his hand rest there a moment. "I'll let Alex explain what's happened in Denver, Sam. I need to check on the health of a young lady I know."

**

In the loft over the barn, as Ellen washed Caroline's hair, Caroline spilled out the story of Isaac Brown's death. Ellen's fingers massaged the tension out of Caroline's neck and scalp.

"Lord," Ellen whispered, "you have bruises on top of bruises all down your back."

Caroline arms were so stiff she could no longer reach up to wash her hair. She didn't know how she'd made it up the stringer to Isaac Brown's office last night. Today's buckboard ride from Isabeau had been excruciating.

She stole a glance at her valise, wishing she had a chance to get at the papers she'd stolen. She'd managed to hide the valise under the dresser so that no one would open it. She wanted to get at those papers, or at the least to give them to Gryf without anyone else knowing he had them. She hoped the files would shed some light on the murders of Jesse and Isaac, but they were off-limits to her until she was alone. In the meantime, she could find out more about the people in By-Gum.

"Ellen, please tell me about the miners of By-Gum." she asked. "I need to understand them better."

225

Ellen shrugged as she massaged Caroline's head. "I didn't meet them until they moved up here – really not until my husband died. Olaf says that Amos, Samuel and Gryf have mined together since Samuel allowed Gryf to join him below ground."

"Where were they then?"

"Cardiff, I think."

"But they tell stories about mining in India and Africa. Why did they leave Wales?"

Ellen hesitated, then seemed to decide to give her all the facts. "This is all Olaf's version, you understand, but he says there was some bad blood between Samuel and Gryf's father and Alex's father, who is some kind of Lord. It got so bad that Alex walked out – left his land and money behind, in protest over his father's unfair treatment of the Williams family."

"Left it all? How does he afford the horses and a ranch?"

Ellen laughed. "According to Olaf, that Alex can turn stone into golden opportunities. To hear Olaf brag on him, you'd believe that Alex has built up two fortunes. I guess he lost a lot of it once – some situation in Pennsylvania. Olaf says he sold a lot of ranch land at a great loss in order to help Gryf."

Caroline noticed Ellen didn't say what he'd helped Gryf do. Since she already knew, she let that pass.

She asked, "What about the rest of the miners?"

"Amos left Wales with Gryf and Sam because he saw them as leaders who could accomplish a lot and who took care of those they worked with. Alex left his father after Gryf and Sam's father was injured by one of Lord Forest's hunting friends."

"So that explains Alex and Amos. What about the other miners?"

"Olaf says Sam and Gryf met Rudy in Switzerland. Olaf and Mac have always worked together. They all met Cornell, John Philpot and Jesse Polgren in Pennsylvania. Cornell was the foreman

226

in an important trial there. Pennsylvania, that's where Samuel met and married Susan, too."

Caroline caught Ellen's eye, wanting to see her reaction to the next thought. "One of these men must pass information to the person who's out to destroy Gryf."

Ellen stopped rinsing Caroline's hair, and thought. Finally, shaking her head, she said, "They've been close friends so long, I can't imagine one of them selling out the others for mere money."

"The killers always know where Gryf is. They know what will hurt him most. They told Kidde where I was going. Someone who knows a lot is causing all this grief, Ellen."

Ellen pointed the water pitcher at Caroline. "It can't be Olaf," she said vehemently. "He worships Gryf."

"No. Not Olaf," Caroline agreed, though she knew Olaf was the reason Gryf had to leave By-Gum so suddenly two days ago.

Somewhat mollified, Ellen's fingers made squeaking sounds in Caroline's hair. "That should do it," Ellen said. "Can't smell any more smoke."

Caroline reached for a towel. "Oh, that feels much better." She wrapped the towel around her head, then pulled her new dress, now her only dress, over her chemise and pantaloons.

"You need to be warmer than that," Ellen said, holding out a long woolen robe Deirdre had left during her last trip out from the house. Caroline gratefully pushed her arms into its softness and tied its belt around her waist. The robe covered her dress completely.

Ellen picked up Caroline's pig-bristle brush and gestured for her to sit again on the end of her bed. "Now," said Ellen, brushing the tangles from Caroline's tresses, "suppose you tell me about that scar behind your ear."

Caroline looked at her. "Blunt. Is that how friends talk to each other?"

"Direct. You don't know about friends? Where have you been, Caroline?"

"I had friends at the university, but they . . ." Caroline decided it was a little early in their friendship to explain that she'd been mistaken for a boy until she was eighteen. "They weren't girl friends," she ended lamely.

Ellen's eyebrows twitched. Caroline was sure she was being misunderstood, but she didn't know how to backtrack.

Ellen persisted, "And the scar?"

Caroline fingered the scar and shuddered. "A mine cave-in. I think it was a roof beam. It might have been rock. I wasn't conscious."

"Honey!" Ellen shivered. "You went back into mines after that?"

"I love mines. This was a freak accident."

"It would turn me freakish. That's a fact." Ellen lifted Caroline's hair to study the scar again. "How long ago was this cave-in?"

"I won't ever forget that date," Caroline sighed. "January nineteenth, eighteen seventy-eight. It's the next few weeks after that I can't remember."

Ellen stopped brushing. "Your father is Carl John Trewartha, isn't he?"

"Yes." Caroline glanced up at Ellen. "Did you meet him, too? Gryf knows him."

Ellen shook her head. "Not me, but the miners have all met him. Admire him," Ellen said, but her tone was brusque, and she had become very businesslike in her brushing of Caroline's hair. "That was in eighteen seventy-eight, as well."

Caroline felt a thread was missing from this conversation. It reminded her of talking to Gryf about her father. "I was there, barely, but there at the verdict. I know what Gryf was accused of."

Ellen relaxed again, but before she could answer, someone knocked on the door to her loft room.

228

Ellen leaned over Caroline, whispering, "Want company?"

Caroline smiled. "No doubt Deirdre again, bearing food. *Come in,*" she called.

The door opened. In the light of the setting sun, all they could see was the silhouette of a tall, broad-shouldered man with curly hair.

"Alex?" Ellen asked.

But Caroline knew by the stance that it was Gryf. He had one leg out to the side like a supporting buttress for his height. "Come on in, Gryf," she said, hastily straightening her protective robe. He ducked his head under the lintel. Once in, he noticed that Caroline's hair was down and wet. "I didn't mean to interrupt. I . . . Alex told me about Isaac . . ."

She stood and gripped his hand, trying to express her sorrow for his friend. "I wish . . . If only I'd arrived sooner."

"God, no!" he said. "You'd have been murdered with him."

Ellen brought the chair from the dresser toward the patch of sunlight by the door, setting it down for Gryf where anyone passing by could see his visit was proper and public. Gryf didn't notice it. Instead of regaining a sober distance from Caroline, he reached up and touched her wet hair, studying its color in the sunlight.

"I don't want you hurt by this madman," he said, his voice dark with tension. "I want you safe. Somewhere away from me."

Ellen coughed. Gryf glanced at her, evidently startled by her presence.

"Gryf," Ellen said, her voice emphatic. "This man who blows things up, he may not be after you alone. Ask Caroline what happened to her on January nineteenth, eighteen seventy-eight."

Gryf frowned at Ellen. "Eighteen seventy-eight?"

"She almost died," Ellen supplied. "Mysterious cave-in. Can't remember the next several weeks."

Appalled, Caroline snapped, "Ellen! I don't tell your stories."

229

Gryf interrupted, "January nineteenth! Caroline? That accident. That probably was no accident."

Caroline felt a chill slide down her back. She now understood that Gryf and her father both believed her accident was related to her father's testimony at Gryf's trial. "Why do you believe that?" she said slowly, "It was just a weak beam."

"The attempt on your father was only nine days earlier."

Ellen lay Caroline's brush on the bed quilt. "Within nine days, you were nearly dead. The mine owners' reach is far."

Caroline's thoughts returned to the hospital, the long rows of beds, the big nurses, her appalling inability to speak. The nurses yelled at her as if she also couldn't hear, and as if she had no mind left. She'd been imprisoned in her unresponsive body, lying on a prickly horse-hair mattress in a room that reeked of sweat and vomit. She remembered her father's first visit. He'd bellowed at the supervisor, and then, he'd hired a carriage to move Caroline to the home of a friend where a gentle nurse was hired, and the family doctor oversaw her recovery.

And there had been a mysterious guard posted outside her door. During those visits, her father's arm was in a sling – a sprain, he told her.

And the next time he came to Kentucky, there had been much whispering in the hall. The one phrase she had caught had not made sense. Her host had admonished her father, "Carl, if you testify, . . . work in Schuylkill."

As she sat, surrounded by memory, she saw Gryf's hand reach for her brush. Feeling the tug against her head, she raised her gaze. He was already brushing tangles from the ends of her curls. His jaw muscles were tense, his attention on her hair. She reached out, put her hand on his arm and stopped him.

"And Isaac was your lawyer in Schuylkill."

He pulled his lips tight, obviously considering what to say. His dark eyes met hers. His deep pain held her attention. "Yes, I was accused of those murders," he said. "And of trying to murder your father."

"Your father told the jury he knew Gryf Williams," Ellen added, "and the person who shot them was not Gryf."

"But," Gryf added, "I was nearby when it happened. I found the murdered men in the alley and called a guard."

"And the tart testified against Gryf . . ." Ellen said.

Caroline saw Gryf stop Ellen with a glare. He tugged on the strand of Caroline's hair that lay in his hand. "Ellen is right to tell me about your accident," he said. "There is a pattern in what's been happening at By-Gum. And January nineteenth, eighteen seventy-eight is part of that pattern."

"But I was in the mountains of Kentucky. He was in Pennsylvania."

"Kidde told you the man could hire murders done miles from where he was, eh?"

She nodded.

"Who else was hurt in your mine?"

She thought about that time, such a gray memory – really no memory except what others told her about it. "No one else was injured. It happened between the day and the night shifts. I was inspecting the timber framing."

"Who sent you to do that?"

"That whole time, I have trouble remembering it."

Abruptly, Gryf sat in the chair near where she stood. His brows drew together as if unwanted thoughts consumed him. "I don't know why," he said. "and I don't know who, or how. But I believe that your father and I, and even you have stepped in the path of a madman."

She knew then that the papers in her valise could not wait for a more proper visit alone to Gryf's office. Ellen seemed as loyal to him as Alex and Samuel. So, even though Ellen was here, they had to go over the papers and try to figure out who was murdering his friends. She bent down, hauling the valise out from under her dresser and began to lift it. As she straightened, she started to speak, but the world around her grayed out. She felt her legs buckle beneath her.

"I've got her," she heard Gryf say.

"It's pain and shock," Ellen said.

She heard the valise fall open and everything spill from it just before she fainted.

**

Propped in bed, Caroline re-stacked the files and handed them to Gryf to put in his safe. Her hatchet now sat in Gryf's lap. He passed his hand over its handle several times as he accepted the papers.

She glanced at him and at Ellen. Their faces looked as grim as she felt. These files had been her hope for an explanation of the murder of Isaac Brown, and perhaps an idea of who attempted to ruin Gryf and By-Gum. Since recovering from her dizzy spell, she'd helped Ellen and Gryf read and study and re-study these files, but not one paper hinted at an answer about the contract.

Several of the files she had grabbed had nothing to do with By-Gum, but were about a case Brown had been working on for a Mr. Thomas Wood who, Ellen decided after careful reading, must be searching for his wife and missing sons.

Other papers were very important to Gryf – deeds to the valley, and claims for the ridge, even claims on the eastern side of the butte.

They found the agreement between Gryf and twelve By-Gum miners, making ownership of the mines mutual and equal. The agreement called for a meeting of all twelve in questions of safety, expansion and in borrowing. Gryf had shown her minutes for several meetings of the partnership, one indicating agreement to borrow from Allied Mines and giving him the responsibility of speaking for the partners in negotiations with Terry Branahan, President of Allied.

But they found no copy, nor even a draft of the agreement with Terry Branahan and Allied.

Deeply disappointed, they stacked the files, and were about to return her valise to her dresser again when Gryf noticed the unopened letters which had fallen beneath Caroline's bed.

"What are these?"

"I stole them, too" she admitted. "They came that day, I suppose. That's the only reason I can figure that Mr. Brown never opened them." To open these herself would be stretching her definition of right and wrong.

Gryf studied the return addresses. "There is one more letter from the solicitor for this wretched Mr. Wood," he commented to Ellen as he handed them over for her opinion, "about his children, no doubt."

Ellen looked them over as well. "Not one of these return addresses indicates a possible concern with By-Gum," she said, handing them to on Caroline, who dropped them in the valise.

"I'll remail them to Isaac Brown's office," Caroline said, "and hope they will be forwarded to anyone handling his estate."

Gryf nodded agreement, then stood. "Ellen?" Caroline saw a quick silent message pass between Gryf and Ellen. Ellen then hurried to gather the tray of food Deirdre had brought them.

"I'll get these things back to the house," she said. "Don't leave 'till I return."

Gryf's gaze held Caroline's attention even as her chaperone whisked out the door and closed it. He looked near to explode, she

233

thought. The gray of his eyes darkened to flint. He set her hatchet on the dresser and towered over her bed, his fists working and his neck muscles taut.

Caroline swallowed around a knot of guilt. "I was going to show these to you," she said, gesturing at the valise on the dresser. "but I wanted to wait until you were alone."

His hand grabbed at the blue pieced coverlet, crumpling the edge of it in his fist. She shrank back against the headboard.

He stared at her reaction. "No! It's not the papers." His voice rasped as he let go of the coverlet. "How can I tell you?" Turning away, he strode toward the dresser, then to the wood stove where he stopped and dropped to his knees. He yanked the stove door open and shoved two more small logs into its belly, but hung onto the door, watching the flames instead of closing it.

Caroline slipped from the far side of the bed, where she could feel safer in the presence of his intensity. Leaning heavily on the headboard, she kept herself upright, though her head whirled with dizzy confusion. She watched him glance over his shoulder and realize that she had put the bed between them.

Gryf slammed the stove door and rose to his full height. "Caroline, how can you be so courageous, and at the same time so afraid?"

She pulled herself up. "I am not afraid."

"Damn you for a liar," he gestured at the bedstead. "You try to save some fireman from his own ignorance. You nearly die in the process. You scurry about Denver in the dark of night – Denver, an oasis for thieves and cut throats. You climb a two-inch wide board up thirty feet into a bombed-out office, steal vital files – yes these are vital to me – and you nearly get caught by some galoot with the same goal who wouldn't think two seconds before cutting your heart out – but me? You can't be alone in the same room with me without hiding behind the bed."

234

Through shimmering tears, Caroline watched as he glanced down at his chest, then his long-fingered hands, speechlessly studying himself while his throat worked around something too hard to say. He looked up at her, his eyes dark, and pleading.

"Am I so very ugly?"

A sob escaped her. "Oh beloved, it is not you."

His eyes widened. In one stride he was opposite her across the bed, not touching the linen, but reaching to her with one hand. "Beloved," he whispered.

She clung to the bed post.

He left his hand out, an invitation to come halfway. "It's not me, you say. They were not miners, you said. Tell me who then?"

Shivering, she reached her other hand toward him, barely able to whisper the truth. "Renegade soldiers."

His eyes closed even as his warm hand closed over her icy fingers. His face shut her out for a moment. Then he gazed at her, the hard planes of his face soft with caring. "Cariad. Beloved," he said. "I am not one of them. You are safe with me."

She dragged in a ragged breath of relief. "I'm sorry."

"Don't be sorry." His voice was stern. "You are wonderful, my favorite engineer."

Through her tears and dizziness, she managed to sniff in a small laugh and smile at him. "Gryf."

"Now you fall back into that bed," he ordered, "and let me cover you with the blankets before you have me shivering as well."

She hesitated only a moment, then lay down. As he pulled the coverlet over her and tucked it up around her shoulders, he whispered. "Better ask Ellen to help you with your night gown or you'll wear out that new dress before it gets a proper life."

She stared up at him. He shook his head. "You don't need to explain the dress. I saw the damage to your plaid dress. And I know Alex. He has an eye for color. His mother was like that, too – could

235

pick out the prettiest fabric within seconds of entering the mercantile. I know. I had to carry her bolts home to the seamstress. The seamstress was my mother."

She started to sit up, but he held her down by leaning on the blankets. "You," he said, "are going to stay in this bed and sleep. Tomorrow, Samuel and I will be blasting the last of the adit and redirecting the stream. No! You will not be there. I can't have an invalid in the way no matter how creative and clever an engineer."

"But I'm responsible."

Gryf pointed a finger at her. "You are a great idea man – uh, person – but the responsible fellow here is Samuel. I left him in charge when I thought Olaf needed rescuing. If I take you up there, it will look like I don't think he can do it right without the engineer."

"But what if . . .?"

"Do you want to interfere with Samuel's moment of glory?"

"Gryf?"

"What?"

"Am I a good engineer?"

"You're an excellent engineer."

"Then I should be on the ridge in case anything goes wrong."

"Darling, if you think about my big brother and how much he wants to be an equal partner in this enterprise, you will not insist on being there."

"Your big brother?"

"Shorter, but six years older. Six years wiser. I trust him."

She fell back against the pillow in capitulation. "All right."

He grinned at her and brushed her cheek with his hand. "That's better." He gazed at her, letting his fingers linger near her lips. "Much better." Leaning slightly closer as if to study her carefully, he whispered, "Say it again."

"All right."

"No. The other."

She stared at his expectant face, loving its crags and lines, his wild black curls and his graying beard. She knew she would never be able to be what he wanted her to be, a woman able to abandon inhibitions for him. She felt tears fill her eyes. Grief for unattainable physical closeness clutched at her throat. Yet, softly, she declared his place in her heart.

"Beloved."

He smiled, a sadness in his eyes that told her he understood what she couldn't tell him. "You'll see," he put his mouth close to her ear and whispered, "You will be all right. We will be all right."

After he was gone, she lay in bed, warmed by his promise that all would be well. Before she drifted off, her more practical self told her he meant to reassure her only about tomorrow's dangerous blasting.

**

The next morning, Caroline fidgeted as she lay on the makeshift camp cot covered with a blanket that Jimmy Freya carefully tucked in. She'd been carried to the hilltop meadow just before Gryf and Samuel left for the ridge. She knew she should be on the ridge, but she also knew from the look of pride on Samuel's face that she had to stay well away from the blasting. This had become Samuel's project and Gryf had faith in Samuel.

All around her, as she dozed in and out of sleepy stiffness, the distaff side of By-Gum watched, waited. Nearby, Marie and Ellen played games with the children in the meadow at the top of the newly built chain and steps. Miguel's children and their mother Teresa came down from the high pasture to play with them.

Throughout the morning, Caroline grew stronger. Good sleep had eased most of her stiffness, but not the tear in her heart when she thought of Isaac Brown.

Lying in the warm spring sun made her feel stronger. From her invalid's bed, she kept vigilant attention toward the ridge on the far side of the valley. This time, she knew her exclusion had nothing to do with being a woman engineer.

As she grew stronger, she considered the implications of last night's revelation. Ellen and Gryf were concerned about the connection they believed existed between her disaster in eighteen seventy-eight and these disasters at By-Gum. Back then, she had once found a a threat against her if her father told the truth.

She believed that connection, but didn't understand how those Pennsylvania deaths could be related to these more recent deaths. The Pennsylvania mine owners would have difficulty discovering where Gryffith Williams had gone. As hard as she had tried to find him, she had only found him by the coincidence of her work with Allied Mines.

She could believe that whoever tried to kill her father may also have planned to implicate Gryf in that murder. However, the connection to these recent disasters was difficult to see and even more difficult to prove.

From what Ellen and Deirdre had been saying, it seemed that disasters seemed to have followed Samuel and Gryf across the world – not disasters of their own making, but clearly aimed at them. Caroline desperately wanted to understand the cause.

Closing her eyes, she savored the other memory of the previous night, of Gryf's fingers on her cheek, his warm gaze on her face, and the joy in his eyes when she forgot herself and blurted out the truth of her love. Caroline knew she would have to tell him the rest of the truth one day soon, but for a few moments, she wanted to dream about life with him.

By noon, Caroline had recovered her strength enough to join the other women as they fed the children. Except for worry about the men, she had begun to enjoy this day with Ellen and her friends.

The miners on the ridge let off small blasts designed to damn the flow down into Mine Number One, and to redirect the underground stream into the culverts and irrigation pipes they had built.

Gryf and Caroline had calculated that the underground stream had not come from the bottom of the huge Moraine Lake that lay behind the natural dam between the mining ridge and the next ridge to the west. The lake maintained a steady level.

They also believed that ever since the morning when Olaf almost drowned, only some of the potential volume of the underground stream flowed down into the mine near By-Gum. Gryf was certain the greatest volume of water still followed its original course between the shale and the granite, perhaps reappearing above ground many miles away. He worried that their efforts to get at the breach in the shale would bring water rushing into By-Gum.

The families picnicked in the upper meadow to keep all safe in case the drilling and blasting accidentally tapped into a new and greater flood.

So far, they'd heard several dynamite booms, yet no flooding had occurred. Below, in the valley, Amos and Rudy kept a watch for increased flow in the breached roof of Number One.

This morning, Rudy had said to her, "This adit was your idea, after all – a fool's idea just so's you kin get the mine to produce fast enough to polish your reputation."

She pretended not to care what Rudy thought, but she was praying that her fool's idea work. She did feel responsible. He was right about that. Caroline kept her fingers crossed and her attention toward the ridge. Well after lunch, after an agreed-on signal of two rifle shots, a critical explosion occurred. One huge blast. On the meadow, every woman and child rose, watching for water from Number One. They held their breath, peering down at Rudy and Amos. Then they heard three small sharp dynamite blasts from up high on the ridge.

The signal for success.

Those on the hillside cheered. Their cheer was taken up by the children. And below, in the valley, Amos and Rudy were seen to stomp around both openings to Number One, gesticulating to one another. Caroline could no longer stand the suspense. She made her way down the terraced steps, hardly touching the chain. At the front of the burro tunnel, she found Amos.

"Is she dry?"

He grinned at her. "Sure appears to be petering out down here, ma'am."

She watched as the output from her pump and Gryf's sputtered into the ditch. What yesterday had been a steady flow, was indeed coming to an end. She glanced down the tunnel where the two pumps valiantly dragged in the last of the water at the bottom of the entry shaft.

"Where's Rudy?" she asked.

"Gone to see the other miracle." Amos laughed and pointed down the ditch. Following his direction, she saw that Rudy had made his way a half-mile downhill to the marshy field – Jimmy's pond. The pond was rising. Even from here she could see that four small rivulets were running down from the flanks of the valley and into the low space.

"Yes!" She whispered. "It waters the pines and collects exactly there – a new reservoir for the town."

Amos forgot himself at that moment. He smacked her shoulder, saying, "I'll be danged. You had it all figured!" Sudden recognition of what he'd done made him color and duck his head. "Gee, Miss Trewartha, I don't. . ."

She laughed and plunked him on the shoulder as well. "We did it! By golly, it worked."

He glanced up at her, disbelieving at first and then catching her elation, raised his arms and shouted. "It worked." He danced a jig around her and then hooked arms with her so they could both dance.

Amos sang out "It works, by-golly. It works, by-gum." To which Caroline added, "It drained the mine called Number One."

After several choruses, they came to a breathless rest, and an awareness that Rudy was standing nearby with a smirk on his face. "Such caterwauling," he groused. "You'll wake the whole town." They glanced up at the meadow and found that all the women on the hill watched them, laughing. The children imitated their dance and sang their song.

"Come on to the school," shouted Deirdre. "The men'll be on their way down. We're fixing to have a celebration."

CHAPTER TWENTY-ONE

Drying her arms on a dish towel, Caroline stood with Deirdre and Marvelle in the doorway of the school kitchen. Several feet away, Sammy and Joey Williams sat on a bench next to their Uncle Gryf. The twin's dark heads drooped toward each other.

Caroline didn't blame the little boys for wishing to stay where oatmeal cookies baked in the wood stove, and where Manuel and Teresa, Ellen and Olaf, Samuel and Susan swirled about the floor to the rhythm of John Philpot's fiddle tune. She, too, wished this party might go on and on. She wanted to forget the work ahead of them – installing a miner's cage to speed the process of cleaning out and shoring up the main mine.

And after the miner's cage, we must . . .

Taking a deep breath, Caroline forced herself to think about celebrating instead of planning. After all that had happened, By-Gum needed some time to celebrate.

In front of her, Sammy's head bumped Joey's. Both boys jerked upright. Sammy blinked and hollered, "Ye dance good, Da!"

Everyone in the room laughed. Gryf put his arm around his nephews. "Righto, Sammy," he said.

John Philpot stamped four quick beats on the floor as he began another tune. Amos Jawarski stepped up to Caroline. "You remember the polka we done by the mine?"

She smiled. "That was a polka?"

"Yup. Kin we do a repeat?"

Caroline managed a curtsy to Amos. "I would love to."

On the schoolroom floor, she inhaled the combination of iron, zinc and sweat that was Amos's special mining smell. He was her friend, just as Ellen was. And friends freed her momentarily from worries about the mine and fear of the man who hired Kidde.

Amos put his hands gingerly at her waist, saying, "Now you take a good grip on my shoulders 'cause we're going round real fast."

And then they were off, whirling three hundred sixty degrees with every four steps. At the end of the song, Amos gasped, "You dance pretty good, Miss Trewartha. I believe you've become 'altitud-inized.'"

She looked at him blankly, and then broke into laughter. "You're right. I am breathing better." Actually, her head was awhirl. She reached out a hand behind her, hoping to lean on a desk. Instead, long, familiar fingers steadied her. She glanced up at Gryf Williams and her heart faltered.

"You're the bravest lady I have met," Gryf joked. "Maybe brave enough to dance with me, eh?"

Heat rose in her cheeks. Surprised at her reaction, she glanced into his soft gray eyes. "If you ask, you'll see if I'm brave," she answered as smoothly as she could.

"May I have this dance?" He bowed, a mock of genteel mannerisms.

"Not if it's another polka," she laughed. "I won't last."

John Philpot ran his fingers up a quick scale and started a sedate rhythm.

"Ah," said Gryf, "May I assume this non-polka gets a 'yes' from Miss Caroline Trewartha?" Without waiting for her reply, he swung her out onto the dance floor. His left hand still held her right, but his other hand slid around her waist. This was not the innocent waist-holding that Amos had done. Gryf's fingers spread up her side possessively. He seemed to be studying her reaction while dancing with a smooth grace.

"I understand I missed quite an exuberant display of joy when you and Amos discovered the mine was draining dry."

She knew if she took her eyes off his face, she wouldn't be able to dance. She loved him, trusted him. Only last night she'd let him tuck her into bed. That gesture had seemed innocent. However, tonight, awareness of his long, warm fingers forced her to face thoughts of intimacy. She wanted, yet she feared.

His gaze held her steady. He leaned closer and whispered, "Breathe, Caroline. We're only dancing. All these people are your friends. You are safe."

She breathed deeply. Tentatively, she smiled at him, and stepped on his toes.

He chuckled, "I guess I'm the one who's brave, eh?"

As they circled the dance floor, Gryf continued to talk, covering her mute stiffness. "You have a way, Caroline. You've convinced me to do things I thought not possible. Tomorrow, I'm going to put Cornell Ivisson in charge of installing the miner's cage – the one Alex rescued from Stemmins. And while the men are working on that, I hope you will ride up to mines two and three with me. We'll figure how to put them into production. We may yet have a profitable season, thanks to you."

She swallowed, "I value your confidence."

He smiled at her. "You have my admiration, and," his hand tightened slightly on hers, "you also have my loyalty."

She glanced up to understand his meaning. He gazed at her with gentleness. "I keep trusts for friends who need to store them. Secrets can be a heavy burden."

She stiffened, "I don't know what you mean," she said, knowing without doubt that he referred to her past – to the very cause of her taut manner as they danced.

"Sometimes," he said in a soft, low voice, "a secret turned to the light becomes neither as dark, nor as controlling as it felt when it lay hidden in our hearts."

He was treading too close. If he ever knew all that had happened to her, he would be sickened. He would never look at her as a colleague, or a friend, but only as . . . as a used and dirtied rag. She had to push his questions away, refuse to acknowledge them.

She raised her gaze to his and said, "Gryf, I appreciate your offer, but I have no secrets that seem a burden."

The slight caressing motion of his thumb on her ribs emphasized what a liar she was. Yanking her hand from his, she backed away, staring at him in fear. Then she turned to run and bumped into the arms of Alex Kemp.

"Here, what's this?" Alex asked, holding her off from him by gripping her shoulders.

"I'm sorry," she muttered and tried to dive past him. Beyond Alex, she caught a glimpse of a tall, heavy-set man leaving the schoolhouse. His dirty hair was caught back in a queue. She stiffened as the man disappeared.

Alex held her firmly, "Did this big galoot step on your toes?" he asked, grimacing toward Gryf.

"I . . I stepped on his." Her voice sounded tense, and louder than she intended. She glanced at Gryf.

"There goes the man with his hair tied back," she said.

Alex laughed. "A man with long hair?"

Gryf's gaze darted about the room. "Where?"

"He just went out the door," she said.

Gryf called to Cornell and Samuel to follow him. With his brother and others behind him, he moved out into the night to search for the man.

Alex studied Caroline, "Why does this man with the long hair, worry you?" he asked quietly.

"I saw him the night we found Jesse Polgren's body, yet I have not seen him working with the men since that night."

"Ah." He nodded. "Can't be too careful after Kidde attacked you."

Gryf ducked his head to reenter the schoolhouse. He caught her eye and shook his head. "He must have gone pretty quickly. Sam and Cornell are putting more guards around the buildings and the mine."

"Can this man be important?" Alex asked.

Gryf's jaw tightened. "He threatened Miss Trewartha. I want him found." He spoke to Alex, but at the same time, his hand reached for Caroline's shoulder, merely rested there, with his thumb moving slowly over her collar bone. She tried to breathe, as he had suggested, tried to stay next to him.

During this one night, she'd felt such deep joy, watching her town celebrate, and knowing friendship with Ellen, Deirdre, Marie, and even the beginnings of warmth and understanding with Marvelle.

Yet, in the midst of celebrating, she'd felt isolated by her role as outsider, threatened by the sudden reappearance of the strange man, and finally, the subtle motion of Gryf's hand had set off her deepest fear. And here was his affectionate touch again.

"I think," she whispered, "that I must be tired."

Gryf's thumb stopped moving. He gazed at her. "I expect you're worn from dancing and working so hard. We don't have to go up to the other mines tomorrow. I think you should take a day to recover from all that's happened."

"No," she blurted. Embarrassed, she glanced up at him. She saw only the gentle caring and the puzzlement. "No," she said more softly. "The season is short. We need to plan for the mines as soon as possible."

"Early to bed, and so forth," Alex said. "I'll walk you to Freya's."

Startled at his offer, she looked to Gryf, expecting that he would take her arm and wave Alex off. However, he merely frowned, swallowed hard and said to Alex, "Be sure her door is locked. I'm going to patrol the perimeters, search for this fellow."

"I'll let Mac know she is at home so he can keep an eye out, and then," Alex said, "I'll return to your place. We've got some talking to do, you and I."

Alex offered his arm and Caroline took it, lifting her chin to walk stiffly from the schoolhouse without looking back.

**

After searching for signs of the long-haired stranger and warning the guards at the mine and work buildings about him, Gryf returned to his home. In his own cabin, he tossed everything off his coat hooks as he searched for his fisherman's jacket. Scooping up the heap of clothes, he threw them onto his side chair. He realized he was counting seconds, losing track and starting over again, counting in his head the number of minutes Alex took to walk Caroline home. In his estimation, it took Godawful long.

He opened his mother's cedar chest and tossed things out of it. When it was empty, he grasped the side of the chest and leaned over it, breathing hot and angry, and confused.

He had thought Caroline was easing up, able to let him closer. Last night she had said that precious word. He didn't even say it to himself for fear he would never again be able to imagine her voice saying it.

And there were other signs she could warm to him, even relax in his presence. Geez! She'd cried on his chest during the night in the cavern on the ridge. She had shared her blanket with him. And then, as they came down from that stormy night, she'd let him kiss her. She even seemed to return his kiss. But, he reminded himself, he'd first kissed her in protest of her lie, the pretense that she cared for his safety only because they had to do business together.

Is she forever going to hide her fear behind the camouflage of work and ambition?

Finding no cotton jacket, he began putting his books and shirts back into the cedar chest. This chest, and a rocking chair that Samuel now possessed, were the only furniture his mother had ever owned. He looked at the worn paper lining of the chest, thinking of the few times he had seen what his mother stored in this small space – one Bible, which he still had, two gray dresses, now Susan's. Wrapped in an old shawl there had been five or six photos, but they were no longer in the chest by the time he and Samuel returned to Cardiff for her funeral. He'd never seen the photos themselves, merely knew that she had them.

He stared at the filigree printed on the lining paper, thinking about the vicious things his father had said to his mother. When he was small, he'd been frightened, certain she would leave. But she never did. She took all the brutal names his father called her in silence and stayed for him and for Samuel.

And then, one day, Samuel, stood over their father's wheelchair and ordered him to hold his tongue or be put out in the streets to beg. Sam was already working in the mines, and their father knew Sam could and would follow through on his threat. Father held his tongue when Samuel was at home. He never again spoke harshly to their mother, but he continued to turn his bitter tongue on Gryf when the two of them were alone.

From him, Gryf had learned that he was an ugly child, arrogant, a thief, and would end his life in the gallows. Gryf also learned, as he grew older, that no man respected his father's opinion. Still, it was not easy to cut the man's voice from his memory.

Gryf shut the chest, pushed himself up and paced the small cabin from the fireplace to the built-in beds, around the table and two side chairs and back to the fireplace. Dark and ugly, that much was true. Is that why she still shies when I touch her? Or was it the other – the thing that must have happened to her?

They weren't miners. Renegade soldiers.

Ellen. Maybe Ellen can help her, he thought. He grabbed up a wool jacket and was about to go back to the dance in search of Ellen. Instead, the door burst open and Alex walked in.

"She's all safely delivered to Freya's," Alex said. "Mac is guarding his farm while we search for the stranger she saw. She says she'll wait for you in the morning, but she'll be gone to the mines after six."

Gryf grunted, "Still bossy, eh?"

"Bossy, but oh so beautiful. What the hell happened here?" He gazed at the mess of clothes on the floor.

"Can't find my Welsh fisherman's jacket," Gryf said.

"Let me guess." Alex put a thoughtful finger to his cheek and wandered across the room in a pretense of investigation. "The jacket is not on the hooks and it's not in the chest."

"You taking up police work?"

"Just trying to help. Do you have storage under these beds?"

"None. Too many varmints under there."

"Hmmm," Alex thought. "Do I remember correctly that after her husband died, you paid the Widow Robertson exorbitant fees for laundering your shirts?"

"I did, until she became the schoolteacher."

Alex's silence made Gryf glance up to see that he was awaiting further explanation. Gryf thought it ironic that Alex should be the one to suspect him of a dalliance.

"Ellen washed my shirts," he said. "The income fed her boys. That's it."

"Ah. So you say."

"You ought to try thinking of women as friends once in a while, Alex. Friendship reveals a whole new dimension in women which can be deeply satisfying."

"I'm convinced. So, Ellen was a friend whom you over-paid to wash your shirts."

"Exactly."

"Nevertheless, is it possible that your fisherman's jacket is at her farm, perhaps in her bedroom?"

Gryf ignored the remark, but he was jogged into a memory of himself searching for things that needed washing. To be sure she made it through the winter, Gryf had taken anything that could be dunked into boiled water. That last time he'd taken her laundry, he'd realized that Ellen was not only proud, but also that she was great with kids. He'd picked up the last load of clothes, paid Ellen in chopped firewood and ten pounds of flour. He'd left that basket in his lean-to. Then he'd called a town meeting to encourage people to offer her the job as schoolteacher. He'd forgotten all about the basket of clothes.

He grabbed the lantern from its hook by the dry sink and flung the door open. Alex followed him out to the lean-to door and offered to hold the lantern while Gryf yanked it open. He stopped a moment to wonder why the lock on the lean-to was broken, then, in haste to find the jacket, he grabbed up the basket.

"Why do you want this jacket now?" Alex asked, holding the lantern high.

"Caroline got soaked the last time we went to the mountains. That tight weave cotton over a wool sweater can keep off the chill. Wish I had two of them, I'd use the other one myself."

Back in the cabin, he dumped the clothes. There was the fisherman's jacket. Relieved that at last something was going right, he lifted it up. Its length would keep her warm. And since it had no buttons, but was pulled on over the head, the wind would have a tough time getting in at her. He had liked this jacket for prospecting because he could put sample rocks into the big front pockets.

"What's that? Iron ore?" Alex pointed to the right sleeve. A dark brown stain covered the back of the wide cuff.

Gryf studied it. He smelled it and jerked his head back. "Blood. Still pretty strong."

"Ellen must have tried to get it out."

"Ellen washed it months ago. This is too fresh." Gryf took the jacket to his sink and poured water from the pitcher onto the stain.

"Do you suppose some animal got into your lean-to?" Alex asked.

"Could be," Gryf said. He scrubbed the cuff. Even with soap, most of the stain was still in the sleeve. "Well, the jacket's got to be dry in the morning, so that will have to do," he said, hanging the coat over the second chair. He pushed the chair near the fireplace.

"Now, Alex, you wanted to talk."

Alex sat down on the side of the bed he used when he visited. "I do. It's about Miss Trewartha."

Gryf tensed, but kept straightening the wet sleeve, waiting for the hammer blow to his gut.

Alex's tone was light. "I told her if she were ever afraid of you again, she should come out my way for safety."

"And she laughed?"

A rueful smile pulled at Alex's mouth. "Actually, she did. However, I gave her directions just in case she ever needs them."

"God help her if you're her back-up plan."

Alex ignored him, turning all serious on Gryf. "As we, she and I, have shared the road from Denver twice, I feel I have come to know her quite well. She is a remarkable woman, Gryf. She's lovely, of course. Anyone can see that. But she was so . . . so fine about what happened at Isaac's. She is, well ... she's amazing."

"And?"

"And . . . are you as interested in her as it seems? Or is it all right if I court her?"

Gryf's grip tightened on the sleeve cuff. He felt heat rise within him. It was unfair of him, but the idea that Alex might want Caroline made him angry. It didn't surprise him. His friend had always had an eye for beauty. But Alex's ease with women caused images in Gryf's mind which made him ill.

Alex must have mistaken Gryf's silence for inner debate. "She is the real thing, Gryf. Not one of those affairs, not like in Philadelphia and Pittsburgh."

"You better treat her right."

"It's okay with you then?"

"No," Gryf stood up to fix Alex with his attention. "I am as interested as it seems. However, she doesn't belong to you or me. She has a right to choice. But you better not hurt her, eh?"

"Best man win, and all that?"

"I hope to God she comes out the winner."

CHAPTER TWENTY-TWO

"I don't think she meant you had to meet her at four in the morning," Alex grumbled to Gryf. They stood in the dark near Gryf's cabin, Alex shivering, but willing to help.

Gryf cinched the saddle. "Maybe, after this, she'll stop sending me orders about meeting her in the wee hours." Gryf figured since he was awake anyway, thinking about her, thinking about Jesse and Isaac, he might as well put wakefulness to use.

"How you going to roust her?"

"Same way Jimmy does it – pebbles on the window, eh?"

"You know she won't even be dressed at this hour."

Gryf glared at his friend for even thinking such thoughts. The truth he admitted to himself was that he hoped to find her sleepy, wearing maybe a thin cotton nightgown. With luck, there would be lace. Hair all a-tumble. One shoulder peeking out. Her slim feet exposed.

Lord, what am I going to do with my mind?

"Got your jacket?"

"Yup." Gryf kneed Sol, making him blow out so he could tighten the cinch. Sol was a clever devil for making you ride with a loose saddle.

Alex tied Gryf's bed roll to the straps at the back of the saddle. Then he flipped up the cover of the saddlebag on the far side. "Deirdre made you some Irish pasties. At least she claims they're Irish." He held up a string-tied packet. "Me, I think they're granite."

Gryf chuckled. "Deirdre's pastry is built to last."

Alex flipped the saddlebag cover down and tied it. Then his face grew sober. "You take care of her."

Gryf stared at him over the saddle. "You should judge?"

"All that before," Alex waved his hand at the past, "all that was harmless kicking up my heels. The girls had just as much fun as I did. They ended up richer for the good times."

Gryf bit down on his lip. "I'm off. Just close up the house, will you?"

"I'm going back to sleep," Alex said. "Out to my ranch by ten this morning. Good riding to you."

Alex stuck by Gryf through everything. The festering sore in their friendship was Alex's attitude toward women. The one fight they'd had as boys was because of some tripe Alex had muttered about Gryf's mother – repeating words that Gryf's father, Rhodri, slung at his wife.

Johanna Williams deserved better. Gryf spent ten minutes beating that understanding into Alex.

Afterward, Alex was polite to Johanna, but as he matured, he treated other women as partners in fun, never believing they had feelings and expectations.

Gryf had seen Caroline respond with ease to the light-hearted banter with which Alex always began his seductions. It worried him that when Alex decided it was time to get beyond the banter, he would ignore all signals that Caroline wasn't ready.

Hell! Last night, he, Gryf, had moved one thumb toward the curve of her breast and she had bolted – beyond thought, beyond control. He could not forget her accusing, hurt look, and he felt every-inch mean for that brief lapse. If she could forgive him, he intended to help her learn about real caring between a man and woman, the kind of caring his brother Samuel found with Susan.

**

Caroline leaned back in the rocking chair in her loft room. After a night of hard work, she relaxed, fingering the barrel of her Regulator Deluxe. It was cleaned and ready for the morning's trip.

254

She was dressed to ward off all interest in her as anything other than a mining engineer, wearing her cotton blouse under her old black jacket-bodice, and her split skirt with the leather seat. She'd laced up her square-toed boots over rib-knit stockings. On the end of her bed lay her mother's paisley shawl and her blue wool cape. She was ready to be as business-like and unfeminine as possible.

She was anxious to started bringing coal from these mines and ready to correct any impression she had left with Gryffyth Williams that she was afraid of him. Mortified by her actions at the dance, she could not have slept this night.

A handful of small pebbles hit the window.

Jimmy, she thought. At this hour? She opened the door an inch and saw below her the shadow of a man leaning all his weight on one leg, leaving the other out to the side. Next to him stood Solomon, chewing grasses and whuffling.

"Gryf Williams!" she flung open the door. "What are you up to?"

"Going up to the mines. Thought you were chomping at the bit."

"That would be Sheba. I'll saddle her up."

"Could you holster the sidearm?"

"Might need it," she laughed, tucking it into her bag. "Isn't Rudy Sperl managing Mine Number Two?"

Gryf chuckled, "I doubt your pistol will change his mind about your ideas. He doesn't take to change."

"Such as women in mines." Caroline slung her saddlebag over her shoulder, shut her door and stepped down the stairs.

His black gaze caressed her face. Caroline ignored the hot feeling his look gave her. "The season is short up here, Mr. Williams. Change has to happen fast if it happens at all."

He shrugged. "What does that mean to a careful conservative like Rudy?"

She waved him to follow her. "I've something to show you."

255

**

Gryf lit the lamp and followed her into the barn. Enjoying the way she strutted when she was busy, he watched her walk quickly to the worktable. She pulled a tarp off the table, revealing a pile of wood chips. Nestled among the chips sat several beautifully carved miniature logs.

"Where did this come from?" he asked.

As she held her pocket-knife toward him, he saw a fresh nick on the pad of her right thumb and a blister developing on her pointer finger. She picked up several of the small timbers and fit them together, creating the skeleton of a box. Each timber had a tongue or tenon shaped at one end. At the other end was a square hole into which a tenon could be fitted. This mortise and tenon arrangement made it possible to build the skeleton cube quickly.

"Test it," she said.

Gryf stared at her, thinking what pleasure it would be to know this woman for many years, and always to be amazed by her resourcefulness and ingenuity. Gryf put his hand on her model, applying pressure down. It held.

"Apply a torqued pressure," she said.

He put his weight completely against one corner, pushing toward the opposite corner. The little cube didn't give in any direction.

"It's often built with diagonal bracing," she said, "but it's very strong on its own."

"I have heard about this method," he said. "By gumption! I never believed it could be this strong."

He saw her stifle a small smile of pride. "Square sets. A Mr. Deidesheimer invented them for deep mining in the Comstock." From the straw nearby, she pulled out another model – several cubes that were interlocked with the next cube in any direction. "Push," she ordered, leaning on the structure herself.

256

His hand brushed against hers as he moved in. She recoiled, but he pretended not to notice. He tested her square sets in every possible weak point, and they held.

"We can rebuild the roof of the main mine, eh?" he said, trying in vain to twist along the length of the connecting cubes. "This is great."

Gryf looked at the model and then at her. "Caroline, did you carve all this tonight?"

She nodded. "I wanted you to see how it could be."

He gazed once more at the model. She had not slept this night either. He had spent the night in restless dreaming about people he couldn't change and a future he couldn't control. However, she had spent the night solving problems for him.

"It will work," he said quietly. "I thank you."

**

In the darkness of five in the morning, stiff and angry, Caroline followed Gryf out of Mine Number Two. Gryf was yards ahead of her, nearing their horses and leaving her to the mercy of his mine manager, Rudy Sperl. The Davy Lamp on Sperl's mining hat illuminated the path with spasms of light as he strutted and squawked behind Caroline. Taking two strides to her one did not make him the least bit breathless, unfortunately.

"Neither you nor the richest cigar-smoking Sir Watch Fob from Allied Mines is making Rudolph Sperl do anything," he muttered at Caroline's left shoulder. "Sperl doesn't hire anybody Sperl doesn't trust. You got that, Miss Treewart?"

Caroline replied. "I merely suggested one advertisement in the Denver train station or the post office."

"Might as well drag in the scum off the sewage pond and put it to work."

Now I've got him, Caroline thought and turned to accost him. "Mr. Sperl, you are a good miner. Hire neophytes and train them yourself."

Sperl squinted at her, "Knee-fights?"

Gryf grunted, "That's tadpoles, minnows . . ."

Understanding spread over Sperl's face, "One or two new guys along-side of several good miners – that's logic. But that's not what you're after is it?"

"One or Two? How can you take advantage of this anthracite bonanza? How pay off that debt to Allied? You have twenty trained miners to three mines? You can't do it."

Sperl waved at the darkness around them. "I seen enough destruction caused by careless mining. And so have you, I wager. So have you!"

Gryf interrupted Caroline's retort. "All right, Rudy. We know what you think of the idea."

Miraculously, Mr. Sperl said nothing more.

As Caroline stared at the little man, Gryf said, "Sol and Sheba are anxious to get on with our trip. We'd best haul ourselves into the saddle before they take off without us."

Caroline took the hint. She mounted, laying the reins on Sheba's neck to wheel her up the mountain. She was chagrined to see the bright light of Sperl's Davy lamp illumine both her hiked up skirt and a long limb of exposed stocking. She yanked down on the errant fabric. Behind the lamp, the lined and deeply shadowed face of Rudy Sperl broke into an imp's wicked grin.

"Fact is, Ma'am," said Sperl, "You got lots of chances to persuade if'n you know how to put your opportunities to good use."

"You're out of line, Rudy!" Gryf said.

Sheba snorted, shook her mane and led out in front of Gryf's roan while Caroline's face flamed.

258

**

A week ago, as Gryf remembered it, his goal had been to welcome C. J. Trewartha to three well-run mines, thank him for saving Gryf Williams from the gallows in Pennsylvania, share a few beers and talk over new developments in mining. During the intervening week, his well-run mines became a memory: Jesse and Isaac were murdered; the gender of C. J. Trewartha had brought dissension between Rudy and other miners, and Kidde had tried to kill Caroline.

The only step forward they had taken this week was to follow her idea for diverting the underground river. She was damned good at what she did. The model of the longwall with square set timbers was going to make mining the seam a great deal faster and safer. She was definitely right about needing to hire more miners. But now that she'd argued with Rudy, it would be difficult to back her idea without causing Rudy to lose face. Even though she was a brilliant mine engineer, her head-butt arguing tactics didn't help. He wondered how she had made such progress up in Wyoming.

Up ahead of him, Caroline appeared to be daydreaming about the sunrise over the granite and sandstone walls of his valley. He heard her whisper, "Catkins blooming. God, what a beautiful day." Then, as if to hide her enjoyment, she stiffened and urged Sheba forward once more. Over her shoulder she said, "Is this the fastest route to Number Three?"

He laughed, "You enjoyed visiting with Rudy so much you're impatient to visit Olaf, too?"

"I'm concerned about economics. The distance to this third mine poses an even greater problem of transportation than at the other two."

"We'll deliver by tram over this hill and down into the Dyfi Creek Valley."

"I see no poles. No cable, pullies or tram buckets. What tram?"

"Five years from now," he explained. "This portion of the seam is the closest to the surface, but it will cost the most to develop, so it has to wait until we can afford it."

She shook her head. "Five years from now the railroad will be running through Parshall and Kremmling instead of here. Five years from now you'll be nearly out of business because you can't compete by delivering to Isabeau by wagon – a plodding day trip when the wagon is full."

"A quiet day trip, I hope," he commented softly.

She turned her back on him, not dignifying his attitude with a retort, but he did not give up on her. He hoped one day she would fall in love with his valley and its quiet isolation just as he had. Then she would not want the smoke and noise of trains. She would find ways to build the overhead tram, improve the road, anything rather than bring trains to the By-Gum.

Gryf's hand rubbed over his dark and homely face, but he felt the tension near his eyes relax. The view before him was of black velveteen, smoothly fitted over slim shoulders and a back so upright it reminded him of the day he'd been mesmerized by a sheer wall of extraordinary blackness – its color absorbed all the warmth of the day and changed through all the hues of black, purple and blue as the sun's light revolved.

Obsidian Cliffs, he remembered. Sharp, smooth. Arrowhead strength, but soft – soft and warm to the touch when I finally climbed down to them.

With difficulty, Gryf yanked his mind away from Caroline's jacket fabric and all the thoughts that naturally followed.

He frowned. Crossing the trail, he spotted horse tracks. Shod horses, not the unshod ponies the Lauriggue family sometimes used. These tracks climbed toward Olaf's mine. Olaf never rode a horse. No one but Olaf had a reason for being up near Mine Number Three

260

this morning. Suddenly, Gryf recalled the man Caroline had seen at the dance last night.

Sol's head rose, his nostrils flared, his ears alert. "Whoa, Sol," he commanded.

Caroline turned in her saddle, her eyes wide with question.

"That set of horse-shoe tracks," Gryf explained. "The Lauriggues don't shoe their horses. They don't much bother with horses – waste of fodder."

"But these tracks couldn't be left by Kidde's gelding," she said, turning Sheba for a better look. "Too much snow and rain since then."

Gryf glanced at the ridges and mountains above them. He had a feeling that their progress had been followed since early this morning. She was exposed to whoever might be within rifle shot, and Olaf had been up here alone since sometime last night.

"We've got to check on Olaf." He grabbed up Sol's reins and ordered, "Stick close to me. Be ready for an attack."

Not questioning his urgent concern, Caroline turned Sheba sharply, following Sol up the mountain to the north.

CHAPTER TWENTY-THREE

Caroline studied the area as she urged Sheba after Gryf and over the hill toward the mine. No hoof prints appeared near the mine entrance. Gryf pulled Solomon to the edge of the mine shaft, grabbed a pole of the head-frame, and called down the black hole.

"Olaf?"

"Comin' up, Boss," Olaf's voice echoed out of the belly of the mountains.

Gryf sagged in relief. "No. We'll come down to you." He smiled over his shoulder at her, swung out of the saddle, slapped Sol's reins around the nearest scrub pine, grabbed his pickaxe and jammed the handle into his belt. Then he strode toward her.

"Guess I worried about nothing," he said, rounding Sheba's left shoulder. "Maybe that was Manuel's sheepherders up there after all." He reached up to take Caroline's waist as she dismounted – acted as if he did that all the time, like it was nothing.

Caroline merely stared at him, frozen in place with those great, long hands of his inches from her, his attention on her face, watching, waiting. Gryf's brows rose, briefly, questioning, then a quick look of understanding and pity flashed across his face. Her cheeks flamed with humiliation.

He lowered his arms and said gruffly, "Forgot. You can do it all yourself, right?" Stepping away, he glanced over his shoulder. "Let's not keep Olaf waiting, eh?"

That challenge allowed her to swing into action. She had a job to do down there. She leapt down, strode toward the head-frame, and there, she nearly bumped into him as they both reached for the rope.

He arched a teasing eyebrow. "Go down together?"

Caroline was through being mocked and embarrassed. She burst out with the first thing in her head. "You're too big." Seeing his laugh lines begin to crinkle, she cast about for a rationale. "This spindly head-frame won't hold both of us."

Gryf glanced at it. "Right you are." He adjusted his pick in its belt loop, swung his enormous boot into the empty space over the hole, wrapped the rope around his body and proceeded to lower himself into the mine. "Be right back," he said, and almost managed to remain straight-faced. At the last moment, his eyebrows wiggled up and down, taunting her. Then his face disappeared into the darkness.

She leaned over the hole and saw only a gleam of dark curls disappearing far too quickly. The rope fairly whistled with Gryf's haste to get away from her.

"Olaf, who the hell . . ."

Caroline heard the full force of Gryf's boot soles slam into the floor of the mine shaft.

"Hell of a ride." Gryf's voice was belabored.

Olaf's bass voice boomed up the shaft. "Thought maybe you was a big ol' hare, fallen in of accident."

She wrapped the rope around herself. Rising out of the dungeon of carbon, she heard a deep Welsh imitation of a breathless, falling rabbit. "I'm late. I'm late. I'm late."

Caroline frowned, with no idea what foolishness Gryf talked.

"Coming down," she called, thrusting her hands into her leather gloves. She stepped into the void.

"Stop!" Gryf hollered. "The rope . . ."

As soon as she did it, she wished she'd checked out a few more details. Her palms grew hot. Her gloves gave off the acrid odor of failing leather. She gripped the rope behind her, to slow the rate of fall by braking, pulling the rope hard up against her thigh, but the rope slid through her grasp as if it were greased.

263

It is greased, she realized.

Below, Gryf yelled, "Grab that end. Don't let it . . ."

"I got it," shouted Olaf. "Damn this muck."

As she plummeted, the heavy fabric of her pant-skirt ripped. The slick rope burned into her pantaloons, abrading her thigh. She clamped down on a cry of pain.

"Boss, she's . . ."

"Hang on."

Caroline fell into Gryf's arms, knocking him backward into the wall of diggings. The four-inch knot at the end of the rope hit the side of her head. As they fell, Gryf yelled, "It got away. Got away."

She heard Olaf whisper, "Both ends o' that rope? They're down here with us."

Caroline relaxed toward the warmth of Gryf's callused fingertips as he explored the bones of her head.

"Got your blankets down here, Olaf?" he asked urgently. "Bring 'em both. Quick, man.

"You hurt?" she managed to mumble.

"*Nag* – No. Just rope-burned palms. Lie there, still-like, my girl." Olaf must have handed him the blankets. Caroline felt the hated prickling on her arms as Gryf wrapped a heavy wool around her shoulders. The thick odor of lanolin invaded her lungs. With a flash of pain and light, she was gone into a nightmare of chaos and dark memory.

**

"Where is yer mam?" a voice asked.

Caroline opened her eyes, squinting toward a dim light. She stopped breathing. Across the swirling darkness, fire lit the face of a wild-haired wraith. From beneath shadows cast by deep brow bones, the ghost studied her. He was poised, a pickaxe in one hand

and a piece of bone-dry wood in the other. Caroline clamped down on a shiver and held his gaze.

And then the wraith spoke, "Ye called for yer mother."

His familiar deep voice broke the spell. "Gryf!" she exhaled, and then dragged in the smell of granite, oil shale and coal.

"Where is she?" he persisted. "You were afraid for her. Why?"

Caroline swallowed hard. Embarrassed, she glanced at the wool he'd wrapped around her – two brown blankets, neither blue nor gray.

"Caroline?"

She picked at the fuzz on a blanket edge and forced herself to give him an answer. "At Gettysburg, in Pennsylvania. There was a battle."

"Aye, so I read – maybe seventeen years ago. She was there?"

Caroline nodded and closed her eyes. After a moment, she was able to speak again, to put him off with a simple answer.

"Mother died. I couldn't . . . stop." Caroline heard the wretched drag of her voice. She didn't want to talk about this. Pushing herself to her knees, she swayed. The walls of the spacious cavern hid in shadows. Nearby, the fire danced and reached for her. Gryf's wraith shadow grew enormous.

"Damn," Gryf muttered as he pulled her down onto a blanket and wrapped the other around her shoulders. She gazed up at him. His hand drew away sharply. "Ye must hold it tight," he said, and then he asked over his shoulder. "Olaf? Have ye found the pine poles?"

Olaf answered from far away. "Got 'em. Give me a hand."

Gryf's long fingers reached out to lift her chin. Studying her eyes with a doctor's interest, he said, "Ye hold quiet a time, till we see what becomes o' that knot on yer head. We can't have ye blackin out when we climb out of here."

Then Gryf rose and disappeared beyond the fire. Caroline lay back, staring at the shadows on the ceiling. Smoke from the fire

265

curled up the shaft. Up and up it rose, fifty feet to the outer surface of the earth. Studying the proportions of the cavern and shaft, she realized their generous size was intended to accommodate two wide miners' cages – just such cages as were listed on the contract Gryf had shown her.

She turned her head slightly, watching for the shadow of Gryf which would announce his return from the side tunnel. She was afraid of him sometimes, but not like the fear in her old nightmare, not helpless, not overwhelmed. Gryf Williams sometimes puzzled her, angered her, kissed her, but he was not evil.

Closing her eyes, she breathed deeply. Sometimes, she thought, he understands too much about me.

She glanced once more at the granite wall near the side tunnel and noticed there was a dark, round opening, three feet above the floor. It had been cut or blasted into the wall of the cavern – a stope, a horizontal tunnel from which coal had been excavated. Vaguely, she wondered if it was the stope Rudy bragged about this morning. Until Jesse's death, Rudy had been the foreman of this mine.

He'd mentioned a natural vent shaft letting air into the stope. It was possible Rudy was just yarning. If he were telling the truth, she wondered how far back into the mountain a miner would have to crawl to get to the vent shaft. Above, she heard the nicker of Sheba and the startled neigh of Solomon. She tilted her head trying to look up to the top of the shaft. The morning sun was directly above – too far away to warm her. Caroline sagged within the wool blanket. Sol whinnied twice more, but she barely heard him as she drifted into sleep.

**

Gryf drew some solace from the fact that Caroline seemed able to sleep safely while he and Olaf built a ladder to get them out of this hole. Then he heard Sol's whinny again. All hope for safety left him.

"Hear that, Boss?" Olaf whispered. "Sol seen someone he don't like."

Gryf whispered to Olaf, "I'll wager it's the buzzard that greased your rope."

He put two pine poles gently down on the floor of the cavern, then crept toward the shaft opening and listened. Above, boots crunched on the rocky talus slope to the north of the mine. An awkward eastern duck tried to yodel.

Here in Colorado? thought Gryf.

The duck's fantasy mate pretended to reply. One stupid hunter calling to another, Gryf thought, holding up two fingers. Olaf nodded his agreement and then pretended to slit two throats.

Those hoof prints should have warned me, Gryf thought.

"Swell," he muttered. "They've trapped us in this cave. We build this ladder, climb the shaft and allow two silly geese with rifles to pick us off soon as we poke our heads outside."

Caroline whispered, "Rudy's stope."

Her soft voice made Gryf jump. In the dim firelight, he saw her eyes try to flicker open. They failed. "Sleep," he ordered her.

Instead, she spoke again. "Rudy said . . . a shaft. A vent in the second stope."

Gryf glanced up at Olaf. "She right about that?"

Olaf shrugged. "Rudy bragged how he'd discovered a natural vent to the meadow up top o' this ridge. Said he was digging that stope to the north when he came on it."

Gryf strode to the hole leading into the wall of the mine. "Mighty low-roof," he commented.

Caroline pushed out one last effort, "Vent. Back door. Our chance."

They watched her face relax into sleep. Gryf reached out. The backs of his fingertips brushed her forehead. Not cold. Not breaking a sweat.

Olaf lay a firebrand with a handful of moss from the cave wall to keep the fire fueled. "Knock on the head maybe made her silly, you think?" Olaf whispered.

Gryf stood abruptly. "We've got to get her to help, so I'm going to find this shaft, if it exists."

**

Fifteen minutes and a hundred feet later, Gryf lay in the deepest darkness, sniffing. The air smelled more and more dead. He was losing hope that Rudy had created or discovered venting for this stope. Alert for any draft which might come down this rectangular excavation, he was also aware of how close above him were tons of mountainside. Rudy was a good miner and had built support-a-plenty within this exploratory stope, but the granite seemed to press downward, closing off Gryf's will power.

He closed his mind to memory, to the mine in northern India, to the desperate hours during which he had searched for his brother, Samuel. As he had done on that day he pushed forward with his toes, forcing his rebellious head and arms to do what his stupid feet were doing, go forward toward death.

Olaf had handed him the one hundred-fifty-foot pulley rope just as he entered the stope. Rope, like Gretel's cookie crumbs, gave Gryf hope for finding his way out of this forest of darkness. Feeling its hempen roughness was almost like having a light. He dared not wear the one lamp they had between them. If a shaft existed, the lamp light might be seen from above and give away their possible back door. Plus, it gave off gas fumes and was danged awkward.

Gryf inched forward in the manner of a worm. Curl toes, push feet. Arms drag torso.

Keep going. Push on. Don't think, just smell. When is the air not good enough?

Three feet further on, his lungs dragged in the odor of pure sage warmed by the sun. Real air. Outside air. Move feet. Push me to it. Faster, faster. Where?

Above him, he felt the draft more powerfully. With great effort in the small space, Gryf turned on his side. His hands groped over the low ceiling of his tunnel. There it was. Perpendicular to the stope, a shaft slightly wider than two hand spans. And far above, a small opening to the light and the air. It was a natural outlet to the surface, not blasted or hacked out of the rock, but a fissure in the jumble of folds. Gryf raised his left arm into the opening.

There seemed to be plenty of room – the vent was in fact wider than the stope. He pulled in his head and shoulders.

A mistake. Too late he realized the problem. A shelf of rock, directly above the opening, narrowed the shaft. The shelf took up only an inch of vertical distance, but it was enough. His shoulders were stuck. He twisted to change the angle – left shoulder and arm up, right down. No help. His breath came fast. Sweat broke out on his face. Outside his trap, his right hand scrabbled at the ceiling of the stope, trying desperately to get a purchase, a grip to pull him out again. Everything he did was without effect on his shoulders. They would not move.

He rolled his head against the wall of the shaft, staring blindly up at the small piece of sky that was within his view. His fingers scraped at the vein of coal back in the stope until moisture built up on his palm and it slid without any effect over the surface.

Gryf wanted to call out but knew that Olaf would never reach him – the stope was too narrow. And if he did yell, the men outside, the ones who trapped them would have perfect knowledge of where he was. He worked and pulled with decreasing effect to move his shoulders from this place between two geologic formations. Two

269

bodies of rock, cracked apart thousands of years ago, rested briefly at angles to each other. When would they move again? What force would set them once more on their downhill journey, crashing together, oblivious of anything fallen between them during their short eons apart?

Gryf awoke again to his danger. He had air but was losing strength and will-power to the demon Fear. His hands felt raw. His arms tingled as if he slept wrong on a nerve. He twisted within the hole and felt his shirt rip. The rock cut into his upper arms, but he would not stop, and he could not let himself imagine. Splaying his feet to the sides of the stope, he used his toes again and again as if they were his fingers. They pulled against the wall of the stope. He twisted left and right, achieving barely a half inch of motion each time, cutting himself with every move. Blood ran down his arm from his shoulder to his elbow.

Minutes. Hours. He did not know how long. The single bit of sky above him turned dark.

Is the sun setting already?

Gryf let go of hope. He dropped his head back against the fissure wall, exhaling. The pain in his raw shoulders and scraped hands flooded through his body. He closed his eyes and waited for cold to overcome his senses.

He imagined Caroline's pale face, the angry red welt on her temple, almost exactly the place where Kidde had hit her before. What damage to her was there? He thought how her dark thick lashes brushed her cheeks as she fell back into troubled sleep. He thought of Olaf, watching her warily, never comfortable around women, but determined in his bull-awkwardness to care for her. Olaf, trying to find enough fuel to keep her from dying of exposure, perhaps building the pine pole escape-ladder as they had planned. But then he would wait. And wait. And wait for Gryf to return with news of a second opening into the mine. And finally, Gryf failing to come, Olaf would burn the pole ladder just to warm her.

Gryf couldn't leave them to die at the bottom of that cold pit. He had to find a way back to them. Had to get out of this stupid fix he'd gotten himself into.

Something hit his face. And again. Another.

Rain drops!

Thunder rolled in the heavens. Thunder roared and cracked. Jagged light silhouetted the rock above Gryf. The rain found the fissure. It dripped onto his face. He licked it off.

Thirsty. That was the problem. Dehydrated.

He lay there a moment, savoring the herbal scent of the mountain storm. The drops came more heavily, plopping on his forehead and cheeks like soft balloons.

Then, the rain revealed its sharp edges, a frost razor. A cold rivulet invaded Gryf's shirt collar. Small drops gathered, sheeting together down the walls of his trap, soaking his shirt, plastering his hair to his neck and forehead.

Soon, a new sound demanded his attention – the gurgling of a slow-draining sinkhole. He glanced down. Water was collecting at his chest. The rain pelted into the fissure and gathered in the bottom where his body plugged the way.

Gryf renewed his efforts to escape. His toes pulled at the walls of the stope. His hands yanked at the coal and rock ceiling. His shoulders moved a quarter inch to one side, creating a small drain, but water came in faster than it could get out. It climbed around his shoulders. It mounted toward his throat.

An oily stench arose from the churning runoff. Slick mucus covered his shirt and the raw sores on his shoulders. The water and the oily residue from the fissure walls brushed his chin. Gryf lifted his jaw, praying for another inch, another few moments of life.

Writhing his oil, blood and water-covered torso, his useless arms and flailing feet, Gryf worked to free himself.

Oh, God. Help.

Without warning, his feet became trapped in the hemp rope still out in the tunnel. He must have tangled them with his thrashing. Within moments, he could not move his feet at all. The rope became a vice-grip pulling his body apart – his feet were yanked down the stope, but his shoulders were still trapped within the vertical fissure. Water washed over his tightly closed lips. It lapped into his nose.

Still the snake of hemp enveloped his legs and jerked him completely under the water. His head hit the floor of the tunnel. Water gushed over his face and rushed past him. He landed in the stope on his back, rain still pelting his face from the opening to the fissure.

Thunder rolled. The reverberations echoed and receded. He was out. Out in the blessed darkness of a man-sized excavation. The rain drained away down the stope.

CHAPTER TWENTY-FOUR

From inside the stope, Caroline signaled Olaf to pull the rope once more. As Olaf yanked Gryf's body out of the fissure, his boot smacked Caroline in the mouth. For a moment, she thought she was going to lose some teeth. Hunched over her hands, she pressed against the pain in her mouth. Then she became aware of the rush of water around her. Within moments, Gryf's body convulsed in wracking coughs. He lay just inches ahead of her up the stope. She reached out, her hand colliding with his thigh.

"Uh! What the hell!?"

"Not Hell yet," she answered.

"Trewartha."

"The same."

"Ye've near killed me . . . hauling . . . pulling."

"You'll be a good four inches taller. Thank Olaf."

She heard him cough again, heaving the last of the water from his throat. Then he lay down. Under her hand, she felt him relax, felt him let life drift back into his body and into his plans for the future.

She lifted herself above his legs and stretched to touch his shoulder. By his hissing intake of breath, she discovered the extent of his injuries. Her hand came away sticky.

"Let's back down from here," she said, attempting to sound calm. "I hate to leave Olaf alone down there against those two."

"They've shown themselves?"

"Taking pot shots, although they seem to hit the walls of the shaft instead of actually shooting down into the main drift."

273

"Thought you were gone, Trewartha," he grunted. "In a coma or something."

"Yeah? Well, the whine of bullets can wake the angels." She inched down the stope, making as much haste as excess skirt fabric would allow. Even shivering with a chill, Gryf could back down a stope with more speed than anybody she'd known.

"How'd you know to come after me?" he asked at last.

"Rope stopped playing out. Olaf's too big, so he had to accept my offer. We worked out a plan, and a signal. I tied up your feet. He pulled you out."

"Olaf's got no weapons."

"He's made a staff out of one of the pine poles."

"That's it?"

" 'Take 'em by surprise,' he claims."

"The first fellow might be surprised – for a moment. Could you hurry, Trewartha?"

That didn't require an answer. Caroline moved, heedless of any pain but the possibility of another shoe in the face. She didn't blame Gryf for his haste. She also worried about what they'd find as they re-entered the cave.

Coming into a dangerous situation feet-first wasn't Caroline's idea of a smart maneuver, but having no choice, she decided to fall on stage with panache. Skirt hiked up, black stockings ripped to shreds, knees and elbows streaked with blood and coal dust, what more could a Baltimore-bred lady ask for in a sober entrance? At least bullets were not presently zinging.

God take care of Olaf, she prayed as she pushed herself toward the main room.

Her feet felt cool air, then the floor of the stope fell away from under them. Someone grabbed her waist, pulling her into the cave where she fell in a heap. Glancing up, she saw Olaf reaching a second time into the dark opening. With a quick, dizzying roll she avoided an unceremonious collision with Gryffyth Williams' long self.

Gryf folded like wet cloth onto the floor of the cave. She saw the gaping wound in his nearest shoulder. Deep. Deep and ragged. She tried to get up, but her limbs would not obey her.

Gryf glared up at Olaf, "What were ye thinking, Olaf Fedje – lettin' her come in there?"

Caroline leaned against the wall, letting Gryf's indignation roar around her while her head settled. His sputtering didn't surprise her in the least. What caught her off balance was Olaf's chuckle.

"Boss, she was yust dodgin' bullets. Isn't that right, Miss Trewartha?"

She leaned her head into her arm and muttered, "Rescue? – that part was an accident. Where are those buzzards, Mr. Fedje?"

"I binged one in his head." Both Gryf and Caroline glanced up at him. Olaf blushed. "A big rock I threw."

Olaf gently pushed Gryf onto the wool blanket and began to remove the rags of his shirt from his shoulder wounds. He began tying a bandage to the left shoulder wound. Silently, Caroline crawled on her scraped knees to Gryf's other side. His blood flowed smoothly.

Not an artery, thank God. She closed the wound, pressing the ragged edges together as Olaf tied shirt fabric over moss to provide pressure.

"This gash will be filled with carbon dust," Caroline whispered.

"Ugly tattoo," mumbled Gryf. "Make a sea serpent?"

"Sure thing, Boss," Olaf grunted. "Left shoulder, nasty eyes, big open mouth, fangs drip. Tail over here on this other arm."

Gryf's jaw was grinding. No doubt pain had reached his mind at last. He reached up suddenly and took her hand in his. He bit his lower lip and gazed at her, the gray steel of his eyes dark, unreadable. "Thank you," he whispered. "Thank you both."

An explosion drowned her reply. Chips of granite showered Caroline's back. A rock carommed off the cave wall near Olaf's head.

"By Thor!" Olaf hissed, diving for the floor, "Them yokels!"

A second shot rang out, hitting the wall of the shaft above them.

Gryf's battered arms wrapped around Caroline, pulling her to his chest. He rolled on top of her. "Close your eyes, *fyngeneth*."

The weight of him surprised her. She took a deep breath, expecting panic to rise, but it did not.

"We'll get out of this," he whispered.

More shots came. "*Pum, chwech, saith*," he whispered after each one. "Five, six, seven. Two men, at least," Gryf growled. "Olaf. They want to scare, not kill."

"Mighty odd attack, all right – them never shooting down into the mine."

Caroline tried to drag in deep gasps. Gryf glanced at her quickly, then levered his weight slightly away from her, giving her room to draw air. He muttered some unintelligible Welsh. Rising on one elbow, he whispered, "Look at me and breathe. Slowly. Quietly." He traced her cheek and briefly down her throat, resting his thumb on her pulse. "No fear, now?" His devil eyebrow rose. "No?"

She shook her head slowly, her gaze on his face. His head moved toward her. His attention dropped to her mouth. Self-conscious, she licked her lower lip.

The air rushed from him. "*Iesu Crist*, "He leaned one inch closer, barely touching her lips with his.

His beard tickled her mouth. Deep inside, her body reacted to the sensation by tightening, then uncoiling languorously. She pressed upward into his lips, murmuring, "Mmm."

He spread his fingers through her hair and pulled her yet closer, touching the corners of her mouth with his tongue. Amazing herself with how much she wanted his touch, Caroline wrapped her arms around him.

And caused him to yelp in pain. She'd forgotten herself, and his torn shoulders. Mortified, she sat up, reaching for his bandage. At that moment, their besiegers opened fire once more. Gryf lifted her in his arms.

"You'll break it open again," she protested.

He shook his head, but she could see his jaw clamp down. She held herself very still, hoping to do no further damage as he carried her toward the hole in the wall from which they had exited only minutes before.

"Hide you in the stope," he muttered.

"But I can...," she managed.

He spoke with grim and forceful tones. "If you don't stay in this stope, you'll distract me while I am trying to fight . . . make me worry about every move, every shot. You can take orders for once."

With that, he unceremoniously pushed her back into the stope.

"And be quiet," he ordered gruffly. "Don't want 'em to guess you're in there."

**

At least he stuffed me in here head first.

She wished she had one more chance to look at his wounds. Now only Olaf could look after him. She had to finish Gryf's attempt to find a back door. Without an exit, they were condemned to outlast their besieger. The mountains' daily deluge might keep them in drinking water, but it would not provide them with food, nor with better weapons for defense. Eventually someone from By-Gum Valley would come searching from them but help from the valley would blunder into the crossfire.

She crawled into the darkness, hoping the air shaft Rudy bragged about this morning proved to be something larger than the fissure in which Gryf had nearly drowned. She wished she'd asked Rudy more questions, and argued with him a great deal less.

For all that he's an opinionated little man, he knows mining and he knows these mountains.

Behind her, she heard more shots and some healthy Norwegian expletives – at least Olaf's voice had the cadence of cussing.

But where is Gryf? Is he hurt? Drat it, man. Speak up!

She touched her lips, remembering the look of desire on his face just before she licked. She couldn't believe what had happened in that moment. She felt her face flush with heat.

And, I must be a sight. Coal and water streaks all over my face. Like himself, a fearful vision, the backs of his long fingers covered with black, his dark curls littered with dust, his beard – so soft and silky.

Her every thought led in unsafe directions. Later she would figure out why she hadn't screamed the moment his body enfolded hers. For now, she had to find a way to save the three of them.

**

Gryf laughed, "Those blackguards'll not come back soon. You fair winged the ruffian that poked his head over the shaft."

Olaf grinned. "Yah. Sometimes I kin bring down a good bird for dinner."

"You ever play a game called baseball?"

"What for?"

"For fun – doesn't put dinner on the table, though. We've got a bit of a breather now. Let's build the ladder in case it comes in handy."

"That wound opened again, Boss. Maybe I redo the bandages first."

Gryf shrugged off Olaf's offer. "It's all right. Just strained it a bit." He leaned closer to Olaf and waggled his conspirator eyebrows. "I put our engineer on the shelf – to keep her out of trouble."

Olaf glanced toward the stope. "She bein' mighty quiet in there. S'pose that head bother more than she say?"

Gryf frowned. He strode to the opening and peered in. "Miss Trewartha?"

Nothing. No rustle of wool skirt. No dark boots.

"Caroline?"

Over Gryf's shoulder, Olaf handed him the rope. "I think she'll be testing Rudy's truthfulness again." Gryf's coal pick appeared over his shoulder. "She be far up there by now," said Olaf, "She's a little flicka, but she is stubborn . . ."

"*Yn wir.* Indeed, she is," Gryf took the tools from Olaf and scrambled back into the stope.

**

Caroline had mentally measured her hips and her other parts against the memory of Gryf's shoulders and decided she was a great deal smaller in all dimensions than he. It was a relief to know it because on this occasion it might mean she could free him and Olaf. She was already in the fissure in a most unlady-like pose – feet on opposite walls, hands clinging to the rocks above, preparing to pull herself up the thirty feet to the opening. Gryf chose that moment to berate her from below.

"What the hell are you doing, Trewartha?"

She jerked, nearly losing her grip. Her first thought was for vanity.

Thank God for the darkness.

Her second was annoyance. "I'm escaping," she whispered.

"Can't take us anymore, eh?" His voice seemed to have multiplied.

"The noise you make will bring them right here, Mr. Williams."

"Top end's a tight fit," he said.

She felt her face go hot. A long moment of silence followed before he seemed to realize what she thought.

"I mean," he said slowly, "the top end of the fissure is even smaller than down here."

"Oh. I . . . it is, but it's worth a try."

"Brought my pick. Can you reach down?"

"How'm I going to use a pick? Might as well ring my own funeral bells."

"I brought the rope too. You can signal us."

"You're planning a distraction?"

"That cave back there echoes bull fierce. Olaf and I can be a big diversion when ye're ready."

"Then pass that rope and pick up here." She barely had strength to let go with one hand and stretch down. Her feet ached from bracing herself against both sides of the shaft. The muscles in her other hand threatened to seize up from being in one position for so long. She felt the pick touch her fingers. He'd pushed it up head first. It was almost out of reach. She managed to hook her pointer finger under the arch of the narrow end. She was afraid she might drop it on him before she had a sure grip.

"I'm outta the way if it falls," Gryf said. His muffled voice proved that he'd moved back from the opening.

Does he always know what I'm thinking?

She pushed away the thought, managed to get her hand clear around the head of the pick and pull it up to her waist. Attached to the handle was the rope. Caroline wedged the clumsy pick head into her skirt belt. It would have been safer if she'd let it hang by the rope below her, but there wasn't enough room to turn it over. She'd have to deal with it this way and hope she didn't impale herself on it.

"Tie something noisy on your end, she said to Gryf. "When I'm ready to hack at the rock, I'll get your attention."

"Yank three times. You'll have exactly half an hour to get out. Then I'm coming back in after you."

"Don't waste your energy, Mr. Williams. I'll be out. And I'll yank the rope five times when I'm in the clear.

**

Caroline couldn't believe the racket two men could keep up. They sounded like a clan feud among Brobdingnagians. The echoes of their pandemonium were rhythmic, even, and designed to cover her own rhythm with the pick. She was grateful and amazed.

She was also in pain. Every muscle in her left foot was cramped. Her back shot with bolts of heat as each blow of the pick jarred her body. But she was determined not to give up. This last slab of shale, wedged sideways across the opening to the fissure, must have fallen from a cliff above. It almost covered the hole. She had chipped away at the softer sandstone uphill from the slab for twenty minutes, dulling the end of the pick. She uncovered a crack in the sandstone and, using the head of the pick as a hammer, she drove a wedge of harder rock into that weakness.

Gryf was due back up here soon. She had to finish before he came or risk dropping rock down the fissure onto his head. Her right foot seized up. In reaction to the sudden pain, she hacked off center. The crack opened and half of the sandstone fell away, bounding down past her left foot, bouncing itself to small pieces before it hit the bottom of the fissure.

After Caroline recovered from shock, she glanced up and saw the edge of the sun. She smelled the sharp odor of pine pitch. She'd created barely enough room to climb out. With two cramped feet and very little energy, she stared at those last few feet and wondered how to move. It wasn't at all clear which foot to lift. The other might give way at the additional pressure. She'd come so close – yet how to finish . . .

A small bird chirped. A marmot whistled. She lifted her right foot and inched her way out into a meadow.

CHAPTER TWENTY-FIVE

Caroline yanked five times on the rope to announce her escape. Then she stretched face-first into the beautiful meadow grass, thanking God for warm sun, for white ground daisies and for the oblivious sow bug marching between blades of wild wheat mere inches from her left hand.

The pungence of pine needles woke her from celebrating. In spite of Gryf's urgings, she determined not to return to By-Gum for help. There was no way she would leave Olaf and Gryf at the mercy of the boulder-heads below.

She untied the rope from her pick handle and tried without success to pull the rope out. She realized it was fastened to something at Gryf and Olaf's end to prevent it from leaving the cave.

They've a plan to use it, she guessed.

Lower down the hill from her, the clank of metal hitting rock sent her diving for dirt. She was certain that had been the sound of a rifle barrel, carelessly moved. Since she was still alive, she guessed the person holding the rifle had not seen her. Or perhaps hadn't a good enough angle to blow her away. With extreme care, she twisted her body, searching for a hat, an elbow, any sign of a human being in that direction. Fifty feet away, she caught sight of a dark, scuffed boot. Its worn heel wiggled as its wearer adjusted his position.

Unless this guy has his shoes on backwards, I'm in luck, she thought. She rose, holding Gryf's pick in both hands to keep it from hitting the rock. Now she could see the fellow, hunched over a rock, aiming his rifle down toward the mine's entry shaft. He was at the very edge of the cliff, where the meadow merged into a jumble of glacial boulders.

If he'd been there long, he would have heard her pick – probably arrived after she cracked that last piece of sandstone, but before she popped out of the shaft into the meadow. He seemed oblivious to the possibility that anyone might be behind him. She took a quick survey of the area between them and stepped onto the mossy clump next to her.

She'd learned that men give away awareness by tightening muscles.

Keeping an eye on his back and shoulders, she stepped from a mound of alpine moss, to coneflower, to thyme, muffling the sound of her approach. The man remained unaware of her. The sun, two hours from setting, rode low near the western peaks, throwing his shadow downhill from her.

With care not to rustle her jacket fabric, she raised the pick. The ugly pick blade caught her attention. Without thought, she turned it. Grasping the blade, she raised the flared wooden handle over the man.

His shoulder muscles bunched. He turned on her, rifle at the ready. She brought the handle down on his head with a dull crunch, then yanked down, deflecting the barrel off to her right as the rifle fired. His body slumped into her knees, knocking her down. She sat hard – staring at her victim.

The wound on his head mixed blood with his blond hair. She scrambled backwards, away from his flaccid tanned face and heavy torso, moaning at what she'd done.

He was waiting to kill us.

"Hardy?" His cohort yelled up from below with a deep rasping voice. "What you shootin' for, you tinker-brained fool?" Silence answered him. The fellow down below barked out a rough, habitual cough. More silence.

284

With no time to waste in remorse, she crawled away from his body, and out of sight of his partner. As she rose, she found herself face-to-belly with a grease-spattered shirt. She darted a glance upward into a familiar, ugly face.

Gordon Rankin of Wyoming.

"Oh, shit!" she muttered.

Rankin grinned down his rifle barrel. "Drop the pick, Miss Trewartha."

"How did you find. . .?"

"Drop the pick or I shoot your hands." Rankin's squirrelly thin voice in contrast with his bully's body had an unnerving effectiveness.

She dropped the pick. She had no doubt Rankin would pull the trigger. No remorse. Ever.

"You a mighty slick woman." He chirped, then spat a stream of chewing tobacco into the meadow grass next to her skirt. "I could swear you fell into that mine shaft down below, but I musta been seein' a mirage, 'cause here you are." He sidled closer, studying her eyes.

Caroline stepped back.

"I did see you bean ol' Hardy there."

"He was preparing to shoot me."

"*Preparin'*! Ain't that just like you, Trewartha. *Preparin' nothin'*. Hardy was shootin'. You whomped his head and his rifle in one blow."

"Rankin, what are you doing here?"

"Capturin' you. I get a deal of gold for tyin' you in knots."

"Real gold? Or fool's gold?"

"And not just for you." Rankin spit again, barely missing her left shoulder. She didn't flinch. "Gotta finish that feller down in the mine, too – that Griffin."

"Who's paying?"

285

He laughed. "Wanta top his offer? You never seen that much gold even at a stamp mill."

So, Rankin had met the author of Gryf's grief. She had to know what he knew. Rankin angered easy, then he justified himself. Thus, she set her mind to rile him.

"Suppose this fellow can't pay you. So, he makes the same offer to another polecat? Cancels his debt by arranging your death."

Rankin glanced around as if looking for the next man in line. His jaw bunched. With a swift snakelike movement, he clamped one hand around her neck. "He's got money, all right. Seen his carriage and his team."

Caroline asked calmly, "Expensive? Rented, were they?"

Her courage was rewarded with a sharp, choking shove. "You talk too much, Miss Trewartha. Now show me how you got here."

Can't let him know about the fissure behind him. He'd use it to burn out Gryf and Olaf.

"I climbed up the entry shaft," she answered, thinking fast to recall the layout near the entrance.

"You? No woman climbs. . ."

"Hand over hand, then I hid behind the boulder near the pulley and rope frame until you turned your back on me."

"And just walked up this hill, I suppose."

"Boulder to boulder. Took the opposite direction from you."

"Phil would've seen you."

"Your man below is singularly unobservant – and awkward. He rolls his smokes with two hands, and has to watch the process." She was betting Rankin had never observed how the man smoked, or rolled either. Used him, but didn't know anything about him – not as much as she knew from one raspy sentence and a habitual cough.

Rankin glared at her, his eyes thin slits, his Adam's apple bobbing with indecision. Shoving her toward the boulders, he squeaked. "Get a move on down the hill."

They both heard a groan from the man she'd hit.

"What about your buddy?"

Rankin flicked his rifle barrel off to one side and pulled the trigger. She jerked her hands to her ears. Through the cotton muffle of deafness, Caroline heard Rankin shout, "He ain't twitchin' no more. Now move." He pulled her toward the edge of the moraine cliff. Her head swam, her stomach rebelled. He cranked his rifle into reload position.

She held her stomach in check. She'd seen Gordon Rankin at work in Wyoming. Towering strength. High voice. Short temper. When he yanked on her arm, Caroline moved quickly around the boulder cliff and down the alpine slope toward the plain where Solomon and Sheba stood, tethered twenty feet from two abused-looking nags.

As they hiked down to the mine entrance, Caroline cast about for a glimpse of the man who had yelled from below when Hardy's rifle went off. She wanted to watch his actions so she could establish a believable timetable for where everyone was when she escaped.

It took ten minutes for her hearing to return. First, she heard the crunch of Rankin's feet on rock, then the shriek of a marmot. Finally, she could hear even the slight breeze that whipped up the ridge from the valley.

Rankin shoved her to the mine shaft. Just before she stumbled into the hole, he grabbed the back of her neck. Yanking her close to the opening, he hollered down.

"Griffin, I got your woman."

He forced her to lean over the fifty-foot drop. She shivered, but yelled, "Rankin, do you and your buddy expect that guy to come out and get shot?"

"Shut up woman," Rankin yanked her back against his chest.

"Griffin, she don't think you care enough to figure a way out."

"I'm not his woman," she hissed.

"Yeah? Well, we'll see." He gazed over her shoulder, down at the silhouette of her breasts under the dusty velveteen. "Body like that, sure gotta be somebody's woman. Mebbe mine."

**

Gryf closed his eyes. His gutting knife hung motionless above the last notch he'd carved on the pine pole ladder.

"The shots we heard," he whispered. "He did shoot her."

"She still hollers good," said Olaf.

From above, the man yelled, "You comin' or not, Griffin?"

"I'll come. Toss a rope over the pulley."

"She feels mighty good," the man's high voice echoed down the shaft.

"Get me that rope!"

The man laughed, a high-pitched giggle that sent nausea through Gryf. "Man's in a sweat to get up here, Phil," the giggler said loudly. "Bring that rope off my saddle."

Olaf took Gryf's knife and hacked at the notch. "Boss, we got to have something to trade for her."

"I'm figurin', man," Gryf said. "I should never have let her do it."

"Yah? You could stop her?"

"Whoa up," whispered Gryf. "What did she say? Ye know any Rankin, Olaf?"

Olaf's white-blond brows lowered, "No Rankin since Pennsylvania . . . That time at the Gap Mine."

Gryf circled his arms in front of his belt. "Big belly? Stank bad?"

"Yah. Big fella. Little voice."

"She said, something like ...'Rankin, how'd ye expect that guy to come out. That's what she yelled."

"Sure sound like it," Olaf said.

"Means Rankin doesn't know yer here, eh?"

"Oh no. I'm not hiding down here. You hoist up there, he picks you off, then murders her."

"No. I'm thinkin' Chess. He has a blind spot – so sure that he's got me check-mated that he forgets to pay attention to the whole board. We take advantage."

Olaf glanced up from constructing the ladder. His florid face slowly lit with a big smile. "Yah, gut. He forget about your pawn."

"My knight."

CHAPTER TWENTY-SIX

"Get that rope over here, Phil," Rankin growled. His stringy-haired buddy backed off, then hurried toward the two nags.

Caroline stood stiff and straight. Rankin yanked her hands up behind her, tying her wrists to a post of the headframe with his thick leather belt. While he tied her, she stared off at the Butte as if sure of her future, and barely bothered by his existence. All the while, her mind was running over two thoughts. First: to keep Gryf Williams down in the mine shaft. The moment he came out, Rankin would murder him. Her second thought was that she knew this vicious man from well before Wyoming – a time and place it was important to recall.

Phil returned, tying two ropes together.

"For God's sake, lower the rope," Gryf yelled.

"Get to it, Phil," Rankin ordered.

Phil snorted. "You ain't goin' near that shaft, I notice. Where's Hardy?"

Rankin jerked his head toward Caroline. "This dame killed him with a pickaxe."

Phil gawked at Caroline. Rankin's impatience tightened his voice even higher. "Roll down the damned rope."

Phil worked the hemp, making sure the big knot rode on the pulley track.

"Don't come up!" Caroline shouted.

Rankin whacked her across the face. "Shut up."

Her face went numb. She tried to hang onto some sense of up and down.

"God, Rankin," whined Phil, "The man said not to . . . "

"Hush your face, idiot," Rankin hissed.

"Rankin," she said loudly, "What rich gentleman wants us killed?"

"Damn you bitch," Rankin raised his arm a second time. "I told you to shut yer mouth."

"Who owns the carriage and fine horses?" she yelled. She tensed for the inevitable blow. Instead, Rankin bent over and yanked her right foot out from under her. The back of her head rammed into the post, nearly knocking her out. She would have fallen, but the belt leather bit into her wrists and held her upright at the stake. Pain ripped across her shoulders and down her arms.

"Nice ankles," Rankin purred as his hunting knife cut through her boot lace. "We'll start here." He tugged her boot off her foot. "Shredded stockings? Kinda inviting i'n it?" He grinned at her, two yellowed teeth and a brown wad of tobacco gapping between his fleshy lips. Her spine chilled, but Caroline kept her face impassive.

"Is this all you're good at?" she asked. "Bullying women?"

Rankin's grin drooped. His eyes narrowed. He dropped her bare foot and trudged to his fire. Shifting his sagging pants up over his belly, he stooped with a grunt and lifted a stick from the fire. Then he turned toward her, waving the red-hot end of the stick.

"Now lady, the only talkin' you're gonna do is to tell ol' Rankin about how you got yourself out of that mine." He approached, keeping the red flame glowing by walking slowly, glaring at her as he approached.

She stiffened her legs, trying to stand tall against the post. "I'm a rock climber," she said.

"Lady," said Rankin, "you lie."

She gazed steadily at him. "You were waddling south at that moment I climbed out."

Rankin's eyelid twitched. His hand with the flaming brand came up for a moment but he stopped himself from burning her face.

"You couldn't have climbed that sheer wall." His voice rose toward uncontrolled anger. She was sure there was doubt in his hysteria.

"I had to," she said loudly, toward the shaft. "Griffin can't climb. He's injured."

Caroline saw the ropes move. She had to convince Gryf to stay down. She raised her face toward the hot poker, calling, "He won't kill me until he has you."

Rankin whirled toward the mine shaft. "I can burn her good. Then I hog tie her to your crazy horse, here, and whack him off down the mountain."

"No," Gryf shouted. "No! The roan's out of control."

Rankin laughed. "I'm firing yer lady right now."

"I'm on my way up." Gryf yelled.

But Rankin, still watching her impassive face, knelt down, carrying the hot stick close to her skirt. She breathed slowly, expecting the harsh smell of melting wool to rise before she felt the fire. Instead, searing pain ripped across her foot. She screamed. Rankin's hand held her jerking foot fast to the ground. He yanked the stick away from her instep. Caroline ground her teeth together.

"Tell me, or I do it again."

"I . . . told . . ."

He touched her foot again.

"Ahhh!"

"Tell me."

Phil launched himself at Rankin, grabbed at the brand and yelled, "He'll have your neck ..."

Through a wall of pain, it dawned on Caroline that, the rich man wanted them alive – or her alive.

Rankin flailed the brand in a wide arc around him, "Back off, Phil."

"I'll kill you, Rankin" Gryf hollered.

The corners of Rankin's mouth twisted upward. Then Rankin turned to Phil, the brand in his hand still glowing. Phil backed off with his hands in the air, a rigid fear quivering his nostrils. Rankin's glare fixed on Phil.

"You hitch our prize hen here top o' that huge horse."

"I don't do good with horses, Rankin. 'Specially big 'uns like 'at."

Rankin stalked to his own horse, yanked a leather whip from the saddle. "I'm gonna hobble him. You take care o' the woman."

"Right." Phil stepped behind her, wrenched the leather belt, releasing its buckle. He pulled her hands in front of her and whipped the belt once more around her arms. With little ceremony, he hoisted Caroline over his scrawny shoulder and approached Solomon with excruciating slowness.

Rankin uncoiled his whip from his left hand. Faster than her mind could follow, the leather whipped back, forth and wrapped itself around Sol's forelegs. Sol snorted in surprise, dancing his hind legs around his front.

"Tell your roan to settle down, Griffin," Rankin called. Sol neighed and reared, sharp hooves stabbing the air.

"Stand at attention," called Gryf. Sol dropped his tethered forelegs, shuddered and kicked out once with his hind hooves.

"Attention," Gryf repeated sternly from the depths.

Sol stopped his dance with amazing abruptness. Despite the sharp jabs to her stomach from Phil's bony shoulder, Caroline's heart leapt, remembering what 'Attention' meant to Sol.

Rankin watched the apparently docile and well-trained roan with a wary eye. "Tell him we're friends, Griffin," Rankin yelled.

Caroline's few hopes sank. From the cavern below, Gryf's reply carried a note of similar disappointment. "Sol. Friends," he called.

Head bowed, Sol shivered then stood silent.

"Now, Phil," Rankin ordered.

293

Caroline felt Phil shudder just like Sol. Nevertheless, he stepped closer to the horse and brought Caroline's feet to the ground. "Hold the damn saddle and pull yerse'f up," he whispered.

Caroline stretched her battered body. Phil yanked her leather-wrapped wrists toward the pommel. "Get," he hissed at her.

She grabbed whatever part of the saddle she could and lifted her still-booted left foot toward the stirrup. The stirrup was surprisingly close to the ground.

Thank the Gods for Gryf's long legs.

She bounced lightly up, swinging her damaged right foot into the air.

Phil jumped back, barely clear of her intended kick. Glaring at her, Phil missed Sol's hip maneuver. With swift, bunched muscles, Sol knocked Phil off balance and into the dust. Caroline landed slaunch-wise in the saddle. She had to grab for the pommel and lean over it to stay up. Sol wheeled to face Rankin who yanked his rifle up, pointing it at her chest.

"Control that varmint or he dies."

"Sol, stand," she said. Sol stood. His head came up.

Don't try anything, Sol, she prayed as she watched his ears twitch. Phil scrambled away on his rear end, hands and feet propelling him through the dirt like a beetle.

Caroline's pulse thudded against her throat. She watched in disbelief as the rope and pulley moved. Phil turned his eyes toward her, but his attention strayed from time to time toward the progress of the ropes and Gryf. Caroline herself was mesmerized by the motion of the pulley and ropes. She couldn't make herself believe he'd be able to hoist himself fifty feet.

Yet, he was rising. The rich man may have wanted her unharmed, but she believed he wanted Gryf dead. Despite the excruciating pain in her right foot, she had to find a way to free herself before Gryf climbed out, so she continued to pull against the belt.

From her perch atop the horse, she noticed dust rising from the far side of the cliff above the mine, spiraling over the place where she had hit Hardy with the axe handle. The dust announced the approach of several horses from the east. No one from By-Gum would arrive from that direction.

Did Rankin expect confederates? In this brilliant clear air, it was difficult to judge distances, but they were coming fast.

She had to get Gryf and Olaf free before Rankin had more help. In spite of the pain, she wrenched at the belt leather, desperately working it as she studied their situation.

"You best hurry, Griffin. I'll smack this horse and he'll give your lady the wildest ride she's ever had."

"I'm coming! Leave her be."

Sol's head moved down his forelegs, chewing at the leather thong. Caroline worked at her own ties. Her skin was raw. The buckle tongue pushed into her skin next to a distended vein. Pain jagged up her arms as well as her right leg. She crossed her wrists and draped a small drooping length of one wrap over the ridge of sewn stitches at the top of the pommel. She pulled back. The buckle moved. Its tongue sank a little within the hole in the leather, and away from her wrist.

Rankin's thin voice called down the shaft. "Mebbe I ought to just shoot you on the way up."

"You supposed to deliver a live man?"

Rankin was silent. He sagged against one post of the frame for the pulley system. "How come you're using just that one arm to pull?"

"Shoulder's cut bad."

295

"Damn. You ain't no more'n twenty feet up. Hang on tight, I'll move you faster than that." Rankin began yanking on the ropes above him.

From below, Gryf's voiced sounded a panicked alarm. "Let go the rope. Too fast. Can't . . ."

Caroline heard the rough rattle of the unwinding rope snapping against the shaft walls. A scream rose from the cavern, followed by a thud. Gryf had fallen.

"Griffin," shouted Rankin. "Damn you Griffin. Why'd you go and do that?"

Caroline, cold with dread, strained for Gryf's answer. Silence echoed up the shaft.

Frantically, Caroline worked her wrist leather back and forth over the pommel. The tongue sank further within the leather. She reached forward, once more catching the loosened loop over the sturdy stitching at the top of the pommel. The strain on the metal was beginning to show in tiny lines of stress at the curve of the pot-metal shank.

"Phil," Rankin called. "Get down this shaft and take care of that bastard. We gotta get him up here in one piece."

Phil peered over the hole. "Jesus, man," he said, "Look at all the blood on his shirt. Gotta be hurt bad."

"Get going."

Caroline took advantage of their inattention toward her, she yanked harder and harder on the loop of belt. Off to her right, the dust cloud of Rankin's probable confederates approached the rise of the hill.

Caroline heard the tongue of the belt pop, felt the sudden slack. She raised her gaze just as Phil's boots scraped on the rocky soil between Sol and his own dark mare. Alert, she stilled the motion of her hands. Her right boot nudged Sol. Sol desisted in his leather chewing, moving his muzzle slowly onto an Alpine plant. Phil glanced in Caroline's direction, frowned briefly, then yanked on the ropes which tied his bedroll behind his saddle.

Caroline breathed deeply, trying to calm her heart and her fear for Gryf and Olaf. As Phil approached the shaft, Rankin raised the rope toward the head-frame pulley. A length of dark brown rope rose into view. It took her a moment to realize the color was drying blood. Gryf lay at the bottom of a cold, dark shaft on a bed of coal rubble. She held herself frozen atop the big roan.

Caroline felt a cold detachment creep over her body. The arch of her foot ceased to burn, ceased even to exist for her mind. Her focus narrowed to the backs of the two men whose actions left Gryf unconscious at the bottom of that tomb.

Phil tied his bedroll to the rope, then straddled the roll to descend. "Got a tight grip on that?" Phil asked as he glanced at Rankin.

Rankin leaned back, holding the rope with both hands. "Go, damn it."

"Hey," shouted Phil, as his head disappeared. "Hey!" he yelled again, his voice muffled by distance and the speed of his descent.

"Stop yer belly achin'," shouted Rankin.

Rankin's method hardly slowed to allow Phil to touch his feet to the ground below. Immediately Rankin yelled orders again. "Now tie him into yer bedroll."

CHAPTER TWENTY-SEVEN

The dust rose higher and wider over the cliff. Caroline went after the belt with a vengeance.

"Whatcha goin' off that way fer?" Rankin' called down.

As she yanked repeatedly on the belt, Caroline leaned forward, trying to hear noises from the shaft. Her left hand fell free of the belt. She grabbed quickly to keep the noisy buckle from falling to the ground.

"Phil, you relievin' yerself? That's enough jokin' around."

"Phil," Rankin's voice grew angry.

She suspected Phil's silence was probably Olaf's doing. He'd no doubt been gagged, trussed, and put out of sight within the mine – upsetting the precarious balance for Rankin. Her job now was to turn the tables on Rankin so that Olaf could bring Gryf to the surface for medical help.

Suddenly, Sol dropped his long nose. Caroline grabbed the pommel to keep from pitching forward. She glanced down and discovered that the lariat had been scythed through by Sol's teeth.

The dust cloud darkened above the cliff.

Caroline wrapped the buckle end of Rankin's belt around her left hand.

"Damn you Phil," shouted Rankin. "Get back where I can see you." He leaned against the post where Caroline had been trussed minutes ago.

Caroline leaned over Sol's neck. "Attention, Sol," she whispered as she gripped his flank with her knees. Sol leaped forward. A small rock shot out from beneath his hoof. Rankin whirled, cocking his

298

rifle in the same motion. Caroline shouted, "Now!" Sol veered to the right. Rankin lifted his rifle to his shoulder.

Caroline snaked the belt out, whipping thick leather around the barrel of the rifle. She yanked to the left, ripping the gun from Rankin's hand sending it exploding through the air. A whining bullet trailed left of Caroline's shoulder.

Sol's great haunches bunched beneath him as he turned a hair to the right before finishing his charge. He plowed into the horrified Rankin, tossing the man into the talus slope at the base of the cliff, beyond the mine shaft and well beyond the fallen gun. Rankin scrambled on all fours, attempting to escape his pursuer. Sol stalked him until the man tried to stand and run, the horse's big teeth came down into Rankin's shoulder.

Caroline nearly fell off Sol in her rush to grab the rifle. She snagged the hot barrel and dragged the gun to the edge of the mine shaft. She fell to her knees, peering over the edge. "Gryf. where are you?"

Blood pounded in her head. Her vision blackened with breathless fear. "Gryyyyffyth!" she cried out.

"Does Sol have him?" Gryf's deep voice rose, as strong as ever.

"You're all right . . ."

"Rankin?"

"Yes. Yes. Sol's holding him at attention. You . . ."

"I'll kill you Griffin," hollered Rankin.

"We're on our way up. Keep that weapon on him."

Caroline rolled quickly, aiming the gun at Rankin. She need not have worried. Sol's grip was unbreakable. Now that she was lying still, the pain in her foot seized her attention. She felt sick and shivery, but she couldn't let vigilance waver.

"Hang on, Sol," she said tightly, as she opened the rifle. Both barrels were empty.

Gryf hoisted himself up onto the edge of the mine shaft. "Aw, shit," he groaned. Her gaze followed his.

Above them all, a band of horsemen lined the crest of the cliff.

**

"Hold still, every man-jack of you," shouted the big man at the center of the horsemen. Caroline glanced at Gryf. His bandages were bright red, but his face held its color.

"Say nothing about Olaf,'" he whispered. "He'll stay down until we find out what this is about."

She looked quickly at Rankin, held upright by Sol. He seemed to have heard nothing of Gryf's whispers. Above him, half of the men stayed on the overlook, their rifles still aimed at Rankin, Gryf and herself. The other half rode the narrow trail between the boulders, coming down toward the mine. To her surprise, she recognized the street urchin from Denver astride one of the horses. The child was a deal smaller than any of the men, but he rode with a stiff back and his head high, as if he were the most important among them.

More surprising yet, Alex Kemp rode with the men. Alex raised his chin and removed his felt hat, waving it toward Rankin, shaking his head from side to side as if in disapproval of something.

"Gryf," Alex called. "Let Sol off duty, my friend."

Surprised, Gryf jerked toward Alex's voice. "What is this?"

Alex swung down out of his saddle, slapping dust from his hat. "This is an unfortunate misunderstanding. How about giving Sol a break?"

Recovering his composure, Gryf ordered, "Sol, guard."

Sol's teeth moved off Rankin's shoulder, but the roan didn't remove his nose from the vicinity of Rankin's ear. Rankin's eyes followed Alex and Gryf, but his body stood as much at attention as when Sol held him there.

Gryf began to rise, but the leader of the horsemen yelled, "Stay down."

Gryf rolled back, sitting on his boots. Caroline could tell he was ready to spring up from what appeared to be a relaxed position.

Alex hunkered by Gryf, checking his arm bandages. "Jesus, where'd this wound come from?"

"What misunderstanding?" Gryf asked Alex.

"Someone told the marshal here that you were in Denver the day Isaac Brown was murdered. He thinks you have motive."

"How could Gryf have motive?" Caroline interrupted. "Brown was his friend."

Alex tightened Gryf's bandage, grunting. "You and I know that, but it appears otherwise to the marshal."

As he drew near, Caroline recognized the marshal who had interviewed her in Denver. The big man swung down out of his saddle, strode toward the mine shaft and looked down it. He seemed to see nothing down there.

"Somebody want to explain to me what you all are doing up here?" the marshal asked, glancing at Gryf's bloody bandages.

Rankin's voice boomed, "I was trying to capture this Griffin varmint. But she come along to rescue him and murdered my buddy up there, top of the cliff."

Caroline's surprise made her speechless, but only for a moment. Then she treated Rankin's accusation with contempt. "Better believe it, Marshal," Caroline's voice dripped sarcasm as she limped toward Gryf. "I can also fly."

"Marshal," interrupted Alex, "we need to get these people some medical attention."

The marshal's face reddened. "I'll take care of this as I see fit." He turned on Caroline, "Where's your boot?"

She stared down at her swollen foot. "Rankin cut it off me and burnt my foot with a stick from the fire."

Gryf stood upright, his face gone gray. One of the men grabbed his shoulders, but he strained toward her, trying to get a look at her foot.

"It's all right, Gryf," she whispered. Even as she said it, pain from the burn shot up her leg. She leaned on Rankin's rifle and drew the injured foot up toward her torso. Sickness took over her body.

Alex put his arm around her shoulders. "Let me take her, Marshall."

"Take her to Deirdre," Gryf urged.

She wanted to stay for Gryf – straighten out the marshal . . .

Alex lifted Caroline as if she were a doll. "Marshal," he said, "we need to get these people back to town before this young lady's foot becomes worse. We've a doctoring lady on a ranch nearby."

The marshal glanced at Caroline, at Gryf's bandaged arms, and at Rankin. "You three are under arrest. Looks like we'll have to ask questions later." He signaled to the men atop the cliff. "We're heading back to town. Bring that body from up there."

Caroline tried to turn toward Gryf, but Alex was already moving to his own horse. He called over his shoulder, "She's cold all over."

Gryf said, "Get her my jacket."

"I'm fine, Alex," she protested. But Alex deposited her on his gelding. As she slumped over the horse's saddle, Alex moved to Sol and Rankin.

"Whoa boy," he soothed as Sol skittered from him.

"Sol, stand," Gryf ordered.

Sol snorted, drawing Caroline's wavering attention. Alex murmured something soothing to Sol that made even Rankin seem to relax. A moment later, the marshal's man moved between Sol and Rankin, tied Rankin's hands and hauled him away from the horse.

From Gryf's saddle bag, Alex pulled out a small kit bag, a package Caroline recognized as one of Deirdre's Irish pastries. Next, Alex yanked out a pair of overalls, a ragged straw hat and a blue cloth. The hat fell to the ground.

As Alex unrolled the blue cloth, the boy from Denver shouted. "That's it. That's the jacket I saw."

With horror, Caroline saw he was right. The jacket, designed to be pulled over the head, was exactly like the jacket she'd seen on the man who leapt from Mrs. Porter's upstairs window. And then, she glanced once more at the hat that Alex had dropped on the ground in his haste. It was the same – the murderer's hat.

Time froze for Caroline. Her eyes took in the evidence. She saw Gryf's face, staring at the boy and then at the jacket. Through a slow change, she saw him understand that something had shifted, some indefinable line had been crossed.

He turned to her, a question in his raised brows, but she could give him no reassurance. His face grew taut as he watched her try to deny the jacket and its meaning. Her heart said "no" but her head asked "why?"

He saw the doubt and turned his face from her.

She shrank within herself, into a black place where love warred with the evidence before her eyes.

"Alex," Gryf called, "Get her something warm. Get it fast. She's failing."

CHAPTER TWENTY-EIGHT

Caroline grew aware that either Deirdre or Ellen were at her bedside night and day. Her foot throbbed within its bandages. She was hot one moment and freezing the next. And her head ached as if a boulder leaned against the back of her neck. Twisting and throwing off covers, she barely heard snatches of conversation when Ellen arrived to take Deirdre's place.

"Deirdre, you must sleep," Ellen whispered. "I'll cover her again."

"She's burning up. Leave her to the air until she starts to shiver."

"I understand," Ellen said. "See if you can slip Gryf a message about how she's doing. The Marshal wouldn't let me speak to him."

"Where'd they put him?"

"In his own office. But they're holding the fat fellow in my school until Duncan and his wagon get here. Why do men think they must commandeer the biggest building for their business?"

"You wouldn't want to be teaching today, believe me. You'd be answering questions from my Jimmy. He's mad as all get-out about them arresting his hero."

"I know," Ellen chuckled. "Mad as a hornet, pesky as a fruit fly. He's been at the marshal all morning."

"That scamp."

Caroline could hear Deirdre's skirts rustle as she rose. She tried to rise, too, so she could ask about Olaf, about Gryf's shoulder wounds, about . . . .. she couldn't remember, and she couldn't lift her head.

"Now Deirdre," Ellen whispered. "Don't go after Jimmy. He's got a right to be angry. And you need sleep so you can come back here tonight."

**

Behind the barn, Jimmy Freya held his throbbing nose and glared up at the boy who had just knocked him on his rear in the dirt.

"Don't care if you can dust me up," Jimmy said. "You didn't never see our Gryf jump out no window."

The tall boy stood with his fists cocked in case Jimmy rose for a tenth time. "Didn't say who I saw," the boy panted. "Said I saw that hat and jacket. Saw a long fella in them duds, but that don't mean I lied."

Jimmy stared at the boy. Since none of the other lads were around to watch, Jimmy made a conscious decision to take a breather. "Beard?" he asked.

The boy shook his head. "Never saw his face."

"Didja get close enough to guess how tall?"

"Nope. He ran kinda low to the ground. Man, he was fast."

"What else didja see?"

The kid looked off, like he was thinking. During this unguarded moment, Jimmy considered bowling him over with a rolling tackle, but he wanted to hear his answer, so decided to wait.

"The fella had real wide shoulders," the boy said, "and he was cat-fast, and quiet."

Jimmy's heart sank. It all sounded like Gryf. Too much like Gryf. "That don't mean much," he said testily, "lessen you seen his face, nor his hair."

The boy uncocked his fists and offered Jimmy a hand. "Can't say that I saw either," he said. "My name's Jack, what's yours?"

"Jim," Jimmy said, deciding the short version sounded tougher. He took the offer of a hand up. "You box good," he said. "Wanna teach me?"

"Sure," Jack said, grinning. "I learned from some real big guys. Mean. You gotta keep your hands ready, Jimbo. Keep your face protected, like this." He danced right and left, holding both hands high. "And move more, so I don't get such a clear shot at your nose."

Jimmy picked up his leaden arms and held them the way Jack demonstrated. "Jacko," he said, trying on the kid's nicknaming style, "Did you know this Isaac Brown, the guy who died?"

"Sure did," said Jack, as he danced around jabbing at Jimmy's raised fists. "I ran errands for him, and he paid good – food and coin."

**

While night turned from black to gray, Caroline's dizziness gave her the devil of a time when she pulled her boot over her swollen left foot. Two days too many had been spent in this bed. She glanced at Deirdre who had fallen asleep in the chair next to the wood stove. Afraid Deirdre would wake and shove her back into the bed, she crept toward the door. She must not waste any more time getting over her fever. Duncan's wagon would come back in three days.

According to Deirdre, the marshal was letting no By-Gum people near Gryf. Marshal Jeffers planned to chain Gryf and Rankin into the wagon to begin the journey to Isabeau and then on down to the jail in Denver. Thus, she had little time to prove the marshal had the wrong man. And she had to do it without getting caught because, Deirdre said, Marshall Jeffers intended to arrest her for the murder of that man at Mine Number Three – fellow named Hardy Gilchrist.

Slipping out the door into the darkness, Caroline pulled her blue cape about her shoulders. Within minutes, she was behind the barn and limping toward the Number One Mine. As she passed the mine buildings, a shadow stood in a small pool of light from a window at the blacksmith's shop. Sneaking up on the shadow, she was relieved to see it was Samuel.

"Hey," she whispered.

Samuel jumped and peered at the corner of the building. "Miss, what are you doin'?" he asked, glancing around, checking to see they were alone as she limped toward him. "Marshal Jeffers finds you out of bed, he'll arrest you."

"I've got to figure out who sent the marshal up here."

"You're still in bad shape."

"Boot's too small. I'll be fine." At the moment, Caroline was not sure how much longer she could stand up, but she didn't want Samuel to know it.

Samuel studied her boot a moment, then whispered, "The marshal says he came because someone tipped him anonymous-like – pointed him to that boy, Jack"

"Why Jack and not me? We were both there when the murderer jumped from the window."

Samuel shook his head. "Maybe whoever it is wants to make trouble for you as well, Miss Trewartha."

"What evidence do they think they have?"

Samuel looked grim. "Pretty damning, beg your pardon. That jacket of Gryf's has blood on it. So does the hat."

She glanced away, "It can't be him," she said. "You know he'd never do such a thing."

Samuel nodded. "I know it. The whole town knows it, but how did the murderer come to wear that jacket? And then how'd he get it up here among Gryf's belongings?"

"Is it a common type?"

"It's common in Wales, but not here. It's good for keeping you warm in a high wind. That's why he packed it. He wanted to have more protection for you during the trip up to the mines. And he knows nothing about the hat."

Her heart thudded once and then seemed to stop.

"Oh, just a second, "Samuel said patting his jacket. From an inside pocket he brought out a telegram. "Fellow dropped this at Alex's. I'd a brought it to you, but Ellen said you were incoherent, and I thought ..."

Caroline tried to smile, "Thank you Samuel." She held it up to the faint light from the blacksmith's shop. "I can't think who . . ." Then she saw the name of the sender, *Hume, President, Allied Mines*.

She ripped open the end and unfolded the gram.

Trewartha, this is to authorize your take-over as manager of By-Gum mines. During Williams' trial, Allied must rescue investment. Sending equipment you requested. If next payment late, will be forced to foreclose. Hume

Caroline stared at the words. For one moment, she was overwhelmed with Allied's show of trust in her as engineer and manager, and the speed with which they sent the equipment she'd requisitioned. Then shame and anger heated her face. Gryf was fighting for his life against trumped-up evidence. Allied stood ready to take over his mines at the least hint of trouble.

Besides, how did Allied hear so soon?

"Samuel," she said, "Read this and tell me about the man who brought it."

Samuel took it. She watched his face. His eyes widened and the color drained. "My God," he whispered. "It's been two days. How could they know about the murder accusation, eh?"

"What about the messenger?" she asked again.

"He rode past Alex's ranch, yesterday afternoon. Said he was headed down to Santa Fe to hunt gold. He was a bit lost. Went right past By-Gum in the night, I expect. Abel at the telegraph office paid him to deliver this telegram up from Isabeau."

Caroline snorted. "Abel, who closes the telegraph office to go fishing? He's never seemed so interested in delivering telegrams in a timely manner."

Samuel shrugged, "I guess he thought you might be leaving soon, Miss Trewartha. Wanted to be sure you received this."

"This is too soon. Someone at Allied planned Gryf's arrest."

"Stemmins? He's in Denver and deals with Allied. Alex thinks he steals everything they send us."

"Sure could be him," Caroline said. "Do you know how to get in to see Gryf?"

Samuel's jaw tightened. "I don't think the Marshal would allow God in there, and certainly not you."

"We need to know what he wants; who he thinks is doing this; what should happen at the mines."

"Miss Trewartha, before they locked Gryf up, he spoke to Rudy and to me. He said we should do as you suggest with the mines. Said you had a model in the barn we should see. You have his full backing."

Caroline stared at him, recalling her months at McFadden, Wyoming with a clarity she'd avoided at the time. In a sudden recognition of the truth, she sank to the stoop of the blacksmith's shop.

"He shouldn't have such faith in me," she said to Samuel. "I believe now that Allied sent me up here expecting me to cause dissension. They expected me to do as I have done in other mines – to think I know best about every decision."

Samuel's face twisted in puzzlement as he knelt to talk to her. "Come now, Miss Trewartha, you're very good at what you do. No one believes you could have caused all that much trouble."

She gazed at his dark face and hopeful, encouraging smile and said, "I'm afraid I could. And I did." She fidgeted and twisted her shawl. "The men hated me before I left."

Samuel put his hand on Caroline's, "You've been very good for us – made us think different than we done, and at a critical time."

Eyes filling with tears, Caroline managed to say, "Sam . . ."

He smiled at her and raised one quirky eyebrow. Suddenly she saw his resemblance to Gryf. His smile broadened as he said, "There's another reason I'm glad you've come."

"Oh?"

"Never seen my brother in such a sweat. Makes me a happy man."

Shocked, Caroline spoke sharply. "Your brother is charged with murder."

"Oh, that's not fun, Miss. It's the unexpected love . . ."

She stood, nearly knocking him over. "That will do."

He chuckled, then whispered, "Better lay low. Soon as the marshal realizes you're on your feet, he's gonna clap you in irons for murdering that Hardy Gilchrist."

Caroline's stomach roiled with renewed horror at the memory of Rankin blowing Gilchrist's head apart. He'd done it merely to rid himself of a nuisance.

Instead of dwelling on that moment, she had to get to work. "Tell Deirdre I'm fine. Tell her to pretend I'm still 'incoherent" and keep Marshal Jeffers out of my room for as long as she can."

"But your foot – you limped over here,"

"If the foot gets worse, I'll find her at night. Meanwhile, I'm able to search for Isaac's real killer. I've got to find out why Gryf's jacket and hat were on the murderer."

310

"I better tell Deirdre right now, Miss. She'll get real scared and noisy if she wakes to find you gone." He started off, then turned back, a question forming in his eyes.

"I'll leave you messages in Sheba's stall," she said.

Satisfied, he ran toward Freya's ranch.

CHAPTER TWENTY-NINE

Pondering the past threatened to paralyze Gryf. He would go crazy thinking about how pale Caroline was when Alex carried her into Deirdre's. He'd wracked his brain to understand his enemy. Failing to find a rational explanation for Kidde and Rankin's attacks, or for Jesse and Isaac's deaths, he needed to plan as if there were a future. He needed to stop thinking about her.

Yet the marshal had said she was failing and incoherent.

Gryf cursed when the shackle on his wrist clunked against the edge of his desk. He couldn't draw smooth lines on his map. Instead, on a blank page, he tested his pen, drawing a flowing river, spilling from the brow of a smooth promontory and fanning out across the valley. Nearby, he sketched a small hill, and behind it another, both rounded and sun-warmed, like the hills he remembered in South Dakota. Under his drawing hand, the lovely hills curved down toward a smooth plain. He shadowed the lower curve of each hill . . .

And then he dropped his ink pen, gazing in disbelief at what he had done. He'd drawn her, naked, lying on a bed, her hair fanned over his pillow – it must be his pillow. He covered his face with his hands, in despair, losing control. He'd be no help to her this way – no help chained to his desk, able only to lust.

Gryf ripped the offending page from his desk and flung it into the back corner of his office. On a fresh sheet, he began writing furiously, listing all the people he had ever made angry, ever crossed in their desire to cut corners in safety, ever forced to pay a fair wage to a defenseless boy, ever threatened with a union strike. The list grew alarmingly fast.

**

The eastern sky flashed a foretaste of gold as Caroline hobbled toward Gryf's office shack. Growing daylight picked out the silhouette of a guardsman on the front stoop. She faded back into the row of burros where she grabbed the nose halter of one animal and let her weary head drop against his neck until the pain in her foot subsided. Keeping the burro's stout little body between her and the shack, she walked the huffling animal away from his feed, working her way toward the corral gate. The animal drew in breath to complain, but Caroline shoved a handful of grain toward his nose. He stretched his neck out and riffled his lips, trying to reach the sweet-smelling oats. Caroline led him on as she crouched out of sight. When she arrived, she let him have the grain, hurried through and re-latched the gate.

"Thanks, my smelly, little friend," she whispered. Busily munching, he twitched his ears. Hunkering low to the ground, she arrived at the fence corner. Hoof beats approached from the opposite direction. She saw the horse and its big rider in the fresh light, plodding toward the shack.

As the horse lumbered around the opposite side of the shack, the guard's attention turned toward the rider. Caroline took advantage of his distraction to run to the back of the shack and roll herself under the raised floor, flinging herself across a quantity of coal dust to be sure she was far enough under to escape detection. She'd nearly rolled into a pile of junk left over from construction – pieces of lumber, rusty metal and the faint gleam of spider webs. She rubbed her hand through her hair and around her dress collar to get out any spiders. The more she brushed, the more she imagined bugs and mice crawling over her.

"Mornin', Marshal," said the guard. "Did Mullen and his crew return last night?"

"Nope."

"Still checking out evidence at the mine up there?"

"Dunno."

Dismayed at how little she would learn from the marshal's tight mouth, Caroline stared through the opening under the front porch, watching his boots as he swung down off his horse. She prayed that Olaf had gotten out of the mine before Mullen and crew showed up. As long as Olaf was free, Gryf had another determined ally, seeking the truth. Perhaps Olaf had scared the truth out of that skinny Phil. They had to know what rich man in Denver hired Rankin and Phil to capture Gryf and her.

The marshal climbed the steps to Gryf's office. He rattled a padlock, inserted a key and yanked the lock from the hasp. Inside the shack, she heard the scrape of chains and the push of a chair.

His chains are heavy!

"Marshal, any news?" Gryf asked.

Marshal Jeffers closed the door. The rest of their conversation was muffled.

Throughout the interview, Caroline could tell that the marshal paced across the shack and back again. The floorboards creaked. She could follow his methodic pattern. The first time he walked above her face, the boards dipped dangerously close to her nose. She rolled off to one side and watched as those boards sank under his weight on his return. She remembered the weak spot in the floor from her first visit there, back on that first day, before she had loved Gryf.

Studying the substructure as she listened, she realized that one of the posts supporting the floor had sunk, weakening the joist it was designed to hold up.

**

After Marshal Jeffers left the shack, Gryf stared at his list of potential enemies. These people ranged the world – every mining

314

community he'd worked in. Some of them had since died – a few in disasters created by their own carelessness. Still, the list was long. It needed narrowing.

Outside, Gryf heard Jeffers tell the guard to get a meal and to send back another man. The guard tramped off the porch. Soon afterwards, Jeffers rode away as well. There was no one outside. The time had come to act on a hope.

Gryf fell to the floor where he'd noticed the boards sagging under Jeffers' weight. Using a stack of books as a fulcrum and his wooden T-square as a lever, he pried at the joint. It took only a moment to lift one board, but in the process, he broke the long arm of the T-square in half. He whirled around, searching for a stronger tool.

Behind him, a small voice said, "Here. Use this."

"Caroline?"

He fell to the floor. Up through the hole rose a curved and rusted piece from the undercarriage of an old buggy. He took the iron and peered through to the ground. There was no one there.

"I'm out of the way," she whispered. "Pry it up."

"Caroline?"

"Get it up, for Pete's sake. That new guard will come."

Gryf applied the iron to the floorboards, mumbling, "Mouth like that, you can't be too bad hurt."

One whole board came up. He stacked it next to the first, and resumed, pulling up the next and grumbling, "Who else appears under the floorboards when you think she's near dead in her bed?"

A third board came out whole. He pushed it aside, sputtering, "Who else?"

"Stop cussing and work," she whispered.

The fourth board came out and he saw her, white-faced and dirty – a beloved rag doll. At that moment, boot steps clomped up the two steps to his porch.

"Put them back," she whispered.

The guard knocked on the door. Gryf called, "Yes?" while pushing the four boards into place.

"Mr. Williams," said a young male voice, "I've got your breakfast."

Gryf pulled his swiveling desk chair over the hole. "I believe you've got the key," he said.

"Oh," the young guard laughed nervously, "So I do. So I do."

Gryf could hear a tray being set on the porch. He pulled his desk closer to the chair and set himself down gingerly. "Get out from under," he said toward the floor.

The guard rattled the lock. Undoing it at last, he opened the door and bent to grab the tray. If Gryf had not been chained, that moment would have been an opportunity to break out. Instead, he leaned back slightly, trying to appear relaxed.

Gryf decided the guard must have been a bellhop in his pre-law-enforcement days. He delivered the tray, uncovering the hot biscuits and scrambled eggs with a flourish, almost making Gryf feel the need to reach into his pockets for a tip. He willed the boy to leave, but the little guy seemed determined to wait and to watch Gryf eat.

Desperate to get rid of him, Gryf said, "I have work to do, young man. And I prefer to eat slowly, and alone."

The boy blushed and moved backwards toward the door. "Oh, of course, sir."

Once he was out and had relocked the door, Gryf covered the meal, hoping to keep it warm for Caroline, whom he suspected of not eating anything for some time. He moved the chair as quietly as possible and stacked the boards next to the desk, reopening the hole.

He poked his head through and found her silently stacking other discarded lumber – building a crib support, just as she would have in the mine if there weren't enough posts to hold up her temporary joist. He watched as she finished, afraid to say anything, lest the

316

guard hear him. When she was done, he gestured her into the shack through the hole they had created.

As he backed away, she slipped up through the hole, sat at the edge and pulled her feet into the room. In spite of the untied boot on her burned foot, she made this maneuver seem a dance. Just as she had on that night ten days ago when he found her at the creek, she crossed her slim legs and rose smoothly to a standing position. Her motion brought back all the anguish he had felt that other night, grief for Jesse Polgren, and certainty that evil stalked his path and had caught up with him once more.

Caroline must have seen those feelings rush through him, for she reached out and touched his face. Without thought, he folded her in his arms. Miraculously, she came, wrapping her arms about his waist, laying her head against his chest. His chain swayed into her back as he held his breath, not moving a muscle, waiting for her to realize where she was, and to pull away.

She stayed.

Only then did he feel how cold she was. Coal dust and cobwebs covered the back and sides of her new green dress.

Holding her close, he whispered, "Let me get you a blanket."

Her big green eyes gazed up at him, alert. "They want to kill your reputation," she whispered. "Whoever it is, they want you publicly humiliated. That's why they murder your friends – so you will be thought reckless, or worse, the murderer yourself."

He bowed his head over her, thinking, Yes, I believe it. "

He said, "Come then. Look at this list." He picked up the paper and handed it to her, reluctantly encouraging Caroline to disengage from his embrace. "These are people I've got into dog fights with for one reason or another. I've crossed out the ones who are dead."

She jerked toward him. "Dead?"

Taking her meaning, he added, "Not by me, I assure you."

She relaxed and went back to studying the names, her posture all serious business, again. "I wouldn't know any of these in India or Africa." she said.

He nodded, already missing the sweet give of her body. He cleared his throat and whispered, "I'm working on the theory Ellen proposed – that one of these men is someone who knew you and your father as well."

She ran her finger down the list stopping at one Helmut Fein. "There's a buzzard."

He handed her a pen. "Mark them. Then we'll talk."

He pulled the office chair between the desk and drafting table, twirled it to face the desk and gently pushed her shoulder so she would sit down. She concentrated so thoroughly that she barely acknowledged all this motion until he put his hand on her shoulder. Then, as she sank into the chair, she reached up, with the pen still in her hand, and touched his fingers, dropping ink on his middle finger and on her shoulder. He watched the ink drip but didn't want to stop her caressing his fingers. Moments passed. She put her hand down to mark an X next to another name – Lyle Bracken.

Conniving, manipulative, sneaky.

Gryf allowed his hand to air dry as he went for a blanket from his cot – the cot the sheriff had allowed him while he was jailed here. He returned to wrap the quilt around her shoulders. As he stood behind her, he stared at her once-shining knot of deep bronze hair. Those were not mere cobwebs that marred her tresses. A spider sat on her amber hair-comb.

"Sit very still, Caroline," he whispered. "I'm going to take a spider out of your hair."

She stopped moving, stopped breathing. He reached with his handkerchief and flicked the fellow on the floor. Her comb fell, skittering under his desk as he stomped on the spider. He turned back to find her hair had fallen around her back, catching in the folds of the blanket – the long tresses of his drawing.

His flesh burned.

The young boy on the porch called, "You all right, Mister?"

Gryf, startled, took a moment to realize the boy couldn't see his aroused state. It was the stomping that drew his attention. "Just getting rid of a spider," Gryf called back.

"You done with that breakfast yet?'

"No. I usually savor breakfast all morning."

Caroline turned her face toward the door. Gryf saw the softness that loose hair leant to her high cheekbones and forehead. He ached to touch the end of her nose, to taste her. In an effort to stop the direction of his thoughts, he reached for the plate on his desk, uncovering it and taking one of the biscuits in his hands. It was still warm. He broke it in half, buttered it and held it out to her.

She, staring again at his list, merely leaned toward the biscuit and nibbled at one side. His heart thudded in his throat as she drew back, chewed a moment, swallowed and then licked her lips, leaning forward for another bite. She stopped, almost at the biscuit and slapped another star on the list.

Dorian Luck.

Yes. He was in Pennsylvania in 1878. Gryf's mind blurred by the racing of his blood, but he remembered this Luck fellow. *The owner of much useless mine property next door to precious coal seams.*

Caroline's mouth touched his finger as she reached for another bite of biscuit.

"Please," he rasped. "Take the biscuit."

Startled, she glanced up. He saw her register what she'd done. He knew her effect on him must be as plain as a blaring mine signal. She took the biscuit from his hand.

"May I have half of the eggs?" she asked, softly.

He dropped his head toward his chest, closing his eyes to clear his mind. "Take what you will," he said, wretched desire robbing him of voice.

"If you don't eat, too, it will all go cold," she said.

"I'll eat. I'll eat."

Inches away from him, he heard her lift the butter knife, heard her scrape jam from the jar, then saw her hand beneath his lowered face, holding the other half of the biscuit out to him.

"You need to eat," she said, "because I'm going to help you escape from here. And then heaven knows where you'll get your next meal."

Gryf raised his right arm, rattling the chain that attached him to his wood stove. She stared at it a moment, her eyes flashing anger in a way he found most encouraging. She thrust out her chin, a bluff he now recognized as a mask for fear. "In this whole town there must be at least one set of metal cutters."

His heart cheered for her sassy, resourceful ways. "There's a pair in my cabin." He fished in his desk drawer, pulled out a key and handed it to her. "I want you to spend your nights there. You can't light the stove, of course, but you'll be a lot warmer than out in the air, and a lot better hidden than in the barn."

"The marshal will search your cabin."

"He's already done that."

She glanced around his small space. "What if we pull this bookcase away from the wall? We can set it diagonally across this corner so I can stand behind it when the marshal comes in." She rose and hurried toward the corner, intending, he supposed, to move the damned thing herself. He didn't even realize his danger until she lifted the paper he'd discarded an hour before.

Horrified, he watched as if in a nightmare as she slowly turned to leave the drawing on his desk. He reached to crumple it as soon as she dropped it, hoping she would not look, hoping she would go back to empty his bookcase without ever knowing what she held.

She didn't get that far, however, for when she placed the sheet on the desk, she glanced at it. Then she stared at it.

Gryf's face went hot. In an absolute silence, she lifted her eyes from the sheet to him. He tried to swallow but couldn't. He couldn't talk, couldn't defend himself . . .

Her hand went to her thick, free hair, pulling it back, perhaps to make it less like the hair in the drawing. She dragged in a deep breath, then bit her lip, glancing once more at the offending sheet.

Gryf slumped to the desk chair, his elbows resting on his knees. He looked up at her and spoke at last. "Yes, I want you," he whispered. "They told me you were dying. This drawing I did from despair, but it was headed for the stove. I never wanted to frighten you with how I felt."

Caroline sank to the floor. "Gryf," she whispered. "I trust you."

Deep, cutting anguish entered his chest. "I would never . . ."

"No," she reached a hand to his, "You don't understand. I have faith in you. But me . . . I can't . . ."

Her declaration stunned him. He folded one hand over hers and reached out to draw the quilt about her shoulders once more. "Tell me. Please tell me, at last," he urged.

She looked away, "My tenth birthday."

Gryf shut his eyes, bowing his head over their hands.

"Mother and I tried to get to Grandfather's farm for safety. The soldiers were renegades. Running away from the battle, they caught us going into the farmhouse. One of them . . . He . . ."

"I know," Gryf interrupted so she wouldn't have to say it, but a coldness crept down his spine. She couldn't seem to talk. It tore at his gut to see her like this. "I understand," he assured her, but the truth was he could not comprehend such monstrous evil.

"The others," she said, "they killed Mother."

321

"Oh, Sweetheart."

"They killed her and then ran down Black Schoolhouse Road. When the battle was over, we had to burn the dead horses."

Her whisper rose. He pulled the quilt over both their heads so she could say it and yet be unheard by the guard. She held tight to his hand, rising to her knees. She went on talking in a soft, hell-driven child's voice. "and then we buried Mother. And Daddy couldn't come home because he was in another battle very far away, so he never got to kiss her goodbye. He wouldn't have known her if he'd come. They beat her face. She was broken and she . . . and she was so . . ." Caroline's adult voice came through at last. "She was so hurt."

With difficulty, Gryf controlled his rage and sought only to let her know he heard and cared. "Caroline, you were hurt, too. You needed your mother desperately."

Caroline dropped her forehead to the back of his hand. He could feel her tears run down his fingers. He leaned close where he could hear her broken speech. "Grandmother said . . . people would hate me . . . and revile my mother. I should never tell anyone what happened, especially not my papa."

Fury swamped Gryf. "Carl never knew?"

"She said he would stop loving my mama's memory, and wouldn't come home to me."

"And your Grandfather agreed with her?"

She nodded. "And Aunt Agatha. Grandma said no one must know. And I would never be able to . . . be able to . . . marry."

He touched her tears. "Why ever not?"

"I'm . . . I'm too broken inside."

Gryf could hardly hold himself together for her. "The doctor told you this?"

She seemed barely able to whisper. "No doctor. I bleed. Still. Every few weeks, and I can't stop it."

322

He felt the thud of his heart in his throat. He'd been a boy when his mother had had to explain women's bleeding to him. "They lied to you," he hissed, almost too angry to help her. "They lied to your father. He should have been told. He could have helped you."

"Sir?" called the boy on the porch.

Gryf started. He hadn't realized how enraged he was, and how loud. He struggled to drag his mind from the heart-breaking sadness in her face.

"I'm just . . ." he tried to remember what he'd said that the boy might have heard. "I'm practicing my courtroom defense," he called through the door. "Just getting ready for my trial."

"Yes, sir. That may be soon, sir. Here comes the marshal again."

She was up on her feet before he was, already moving the drafting table off the rug and opening the hole to the foundation. He helped her slip through, then shoved the quilt in after her.

"Wrap up in this," he said. "You can't take ill."

She accepted the quilt, then gazed up at him, her face tear-stained, and with that brave jutting of her jaw that he loved. "Gryf," she whispered, "If I'm not here, I am at your cabin, or near it."

"You can love, Sweetheart. Never believe otherwise."

She glanced at him once more.

He said, "Tell Ellen about the bleeding. She'll help you."

She nodded, a small light of hope entered her gaze, the she rolled away from the hole.

He had the boards and desk in place just as the marshal twisted the lock. With one hand, Gryf crumpled his drawing and stuffed it into the wood stove. Beneath him, he heard a small scraping sound. He thought it was Caroline pulling herself out from under his back-foundation plank.

The office door opened. Sun shone into the room for the first time in two days.

CHAPTER THIRTY

Silently barring the door of Gryf's cabin, Caroline leaned against it and caught her breath. Gryf's cabin had been ransacked. She was certain this had to be the work of Gryf's enemy. The meticulous marshal wouldn't search in such a destructive way. She cast her glance over the mess. There had to be a way to figure out what the person was looking for.

The great room enclosed two built-in narrow beds, their mattresses pulled to the floor and ripped. At the end of the room, the wood stove was overturned. Ash still fluttered about the room. Kitchen utensils were thrown down. A large trunk lay open and empty. In the smaller, back room, the light from a window showed her that all Gryf's hunting and fishing gear as well as his supply of dried food had been destroyed.

The person seemed to have been frantic, angry and in a hurry. And he, or she, sought something small – papers, maybe the contract. A will. A letter, perhaps.

Caroline had time to put all to rights, if the person did not return for another search. If she let herself stop, the dull pain in her foot would overtake her. She would stay here only until darkness. While here, she would at least find a metal cutting tool to free Gryf. And while cleaning, perhaps she could find out more about the person who hated him so much.

By noon, the sun shone through the thin sheet of mica Gryf had fitted into his cabin window. The light warmed her back and shoulders, casting shadows onto the fancy paper that lined his empty blanket chest. She knelt beside the chest and set to work salvaging his quilts and clothing.

324

She folded a clean shirt that lay near the chest, then changed her mind. Unbuttoning her ashy green dress, she shimmied out of it. She pushed her arms into the sleeve of Gryf's worn shirt, then stepped into a pair of trousers. Buttoned, they were so large they threatened to fall off her. She reached into the pile of clothing for a neck scarf, sent it through the waist loops and cinched it about her. Then, after rolling the legs up four times, she could walk.

Resuming work on the mess, she felt safe and warm in his clothes. As she leaned over to lay a shirt in the trunk, she noticed a slight bulge in the paper lining. Running her fingers over the raised area, she felt something move between paper and solid wood. She smoothed it upwards toward the top of the trunk wall. A corner of firm, glossy paper pushed up through the dried glue at the lining edge. She pulled the piece out and was amazed to find a brown and faded photograph. Turning it right side up, she studied the subject.

A man, dressed in riding boots, fitted jacket and flared pants stood beside a horse – a man who looked like Alex, but not like Alex. Here was the same wavy, almost untamed, blond hair, firm jaw, broad forehead and slender nose. But where Alex was polished and sure of himself, this young man appeared tentative, vulnerable. He held the reins of his hunter with one hand. With the other, he lifted a cup from a tray proffered by a grave young woman whose plain dress was covered with a white apron. Her black, straight hair had been pulled back into a loose knot which gave her an air of elegance despite her servant's dress. The young man gazed at the servant woman with unmistakable affection. A softness around his mouth and a shining admiration in his eyes told all.

He loved her.

Outside Gryf's cabin, the *callop, callop* of horseshoes sounded on the road. Caroline flew to the back room and untied the leather string latch on the window that opened into the back yard. She had an alternative exit, if she needed it. The horse and rider moved on.

325

Returning to the trunk, she studied the photo again. This was an odd pose. The few photos taken for her wealthy grandfather were always stiffly formal – never this imprinting of an unguarded moment with a servant. Caroline felt sure the young man had directed the photographer to capture this woman's image as if by accident.

Gazing more closely, she realized with sudden sadness that the high line of the woman's apron barely disguised her pregnancy. No matter how much love there might have been between them, this young man would be no match for the hatred his kind would heap on her and her child.

She turned the photograph over, expecting to find that this was a younger brother Alex had left behind in Wales. Only the name and location of the photographer were handwritten there. *H.M. Evans, ffotograff, Machynlleth, Cymru* – and a date, *1851.*

1851. About thirty years too early to be a brother. Yet this clearly was some relative of Alex's, so Caroline was puzzled at its being hidden in a chest belonging to Gryf. Still, she decided, this ancient business should not concern her. She tucked the photo back into the lining of the chest and set about clearing up the mess while searching for anything that might shed light on the one who hated him so deeply.

Several times during the day, the marshal's horse could be heard loping up and down the road. Late in the afternoon, he stopped in front of the cabin. Caroline rushed into the storage room and opened the window. She upturned the mop bucket to use as a footstool. She was seated on the window-sill, ready to swing her legs out when she heard Samuel's voice next door.

"Marshal?"

"Ayyup?"

"Could I show you something that might help in your investigations?"

"What ya got there?"

She heard his boots squeak as the marshal trudged toward Samuel and Susan's cabin.

"Letters from a miner friend in Pennsylvania – shed some light on that earlier murder."

Caroline hitched down onto the bucket and pulled the window near shut. Listen as she might, she could hear no more of their conversation. She felt certain that out of all the times the marshal passed on the road, Samuel had waited to hail him at a time when he might be about to enter this cabin. Either Samuel was aware of her hiding here, or he wanted to keep the marshal from finding something in the cabin.

Could Samuel have caused this mess? What could he gain from discrediting Gryf? Would he inherit these mines?

Knowing how deeply Gryf loved his brother, she prayed that Samuel was not the cause of his grieving. As the sun sank toward dusk, Caroline had plenty of time to think. The more she worked and thought, the more she questioned the speed with which Allied learned of Gryf's arrest. Moreover, their sudden willingness to send tools about which they previously had stalled, that smelled of low intent. She needed more information about communications between By-Gum and Allied Mines, and she had an idea what she'd have to do to get it.

After dark, she slipped out of the cabin and crept toward the lean-to at the side of Gryf's cabin. Grasping the door handle, she saw there had been a lock on the door, but its shank was cut and left to hang as if it still worked. In the darkness, she felt the shank and found grooves like those made by the type of tool she sought. Someone had hacked at the shank with a metal cutter. She opened the door carefully, expecting to find a jumble of tools. In the darkness, however, she could see nothing but the dirt floor and on each side of the door, shelves lined with neat jars and vats – Gryf's

327

other preserved food storage. Its organization testified to his usual neat ways.

She thought, whoever trashed the cabin last night was sure they would find nothing in here. Why?

She stepped inside, listened for scuttling feet, but heard none. Toward the back of the shed, her boot bumped into a large basket. As it scooted away from her accidental kick, she heard the sound of metal scraping against rock. She lifted the basket and tested the floor area with a sweep of her toe. As soon as she kicked it, she knew what it was – the metal cutting tool she needed – fence mending pliers with a powerful cutter in the blade.

She remembered Deirdre saying that Gryf found his fisherman's jacket out here when he expected it to be inside the cabin. Someone might have stolen it, used it and returned it to the shed as incriminating evidence. That would explain why there was no need to search the shed. The person had already done that on a previous night.

She decided on a course of action. Someone in By-Gum was a traitor to Gryf, of that she was sure – and they had a connection with Allied. That connection would account for the speed of Allied's response to Gryf's predicament. There was one place nearby where she might discover the traitor's identity – in Isabeau, at the telegraph office.

**

Her pebbles seemed to explode against the shutter. Caroline feared they would wake the whole house. The shutter above her creaked open.

"Who goes there?" Jimmy whispered, "Friend or foe?"

She smiled. "Friend." *He's been reading adventure magazines.*

"Miss Trewartha?"

She stepped into the moonlight. "Jimmy, come down," she whispered.

Jimmy pushed the shutter back against the house siding and climbed out onto the porch roof. To her astonishment, a second boy followed him from his bedroom. Within seconds, she recognized that scrawny body. It was the street urchin from Denver. Her heart sank. There'd be no helping Gryf when the very boy who had spoken against him knew she was no longer unconscious in the barn loft. She backed up, ready to disappear, but reluctant to leave without commissioning Jimmy for Gryf's safety.

Both boys dropped silently into the shrubbery, but the taller boy hung back as Jimmy strode toward her.

"Miss," Jimmy whispered harshly as his little arms grabbed her about the waist. "Mum said you was in awful shape."

She hugged him. "I'm getting strong."

He glanced up at her. "You look swell," he said. "But this is Gryf's shirt."

She whispered, "I'll tell you about that later." Glancing toward his companion she whispered, "I need to give you a secret job. And you mustn't tell your friend."

"Aw, Jacko's all right," he declared. "He didn't finger Gryf on purpose."

Aware of the effect of Jack's street talk on Jimmy's vocabulary, Caroline realized the Denver boy must be Jimmy's new idol.

She decided to have it out with the older boy here and now. Speaking toward his skinny shadow she said, "Since 'Jacko' got our Gryf arrested, I'd say he's a long way from 'all right'."

"Miss," said Jack, stepping forward, "I worked for Mr. Brown. We was good friends. I want to find the guy what done 'im in. Jimmy here says it wasn't Mr. Gryf Williams, an' I know he believes that, certain sure. But I gotta know who it was."

"What about your connection to Marshal Jeffers?"

"He come lookin' for me on account o' someone reminded him I was at the scene o' the explosion. I said I'd help him find the one if'n I could."

Caroline decided to take Jack at face value. She turned to Jimmy and said. "You don't want to put Jack in an awkward position – make him choose between honesty to the marshal and safety for Gryf, so keep this under your lid." She walked a little bit away. When she glanced back, she was relieved to see that Jack had turned away from them, and Jimmy was following her. Out of earshot of Jack she whispered to Jimmy, "You take these fence-mending pliers and climb under Gryf's office in the dark of night. Knock lightly. Gryf'll open a hole in the floor and let you in."

"Cut 'im loose?"

She nodded. "Somebody's been mighty free with my dynamite around here and we don't want Gryf trapped if they start to blow things up."

"If'n you know about this hole, how come you didn't just go there?"

Oh, how much I want to see Gryf again . . .

"I've got to investigate some ideas," she said to Jimmy. "I must go tonight"

When Jimmy hugged her good-bye, scrawny Jack, whispered loudly toward them, "Miss, ifn' I was a grown up that people would take serious, I'd be tryin' to find out who told the marshal to come lookin' fer me. I'd be wondering about that deputy in Denver, the one that come on the scene of the crime directly with the fire engine."

Caroline stared at Jack. In the moonlight, he seemed such a twiggy-haired boy, but she remembered his quick-minded leadership of the other lads as they pursued the man who jumped from the window. And now, he was following the same mental trail

330

she intended to search out. "Jack," she said. "I'm sorry your friend died."

"Mr. Isaac Brown paid me to do errands," Jack said in solemn tones. "Helped me learn my numbers and letters. I want to know who killed him."

"What else would you be searching for, if you were a grown up?"

"I'd be wanting to know who told the marshal Mr. Gryf was in Denver when ever' body else says he went to Sapinero."

Caroline stared at the boy. She could have hugged him for his clear-headed ways. Living on the streets of a bustling, hustling town had made him unusually capable of smelling a lie.

"Young man," she said, "I believe I can count on you and Jimmy for secrecy. I could use your help. Could you saddle Sheba without waking any guards?"

"We'll saddle Sheba," Jimmy whispered. "The marshal's man at the barn is fast asleep on Papa's beer. We was hoping you'd show up, me and Jack."

Caroline's head swam with the implications of this statement. "What else are you and Jack planning for?"

Jimmy shuffled a bit, "Sorta hoping you'd figure out where this come from 'fore it was in Gryf's saddle bag." Behind Jimmy, Jack held out a ragged-edged straw hat.

"That's . . ."

"Yes'm."

"Jimmy, did you . . ."

"Marshal forgot it on our table. I been taking care of it. Gots a label inside. Maybe that'll help."

As she reached for the hat, Jack said, "Come on, Jimbo. We gotta get that horse out afore that fellow wakes."

**

At two in the morning, Gryf lay on his bed imagining Caroline safely hidden in his cabin. He hoped to God she would stay there through the night while Jeffers hunted for Rankin. Someone who knew the schoolhouse in detail had sprung Rankin during the previous night – up through the hidden ladder that pierced the storage room ceiling, then out the bell tower and down the roof. Jeffers' second visit today had been to question Gryf about Rankin's escape.

Caroline would be all right, if she stayed put. He hoped she was warm enough without a fire in the wood stove. There were plenty of his mother's quilts in the blanket chest.

Stay home, Caroline.

Tilting his head back, he imagined her exploring his home, watched her touching his chair, shaking her head over his dirty boots, laying her slender fingers on his mantel, brushing her palm over his wood carvings where they sat on the shelf. She would tire, he thought. She had been through so much in the last ten days. Her eyelids would feel heavy, her foot would throb. She would head for his sleeping bench. In his mind, he breathed in the scent of her on his pillow. His foresight, thank goodness, had nudged him to change the sheets.

He sat upright. Alex might stop for the night, as he did often, too tired to ride out to his ranch.

Don't, Alex, Gryf thought. Please don't.

He heard a soft knock on his office floor. Relief washed through him. With quiet haste, he moved his desk and his rug to have Caroline safely near him. When he pulled away the last board, the pinched face that appeared was Jimmy Freya's.

"Where's . . .?" His question halted as Jimmy put a finger to his mouth. Jimmy's other hand reached up through the floor. In his small square fist, Gryf saw a pair of fence-mending pliers, with

332

wicked metal cutters in the inner portion of the blade. Gryf grabbed the pliers and then hauled Jimmy up through the floor.

Once Jimmy was standing before him, Gryf rasped his concern. "Where is she?"

"Gone down to Isabeau, sir," Jimmy whispered.

"Goddam," Gryf hissed. "On foot?"

"I saddled Sheba for her."

His skin grew cold. "Sheba? Don't you know what's going on here?"

"It's okay. The guard at the barn took sick on Dad's hooch."

Gryf's stomach tightened with fear. He leveled his gaze on Jimmy. "Rankin has escaped," he said. "Jeffers told me this afternoon."

Jimmy paled. "He's out there?"

"Who's with her?"

Jimmy shook his head, a maddening, slow motion. "I tried to go," he assured Gryf, "but she said Mom would kill her. Plus," he pointed to the pliers, "I had to give you these in case some guy tried to kill you in here."

Gryf closed his eyes. In his mind, he saw each of the places on the road to Isabeau where a man might wait for prey. His spine shivered at the memory of one tight turn that hid a sudden drop.

"I have to get out of here now," he said. "Hold this chain tight, so I can cut it."

Jimmy took the chain between both hands at a place near Gryf's wrist. At Gryf's direction, the boy held the links down against the top of the heavy desk. Gryf plied the tool against one side of one link, leaning with his free hand on the upper armature of the plier. The cutter made a small groove in the link. He raised the arm of the tool again, and leaned all his weight atop the cutting arm. A deeper groove appeared, halfway through the link. Once more, he opened the tool and once more he put his weight into the cutting arm. He felt a sudden give in the metal. As it popped, the office door burst open behind him. The boot step was too familiar.

Marshal Jeffers placed a hand over the pliers. "I'll take these," he said. "And then you and this boy here can tell me how you helped Miss Trewartha escape."

As Gryf put an arm around Jimmy, he felt the boy slip something into the pocket of his overalls – something round and heavy.

CHAPTER THIRTY-ONE

The town of Isabeau slept as Caroline entered. Saddle-sore, road weary, and jittery from hearing every night bird along the trail, she crept down the railroad track into town. She hid Sheba in the barn near the railroad station, took her revolver out of her belt and moved from shadow to shadow down main street until she found the door of the telegraph office. If she could find a way into the office, she'd have a little time to investigate by herself before the telegrapher arrived.

Expecting nothing, she twisted the doorknob. The door creaked open.

"Miss Trewartha, I presume."

She jerked at the voice, afraid the marshal had caught up with her. Raising her revolver, she peered into the darkness. Behind the counter stood the shadow of a stout man. From his profile against the window shade, she could tell he chewed on a fat cigar. "You know me?" she asked.

He nodded. "Had a mighty lot of correspondence go through this office because of you."

"Abel?"

"The same."

"What correspondence?"

"Started when Allied Mines changed hands – warnings to Gryf Williams to expect you."

"And recently?"

"Warrant for Gryf's arrest. Then yesterday, a warrant for you."

She eyed him, waiting for him to make a move against her.

335

"The *Wanted* description didn't say the dangerous criminal was a dame wearing a fella's shirt, and pants so long she can hardly walk in 'em."

Afraid to let her attention waver, Caroline slipped inside the door and allowed it to close, then she raised her revolver toward him again. "What do you know about me?"

He merely shrugged and said, "Hardy Gilchrist was in town two days before you arrived from Denver with that big crate."

Surprised at his offer of information, Caroline wondered at his purpose. From what she'd heard, Abel did nothing Abel didn't want to do. "Who else arrived with Gilchrist?" she asked.

He shifted the cigar to the other side of his mouth before he answered. "Several men – a fat gut, a little runt – ain't seen most of them since then, except the fellow who signs himself 'Mr. Thomas Wood'."

That name. She knew it. "This Thomas Wood looks like . . .?"

"Like some ranch hand. Boots. Chaps. Suntan that's permanent from living outdoors year-round. Real big. Lean face. Wears a tail of hair"

She felt her mouth open and shut, gawping at Abel like a useless mule. All she could think about was that the fellow with the queue had arrived with Gilchrist, and others – men whose description fit Kidde and the little dynamiter who died in the cavern under the ridge. And all of them came well before the explosions that killed Jesse Polgren and flooded the main mine.

Then she realized what else Abel had said. "This man signs his name as Thomas Wood? You mean he's been in here to send telegrams?"

"Yep. You about to send one yourself?"

"In the dark?"

"Pull down the door shade," Abel said. "Then we can get some work done without announcing ourselves to other visitors."

Alone with this man in an isolated office? She was on her guard immediately. "What work?"

"I figured it would be Gryf, comin' in here to investigate. I figured that right up until Denver's Marshal Jeffers and his crew whipped into town on the train looking for Gryf. After that, I decided to sleep here – wait and see who did come."

"You figuring on helping anybody who walks in your door?"

"You've been given authority to manage the mines. Took that message yesterday."

She couldn't guess who had Abel's allegiance, but she needed to know. "Do you think Allied has the right to give me that authority?"

"Nope. What do you think?"

Since he'd given a hint of his thoughts, she decided to tell him the truth. "I think someone in By-Gum seems to work for Gryf but works instead for Allied. How else would Allied know he'd been arrested?"

"That's been on my mind. Frankly, I'd rather work with Gryf Williams than a company that treats a man like scum soon as he's arrested."

Well, she thought, we're within striking distance of an alliance.

Hoping to ease her way toward investigating his telegraph records, Caroline pulled the tattered straw hat from under her cape. "Do you know anyone who owns a hat like this?"

Abel studied the wrecked hat brim. "I know a lady who sells such lamp shades. Don't know anybody who'd admit to owning one."

"It was worn by the murderer of Isaac Brown."

"Then I'd ask old Letitia Heenie – sells just this kind of trip-trap. She's gone to Denver to replenish her stock, but she's due back in two days."

Caroline's hope fell. In two days, the marshal would have Gryf and Rankin on the train to Denver. "I've got to talk to her."

337

"I'll ask her for you, if you decide to trust me. Bring you the word myself."

Studying his unwavering eyes, she knew she must trust him. She lay the hat on the counter. "Thank you, sir. That information is vital to Mr. Williams."

He nodded. "You plan to send a telegram, or just discuss haberdashery?"

She stiffened her courage and pulled down the door shade. Abel struck something. A flare of light sent Caroline ducking below the counter until she recognized the sulfur smell and realized he'd merely scratched a light stick for the lamp.

So much for complete trust, she chided herself.

As she rose from her hiding place, Abel seemed to notice neither her disappearance nor her reappearance. He adjusted the lamp to burn low so it couldn't be seen from outside. With his sleeves rolled up and his glasses sliding down his nose toward the fat cigar in his mouth, he looked exactly like the man Gryf had told her about.

Nevertheless, instead of asking him revealing questions, she requested a telegraph form. Using the cipher she and her father had once worked out, she asked Dad to ferret out the truth about Allied's ownership, and about Terry Branahan. She signed her name, also in code, so that the corrupted Denver agent could make no connection between this message and her. She paid for her message to be sent to Philadelphia, and watched Abel rattle it off into the telegraph machine in a professional, speedy manner. Praying that she'd trusted the right person, she plunged into the search for Gryf's enemy.

"Four days ago, Mr. Kemp sent a telegram from here to Isaac Brown, Mr. Williams' lawyer."

He hesitated a moment, then lifted the lid on a small oak box he kept nearby. Inside, he had filed telegrams, evidently in chronological order. He thumbed through. "Here it is. Told Brown you were coming to visit."

"That's the one. Later that evening, Mr. Kemp sent a message from Denver, asked you to reply to him in the Denver office."

Abel looked at her for a long moment, working his lips and his cigar in and out as if he were thinking, then said, "You know I shouldn't talk about the contents of other people's messages."

She felt as brilliant as a moss-covered rock. She couldn't think of a way to get the information she needed without completely breaking his professional ethics.

Needle his professional pride.

"Someone diverted the replies you sent to Alex that night," she said. "Our investigators followed their delivery to people of questionable character. Your telegraph system isn't as secure as you might hope."

His face went blank. "That right?"

"Yes, 'tis. And I think that's why Mr. Williams' lawyer was murdered. Earlier that same day, Mr. Kemp's message from here to Brown must also have been diverted."

She saw Abel's jaw tighten. She knew she risked his anger, risked even more if he was the one who sent messages to the wrong people. Still, she had to discover what was going on – had to know who to trust, so she pushed on. "Someone besides Brown learned we were coming," she said. "That person didn't want me talking to Gryf's lawyer, so he got rid of him."

Abel chewed on his cigar, staring at his hands. He fingered the box edge, as if caressing the smooth orderliness of it. Abruptly, he turned and hauled down a notebook, opening it on the counter. "Let me enter your telegram into the log, Miss Trewartha."

She sagged against the counter. He would not help her find out who was sabotaging the mines and setting Gryf up for a murder trial.

Abel pulled out his cigar and began to leaf through the book, "This here is the log of all the telegrams in and out this year," he said. He took up a pen and began inking in the date.

"March 12, 1880," he said as he wrote.

"Mr. . . ., Abel," she said. He looked up at her, his eyebrows higher than his glasses' rims. "Today is May twenty-fifth."

He glanced back at his book, "Oh. So it is. Not March twelfth at all, is it?"

Leaving the date, Abel moved to the next line and wrote the proper information. Caroline watched how carefully and completely he noted the date. With meticulous care, he checked the spelling of her code name, and of her father's code name as the recipient. Puzzled, she glanced again at the previous line, which he did not cross out as a mistake.

Abel finished his logbook, left it on the counter and filed her own message in his box.

"Miss Trewartha, I surely do need a cup of coffee," he said, chewing his cigar in a slow circular motion. "You've seen how I log in my messages, so you can take messages for me to send when I get back. Do you suppose you could watch the office while I dart down to the hotel dining room?"

She stared at him.

"Just be a half hour," he said. "and I could bring you a mighty nice biscuit for your trouble."

Certain he was either very clever or very loco, she also realized this was a gift chance. "I'd be delighted to help you out, Mr. . . . ?"

"Mr. Klauswitz," he said, stuffing his unlit cigar back in his mouth. "Abel Klauswitz. Much obliged, ma'am." He tossed a coat over his arm, rolled down his right sleeve and stepped out onto the board walk. As he left, Caroline saw him twist a key in the door lock. By the time he slammed the door, it was too late to escape that way.

rescue Olaf – nothing to support his claim to have been called there when she was in Denver, witnessing Brown's murder.

Then, she found a recent telegram to Marshal Jeffers, written in a crabbed hand.

Advise yu find boy in Denver name Jack Dorset. Bring By-Gum, immediately. He cin identify murderer Isaac Brown.

Mr. Thomas Wood

The spelling went askew in simple words, but was meticulous in longer ones – an odd carelessness, Caroline thought. Only a day later, Mr. Wood sent a second message, this time to Morton Hume, President of Allied Mines. It read

Send machinery. Predicted trouble requires message we agrede on. All do speed.

This message showed the same combination of care and inattention in spelling, as well as the awkward handwriting. Caroline pondered the message behind the message. It was the fellow with the queue who sent the message to bring up the marshal and Jack. It was this same fellow who communicated with Allied.

She peaked behind the shade on the Main Street window. No one seemed to be out there – no posse, anxious for her arrest. But she must hurry. She needed a clue to Mr. Wood's purpose and plan. And she needed it before Abel Klauswitz found the sheriff.

An idea flashed like sunlight. The tail-haired fellow, Mr. Wood, copied a message written for him by someone else. That would account for the misspellings – short words he thought he knew, long ones he copied carefully.

The clack of the telegraph apparatus sent Caroline's heart into her throat. The thing clattered for several moments, then sat still. Was this an answer from her father already? There was no way to receive it with Abel gone. She watched the machine sit, mute and shining. And as it did nothing, she thought about how telegrams reached By-Gum. She needed that reply from Dad, yet she didn't want to be here when Abel brought the lawman. If she were not here, Abel might send the answer to By-Gum. Maybe the marshal would intercept it, see it was in code and send it to a cryptographer. Perhaps it would be given to Gryf. It all depended on who Abel asked to deliver it – it could go completely astray just like the message Alex received for her from Allied, delivered by a fellow who got lost in the night and never saw the town.

Back to the logbook, she read the name of the courier Abel had used to send Brown's March 12th message to Gryf. *Joe Bosco.* Glancing through the logbook, she saw the name of Joe Bosco as messenger delivering many messages before March 12th. After March 12th, his name never appeared.

At that moment, the machine clattered once more. Even as her heart slowed, the door to the office burst open and in stepped Abel – Abel, by himself.

"Everything all right?" he asked as he closed and relocked the door. Wary of him, Caroline lifted the heavy ledger, ready to use it if necessary. He glanced at her and at the book. He carried a plate, covered with a linen napkin. He set the plate on the counter next to her.

"Your biscuit," he said. And when she didn't move, he glanced at the locked door. "Don't like to encourage business before ten in the morning."

She lowered the book, slightly. "Thanks," she said, and uncovered the biscuit.

His machine clacked once more. He stepped behind the counter and tapped on the key, plopped into his desk chair, pulling his much-chewed cigar from his pocket while he waited for a reply. "Wouldn't be surprised if this were your answer," he ventured. "I put an urgent on it. Boys down the line do their best to get things rolling when I do that."

"What happened to Joe Bosco?" she asked.

Abel's eyebrow shot up. His cigar rose like a semaphore. "Don't know. Bosco always said he was going to move on. Maybe he did. Maybe he fell off his horse."

"Did Gryf ever get that message?"

"It needed a reply. It never got one. I'd have to guess he didn't."

"You never asked?"

"You walked in here an hour ago. Showed yourself to me – a stranger – in spite of an arrest notice for you just coming across the wires. I thought to myself, a powerful want of information sent you here. And that was the first time I thought I should have followed up on Bosco and that telegram."

Caroline flipped open the logbook. "Who carried the recent telegram from Allied Mines to me?"

He didn't have to say it. In the logbook she saw it was carried to By-Gum by Mr. Wood.

Abel's machine gave another dit-dit-dit. For the next minute, he transcribed the code, while she ate the warm biscuit. Thirty seconds after the machine stopped, he finished writing. He waved the paper to dry the ink as he stood up.

"Sign here," he said, flipping the logbook open to a fresh page. She flourished the 'T'.

"Your papa loves you," he said as he dropped the message on the counter beside her.

She glanced at him. He deciphered our code!

Abel smiled. "I learned all kinds of codes in the Union Army. You been asking the right questions. You're a friend of Gryf. I'm a friend of Gryf. You're safe with me."

Caroline took a deep breath and relaxed at last. After all, he did give her time to find out what his logbook could tell her.

Her father's message read:

Danger! Money behind Allied takeover is family named Gwydden – means forest or trees in Celtic. New emblem on Allied stationery is fighting cat with wings. Claws out. Careful. Branahan found dead in empty mine in Schuylkill. I once exposed owner of same mine for misrepresenting mineral and carboniferous content to my client. Attempted bribe. Vicious. Owner's name was Thomas Wood.

Am on my way. Love, Dad

Stunned, Caroline read the long telegram three times. The name Thomas Wood, over and over again. Celtic-Welsh, and English. She remembered the letter in her room above the barn, the letter she'd thought had no significance – a Mr. Thomas Wood searching for his sons – an obvious trap, laid for Gryf – a man so dangerous her father dropped everything to come to Colorado.

The cat with wings – the filly behind Isaac's office had such a brand. The horse belonged to the murderer. The same symbol on the ring on the hand of the man in the cave. Gryf knew who it was that used that symbol.

Gryf. She must return to By-Gum immediately. She had to warn him.

She looked up into Abel's thoughtful eyes and said, "If anybody named 'Wood' comes in here, you nail his hand to this counter."

Abel's cigar stood straight up. Gazing at Caroline, he said, "I surely plan to". He reached under his counter and hauled out a Winchester rifle. "Take this and this box of ammunition. Gryf wants you safe."

She stared at him until he pushed the box into her hand.

He said, "Now you go out the back way through the storeroom."

She holstered her revolver, took her message, and the rifle, and started toward the back, but Abel said, "I got two questions."

Glancing over her shoulder, she waited.

345

He said, "Do you trust Duncan?"

"Is there a reason I shouldn't?"

"Nope. I asked him to make sure you got back to By-Gum safely."

"Why him?"

"Gryf bought him that wagon and gave him his team. Said he needed a good man on the roads."

"Then I trust him. And question two?"

"What's your Dad look like?"

"Blond turning white, taller than me, shorter than Gryf. Red mustache and beard. Why?"

Abel lifted a wooden toolbox. "Don't want to maim the wrong man."

CHAPTER THIRTY-TWO

"You're too late," Duncan said as he fiddled with Sheba's bridle. "There's already a wagon gone to By-Gum. Fellow name of Stemmins brought the steam engine what lifts a miner's cage up the shaft."

Caroline slumped against the door of the livery barn. Any other day, she would have been elated to have that engine. It meant getting the coal out faster. But getting out coal was no longer her main concern.

"The marshal," she said, "will commandeer that wagon to bring Gryf and Rankin to Denver."

"Beggin' your pardon, miss," Duncan said, "but he'll be lookin' to transport you, too. According to Abel, you been accused of murderin' one of Rankin's buddies."

Caroline's stomach turned at the memory. She pushed away from the door, stowed the Winchester and box in Sheba's gear, then tightened the cinch on Sheba's girth before she could talk.

"I bollixed the guy with a pick handle, but Rankin killed him." She flipped the stirrup apron down over the cinch and grabbed the pommel and saddle to hoist herself.

Duncan hoisted his saddle over a large gelding. "I'll take you to Gryf, Miss Trewartha, and then I'll make that Stemmins' wagon useless."

"Good idea, but tough to accomplish. Marshal Jeffers will have set up a search for me by now."

Duncan patted the withers of his horse. "Methuselah here can smell another horse miles away. Best lookout we got."

Glancing at the gelding's bright eyes, she frowned. "Methuselah – Is he very old?"

"Nope. Gonna become very old, with me." He shot a tentative smile over his shoulder at her.

Surprised at this show of humor from one so taciturn, she laughed, and added, "May you live to be ancient, and enjoy every year of it."

Duncan blushed as he offered her a hand up onto Sheba, but Caroline had already pulled a sawhorse next to her mount and was swinging her leg over. After pulling bandanas over their faces to keep out the trail dust, Caroline and Duncan urged the horses onto the steep path.

For the first hours of their ride, Caroline kept her hand near the Abel's Winchester in her saddle holster. Duncan kept his buffalo gun slung over his arm. Duncan elected to stay behind her, saying "Gryf'd pull my teeth if someone was to hurt you. I'll stay back here, 'cause I can see in front and I can feel those behind me."

Moving into the last hour on the trail, Caroline pulled the Winchester from its holster. She tightened the ammunition belt at her waist and stood in the stirrups. She wanted a better look at the terrain. She also had a cramp in her right leg that needed stretching.

"Don't give 'em any taller target than you gotta, Miss." Duncan drawled as he rode up beside her.

Before she could comment, Duncan's gelding screamed. Methuselah rose on his haunches, came down with a thundering of hooves. In his pain, he shouldered Sheba to the side and took off up the steep, narrow trail.

Then Caroline heard the crack of a rifle. There was no need to tell Sheba what to do. Sheba bolted up the trail with Caroline gripping the saddle aprons between her knees, holding on to Sheba's mane with one hand, and to Abel's Winchester with the other. There was nothing for it but to trust the mare and stay low.

She held so low over Sheba's back that the pommel hit her in the stomach when the mare's muscles bunched for each new stride forward, but Caroline was more aware of the third shot behind her.

As Sheba rounded an abrupt curve in the trail, her hooves skidded on the rocks. Her hind legs scrambled in the effort to keep from sliding off the trail. The mare, in agonizing desperation, flailed for purchase on the edge of the cliff. Caroline lifted herself up, pivoted her knees and threw her own weight toward Sheba's ears. As if encouraged by this instinctive move, Sheba grabbed for earth with all four feet, righted herself and tore off again down the trail.

Caroline was sure that each leap forward would bring her completely off the horse's back. Her left-hand fingers were painfully twisted in Sheba's mane. Any fall would leave her dragging next to the mare.

Sheba's gait changed abruptly from headlong gallop to sedate trot. The mare raised her neck as if a sulky were harnessed behind her. Caroline regained the grip of her knees. Untangling her fingers, she discovered the reins looped about the pommel. The rifle seemed to be glued in the stiff grip of her other hand.

Ahead, she saw no Methuselah and no Duncan, and no apparent reason for the sudden control after Sheba's headlong panic. Sheba's quick trot covered trail at an enormous rate, slowing slightly as they approached the next bend around a rock palisade. There, one hundred yards in front of them, Methuselah slumped in the middle of the trail. No Duncan sat in the saddle.

Above them, columns of ancient, cooled magma leaned over the narrow road. The winter ice atop the cliff melted, becoming waterfalls, tumbling down the cliff face. Scanning the top of the cliff, she could see no sign of a rifleman, yet, Caroline's neck cooled with awareness of malevolent watchers.

She knew he'd be a fool to step close to the edge of that melting ice field. As long as he stayed back from the edge and she stayed in the shadow of the cliff overhang, she would be safe. She turned her attention to the near-vertical slope on the downhill side of the trail. Her throat closed on a moan as she saw Duncan's body, prone, seventy feet below amidst rocks and sage-covered soil.

Reigning in Sheba, she swung out of the saddle. "Duncan. Duncan, can you hear me?"

Tense, afraid to be given away by her own echo, Caroline watched his body. Nothing. She imagined the rise and fall of his back that would signal breath. He was a good man. And Gryf couldn't stand to lose another friend.

Thirty yards down the trail, Methuselah shuddered above a dark patch in the dust. From his saddle, loops of rope hung, neatly tied to a thong. She glanced at Duncan and saw no change, no movement. Sheba nickered and cantered down the trail toward Methuselah. Caroline followed on the run, aware now of stiffness in every place where the pommel had bruised her body. By the time she arrived, Sheba licked Methuselah's wound. Caroline pushed Sheba aside and discovered that a bullet had entered his right shoulder, leaving a small hole surrounded by bruised flesh.

"Don't worry, old boy. I'm going to get Duncan and then we'll get you home. That's a promise."

Sheba nudged Caroline away from the wound. Caroline looked both horses in the eyes and found only dull pain in Methuselah's gaze, but a brilliant determination in Sheba's. She trusted that look. Sheba had proved worthy many times over.

"Take care of him, girl. I'll be back."

Lifting Duncan's big rifle, ammunition belt and rope Caroline ran back up the trail. A quick look at the cliff tops revealed no one, but she figured it was only a matter of time before the rifleman showed up to finish what he'd begun. She wanted all the tools for survival with her.

350

Even as she thought it, she heard the plod of horse hooves on the trail behind her. She turned to level the rifle at her attacker, but a heartening scene met her. There, following her, Sheba guided Methuselah – keeping him moving slowly toward Caroline's position above Duncan's body. For some reason, Sheba deemed it important not to be separated. And somehow, their closeness gave Caroline strength.

Caroline took another look at the gelding's shoulder, and then, remembering his second scream of pain, she looked for other wounds. An ugly bullet had smashed into the leather of the saddle. Blood already dried on the stirrup apron, but when she lifted it, she found the bullet had not pierced the thick leather

The blood must have come from Duncan's leg. Caroline reached for the bandana at her neck and felt relief to find it still there. She studied the rocks and scrubby trees nearby and decided they were too weak rooted to use as pulleys. Taking a chance on Sheba's stolid character, Caroline wrapped the rope once around the pommel of Methuselah's saddle and quickly tied one end to Sheba's pommel.

"Back, Sheba." she ordered. And Sheba backed, keeping the rope running smoothly around Methuselah's pommel. "Sheba, whoa." Sheba stopped. Methuselah didn't move a muscle.

Gryf must have trained them both, she thought.

She unfurled the rest of the length of rope and saw that it lay a few feet short of Duncan's inert body. Gently, she coaxed Methuselah closer to the edge of the path. He complied gallantly, but his eyes still glazed with pain.

"Methuselah, I need your help. You must stand firm, old boy."

From the roll behind her saddle, Caroline pulled the tightly woven wool rug that served as a ground blanket. After a moment's debate, she hid the rifles in the shrubs along the side of the trail. They would hinder Duncan's rescue if she took them with her. Yet she didn't want rifles available for the men who stalked them. Slinging the leather ties of the rug-roll over her shoulder, she tied the rope around her waist and backed down the slope, step by precarious step toward Duncan.

Let him be alive, she prayed. Let Duncan be alive.

As she lowered herself, she aimed for an area behind Duncan's legs, hoping that if she loosened any rock, it would not roll toward him. She knew from the lowering of Methuselah's head that she could not count on his help for much longer.

Reaching Duncan's elevation, she moved toward his body, freeing the rope from shrubs and rocks as she crossed the slope. He had lost a great pool of blood from his leg wound. His breathing grew shallow.

She joined her neck scarf to his and turned the two of them into a tourniquet, stopping the bleeding of his right leg. She tightened the scarves with a juniper twig, then turned his body into the wool rug.

Twisting the two leather thongs together, she tied them around his chest and wove them through four spots in the wool. Then, she untied herself from the safety rope and tied it to the end of the rug nearest his head, forming a travois.

"Back Sheba," she called. Sheba backed. The rug fibers strained against Duncan's weight. The rug pulled taut and began to move slowly uphill, directly toward a rock.

"Sheba, whoa."

Caroline climbed above his body, loosened the rope from the rock, directed the travois to its right and called out to Sheba again. Climbing above him, and beside him, stopping and pulling, Caroline cleared the path for Duncan's carpet.

By the time they arrived at the trail, Caroline sweated almost as much as Duncan's shocked body. She hastened to untie the rope from Sheba and Methuselah, then grabbed Duncan's bedroll from behind Methuselah's saddle. She spread it over his chest and then loosened the tourniquet from around his leg.

"May you live many years," she muttered as she worked. "Live to be Methuselah."

The bleeding did not resume right away. That heartened Caroline into hoping the bullet hadn't hit an artery. When blood did come, it slow dripped. She tightened the tourniquet again and set about figuring how to get Duncan over Sheba's back.

As she stood, she realized the question had become moot. There in the road beyond her stood a man glaring down his rifle barrel at her. She dropped to the ground, hollering at the horses, "Hah! Hah!"

As Sheba and Methuselah bolted up the road, creating confusion with their dust, she rolled into the bush that hid Able's rifle. Caroline came up ready, but she couldn't shoot. Amos rose from the road behind the man. She flopped back down and hugged dirt. The rifleman's shot whizzed over her head and thudded into the ground ten yards beyond her. She waited.

As soon as she heard the clang of a shovel, she sat back up and watched the rifleman's slow crumple to the roadbed. At his back, Amos stood ready to deliver a second whack.

Behind Amos, Rudy Sperl crept from the shadow of a rock outcrop. Fearing for Amos, Caroline shouted, "Behind you ..."

He wheeled, bringing the shovel around. Rudy dodged. Amos dropped the shovel and reached out to steady Rudy. Caroline heard Amos' ragged voice saying, "Sorry old man, I thought we had a 'complice or somethin'."

"Miss Treewart there thinks I *am* an accomplice."

The rifleman groaned. Amos rounded on him. "I'll hog-tie this one," he said to Rudy. "You signal that boy."

Rudy faced toward By-Gum, put two fingers in his mouth and let out a shrieking whistle.

Caroline called down to the two men, "Can we get Duncan to Deirdre, quick?"

Rudy glanced at her. "Can if you don't lop off my head."

"I'm sorry. I thought . . . well, you know what I thought."

" 'Fraid I do," said Rudy as he strode up to bend over Duncan's body.

Below them, she heard the bump and rumble of a heavy wagon. She glanced at Rudy.

"Us and the boy heard the rifle shots," he said. "Come to investigate." He wrapped Duncan tightly in the bedroll as he continued to talk. "There sat this wagon, crosswise of the road and nobody driving it. Left the boy and a gun. Me and Amos got real quiet and kept climbing. We seen you bringing Duncan from below, and then we seen this fellow waiting for you. So, we got ready to take him."

"I'm sorry about suspecting you."

Rudy glanced up at her. "I've give you a bad time, Miss Trewartha. 'Spose you couldn't tell it was worry, not mean-ness."

Caroline noticed he hadn't messed up her name – the first time since she arrived at By-Gum. Embarrassed by his understanding glance, she turned to catch the horses.

Sheba's curiosity brought her peaking around the next corner up the road. When Sheba saw friends, she nickered at Methuselah, encouraging him to join her. On the downhill side of the road, a big work wagon rolled into view, driven by Jack – the boy from Denver. He turned the wheels into the cliff and applied the brakes like a veteran.

Caroline bent over to search in the pockets of the fellow Amos beaned. His papers included a receipt from Samuel Williams for the steam powered motor. They had found the infamous Stemmins. He must have delivered the elevator motor and then, on the way back to Isabeau, decided to take out the mining engineer. If Duncan hadn't

354

ridden up next to her at that moment, she would be the one bleeding to death on the road to By-Gum.

**

Once Duncan lay safely on the straw in the back of the wagon, Caroline checked the horse's wound and then tied Methuselah behind the wagon and let Sheba follow. She climbed in next to Duncan, scanning the cliff tops above them for other snipers. She held Abel's rifle at the ready and kept Duncan's buffalo gun nearby. Jack clucked at the team and started after Amos and Rudy who, despite their age, were nearly running back to By-Gum. She kept glancing at Duncan, whose skin was cool to the touch, yet wet with sweat. They had to get him help as soon as possible.

"Miss," Jack said over his shoulder. "Marshal's got Jim Freya in custody at Jim's own house. Blames him for you escaping."

"Jimmy! Will the marshal take him to trial as well?"

"Can't tell. But Marshal Jeffers is real angry."

"Is Gryf still chained?"

" 'spect so. The marshal caught Jim trying to cut the chain. He took Jim and the fence cutters away."

"As long as he's chained to that stove, Gryf's at the mercy of this man who wants to kill him.

"I think I kin find a hack saw from the carpenter's shed."

Caroline glanced at Jack. Within the last few days, he'd developed from a boy to a very steady young man. There was a new strength to his jaw. She believed he would do all he could for Gryf. "We need your clear mind, Jack," she said.

He colored brightly but didn't respond. A few minutes later, he spoke over his shoulder, as if he were aware they might be watched. "I'll take that injured horse to Mac. First, I'll let you off near town. Mr. Gryf says you should go up to Mrs. Ellen Robert's ranch."

"How'm I going to figure out who killed Gryf's lawyer if I hide out up there?"

"How you gonna do it if the marshal catches you?"

That stumped her. At least she could lay low at Ellen's long enough to get an idea what to do next. She had no fix on where the man with the tail of hair hid out when he wasn't passing telegraph messages for 'Mr. Wood' – the man who wrote the messages for Tail-Hair to copy. Perhaps Ellen could help her figure out who 'Mr. Wood' really was.

Meanwhile, she watched the cliffs and asked Jack about the comings and goings at By-Gum so she knew who was accounted for, and who might have betrayed Gryf to the sheriff. Everyone except Olaf had been in and out of town during the last two days since she left for Isabeau.

Jack offered, "Jim told me to keep a look-out for this big guy, Olaf. Said he was not old, but with white-yella hair. Ain't seen 'im yet."

"I think Olaf's going to help Gryf if he can figure a way."

"I kin help him."

"Jack, would you to take a message to Gryf."

"Believe I kin get into that shack. Marshal don't know he should watch me."

"Tell Gryf that the man behind all these murders signs his name to telegrams as Mr. Wood. Mr. Wood tells Hume at Allied Mines what to do, as if he were Hume's boss. Allied is now owned by a family named Gwydden."

"What kind o' name is that?"

"Celtic, I think." She checked her message from Dad, then made a quick decision. She hauled out an old phosphorous stick and used it as a pen. Caroline translated the coded telegram and then pushed it toward Jack. "Careful with the charcoal writing. Give Gryf this telegram, it will explain."

With his free hand, Jack folded it carefully into his pocket.

Caroline said, "And tell Gryf that the man with his hair in a tail brings Wood's messages to the telegraph office at Isabeau."

"Mr. Wood, Hume at Allied Mines, the man with tail of hair," Jack repeated. "Got it."

As they topped the last rise before turning into town, Jack slowed the wagon.

"We'll do our best for Mr. Gryf and Duncan, Miss. You roll out and hide in that Juniper. We'll get everybody's attention when we whoosh into town with all this trouble. That's when you can make your getaway to Mrs. Robertson's."

"Jack, how come you to care about Gryf and Duncan?"

"Jimmy and his family, they take good care of me. I figure I can take care of people that's important to them."

"You're a good man, Jack."

He stared straight ahead. "I'm trying it. Now roll out right quick."

CHAPTER THIRTY-THREE

By the time Marshal Jeffers stomped onto the porch again, Gryf had filed halfway through one link on his chain. When the marshal stuck his key in the padlock, Gryf dropped the sharp rock Jimmy left him back into his pocket, and tried to act calm.

The door swung open. Olaf and Ellen stood on the front stoop, behind the marshal. Fearing Jeffers was about to arrest them for some new death among his friends, a cold dread swept Gryf.

"Have you found Rankin?" Gryf asked. The marshal shook his head. Gryf closed his eyes, but horrific images came to him anyway. None of Gryf's people had reported seeing Caroline since she left his office yesterday morning.

Jeffers paced into the small room, glancing with apparent satisfaction at the new boards his guards had nailed over the hole in the floor. "Williams," he said, opening the door wide so Olaf and Ellen could enter, "these two people have brought me a witness to the goings-on up at the mine."

Gryf breathed again. He glanced toward Olaf and held tight to the weakened end of his chain. "I found this fellow that was up there with Rankin." Olaf said, looking as innocent as a giant daisy.

"This Phil Hunt," drawled Jeffers, "he come with a story about some rich fellow down in Denver hiring them to bring him Miss Trewartha, and to get rid of you."

"What rich fellow?" Gryf asked.

"Phil Hunt says he never saw the man. Only heard about him from Rankin."

Gryf sat down. *We get only glimpses of this fellow.* Aloud he asked, "What else did Phil hear about him?"

The Marshal shrugged, "He wears swell clothes and a big gold ring with some kind of fancy animal on it."

Gryf thought, the winged cat rings? The only clue to the murderer's identity is the games keeper's ring on that little weasel in the cave. For Alex' sake, Gryf hoped the ring was a decoy. Yet after Rhodri Williams was shot and dismissed, who would have access to that ring but the Lord Gwydden, Alex's father? And Alex discovered that his father left England for America months ago.

Gryf believed Olaf had made a deal with Phil in order to get him to come in and confess, but he didn't know how much blame Phil was opting to take, and how much to load off onto him and Caroline. He glanced at Olaf, but it was Ellen who filled in the missing information. "Marshal, tell him about Gilchrist . . ."

"Miss Ellen . . ." Marshal Jeffers tried to stop her, but Ellen blathered as fast as Deirdre while she spilled the tale.

"Miss Trewartha couldn't have killed that Gilchrist fellow," she said. "Phil Hunt said she had no rifle when Rankin brought her down from the top of the hill behind the mine."

So, there it is. Phil spoke on Caroline's behalf. I will speak for him.

"Jeffers," Gryf said. "This Phil person, he tried to stop Rankin from burning Miss Trewartha's foot. I could hear him from down below."

"That right? Somethin' funny here," said Jeffers. "Want to tell me what it is?"

Again, it was Ellen who spoke. "Something is not funny, sir. Some evil person wants Gryf Williams dead and Caroline Trewartha kidnapped."

The marshal rounded on Gryf. "You got any idea where he might be?"

Gryf leaned toward Jeffers. "Some coward has been sending buzzards to murder my friends. And now he wants to kidnap the woman I love. If I knew how to find that person, he'd be dead."

**

At Ellen Robertson's ranch, Caroline could rouse no one, not even Ellen's boys, who were probably in town with her. This didn't surprise her. Ellen had been staying with friends in town while she and Deirdre took care of Caroline.

She wished for that care again, at this moment, because her foot hurt something fierce.

Since it was dark, she bedded down in the sweet hay of an empty stall in the barn. Nearby, two oxen and a horse munched, and whuffled, and settled for the night. She twisted about in the hay, trying to calm the itching in her healing foot, and also make sense of the pieces of the puzzle that she had.

She knew that 'Mr. Thomas Wood' wanted to leave Gryf in financial ruin and hanged for murder. She also knew that at one time or another, several men probably had worked for 'Wood' – Kidde, Rankin, Phil, and the man with the queue who delivered telegrams in Wood's name. But someone in town, someone Gryf thought was a friend directed all these people. Somehow, Mr. Wood's people knew that Caroline and Gryf would be at Mine Number Three the day after the dance. Most recently, someone had hired Stemmins to come after her and Duncan on the road from Isabeau. When she left By-Gum, yesterday, only Jimmy and Jack knew she intended to go to Isabeau. Was she wrong to trust them? Did Jimmy or Jack trust the wrong person?

If she knew who the boys told about her trip to Isabeau, she would have a short list of suspects. But she couldn't get to Jimmy and Jack safely. Wood could be anybody at By-Gum. She was certain he was at By-Gum. Some incidents had to have been set in motion by a person who worked among them, a person who knew where they intended to be. Perhaps one of the mine partners . . .

Cornell Ivisson? He's a relative newcomer to the group – was he sent to spy? But it was his work on the jury that exonerated Gryf.

Or could it be Olaf? Rudy? Amos? Mac Freya?

Mac Freya? She didn't want it to be Jimmy's father. Yet because of Deirdre and Jimmy, Mac had more knowledge of her comings and goings than Cornell and the other mining partners.

Alex? She supposed he might gain, if he were in Gryf's will. But he had his ranch and no apparent interest in mines outside of his friendship with Gryf. Down in Denver, it was Alex who dealt with the marshal's suspicions of her. And he'd convinced Stemmins to start delivering parts for the mine – the steam engine that Stemmins brought today was the first installment on that promise.

And after the delivery, who told Stemmins to come after Duncan and me?

Of one thing she was certain. The betrayal could not have come from Rudy or Amos. If they were part of the plot, they would not have rescued Duncan on the road.

Samuel? He signed Stemmin's receipt for the engine. Does Samuel Williams stand to inherit the By-Gum Mines if Gryf dies?

Caroline didn't want to believe that either. Yet money was a powerful invitation to murder – maybe powerful enough for a brother.

Then she dismissed the idea outright. It wasn't Gryf's murder that the hidden Mr. Wood wanted. This was, foremost, an attempt to ruin him. Mr. Wood plotted to destroy Gryf 's reputation before the world, if that included standing trial for murder, so much the better.

Caroline suspected that Ellen had it right. There seemed to be a connection between the 1878 attempt to murder her father and the effort to destroy Gryf this year. Her father believed so strongly in the connection that he was in haste to come to Colorado. If

Gwydden and Wood were the same man, as her father's telegram suggested, Carl Trewartha had made an enemy of him by exposing his shady land dealings in 1877. But how had Gryf crossed him?

The murder of Isaac Brown was a trap for Gryf, just like the Pennsylvania murders. But who sent the telegram luring Gryf to Sapinero?

Caroline had been back and forth through Abel's logbook and had not seen that telegram, or any like it.

Pacing now, she tried to think about what she knew of each man at By-Gum. With most of the men, Gryf had a long history. Because of that history, Gryf trusted them. He'd invited them to become partners in this mining venture. Only Garland Wright and his wife Marvelle had invited themselves. Garland's attempts to teach the Indian and Basque sheepherders about the Gospel took him away from the valley for long periods. Those mission outings, however, could be a cover for trips of an entirely different nature to Denver and Isabeau.

Garland seemed singularly ineffective as a minister. Although Deirdre gave lip service to his good works, no one in town thought too much of his piety; Marie even asked that he not preach at Jesse's funeral. Yet, he seemed just as ineffective at evil.

Marvelle was judgmental, until she got involved with the children. Was she merely acting on that day? Could she act that much?

Caroline hugged her cold arms about her body and paced the hall outside her stall. "I need to talk to someone who knows all these people as well as Gryf."

Ellen's brown mare lifted her head over the stall door. The mare's big eyes followed Caroline's movements with calm curiosity. Caroline stopped and contemplated the horse. After a few moments, she said, "I think Ellen won't mind if I borrow you. Let's go to Alex's ranch and get some help. As the one non-miner, Alex has a different perspective on all these people. I need to know more about how John Philpot came into this group. And how Garland Wright found out there was a town up here to evangelize."

The horse stretched her neck out toward Caroline.

"I know. Alex is liable to think I came for his charming company. The man does not underestimate his worth, but," she patted her revolver in her pocket, chuckling, "I think I can get him to believe this is not a social call."

**

Gryf stood next to his desk lamp, studying the note from the boy, Jack. Ellen had slipped the note and a telegram into his pocket when she hugged him goodbye.

"Miss Treaworthy says tell you man named Wood sends telegrams to Hooume at Allied. Miss T will lay low at Miss Ellen's until safe."

Gryf lowered his head and thanked God for the news that Caroline was 'laying low' at Ellen's ranch. Then he glanced at the charcoal translation of the telegram from her father.

Danger! Money behind Allied takeover is family named Gwydden – means forest or trees in Celtic. New emblem on Allied stationery is fighting cat with wings. Claws out. Careful.

Gryf's mind froze on seeing the word 'Wood' and then "Gwydden" linked to Allied Mines.

This confirms it. The man with the ring in Denver is Lord Forest.

Thomas Dunbar Kemp, Lord Forest, The Earl of Gwydden – Alex's father. Lord Forest once such a quiet man, gentle and thoughtful. However, the gentle man became implacable on that afternoon in Gryf's ninth year when he carried home his game keeper, Gryf and Sam's father.

363

Lord Forest had driven the wagon himself, bringing Rhodri Williams into the door yard at their cottage. Rhodri cussed and hollered, all the while bleeding from a shot to his back. The accident happened during the hunt. The village doctor, still dressed in hunt woolens and boots, met Lord Forest at the door, then closed himself into the back bedroom with Rhodri. In the front of the house, Lord Forest began piling their few possessions onto his wagon and yelling at their mother, "I want you gone – gone so far even I cannot find you."

And when Gryf and Sam had tried to fight with him, Lord Forest had grabbed them both with a strength they'd never have believed he possessed. He held them easily, one on each side, flailing in futile efforts to hurt the man.

"All along you were right, Johanna." Lord Forest announced. "Rhodri Williams sold his finest possession for position. God knows I was besotted enough to buy. And now we all shall pay."

Gryf remembered hearing the anguish in his lordship's voice even as he and his brother fought the man. Their mother calmly called her sons to attention. Lord Forest dropped them both in the mud of the road. As they scrambled away from his reach, their mother did a remarkable thing. She stepped toward the lord of the big house and brushed mud from his coat front. He grabbed her hand and held it away from him, saying, "Get to the bank. Ask for Mr. Scott. I won't have you anywhere near us."

Johanna Williams glanced up at him. Gryf remembered the deep shadows beneath Lord Forest's eyes, and the firm set of his jaw as he returned Johanna's pleading look with no softness. His mother straightened her shoulders, turned to Sam and Gryf and ordered them to finish bringing out the household furnishings.

Gryf had never understood that moment in their lives. And the next years, what with moving frequently and dealing with the vicious anger of their paralyzed father, he'd taken little thought to it.

364

He only understood that the source of stability in their lives was gone. Their father was shot by one of Lord Forest's friends, and the great lord couldn't move fast enough to get rid of the evidence. A few hours after their banishment, Alex followed Samuel and Gryf down the road toward Caerdydd. He'd hidden in the roadside hedge until her mother took Rhodri to a doctor. Then he brought them food, and warned them to steer clear of his father's anger. He had wanted them to write to him in secret and send the letters to one of the tenant's cottages.

Later that year, Alex, too, had left his home. He never again returned.

Now Lord Forest seemed to have found them all. Gryf read again the rest of the long telegram.

"Branahan found dead in empty mine in Schuylkill. I once exposed owner of same mine for misrepresenting mineral and carboniferous content to my client. Attempted bribe. Vicious. Owner of mine was Thomas Wood."

Terry Branahan, another victim. Bile rose in Gryf's throat, rage and a deep sadness. It was true what Kidde had claimed, the man was rich enough to hire murders done in places miles from where he was.

Incredible that Lord Forest was the one behind all these murders – even in the earlier attempt to bribe and then murder Caroline's father.

And, thought Gryf with a start, Caroline Trewartha has never in her life 'laid low'. She's out there, still in danger, still looking for evidence to save me.

He stashed telegram and note, and yanked the stone from his pants pocket. Setting the chain against the metal housing of his typewriter, he reared back and smashed the last quarter inch of the link to a pulp. One violent blow was all it took.

And that was all the noise it took to bring the young guard into the room. Ready for him, Gryf lunged. Grabbing the man's rifle with one hand, he wrapped his other arm around the young man's neck, covering his mouth. The guard had enough presence of mind to bite Gryf's palm, but not enough strength to wrench himself free. Ignoring pain, dragging the man with him, Gryf dropped the man's rifle on his desk.

The fellow had spunk, Gryf noted, as he stopped a loud holler with an old rag. He never realized until that moment just what a boy he was dealing with. Fear made the kid's blue eyes fill with tears. Gryf held the boy's jaw, made him look at him. "I'm not gonna kill you, son."

He shoved the guard into the desk chair, ran the chain around his shoulders and the chair, pushed the chair closer to the wood stove, wrapping the slack in the chain around the man as they moved. Then, Gryf tipped the chair on its back.

Gryf leaned over and took the boy's ammunition belt. "You're good in a fight, but I had all the surprise." He backed up and grabbed the rifle from the desk, saying, "When this is over, I'd like to offer you a job."

Before he left, Gryf didn't mention that the job would involve a whole lot of training in self-defense. The kid was green, and the marshal hadn't given him any idea how to stay alive.

He glanced out the door into the night, checking out each shadow. After he pulled the door closed, he climbed down the side of the porch and stayed as low as sagebrush while he headed for the carpenter's workshop and his brother. He tossed a pebble at the window near Samuel's usual workbench. Samuel was certain to be here, where Gryf could get at him if he escaped. Samuel better hurry. The growing light of a wet dawn made it easy to be seen.

"Meet you at Number One Tunnel," Samuel whispered through the opening at the bottom of the window.

366

Gryf wheeled and ran toward the mine, racing past the spindly headframe, the engine house, and around the contours at the base of the long ridge to the tunnel opening. He disliked the idea of being inside something after spending far too long in his office, so he climbed a hundred feet up the ridge to a pair of scrub pines where he hunkered down to wait.

Samuel came. Gryf hissed at him. Samuel gestured to Gryf to meet him at the lake – the lake they had created by diverting the stream. Minutes later, Samuel entered the plantation of pines and aspens where they grew down close to the new lake.

"Hope you didn't hurt that guard."

"Tied him in my most comfortable chair. Have you seen this note from the boy from Denver, eh?"

"Jack Dorsey can write?" Samuel took the note and lit a small candle. As he read it, Gryf saw the blood drain from Sam's face. "Gwydden. Wood. Lord Forest? – that old buzzard?"

"And there's this telegram from Caroline's father," Gryf added.

Sam read it, shaking his head. "As far back as Pennsylvania – so much planning smells like powerful hate."

"Hate for what?" Gryf asked.

Samuel shook his head. "We weren't exactly his favorite people, but we left when he ordered us out."

"Sam, this doesn't make sense."

"Maybe Caroline got it wrong."

Gryf started at the friendly use of her Christian name.

Samuel must have seen his reaction, because he glanced carefully at Gryf. "Maybe Caroline's not wrong, but Jack. How careful is this Jack? Why'd she give this message to him and not to Ellen?"

Gryf stared at Jack's handwriting. Then he reread the end of the message. "*Miss T will lay low at Miss Ellen's until safe.*"

"Ellen wasn't at her ranch when Caroline got there,' Gryf said. "She was in By-Gum helping Olaf bring in Phil Hunt. And Caroline wouldn't stay at Ellen's if she thought there was something she could be doing."

Samuel shook his head. "Doesn't sit still much, does she?"

Somehow, Sam's tone of affection for her annoying traits warmed Gryf. Still, Caroline's tendency to action presented grave difficulties. "Trouble is, where would she go?" Gryf stuffed the notes back into his shirt pocket.

"Probably looking for answers," Sam said. "Avoiding the marshal. She might have tried Alex."

Gryf flinched. *All night at Alex's ranch.*

Sam must have realized what he'd be thinking. He put a hand on Gryf's arm. "Alex wouldn't."

Gryf paced farther into the trees and back, trying to control his pounding heart. He told himself to stop acting like a jealous lover, but his knowledge of Alex's habits with women would not allow him to dismiss his fear. "When has Alex ever restrained himself if he thought there was the least invitation?"

Samuel glared at Gryf, then let out a sigh. "Yer right." He edged toward the lake, evidently checking for surprise visitors. "It's clear, so far, but don't forget that Rankin is still out there somewhere, too."

"And Lord Forest is somewhere, getting more and more desperate," Gryf added. "It'll take forever to get to Alex's on foot."

"You run downhill of By-Gum, then edge back along the creek. Hide among the aspen. I'll bring Sol. Meet you at the creek-crossing near the trail up to Alex's ranch."

Gryf stared at his brother. "Thanks," was all he could get out of his tight throat.

"*dim problem.*" Samuel waved his hand.

368

CHAPTER THIRTY-FOUR

In the dark hours of morning, Caroline stood on the porch of a large log cabin. She took a deep breath, chiding herself for conjuring last minute doubts about Alex. All the way from Ellen's she'd been entertaining a mental debate about talking to Alex. She knew such questions were mere camouflage – anything to hide her greater fear of his male ego.

He is just a man. Ever since I graduated, I've dealt with interested men. He is nothing to fear. He knows these people.

Foolish ancient fears were not going to keep her from getting Gryf the help he needed. Besides, she had Ellen's horse and could leave if he became too amorous. Before she could change her mind, she knocked on the thick door. The size of the logs surprised her. She was certain trees this size did not grow at this elevation. They must have been hauled up here from a long distance.

Alex opened the door. He wore a silk robe of gold and green over purple pajama pants. Caroline couldn't help thinking he had a fine eye for color, but his startled glanced made her think she shouldn't have come.

"You're alone?" he asked, gazing around in the black night of the door yard.

Bluff bravery, she told herself. "I'd a' brought the Queen's Navy, but the admirals was busy at Trafalgar."

He laughed. "Sorry. Just couldn't imagine you taking me up on my offer of a tour."

"I need information."

"Ah, business."

369

"You know the mining partners as well as any. And it's got to be a person at By-Gum."

Alex gestured at someone behind Caroline. She whipped about, startled to find a young man at her back.

"Take Miss Trewartha's mare to the barn, and bed her down," Alex said.

The man tipped his hat at Caroline and turned away. Reluctantly, she watched the mare take a carrot from the young man's hand as they walked toward the barn.

"I'll take care of you," Alex said, holding his hand out to her. The smooth way he said it made her step back, but he smiled at her and offered his hand with such openness that she accepted. As she climbed his steps, he touched her hair and retrieved a straw. "It appears you slept in a barn."

"Been hiding out since someone attacked Duncan and me on the road back from Isabeau."

"Isabeau? What were you way down there for?"

She glanced at him, feeling she'd missed something, or he had. "In case you're interested, I'm fine, but Duncan was hurt pretty badly."

He seemed not to notice her cutting tone. "And where is Duncan?"

"At Deirdre's, I hope. Amos and Rudy took him there."

"Why were you in Isabeau?"

"I needed to know who told Allied Mines that Gryf had been arrested. I believe whoever did that must be the true murderer of Isaac Brown."

"And did you have help from the telegrapher in this search?"

She decided to obscure Abel's part in her discoveries. "I went fishing by myself." Before she could elaborate, he'd ushered her inside the parlor.

She gazed at an amazing room – much larger than the outside of the cabin would have hinted. Its walls had been whitewashed. Heavy furniture created a dark atmosphere, even though there was a glittering chandelier of candles in the center of the room. Bookcases lined most of one wall. Atop the bookcases were stuffed birds and mammals, an owl, an osprey, a lynx. In the candlelight, their shadows appeared to move, crouching to spring upon their prey. None of the animals seemed to have been damaged by shot.

"You hunt with arrows?"

He pursed his mouth in disdain. "Too uncertain." He rang a bell as he talked. "But I don't want to bore you with tales of the past. You're quite well read, Miss Trewartha. Let me show you my library." He pulled down a leather-bound book. "This is *Al Aaraaf*, by Edgar Allan Poe – a fine work, but nowhere near as fun as his *Berenice,* which I have somewhere nearby."

As he reached for a volume, Caroline stopped him with a hand on his arm. "Alex, someone from By-Gum has been trying to frame Gryf for murder."

"Later, my dear. After the servants are gone."

His elegant British calm annoyed her. It annoyed her even more that, as she started to confront him, a woman appeared at the library door carrying a tray of tea service.

"Tea at five in the morning?" Caroline asked.

"You've been out in the cold," he said, as the woman poured a cup and set it on a low table where a coiled ceramic snake surrounded a vase filled with meadow flowers. Alex waved a hand toward a chair.

Caroline ignored his invitation to sit, stepped to the table, lifted the cup and warmed her fingers on its porcelain. The woman glanced at her in mild disapproval.

"Thank you, Gillian." Alex dismissed. A line of humor played at one side of his mouth. When the woman had left, he turned to

Caroline shaking his head and chuckling. "I happen to know you had the most genteel upbringing that Maryland and Pennsylvania can afford. Don't play the country buffoon for my people."

"So, who do you think is doing all this?"

He frowned as he laid down the book. She waited impatiently while he poured a cup of tea. Finally, he said, "If I had any idea, that person would be on the rack in my dungeon."

"I wish you truly had a dungeon for such fiends." Caroline sank into the nearest chair. "It is a man named Wood – but I don't think that's his real name. The fellow I saw the night we found Jesse Polgren's body – the fellow with his hair pulled into a queue, he transmits the messages, but he misspells simple words, so I don't think he is the author of those messages. If we could just find him, I think we could wring the truth about the real Mr. Wood out of him."

He stared at her a moment, and then asked, "What'd you do? Storm the telegraph office and steal Abel's files?"

"Something like that."

"And you told Gryf about this 'Wood' person?"

"Nobody can get in to see Gryf."

"Yet you wear his shirt and pants. I'd say you've become quite close with him."

She thought she detected a hint of jealousy in his voice, but she waved her hand, dismissing the clothes and the closeness. "I stole them, too," she said. "And now the marshal's after me, so I hid out at Ellen's."

"And who did Ellen think Mr. Wood was?"

"Ellen wasn't at home. I thought maybe you'd know."

He lifted a cup of tea and sipped it, as if doing so would help him think. "I have an idea who Wood is, but I can't be certain. I don't want to incriminate anyone without proof."

Caroline could hardly believe his uncooperative attitude. "Don't be so ripping refined. Spit out the name."

Alex jerked. "Damn," He wiped scalding tea from his pajama sleeve. He set the cup down and continued wiping at his wrist while he talked. "If I tell you, and set off a man hunt for him, he will be forewarned. I need to consider the best way to proceed."

"This person is trying to murder Gryf's friends. What if you're next on his list?"

"I must make some difficult decisions, Caroline. I'm not going to make them while you berate me. Nor am I going to make them while dressed in a robe, if you don't mind. I will think while I change. I'll have an answer for you in twenty minutes."

"You are too boffing calm." She gestured out the library window, "We've got no time. The sun's going to rise in a couple of hours and Wood could be at it again."

"Maybe a little sunlight will help make things clear." Alex stepped into the hall and closed the library door after him.

Angry at Alex, and wishing she were back in By-Gum where she could talk to Gryf. Caroline fidgeted with the wood carving on the chair, then rose and paced the floor.

A sudden notion set her mind spinning in new debate. Alex didn't ask about the attack on Duncan and me because he already knew.

She started toward the door, intending to leave, but halted in mid-step. It couldn't be. Alex is Gryf's oldest friend.

Then another thought gave new fear. He asked about the telegraph office before I mentioned telegraphs. He knew I would have to find my answers in Abel's office.

As she stood near the library desk, she noticed a file among the books to her left. Pulling it out, she saw the words "By Gum Loan Contract" in what she now recognized as Isaac Brown's handwriting.

She knew.

373

Alex had killed Brown and planted evidence in Gryf's saddle bag.

She whirled toward the library window, meaning to climb out and rescue Ellen's horse from the barn. Even as her pant leg knocked his book from the table, she asked "Why?".

As she bent to rescue the volume, she recognized another fact. It was Alex who brought to town the telegram that sent Gryf to Sapinero.

There was no such telegram in the logbook.

That's because Alex created it. What's more, Alex delivered the telegram that gave me authority at the mines.

Then his story of the lost messenger was a lie.

The book in her hand fell open to the frontispiece. In a glance she saw several things that made her heart stop. The title read, *Cobwebs from an Empty Skull, Ambrose Bierce*. On the opposing page was a book owner's stamped engraving – a cat, its fangs bared, and its claws extended. The beast stood on its hind legs, offering to fight an unseen enemy. Long-fingered wings, like those of a bird of prey, grew from the cat's back – the cat her father found on the stationery for Allied Mines. The same cat she'd seen branded on the horse Isaac's murderer had expected to use for escape.

Beneath the cat, in fine script, she read the words. *llfyr*, Thomas Dunbar Kemp, Lord Forest, Earl of Gwydden.

Alex is Mr. Wood – Get out! Now!

Dropping the book face down, Caroline ran to the double-hung window. It rose smooth as wood on wax, but the weights clanked. She dove out, rolling to her feet, where she came up facing a large gun barrel and the young man who had taken Ellen's mare. She whirled back to the window. At that moment, the library door opened. Alex Kemp moved quietly into the room. He picked up the book from the floor. He saw where it lay open to the frontispiece and the cat and shook his head.

Bending over to look out the window, he said gently, "You may as well come back in. You are well guarded."

Seeing another shadow behind the young man, Caroline decided to play along for a time. She ambled toward the porch. Kemp met her at the door, grabbed her arm and pulled her into the library.

"What's with the winged cat?" she asked, as much to keep him talking while she was vulnerable, as to get information.

"It's a Griffin," he said. Sadness softened his voice. As she straightened, she looked into his eyes. There she found the same gray-blue color as Gryf's eyes, but with an overlay of brittleness, like ice.

Stunned by what she now knew, she couldn't think what to do.

"Alex," she said softly, "Is he dead? Are you now the Lord Forest, Earl of Gwydden?"

"No, damn his eyes. He lives. Me – I am a mere viscount – if that much. He disowned me years ago."

"Disowned?"

"I should have shot the bitch," he muttered. "Rhodri Williams meant nothing."

She recognized the name Rhodri Williams as Gryf and Samuel's father. Uncertain who he was calling bitch, she asked. "What did it matter if Lord Forest disowned you? You are rich in your own right. What can a title matter?"

"Oh, titles are very important. Believe me. Samuel's father wanted a title – game keeper to Lord Forest. To buy that title, Rhodri Williams sold his own wife to my father's pleasure."

Caroline remembered the photo. The servant woman, carrying a child. The man, smitten with love. How that must have hurt the older boy, the son whose mother was not loved.

"You and Gryf were friends . . ."

"You've disappointed me, Miss Caroline Trewartha."

She knew he referred both to her misunderstanding of his manipulative character and to her failure to forward his plans. "So," she whispered, "you hired me to make sure By-Gum failed."

He glared at her. "That's how it should have been. Everywhere else you've worked, you left the men at each other's throats. You didn't even see it – too busy using your mind to get things running. All you've thought about was to make money for the company so as to solidify your engineering reputation."

Humiliation burned in her chest. He had it right. She had been like that – especially in Wyoming. The more they objected to a woman in her position, the more she leveraged her power as inspecting engineer to force capitulation.

"Why do you hate him so much?" she asked.

He appeared not to hear her. Instead he ranted to the animals of the library. "He has lust in his blood. Inherited it." He turned his steel gray eyes on her. "I knew you'd set his mind singing. You would make his body burn. Distracted enough not to see the catastrophe until it crushed him."

"Alex . . ."

"But at By-Gum you decide to be different. Here, you decide to make friends with these idiots. You decide this time to care about the people around you."

Caroline stared at him. He had become so fixed on his lifelong hatred that he couldn't see the love and friendships he might have had. From the moment she met Jimmy and Amos, she knew that the people of By-Gum would give her a chance. Then she met Deirdre and Ellen. For the first time, she was with people who wanted her to stay.

"These people cared about me," she whispered. "And they cared about you . . ."

He held up his hand to silence her – or to ward off her image of all he had foregone in taking his revenge. "We've a journey to make." He took her arm in a firm grip, opened the library door and called, "Emmet. Is that mount ready?"

Through the front door and into the entry hall strode the man with the dark blond queue. Caroline's heart thudded in her throat. Fear crawled down her spine.

"The horses await," the man said, "and the dynamite's all packed, my lord."

"I may need your assistance getting Miss Trewartha astride her mare."

At the man's lewd grin, Caroline shied. "I won't give you trouble, Alex."

"Better yet, put her on my horse," Alex said, pulling her forward and out the door to the porch.

Without preliminaries, Emmet wrapped an arm about her waist. His other hand shoved between her legs and grabbed her right thigh. He lifted her, tossed her leg astride Alex's big roan and let his hand linger between her thigh and the saddle. She kicked her left foot into his chest as she grabbed for the reins. Emmet scrambled backwards, but Alex's firm grasp on the reins thwarted her attempt at escape.

"My lord," Emmet gasped, "you've a job of taming ahead of you."

"After the important matter of the dam." Alex pushed his foot into the stirrup and swung up. Caroline thrust her elbow into his chest, but he grabbed at the scarf in her waistband and held her in the saddle while he finished mounting. With his great height behind her and his arms around her at the reins, her efforts to fall down the far side of the saddle were completely stopped. With one hand, Alex held both her wrists, and then wrapped his legs about hers to keep her from kicking.

"Emmet, tie the young lady's arms at her waist."

As Emmet wrapped the rope about her arms, he let his hands explore parts of her nearby.

Alex's foot knocked his man's arm from her body. "Tie the knot and leave off touching." Emmet didn't even flinch. He wrapped the rope around her arms and waist three times, leaving her hands able to grasp the pommel, but to reach no further. He tied the knot without any other motion.

Alex regained his stirrup and spurred his horse forward. "Bring the other horse to the top of the ridge. Then I want you back down here, taking care of the ranch in case the marshal comes this way."

"Want this one all to yourself, do you?"

Alex's grim silence did nothing to allay her fears. Through the veil with which her mind covered reality, Caroline saw that Alex turned his roan into the woods instead of following the trail back toward Ellen's and By-Gum. Within minutes, he leaned over her and urged the big horse almost straight up the side of a steep hill. As her knees held tight to the horse and her fingers sought his mane for security, she became aware that Alex's ranch was a small valley near the ravine where Jesse's body had been found.

The top of the ravine was one of several ridges that led up to the higher mountains above By-Gum. Alex's horses mounted the ridge west of the one under which lay the seam of coal. This ridge led to the glacial debris that formed the natural dam. Behind that dam was the huge mountain lake she'd seen on her first ride up the butte.

Is that mount ready? Alex had said.

Ready, both the horses and the dynamite.

CHAPTER THIRTY-FIVE

Gryf hid in the snow slickened woods where the cold creek crossed the trail to Alex's ranch. It would be difficult for Samuel to sneak the horse to Dyfi Creek without being followed. Still, Gryf's worry for Caroline made him fume. Pre-dawn gold lit the sky by the time he finally heard hoof beats on the trail. He almost stepped into the path to meet Sam, but the unfamiliar sound of ringing spurs made him duck. An unknown horseman urged his mount up the trail toward Alex's ranch. As the stallion neared, Gryf blinked.

The past is too close.

He stared at a rampant griffin branded on the haunch of that animal – Lord Forest's crest. The rider wore his hair in a long, dirty queue; here was the man Caroline had seen at the celebration.

And when else did she meet him? The night we found Jesse's body . . . in this same ravine.

As he hunkered beneath the tall angelica, Gryf felt dread rise through his body. Lord Forest must have taken over Alex's ranch. Caroline was in danger. If Alex guessed his father's methods and confronted the man, Alex himself would be in danger.

His crest on Allied's stationery, and the purchase of Allied Mines by a Mr. Gwydden pointed directly toward Lord Forest as a man capable of killing anyone – Terry Branahan, Isaac Brown, Jesse Polgren. Gryf must get to Alex's before Lord Forest harmed her, or his own son.

Suppose it was Lord Forest who shot our father that morning, during the hunt. If it was not the accident he made it out to be, does he believe we know of his guilt?

Another piece of the puzzle fell into place. Alex knew the truth. That's why he left his father and never looked back.

He'd lost his son. Blamed Gryf and Samuel. That alone accounted for the many years of pursuit, and so many efforts to . . . efforts to what?

Caroline was right. The man had never tried to kill him or Samuel. All his effort had been turned to discrediting them, mostly financially, but twice, by framing Gryf for murder.

How would that bring Alex back to him?

Deeply worried for everyone at the ranch, Gryf started through the woods, through mud and snow drifts, paralleling but shunning the trail to Alex's ranch. Minutes later, he heard another rider approach. This time, Gryf waited until Samuel was in sight before he showed himself. To his surprise, Olaf accompanied his brother, riding Sheba, his skis tied behind her saddle.

"You on a horse?"

"Gonna get our flicka back, Gryf." Olaf raised his rifle.

Samuel jumped down from Sol. "Couldn't convince Olaf it was just Alex and his wandering hands that had you worried."

"It's not just . . ." said Gryf. "Two minutes ago, Caroline's man with the queue rode by on a horse that had Lord Forest's crest branded on his rear. Something is going on. I'm worried about both Alex and Caroline."

"What would Lord Forest do to Alex?"

"Alex would be furious if he discovered his father master-minded the murders of Jesse and Isaac. He might confront the man. Force his hand . . ." Gryf swung up into Sol's saddle.

Samuel grabbed onto the stirrup apron to get Gryf's attention. "Gryf, Lord Forest wasn't like that. He sent us away, but he . . . well, I always had a feeling he did it to keep us safe."

"Safe from what?"

"From whoever shot our *Da* that day."

For the first time, Gryf questioned his memory of events. He'd remembered Lord Forest's anger, his abrupt orders, his hardness toward their mother. But there was that gesture, his mother brushing mud from the front of the man's coat – a gesture of . . . affection. A gesture completely at odds with the rest of what he saw.

"What do you know, Sam? What that I don't know, eh?"

Samuel glanced at Olaf as if gauging whether to say something in his presence. Then he directed his complete attention toward Gryf. "It may not be him doing this. That's all I know. Don't trust anyone."

Samuel was holding back, but Gryf couldn't leave Caroline there while he whittled it out of his brother. "I'm getting her out of there. That's it."

Samuel started to say something more, then merely warned, "Watch your back. I'll return to By-Gum – distract the marshal from searching for you down this way."

Gryf nodded at Samuel and turned Sol down the trail to the ranch. Olaf and Sheba fell in right behind him. The farther up they rode, the deeper the snow became.

As they approached the last bend to Alex's ranch, Gryf dismounted and led Sol into the Aspen woods. Olaf followed. When they could barely see the out-buildings, he gestured Olaf up beside him.

"Can you keep a watch from that corner of the barn?"

"What's this Lord Forest look like?"

Gryf closed his eyes and the man appeared before him as clearly as if he'd only sent them away last week. "He's tall, blond like Alex, but twenty-five years older."

"Curly hair?"

Gryf nodded. "Always brushed smooth when I knew him." Gryf shuddered at what that smooth exterior must have hidden.

381

Olaf started toward the buildings, whispering, "Wait till I'm at the barn, Gryf."

"I will. Then I'm up to the door like an ordinary visitor."

Gryf watched and realized that for such a big man, Olaf could be amazingly quiet even though he had to lift his boots high to run through the snow drifts.

Olaf positioned himself at the barn and then nodded toward the house. Leaving Sheba in the trees, Gryf rode Sol to the door yard, dismounted and climbed the porch steps. As he raised his hand to knock, a voice behind him said.

"He's not home."

Gryf jerked around and found Olaf, blood running down the side of his face, his hands raised behind his head. The man with the queue used Olaf's own rifle to prod him forward. Gryf's heart pounded. He'd been careless. Another friend was in danger because of him.

"Mr. Kemp left me in charge here," the man said, "and I want to know what this fellow is doing sneaking about the property."

At that moment, a woman in an apron burst from the front door of the cabin, nearly bumping into a surprised Gryf. "Emmet, what's going on?" she asked.

A strong-looking young man followed her, carrying a paring knife and a potato. He was also staring at the man Emmett. Gryf had never seen these people before. As he kept an eye on that paring knife, Gryf's fear for Caroline and Alex deepened, but he kept his voice calm.

"We are friends of Mr. Kemp," Gryf said, "and have reason to believe he may be in danger."

Emmett snorted. "Danger? From what?"

This man is Alex's danger. "Who are you?" he asked.

"Gillian," Emmet gestured at the woman. "You and Rafe get on down here near me. I'd rather not shoot you accidentally." The woman and her helper stumbled past Gryf.

Gryf said, "I've never heard of any of you. What have you done with Alex Kemp?"

"Kemp's never been in danger I know of," said the young man.

"He's gone to . . ." the woman began.

"Shut up," ordered Emmet. He shoved Olaf closer to the porch rail. "See that piece of wire on the chair seat?"

"I see it," Gryf said. The wire lying on the porch rocker was barbed, maybe a coil left from some fence-mending project.

"Tie this big guy to the rail."

Dread swept through Gryf, but he lifted the wire, testing its weight, figuring how to throw it, how to avoid Olaf's face. Out of the corner of his eye, he saw a quick ghost of motion run between Sol and the backs of Olaf and Emmet. Gryf hoped he'd read that low-running style correctly. Slowly, he turned to face Emmet and his companions.

"This wire will cut Olaf."

"Not if he stands real still . . . and you tie real careful."

Trying to keep his shaking anger from showing, Gryf stepped toward the rail, holding the wire in his right hand. Emmet stepped back from Olaf, aiming Olaf's gun at Gryf, but teetering on both feet like a hunter ready to move in any direction. "Get it over with," he hissed.

Gryf prayed he'd read the man's jumpy habits correctly. He let fly, throwing the wire to the man's left. With unbelievable speed, Emmet raised the rifle and shot the wire as if it were a grouse rising from the snow drifts.

In that moment, Samuel rose, tackling Emmet low and from the right. Gryf grabbed at the barrel of the rifle, ripping it from his hand. Olaf pinned him to the earth.

Gryf aimed the gun at the woman and the young man. The youngster raised his hands and dropped the knife and the potato. The woman covered her mouth with both hands and started blubbering. Gryf lowered the rifle sight to the man's hand where Olaf had it slammed it against the wet and rocky ground.

"Where are they?"

Emmet squirmed, but Olaf leaned into his chest. The breath wheezed out of him. The woman started forward, "Jesus, Mary and...," she cried. Gryf raised the rifle toward her.

"You move again, I shoot him first."

After a moment of frenzy, when Gryf feared the man would never breath again, Olaf let up, slightly. Gasping, Emmet said, "He'll kill me."

"Die now then, or take your chances later."

Emmett glared at Gryf. Olaf began to tighten his arms around his chest. Emmett shouted. "He took her."

"Lord Forest?" Gryf asked.

"Yes. Lord Alex."

Samuel glanced up at Gryf. Gryf shook his head in denial. "No. Lord Forest, his father."

The man twisted his face in contempt. "Him come here?" he coughed out. "Soon as you're dead, his father's as good as dead."

Stunned, Gryf couldn't think. It was Samuel who faced the truth first, asking, "Where did Lord Alex take Miss Trewartha?"

"I'll not say."

Samuel said, "Then kill him, Olaf."

Olaf began to squeeze. The fellow's face went red as he struggled to free himself and breathe. The woman whined. Within seconds, the man's lips were blue. Olaf let up. Emmet wheezed and coughed, dragging in air.

"Where did Alex take her?" Gryf asked.

"To. . .the. . .ridge."

384

"Where on the ridge?"

"The lake."

Olaf raised his head, gazing up toward the ridge. "He'll drown her, Gryf."

Gryf gestured with the gun. "Tie this man with the wire, or what's left of it. And take these people into By-Gum to lock them up."

"Not down there," hissed the young man. "We'll drown too."

"Shut up," Emmet shouted. A fit of coughing interrupted his hoarse cry. Gryf turned the rifle barrel toward the young man.

"You. Why would you drown."

"He's got all that dynamite packed on the other horse. He's gonna blow the lake."

Olaf stood, bringing the coughing man with him.

"Olaf," Gryf said, "You and Samuel bring them in the barn, tie them up and hie yerselves to By-Gum to warn them. I'm after Alex."

Olaf turned to Samuel. "You ride down. All this snow…I'm getting my skis from Sheba. Straight down is faster."

"I left my bread in the oven," cried the woman.

"Hell, woman," hissed Olaf, shoving her toward the barn. "Don't you have a brain?"

CHAPTER THIRTY-SIX

Alex's horse trudged up the snow-filled and narrow trail. A wall of rock loomed in front of them. Caroline let her eyes follow the rise of the steep moraine. Up, and up the rock rose, spanning the space between two buttressing ridges, twice the height of the tallest church spire she had ever seen in Baltimore. Below the dam, the valley lay parched, yet Caroline could smell water and algae from the vast lake that lay in wait behind the thick rubble.

She remembered when she'd ridden up here to avoid being followed by Kidde. Discovering the lake behind the glacial moraine had been like unwrapping a gift of extraordinary beauty – crystal water, alpine plants poking up through ice and snow, and birds swooping down from their nests near the peaks. Today, however, with Alex's hard arms around her, his stony silence and the presence of a pack-horse laden with dynamite sticks, all she could think of were thousands of gallons of water, poised above By-Gum.

Through the dark hours of their night ride, she had watched in vain for any lantern, another human being. When daylight came, she hoped for a friend who might be in the mountains – any who might see her with Alex, and the dynamite, and warn Gryf.

As the sun rose, Alex yanked her blue cape and paisley shawl about her, covering the ropes and making it appear she was riding with him by choice. Gryf would never believe it.

The Griffin crest branded on Emmet's and Alex's mounts convinced her that Alex was the tall man she'd seen jumping from Isaac's window. She had no doubt it was Alex who hired the man who died while exploding the cavern under the ridge. Alex must have directed Kidde, Rankin, Stemmins and God knew who else in his efforts to ruin Gryf.

Alex lured Gryf to Sapinero and herself to Isaac's house. He engineered the murder of Isaac, by telegraph from Isabeau, then misdirected her carriage and arrived at the lawyer's house before her so he could be seen by witnesses, dressed in Gryf's clothes. He had hoped for her own death when she opened Isaac's door.

Now, in his efforts to destroy Gryf, Alex planned to drown the families of By-Gum in a flash flood. She rode in silence, waiting her chance for . . . for whatever presented itself so that By-Gum might be saved.

Behind her, Alex suddenly chuckled. Caroline realized how uncanny it was that his low voice had a brittle edge, making it distinguishable from Gryf's gentle tones. With no other warning, Alex moved his right hand from the reins to her thigh.

"Cut that out, you buzzard."

His hand moved her pant leg up to expose her knee. "What can you do about it, Miss High Collar?"

She raised her leg quickly, throwing his hand off for the moment. "I'll find something."

"Ah," he laughed, tightening his grip around her waist and laying his hand on her leg again. "In the meantime, this can be ever-so-pleasant."

Her foot came up once more, but this time, she kicked his horse in the jaw. The big roan jerked against the reins, threatening to break into a gallop. She kicked again. He reared. Alex had all the work he could do to hold onto the saddle with his feet and knees while fighting the horse down.

"Damn you, woman," Alex howled. Then he grunted as the roan rose once more, twisting against his reins, trying to bite at anything that might be blamed for his pain.

Caroline breathed an apology to the horse, but she no longer felt helpless in the face of Alex's attentions. She knew now that she had

387

a choice – to hurt and be hurt, or to put up with Alex until she could find a better way to get out of this situation.

By the time he controlled the horse, Alex was furious with her. His hand grabbed at her right ankle, pulling it between his boot and the stirrup apron, trapping her. Her position was now so precarious that any move she made would result in being thrown and dragged. She forced herself to breathe slowly, pushing down the sensations of nausea his exploring hand gave her.

Caroline felt herself break into small pieces – each part drifting away from her center. Nothing he touched belonged to her any longer. When he invaded Gryf's shirt, holding her breast in his hot palm, she made herself think of alpine grasses and of snow – of anything clean.

He whispered into her ear, his breath hot. "I knew you would be a luscious handful."

She pressed her lips together to keep from crying. The farther they rode, the more he tried to get a reaction from her. Brushing his fingers over her, he ran his hand from the rope down her belly toward the saddle. She stiffened. He tried to untie the scarf which held up her pants, but the rope, wrapped about her waist and arms, made the job too difficult.

"Later," he whispered, "I will own all of you soon enough." Thwarted in his efforts, he ran his hand roughly again up her thigh.

She thought of the care with which Gryf treated her, his coaxing smile, his gentle kiss. Alex touched her where she wanted only Gryf to touch her. Her tormented mind pictured Gryf, chained to the heavy stove in the lowest part of the valley. She forced herself stop imagining his fate.

But her mind brought the image of Jimmy, held prisoner in his own house, directly in the path of the water – Deirdre and Mac and Keir, trying to get him out in time. Ellen and the school children,

Marie Polgren, Amos, Rudy, Cornell, John and Nan Philpot, and that little scamp from Denver.

Marvelle and Garland. Are they in the hills? Manuel, Teresa and Juan Jesús?

Caroline prayed that one of them might see the packhorse and realize what the poor beast carried. *Someone please stop us. Stop us before we climb the moraine.*

Alex leaned forward, touching her neck with his mouth. She felt the soft nuzzling of his lips. Her stomach clenched.

"They will know you came with me – believe we enjoyed each other. You helped me destroy them. Disappeared with me."

So, she thought as bile rose in her throat, he too has been looking for others.

Alex's booted legs pulled her trapped ankles further apart. In spite of the split skirt pants, he burned her flesh with humiliating invasion. Caroline closed her eyes. Beyond the tumult in her mind, she heard the cry of a hawk. Taking her mind into the wind, she imagined herself a bird, flying far above the insignificant figures on the roan – barely noticing the struggle of the woman against the man.

I have to return. For Jimmy, Ellen, Gryf . . . I must stop him.

With painful force, she brought her mind back to the ridge, close enough to be ready to act, not close enough to allow him to destroy her. She studied the snowy terrain, putting a fragile wall between her mind and his hands. On the ridge to her left, she spotted the head frame, the pulley and ropes above Mine Number Three. No work horses stood outside the mine. It was as if, with Gryf arrested, no one had the heart to work the coal he'd found for them. Then, she remembered that Olaf feared horses. If he worked the mine, she wouldn't be able to tell from here.

She glanced at a sudden shadow of movement near a boulder atop the mining ridge, but lost sight of it when Alex's tongue suddenly touched her ear. She jerked, but he bit down hard. Sharp, excruciating torment forced her mind to admit his existence. No longer able to keep her mind free of her body, Caroline closed her eyes. A white figure played across her inner vision – a rotund man seemed to watch her torture with glee.

The ridge rose with sudden steepness, forcing Alex to pay attention to his roan. The horses scrambled up where the ridge formed one side of the lake, then plodded along next to the top of the natural dam. It was only a foot and a half wide. On one side of that small margin rested deep, cold water, still with ice edging the blue. But to Caroline's left, the face of the rocky moraine dropped two hundred-fifty feet to the valley between the two ridges.

Alex urged his roan away from the moraine dam, along the western ridge shore of the lake. The far side of the lake was formed by the upper reaches of the eastern ridge, the ridge above the coal seam.

A small grove of aspen enjoyed wet soil, growing sturdy, straight trunks. The silver-barked trees leant an air of permanence to the precarious balance of the power – rock against hundreds of cubic feet of water.

Alex halted the roan. Wrapping his reins about the pommel, he swung his leg out from behind her. Leaving her in the saddle, he stepped to the ground near the trees. Caroline flipped the reins off the pommel so the roan could drink. She had little mobility, tied as she was with her elbows close to her waist, but she was able to do this poor animal a favor.

Alex, not noticing what she had done, pulled on the rope at her waist, making her body tilt toward him. As she fell, he caught her against his chest. She turned her face from his lips. He whispered into her hair, "Even dirty and tired, you are a beauty."

"You . . . are always disgusting."

He snorted, and let her drop in a dry spot under the aspen. She landed with a thump on some very hard rock. The feeling was beginning to return to her legs, but she had no command of them.

Alex took off his Stetson hat and slapped dust from it. He gazed down at her. "I could take you with me."

She remained silent.

"Your silence may save you. Begging for your life would be boring."

She turned her face toward the top of the far away butte. He slapped his hat again, and, apparently disgusted with waiting for her to say something, began unpacking the heavy saddle bags. As he pulled them out, she recognized her own dynamite sticks from their careful wrap of absorbent material.

"How long have you been planning this?"

He kept working. "The first week we were here, a year and a half ago, I rode over the entire butte and the ridges leading to the heights. I searched for two things. First, a way to destroy Gryf completely. Second, a home of my own out of the path of that destruction."

"Why wait until now? Why murder Terry Branahan and buy Allied Mines. Why Isaac Brown, Jesse. . .?"

She stopped, because he stopped working and turned his whole attention upon her.

"You have figured out too many things in the last two days. I think you know enough to have earned your front row seat at this circus." He strode toward her. She grabbed vainly for a root to hold herself among the trees, but managed only a handful of hopeful spring grass, which did her no good as an anchor. Alex hauled her unceremoniously onto her wobbly legs and propelled her out onto the foot-and-a-half wide moraine. At the middle of the dam, he held her over the water. "You see how deep that is?" He kicked a rock off the narrow path. It broke through the thin ice and rolled through the water.

They both watched it disappear into the clear depths, still plummeting as it left the light.

"It is as deep as this." He whipped her body toward the other side of the dam, forcing her to lean out over the near vertical drop. She gasped, feeling herself roll out of his arms. Headed for the abyss with tethered arms and no hope, she closed her eyes and tried to curl into a ball.

At the last instant, he jerked on the rope at her waist. It ripped into her stomach and arms as he hauled her back onto the dam. A rock dislodged by her feet bounded toward the bottom of the slope, sending echoes from farther and farther away.

"You will stay here," he said, shoving her down onto the dam's narrow lip. "Try to move in either direction and you drown or fall."

Caroline, her raw-skinned arms held stiffly at her sides by the rope, splayed her hands into the precious warm rocks beneath her. Dropping her head against her knees, she tried to stop shaking. Though the sun beat against her back, it did not warm. She heard Alex's boots as he walked toward the pack horse.

"Why?" she asked, her voice a reed in the hot air.

"Because everything else has failed to bring him down."

"But such hatred?"

He yanked the last saddle bag from the old horse. "His father deserved to die. I did better than that. I made him an invalid."

She shuddered at the vicious tone of his voice. He could do anything in the name of hate.

"I should have killed Johanna. Her husband was nothing."

"And Gryf?" she asked.

"Because of him, I have no future and no past."

She stared at him, incredulous. "You have enough resources to take over Allied Mines, yet claim you have no future?"

392

"Money is nothing. I can create money merely by looking at a piece of property."

"You had a future with Gryf."

"Not the future I deserve."

"No," she agreed. "Not the one you've earned."

"Your opinion is worthless." He set the saddle bag down and began to pay out the wicking. "When Gryf is gone, my father is next. I will be Earl of Gwydden – at the center of power, with Disraeli in the House of Lords – a power my father never dared put to good use."

She glimpsed at last the drive behind Alexander Kemp. "Did he disown you when you shot Rhodri Williams?" She noted how his eyes narrowed.

"You are as good as dead." With a contemptuous sneer, he threw the saddlebag over his shoulder and strode to the edge of the dam.

Caroline stared out over the vista below her. Her precarious perch on the dam put her midway between the ridge she and Alex had climbed and the one under which the mines had been excavated. Between the two ridges lay a funnel-shaped valley of rocks and sand, with long deep patches of melting snow. When the dynamite exploded and the dam collapsed, she and the water would rush into the funnel – tons of water, roaring headlong toward the town which lay directly below. Ripping up houses and barns, taking mining equipment and shacks with it, the wall of water would crash against the cliff south of town. It might reach even as high as the plateau where she and the women had built the safe haven above the valley.

But the families would not be up there. They had no idea what was about to happen to them. They would be caught in the maelstrom. The flood would bash against the southern cliff. Granite would force it to turn. It would grind around to the left, following the bed of Dyfi Creek, taking all with it as it spilled itself over the stark drop across the switchbacks of the trail to Isabeau.

How can I warn them?

She closed her eyes, trying to conjure a mental connection with Gryf. Emptying her mind of all fear, she imagined him in his office. An open door met her mind's eye as she climbed the porch stoop. She saw his office as clearly as if she had been there. However, she couldn't find him. She gazed about the vision-blurred office and found only an empty chair, turned on its back near the wood stove.

She opened her eyes, slowly. She'd never before thought she could project a message to anyone, yet not making that ephemeral connection left her dejected. She had to find some real way to warn Gryf and the town.

Drawing her mind back to the present, she watched Alex descend the steep incline of the rock dam. He followed a narrow path he must have hacked out on some previous visit. An ingenious, strong and determined man – Alex could have led men in any country. Jealousy and hatred twisted him, creating an evil shadow of the man he might have been.

Behind him, as he climbed down, he played out a long fuse. Seeing that he had the new safety fuses – her fuses, Caroline realized she could calculate what he planned by watching him. At six inches of burn per second, he had already left a thirty second length of fuse behind him.

At that point, he took one paper-covered roll of dynamite from his backpack and placed it in a pre-drilled hole. She knew that type – sodium nitrate mixed with wood pulp to give the nitroglycerine added whomp. That one stick represented enough explosive to lift her and a good chunk of this dam as high as the crest of the butte. Counting the sticks as he placed them, she realized that he had no idea how much power he'd brought with him, but he did have a good idea where to place explosives for maximum effect.

He had not glanced toward her since she asked her probing question. Taking advantage of his disdain, and the growing distance between them, she clucked at the horses. She scrabbled together the blades of grass she had dropped when he threw her here. She waggled them at the horse. The pack horse glanced her way. He showed no interest in the greenery Caroline waved feebly in his direction. She clucked again.

To her amazement, the pack horse stepped toward her, still nuzzling at the drifts for water, still not looking at her, but one step closer. Caroline glanced down the steep slope to Alex's location.

He moved across the slope systematically and then moved down in a V-shaped pattern. He seemed to know that once he started the break, the water would finish the job for him, thrusting the dam debris out of its way as it rushed downward.

To Caroline's surprise, the pack horse touched her shoulder with his nose. She offered him the little bit of grass she had, and as he munched, she grasped the dragging rein that lay within her reach. Below her, Alex's head disappeared beyond the curve of the slope.

Caroline gathered her feet under her and scooted her bottom close to the pack horse's forelegs.

"Stand," she said, and could almost feel him dig in his heels at her command. Able only to lean her back against his legs, she pushed up with her legs. She walked her back up his fore legs. Her need for support was too great even for the stolid pack horse. He took a step back. Half-risen, Caroline fell, scraping her face against the horse's leg. She tucked her body in an effort to keep from tumbling over the sheer drop. Instead, she hit her shoulder against a rock at the edge of the lake, knocking it into the water.

"Caroline? Are you all right?"

Alex! As if he cares for my safety.

She gasped for air, then answered him, her voice as cold and clear as cracking ice. "I'm enjoying afternoon tea. And the view."

"Huh," he grunted. "The view will be more interesting in about twenty minutes."

The pack horse, frightened by her fall near the water, had backed away. She must get up on her own. She sat, cross-legged, leaned slightly forward and began to rise without the help of her hands, or the horse. Her legs ached from the long ride without the aid of stirrups. They shook beneath her and threatened to cave-in, but inch by inch she rose. At last, she stood, teetering on the edge of the world, with one good foot and one still weakened from burnt muscles.

She could see Alex moving farther and farther down the slope. If he were to glance up, he would see her, standing helplessly on the narrow ledge between water and the precipice. But he didn't look.

Her legs became accustomed to standing. Slowly, she tottered toward the ridge of the coal mines, almost two hundred feet away. Her paisley shawl dropped from one shoulder, but she had no way to raise it. As she glanced at it, she saw its reflection in the placid water. An idea made her shimmy the rest of the shawl off and let it drop onto the lake. It spread out like a lily pad, floating with slow movements on the water.

Once again, she worked her way toward Gryf's mine ridge and off the dam. And, glancing at the end of the wicking, she knew she could not reach it. Trying in vain to destroy it would only attract Alex's attention. The best she could do was disappear.

She moved down the ridge as fast as she could go. Her first goal was to get over the rise to the far side of the ridge so that Alex could not see her when he climbed to the top of the dam. She stumbled because she took too long a stride and had to take mincing little steps. Her arms could not help her balance. As she ran the last one hundred feet, prickling awareness warned her that Alex might glance up at any moment. She reached the crest of the mining ridge and skittered precariously down the steep side away from where he

396

was working. Her last glance back gave her a view of him thrusting a stick of dynamite into a hole twenty feet below the top of the dam.

Once over the rise and out of his sight, she worked her way down the ridge toward the third mine. Perhaps Olaf had come to work. He must know and escape the danger.

A warning rifle shot . . . anything.

With each step she took, she muttered to herself. "Let Olaf or Manuel be there. Even Garland Wright. Anybody. Anybody."

She remembered that it had been only five minutes ride on the horse from the mine to the dam, but on foot, it seemed to take forever to get there. She kept her eyes on the rocks and the small meadow at the top of the vent shaft – the meadow where she had whacked Gilchrist, right before she met Rankin. She was getting closer, she had to get there, get Olaf out of the mine, make sure he was safe. She had to get . . ..

"Caroline!" Above her, and beyond the rise of the ridge, she heard Alex's shriek. "Caroline!"

He cried out as if in wretched distress. She could have believed anger, but his tone was inconsolable grief. How could he despair over me? He intended to kill me.

Then she understood. By throwing herself into the lake she had deprived him of the chance to use and then murder her. She hoped his false tears wet all the wicking he'd laid. She might yet save Olaf – dear God she wanted to save Olaf.

Stumbling and righting herself took enormous energy, and a frightening amount of time. She raced in her awkward little steps toward the meadow above the mine, glancing back over her shoulder to make sure that she still could not be seen from the top of the dam.

As she turned once more to run, she bounded off the belly, and the gun belt, of Rankin.

He held her upright by the shoulders, grinning at her with his tobacco-filled mouth. He spit, hitting her in the chest, and laughed his high, nasal giggle, "Why the very person I hoped to see before I left the territory."

CHAPTER THIRTY-SEVEN

Sol, lathered and winded, pushed gamely upward, carrying Gryf high into the snow-covered valley between the two buttressing ridges. Gryf knew he was in the path of the wall of water, but he couldn't take a chance on being caught on the wrong ridge when he spotted Alex and Caroline. As they neared the third mine, Gryf saw Alex far above him – Alex, alone. Breathing hard, Gryf leaned over Sol's neck, urging him upward as Alex climbed up from the face of the dam onto its lip. Alex ran along the dam, looking about him as if in frantic search. Gryf lost sight of him for a moment, then realized he had bent over the lake water. When Alex stood again, he faced the lake. In his outstretched arm was a shawl, its fringe dripping water.

Alex cried out Caroline's name, as if in despair. Gryf's heart stopped.

She has drowned.

In that moment, the sweat running down his face, the pungent odor of sage, the hot air rolling from Sol's withers, every detail burned into his mind because she had left him.

Alex seemed to spot Sol and Gryf near the mine shaft. He shrieked her name once more and threw the shawl down the face of the dam, then raced toward his horse.

The shawl floated for a moment, buoyed by the updraft, then its waterlogged weight dragged the fabric into a ball. It plummeted, collapsing against the boulders.

Gryf's breath left him as the shawl fringe fluttered. When he dragged his attention up to the dam top, Alex was lighting a long fuse.

**

"So," Rankin said, glancing down Caroline's body. "Some man trade clothes with you and wrap you in rope for decoration?" He laughed so hard at his own humor that he loosed his grip on her. Caroline yanked her shoulders free of Rankin's hands and tottered awkwardly backwards.

She saw that the vent fissure lay mere feet behind Rankin. In the week since she climbed out, the grasses had grown up to camouflage the opening.

She faced Rankin and the afternoon sun just as Rankin shuffled up in front of her. As she hoped, he stopped just to her left, with his back to the vent, casting his fat shadow over her. She prayed that he was still afraid of her, even tied like this.

"Can't go very far in that ropey get-up," he chuckled in his nasal voice.

"How did you get away?" she stepped toward him, eyeing his rifle blatantly. He raised it across his chest and stepped back from her.

"Ain't nobody tol' you?" he rocked on his toes, watching her carefully. "I been out here three days. Marshal rode past me lots of times, but I know a few places up here don't nobody know about."

She glanced up toward the dam, then back at him. "You know where Alex is?"

"Sure. He tol' me how to escape that school. And I seen him ride up that other ridge with you – seen him kiss your neck and such." He glanced suggestively at the open buttons above the rope. At that moment she remembered him looking at her in just that way – long ago, two years ago – that night in January.

She steeled her courage for what he might do but lurched toward him. "It was you."

400

He stepped back once more and glanced up at the dam. "What are you talking about?"

She leaned toward him and his gun. "At the Carr Mines. You told me the mine manager wanted the framing in the lowest tunnel checked between the day and the night shift."

"Sure, it was me. Your father needed convincing not to testify in a certain trial."

"And Alex Kemp hired you to do it."

"Woulda made plenty, but you lived."

"Kemp is desperate to find me."

Rankin snorted. She saw he was about to work up a spit, but she moved in on him once more and said, "He's very desperate to find you as well. Says he owes you."

He pulled his rifle closer to his body and stepped back again. "You stay where you are, Miss. I don't want to shoot you."

"That thing isn't even loaded." She strode forward.

"Loaded both chambers mysel . . . Aah!"

As he stumbled into the hole, one leg went straight down the vent shaft, the other twisted to the side at an awkward angle. He screamed in pain. She rammed her body into his right shoulder. His rifle flew out of his arms and up the rocky incline behind the hole.

She raced around Rankin's grasping hands to grab up the gun and run to the overlook. This was her chance to signal the town. Using her hands and her tightly tied forearms, she lifted the heavy rifle, aimed out over the rocky valley, and pulled the trigger twice.

Behind her, Rankin shrieked. Above her, the first stick of dynamite exploded. She jerked about, staring at the top of the dam. Rock flew into the sky. Another and another explosion sent more rock, sand and water into the air. She stumbled back from the edge of the overlook, yelling "Olaf. Olaf get out."

Rankin grabbed at her skirt as she fell near him. "Save me." He shrieked. "Get me out."

401

She yelled, "Let me stand so I can pull you out."

"No. You die here with me."

A second series of explosions rocked the ridge. Stones rained down around them as water spilled over the widening crack in the dam. Below the crack, puffs of smoke announced more explosions. The lower wall of the dam bulged toward them. Suddenly, Rankin flopped against her, a gash in his forehead – he'd been hit. More rock pelted her own shoulders and head. She rolled from his slack grip, seeking in vain for a hiding place from falling projectiles. Even as she rolled, she heard the shriek of a frightened horse. Alex's roan, she guessed, but then she heard hoof beats nearby.

He's found me.

Almost with relief, she felt the first wash of the backwater. The lake tumbled out so fast, that the sides spilled up over the ridge. She and Rankin would drown. Alex wouldn't be able to get at her.

She felt rough hands lift her body onto a saddle, stomach down. She felt a large hand hold her back as the rider rose into the saddle. His horse moved without waiting to be told. The rider leaned his body over hers as the big horse screamed and galloped up the mountain toward the dam.

She recognized the gray and black of Sol's mane as they whipped across her face.

"You're going the wrong way," she gasped.

"Alex is in danger."

Gryf's voice.

"Rock kills," she managed to get out. But less and less rock was landing around them as they rose. The last explosions rocketed. The lake rushed downward, gouging away the sides of the ridges just as the glacier had once done. She could hear the rumble of boulders being pushed down the valley toward By-Gum.

"The town," she yelled. "Olaf."

"Olaf and Samuel are warning the town. I hope . . ."

"How did you . . .?"

"I heard your blunderbuss. Near took off my left ear."

With the pounding of Sol's hooves, Caroline gave up trying to talk. Above them, the water roared out of its confines. She prayed that Olaf and Samuel were in time. *Please take care of Ellen, Jimmy, Deirdre . . .*

"Whoa," Gryf flung himself out of the saddle. Caroline raised her head long enough to see that Alex had miscalculated the power of water. Trapped in a swirling pool at the edge of the ridge, his legs were caught by the weight of the mud and rock that he must once have thought to be solid ground. Gryf reached toward him, holding his rifle out as a lifeline.

"Grab hold, man," he yelled.

Alex stared at the barrel, as if afraid Gryf meant to shoot him.

"Grab it and come to safety," Gryf roared.

Alex jerked back from Gryf. The water swerved in ever widening patterns. Gryf didn't see that his own boots were now surrounded by unstable ground. He took another step toward Alex.

"Sol," yelled Caroline, "Gryf! Attention!"

Sol bounded forward. Her body slid from the saddle to the rocky ground, hitting her shoulder and hip. She tried to rise and saw Sol take a solid grip on Gryf's overall strap. Sol backed up two steps. The ground beneath Alex gave way. Alex glared at Gryf. His arms flew up, desperate for something to grab, but it was too late. Alex disappeared over the edge of the ridge, down into the valley.

**

Caroline's body ached, every inch. As Gryf unwrapped the ropes from her waist and arms, she saw him wince at what he saw there. She was too worn to look. Even when her arms were free, she couldn't feel them. She lay in the afternoon sun and cried. Having done what he could to make her comfortable, Gryf leaned over her,

403

caressing her muddy hair, her scraped face, the torn sleeve at her shoulder.

He seemed to be in shock, almost singing to himself as he checked out her bones and reassured himself she was whole. All she had strength for was to watch him with a grateful heart.

At that moment, he glanced at her open shirt buttons and seemed to realize what they meant. He leaned his forehead against the ground next to her ear and cried. Between gasps of sorrow, he whispered, "I'm sorry. I'm sorry. I should have stopped him. Stopped him. Known. Oh Sweetheart…"

She reached up and caressed his face, wiping tears from his cheek.

Moments later, she drew in a long breath and found enough voice to whisper, "I tried to stop him."

"I know you did, *cariad*. I know." He rose slightly and stared off at the place where Alex had been, mere moments ago. "Why did he do it, Lass?"

"I think I can show you why." Then she thought of what was happening below them. "If it's still there."

"Something in town?"

She nodded. "Are they safe?" Her voice faded. He leaned over her, speaking directly to her face, as if she were deaf.

"We've got to get up and help them."

"I can't seem to move," she whispered.

"Sol and I will carry you."

CHAPTER THIRTY-EIGHT

As Gryf carried Caroline into town, a stench greeted them. None of his friends were in sight. His heart thudded with fear. He pulled Caroline's body close to his chest as he surveyed the damage. Freya's house and barn were destroyed. Every building in the town had suffered major damage. Only two cabins still stood, but even those had been shoved far from their foundation rocks. Every outhouse had disappeared into splintered sticks. The smell rose from their uncovered holes. Swallowing hard, Gryf raised his gaze to the high meadow. The sight of twenty-canvas tents and a hundred milling people brought tears spilling down his cheeks.

They survived.

Samuel saw them first. He raised the alert and the town's people poured down from their haven to greet them. Running on stubby legs, Garland Wright shied away from Sol's muzzle. Marvelle fell to her knees and shouted, "Thank you, God. Thank you, Jesus."

Grinning, Samuel and Susan picked up their twins and whirled them around, singing a joyful, tuneless happiness while Jimmy Freya reached for the reins and led Sol into what had once been the school yard.

Leading the procession, Jimmy talked as blue a streak as ever his mother produced. "Mr. Williams, she'll be all right, won't she? She looks kinda peaked. Ain't she breathin'? We was that worried, ain't nobody said anything for two hours, just starin' out at the ridge, hopin' and hopin' to see ya . . ."

At the back of the crowd, Olaf stood next to Ellen Robertson, tears running down his face. His skis stood upright in a snow drift behind him. Ellen kissed Olaf and then strode toward Sol, her gaze on Caroline.

In her first sign of awareness since the flood, Caroline reached a hand toward Ellen, who held tight. Neither said anything, but Ellen helped Gryf lower Caroline to the stoop where his house once had been.

Before Gryf could wave her off, Deirdre enveloped Caroline in her arms.

"You saved us," she chirruped. "And aren't we thankful to have been above, on our own Mt. Ararat as the lake water flashed through town. It was the world's worst fright we had for you and our Gryf when we saw that wall of water . . ."

Gryf glanced at Mac. Mac seemed to understand. "Now darlin' wife," Mac said. We've got to leave that little girl to recover herself. She'll be needing good hot food. You come with me and get the lads and us organized to fix soup for all." Deirdre kissed Caroline's cheek several times and hurried off to do as Mac suggested.

Manuel Lauriggue and his family arrived soon after, bringing supplies from their own stores, including many dry blankets to keep the homeless warm.

Climbing down from weary Sol, Gryf wrapped Caroline in one of Teresa Lauriggue's fine wool serapes. He remembered her paisley shawl crashing against the boulders. On impulse, he held Caroline's face between his hands, rested his forehead against hers and closed his eyes. Her shivering hands grasped his wrists and held on.

Still she could not seem to speak. She had not spoken much since Alex went over the ridge into the roaring lake water. When they had ridden past Rankin's trapped body, she'd whimpered, turned into Gryf's chest, and not made a sound since. Here in By-Gum, finding all safe, she continued to shiver uncontrollably. Gryf pulled back and glanced at her.

"Where are you hurt?"

She shook her head, a motion so slight that he was not sure she had made it. "I'll find ye a place to sleep – dry, and warm," he promised.

She closed her eyes. Helplessly, he turned toward the rest of the town, mentally assessing the damage, searching for a place of safety for every member – especially for her.

Samuel took Sol. "I'll rub him and feed him."

Gryf nodded. Then he studied the devastation. The blacksmith's shop still stood but was ripped open at one corner. The school had been broken into two separate open squares. He followed the gouging, ripping path of the water and found desks, benches and wood stoves and mining tools had been driven by the water until they hung up in the turn of the creek bed, or smashed into the rock below the high meadow.

He saw a signal between Olaf and Samuel and realized they had discovered Alex's body, come to rest at the corner of the blacksmith's shop. Gryf gestured to Ellen. Ellen nodded and held Caroline against her, waving for Gryf to go. He groped through the muddy work yard to the spot where Alex lay. Alex' clothes were sodden. One shoe had been ripped by the water and rock. A large gash yawed near his hair line where he must have hit rock on the way down.

"I'll build this coffin," Samuel said, waving Gryf off. "Take her up to your tent."

Gryf glanced from Alex's body back toward Caroline's pale skin and darkened eyes. He drew in a deep breath, holding his head back, as if glaring at the sky could erase his distress. Samuel stepped between Alex's body and Gryf. "He's dead. You're alive, and she's hurting. Can't anybody undo what he done to her, but we can take care of each other."

Gryf looked once more at Alex's bruised body. "What hell was he living in?"

"A hell he heaped on himself."

Gryf studied Samuel's worried face a moment, then strode toward Caroline.

**

Caroline felt the heat of him as he scooped her into his arms and climbed to the tent city above the valley. Safety. He was safety in all this chaos. At the door to one of the tents, she heard Ellen's voice.

"We've started cooking fires," Ellen said. "You lay her inside, then bring hot water. She'll be better with a friend for a time, and a hot bath."

"I'm not leaving her," he said and shoved aside the tent flap. Inside the tent, there was warmth, a mattress on the ground, and some of his gear. Light poured through the canvas walls. He lay her gently on the mattress, wrapping the serape more closely about her. She allowed sleep to overtake her.

Hours later, Caroline awoke in his arms. She no longer shivered, but her head ached. Ellen entered the tent, put a hand on Gryf's shoulder and nodded toward the door.

"She needs a mother," Ellen whispered. Caroline realized she was right. The terrible tension inside her came from trying to blot away all that had happened since she arrived at Alex's house. Alex had done what the soldiers did – everything she thought she could keep from happening again, well nearly all of it. Not that. Not what killed her mother, and left her own body so battered she couldn't eat properly for months. And she had never wanted Gryf to know she'd been treated that way – by a man he thought he loved.

Gryf kissed her forehead. "I'll bring hot water for you, Sweetheart."

While he was gone, heating the water, Ellen rubbed Caroline's arms and legs, warming her feet and hands and singing simple nursery rhymes as if Caroline were a hurt child. She lay on the mattress and let Ellen baby her. Soon, she heard Gryf bring in a tin washtub.

"This tub is mighty banged up, but I found it down by the schoolhouse."

"Set it there," Ellen said, "Then scoot."

Several trips with hot water followed. Then, reluctantly, he did leave them alone.

Minutes later, Caroline eased herself into the bath, where she almost fell asleep. As Ellen washed her hair and scrubbed her back, Caroline stared about the tent. Amazingly, there was a small wood stove hooked up in the corner. As soon as she saw it, Caroline realized that the stove in Gryf's cabin must have been overturned by Alex, in search of something. She believed she knew what he had so desperately wanted to find – the papers she'd discovered in the lining of the trunk.

Miraculously, someone had thought to rescue Gryf's trunk. It sat in the tent corner opposite the stove. She breathed a sigh of relief at the sight of it. When she dried off, she found a clean night gown waiting for her.

"It's mine," Ellen explained. "Olaf and Samuel warned us of Alex's plans. We packed everything we could and climbed to your meadow – set up a chain gang to haul supplies out of harm's way – your suitcase and papers, too. We even stored Deirdre's sourdough starter up here."

Caroline smiled at the image – Deirdre saving her starter. Slipping the flannel over her head, she felt human for the first time in several days. "Now your turn," she said to Ellen.

"You're talking again!"

409

"I'll be fine." Hearing resonance in her own voice, Caroline realized she was already much stronger. And that was when she had the courage to tell Ellen about the renegades and the bleeding.

Ellen explained to Caroline everything that her aunts and grandmother should have told her long ago.

"Why did they lie to me?"

Ellen shook her head. "To control you, perhaps. Embarrassment in a judgmental community. Who knows?"

"They made me hate myself. It made me pretend to be a boy."

Ellen laughed. "It's what made you be enough of a boy to fool the professors at college, right?"

Caroline looked up at her, surprised that she'd guessed.

Ellen said, "I can't think of many girls who haven't dreamed about fooling old men exactly that way. Think if all girls had such a chance to get what boys get for an education."

Caroline smiled. "I did that." Then she looked down at herself. "Well, I did it long enough, and then I couldn't."

"By the time you became beautiful, you also had become an excellent engineer. You became more than them. And I love you for pulling it off."

Caroline felt so warmed she could hardly speak. "Thank you, Ellen."

Ellen smiled and hugged her. "You sit on the bed and talk to me while I take my bath," Ellen suggested, "then we'll get Marie and Deirdre in here. Right now, they're bathing the children in Marie's tent."

Caroline sat. "Poor Gryf. He's going to have a long line of bathers between him and his home."

"With the outhouses knocked over, and debris mucking the downstream waters of Dyfi Creek, we've got to avoid illness. After cleanup, the men will bathe in Samuel's tent."

Afraid of the answer, Caroline asked, "How is Duncan?"

"He's getting better."

"He was hurt so badly by Stemmin's bullet ..."

"Yes," Ellen said, "It will take time to recover so much blood. But Deirdre is making sure he gets the biggest portion of meat from every stew."

Relieved, Caroline laughed. Then she asked, "Everyone is safe?"

Ellen nodded vigorously. "Everyone. The buildings are destroyed, but the people are here."

Caroline said, "I borrowed your horse."

"Olaf says she's in Alex's barn. We'll bring her down tomorrow, and all the fodder for everyone's animals."

"How will we feed each other when the crops near Freya's are all ruined?" Caroline asked.

"Samuel says Alex has a lot of food stored in his place. Sam even brought that stupid servant from Alex's ranch this evening. She is the sister of Emmett, the man with the queue. And the other one is her son. When Samuel and Mac put together those three people's separate, garbled stories, it looks like they all had a grievance against Alex's father – servants he fired for some reason."

"So, they joined Alex to get revenge," Caroline guessed.

"Revenge? Why did Alex want revenge?"

Caroline stopped, surprised into realizing that she'd been about to spill something only Gryf should know. Ellen seemed to catch on quickly, ducking her head, rubbing soap berry into her hair and changing the subject. "We've got to bring the oxen and horses down from Lauriggue's pasture to help rebuild the town. Not even Mac's barn is standing."

Overwhelmed with the work ahead, Caroline asked, "How are we going to resettle the cabins that are still intact?"

Ellen grinned. "We've got tools. You will not believe the huge winch that Abel attempted to deliver to us this morning."

"Abel? The telegrapher?"

Ellen glanced at her, "He also brought the straw hat to the Marshal. Said Letitia Heenie, down in Isabeau, told him "That nice young man, Alex Kemp, bought this hat.""

Caroline lowered her head, remembering the two different Alex Kemp's she had known – one a teasing, gentleman with many friends, the other a vicious murderer filled with hatred. Pushing Alex from her mind, she asked, "Did the flood smash the winch Abel brought?"

"No," Ellen said, allowing the change of subject by resuming her washing motions, "We sent Abel and two other wagon-loads of machinery right back up the road to the highest point. There was a long, awful moment when we thought the flood had reached them. Then we saw the water turn and go over the drop across all those switchbacks toward Isabeau."

Caroline imagined their moments of fear as the water rushed toward them, wondering if they were high enough, if it would undermine the cliff beneath the meadow and drag them into the maelstrom – holding tightly to the children, watching, praying. She put her head in her hands and shuddered. Ellen gazed at her from the tub.

"One other thing Abel brought up," Ellen said. "A Mrs. Porter found a great coat with a fur collar and cuffs in her guest bedroom. She wanted the marshal to have it because it had to have been left there by the murderer."

"Alex's coat," Caroline whispered.

"Yes. Samuel recognized it. And he knew what it meant."

Caroline let her head lean on her knees. "What twisted his mind?"

Ellen whispered, "Did Alex hurt you, my friend?"

Caroline shook her head. "He . . . he tried, but . . . he had to blow up the dam before he could . . .." Remembering the long ride from Alex's ranch, she pulled the serape about her again. "He . . . I

412

couldn't do anything to stop him. At first, I felt helpless. Then, only anger." She couldn't meet Ellen's eyes, staring instead at the blanket chest.

"I'm sorry," Ellen said. "I wish it hadn't been you who found him out."

Caroline gazed at Ellen. "It's Gryf I worry about. He nearly died up there, trying to save that scum."

Ellen nodded as she lathered her hair. "Alex always felt his wealth and good looks gave him rights, but I never thought it was more than being a spoiled son-of-a-lord."

"Did he . . .?"

Ellen shrugged. "After my husband died, Alex made one wrong move. I threatened him with a gun. He laughed and left."

Caroline tried to smile, but tears raced down her cheeks instead. "I'm glad I met you." She rose, a little wobbly, but strong enough to fill a pitcher to rinse Ellen's hair.

"We'll do fine." Ellen said, and bent her head to take the rinse.

**

In the darkness, Caroline woke with a sense of warmth. She saw that the interior of the large tent had been changed. She lay on a real bed instead of a mattress on the floor. Beyond the bed, a wall of blankets surrounded her. Someone had constructed a way to keep her warm.

Aware of a low firelight somewhere beyond the blankets and the tent walls, she turned toward it. Next to her, Gryf sat in a rocking chair – a chair that had not been in the tent when she fell asleep.

"Where'd the rocker come from?"

He dragged in a long, slow breath before answering. "Samuel loaned it to me. It belonged to our mother." His dark gray eyes watched her, testing a smile as she rose on her elbow.

"*Cariad*, you are safe with me," he whispered.

413

"This I know, Beloved." She saw him swallow hard before he leaned forward and took her hand in his.

"I'm sorry," he said. "I never saw what he'd become."

"He didn't want you to see it," she whispered. "He put great energy into making you believe in him."

"I thought I had come too late, that you had drowned." His voice broke. He bowed his head over her hand, touching her fingers with his lips.

She pulled him from the chair to the edge of the bed and caressed his startled face with her hands. "All the way to the lake," she whispered, "I wished I had shown you how much I love you."

He held her hands near his face. Turning, he kissed her palm – a chaste and careful kiss. But with her other hand, she caressed his ear. His gasp surprised her. Caroline pulled herself to a sitting position, bracing her hands on his shoulders. She realized only then that Ellen's taste in gowns was somewhat more daring than her own had ever been. The gown exposed her throat and shoulders. Gryf stared at her, and yet attempted to keep himself from staring. She leaned toward him, touching her lips to his, caressing his beard with one hand and his ear with the other.

He leaned into her kiss and the sensuous caress. When she stopped to breathe, he smiled. "Do you mean to do this?"

She nodded.

"It's not just a reaction to fear?"

She shook her head. "It is what I should have done the night you came to my room above the barn. I promised myself, if we lived, I would let my love for you be more important than my fearsome memories."

He studied her face, then allowed himself to gaze at her body. In the low light, she saw the lines near his eyes go soft, just as they had when she first argued with him. This time, she reveled in his

414

appreciative enjoyment. She sat up straighter, offering to his view the roundness she once despised. His glance returned to her face.

"You are changed."

She glanced down and saw how very much the gown showed off her body. Still, embarrassed at her own brazen ways, she managed to be honest with him, forcing her words through the tightness in her throat.

"All day, I wanted it to be you, touching me."

"My God," he rasped, wrapping his arms around her back and pulling her to rest against his chest. There she found safety and release. Crying, she began to let go of the long day's horrible fears and humiliations. As she wept, he massaged her back, her shoulders, her neck. Murmuring soft Welsh words, Gryf rocked her until her tears were exhausted. For a long time, she rested against him, then reached around his back, drawing tension from his spine and shoulders as she talked.

"I never again want to wish I'd given you my love." She glanced up at him. He bit his lip. She touched her finger to his mouth, making his body jerk. "I want to be yours" she said. "I want to lie next to you, touch you. I want to give you all that I am and bring you peace."

He sat very still. After a long moment, he whispered. "Tomorrow?"

"Tonight."

As he studied her, his brow furrowed. After a moment, he nodded and then let out a long breath. "Caroline, will you to stand on this rug and take off that gown?"

She hesitated only a moment, realizing he tested her resolve. She pushed aside the quilt, set her feet on the rag rug and stood before him, embarrassed and determined. She crossed her arms in front of herself, reaching for the fabric. He stopped her motion with his hand.

415

"Wait." He stood and lifted his shirt over his head. His shoulders glistened in the low light. The curls on his chest encircled his nipples and darkened his sternum, outlining his muscles. Glancing at her, he smiled – a tentative warmth.

"Tell me when to stop." He reached for the buttons at his waist.

She took in short, courage-gathering breaths. As he bent to take off his work pants, she lifted her gown over her head. When he straightened, his eyes opened wide in surprise, and then he sighed. She glanced at his face. His dark gaze returned frequently to her eyes, as if testing his effect on her. Seeing her unflinching gaze, he returned to caressing her naked body with the warmth of his appreciation.

"More beautiful even than I imagined," he whispered. "I've lain in bed, staring at my rafters, remembering your supple strength, the red lights in your hair, the fear in your eyes, and never once believed we would have this moment."

She saw how the sight of her changed his body. She too felt changes, fever and excitement at the nearness of him, yet also daring beyond what she'd ever known. She reached out to touch his arm, but he wrapped his arms about her, pulling her closer, slowly closer until her belly touched the heat of him. She stepped toward him, feeling his smooth skin rest against her.

His voice was rough with passion. "*Cariad*, ye'd best agree to marry me."

"After I know we can do this."

His chuckle was low and sensuous. "It's fair evident at least, that I can." He moved his hands on her back, exploring her spine, running his thumbs up her sides to brush the outer curve of her breasts. She pushed closer to him, letting her nipples touch his chest.

"Ahh!" He dropped his head back, his mouth open. Watching his face tighten with pleasure, Caroline marveled at how safe and clean she felt while next to this wonderful man.

Gryf smoothed one hand up to her neck. Tilting her head back, he touched her lips with his, tasting the edges of her mouth. By barely touching her, his kisses brought warm turmoil to her whole body.

To control sensation, she crossed her thighs, causing her to thrust one knee between his legs.

"Never do that," he gasped.

"I'm sorry," she whispered, trying to jump back. But his hands took her hips, pulling her more tightly into him.

"Lie down, Sweetheart." He bent over her, levering her onto the mattress.

As soon as she lay on her back, she felt helpless, like a ten-year-old thrown down, pinned to the dirt in a corn field. The dry *tsk-tsking* of cornstalks roared in her mind. "No!" She twisted to her side, nearly causing him to fall from the bed.

He sat up, breathing heavily, his mouth pulled tightly against his teeth. A moment later, he opened his eyes, studying her. "Please, sit up," he said, while offering her a hand.

She rose. He kept his attention on her as he lay down on his back, exactly where she had been moments ago. Pulling the quilt over her shoulders, he whispered, "Touch me, Cariad."

She hesitated.

"My shoulders. My arms."

She reached out, testing her courage again. Within moments, her body warmed to him. She took his hand, placing it on her thigh. In the low light, she watched his gaze caress her breasts, while she brushed her hands over his shoulders. His hand moved slowly over her thigh, down to her knee, playing with the soft skin along the inside of her calf. Her most private self, hot and moist, ached for his touch.

And then she knew. He had the same ache in him. Caroline moved her hand from his arm to his chest, brushing across his taut nipples. He closed his eyes and gripped her knee, turning his body toward her hand.

She watched his reaction with awe. *I can satisfy his desires.*

Soft caresses across his abdomen brought a low moan from him. He opened his eyes to watch her face.

"I love your hands on me," he whispered. "Strong, light. Silk across my skin.

She let her hand trail down his body, skirting his center to tease him with fingernails against his hip bone and on down his thigh. He tightened his lips, holding back frustration.

Then she saw his eyelids crinkle – a sure sign of his humor rising. His hand, which had gripped her knee when he was enjoying her caresses, smoothed its way slowly up her thigh. She rose on her knees, almost without thinking, as if to escape his approach. If that were her body's intention, she soon realized that kneeling was no escape. Instead, it left her vulnerable.

His hand held her taut thigh as he rose. Sitting, he leaned a little forward and took the nipple of her breast into his mouth, scraping it lightly with his teeth. Her body jerked. She gripped his shoulder and pushed toward the disturbing motion of his mouth.

"Uhmm," he sighed. His lips sucked her breast. His hand inched further up her thigh. She wanted him to arrive, to get it over with, to stop tantalizing. Her pelvis leaned toward him. His fingers moved closer. He sucked with more vigor at her nipple. His free hand smoothed its way up the back of her leg. Every part of her body wanted him, more, closer, stronger. But he continued to touch her lightly, insistently.

Gryf pulled back his head to study her face. To her embarrassment, she moved so that her breast sought out his lips once again. He gave a low laugh and kissed her breasts, and then whispered. "I want you. Wanted you like this for so long I thought I was going to explode with frustration."

"Show me what to do."

"Touch me, Caroline."

She drew back, not at all sure what he meant. Then he dropped his hands to the bed and leaned back slightly so that she could see how turgid he had become through their play. She glanced up again to his face. He was watching her, patiently, but his chest rose and fell rapidly, as if he were trying to control deep pain.

Reaching tentatively, she tested the feel of him against her finger. His hips thrust up toward her, his long legs dropping open.

"Please," he whispered fiercely.

She brushed her fingers down his length. He fell to the pillow, exposing himself completely to her. For the first time, she realized that at the base of his shaft, there were two round parts. To her, they seemed tender and easily hurt. She had a rush of desire to care for him. She bent over, touching her hand to his warm member and let its smoothness grow even greater as she felt him. Moving her fingers down his length, she cupped his roundness.

His body pushed hard up into her hands. "*Cariad*!" he groaned.

His hands took her shoulders, pulling her away from her ministrations. "Enough!" he rasped, and pulled her onto his chest, folding one arm about her back, cupping her head to his chest with the other.

His breath came in gasps for long moments. Then he whispered, "I never thought ye could drive me so wild."

They lay there, Caroline not knowing what to do next, but sensing she had taken his request much beyond anything he'd expected. She might have been embarrassed to have been so forward, but she found herself instead, thinking about how soft his body was down there, and how sensitive. She found herself wishing to try new ways to bring this ecstasy to him.

Then his hand sought out her breast, and she pushed it toward him.

"My love," he moaned. "Ye'd best lie very still or I won't be able to keep from hurting ye."

She held very still. "You cannot hurt me."

"I can, sure as anything, take you faster than you're ready for."

Beyond embarrassment, beyond any thought, she knew only the desire to have him touch her more solidly, to bring this long wanting to some fruition. She had no idea what might stop these sensations. She just wanted to be known in some complete way by his hands and his body.

He touched her with one finger.

A wave of sensation began from deep within her, rising and ebbing. "Gryf!" she cried. "Oh!"

He seemed to have been waiting for this moment. His fingers moved, caressing.

"Hold on to me," he whispered as he kissed her ear. "Hold on tight, Sweetheart."

She gripped his shoulders.

"Yes," he murmured. "Yes, Darling, let it come to you."

Then suddenly, he stopped touching her. As he rolled to his back, she cried, "Please."

He smiled tightly, pulling her quickly on top of his chest. "Put your legs astride me."

She looked blankly at him.

"Now," he ordered, pulling her thigh across his belly. She glimpsed his meaning and moved. His long hands gripped her hips.

"Yes," she sighed, sinking toward this new caress.

"Slowly," he groaned. "I am bigger than my fingers."

But she wanted the warmth and the smoothness of him against her unsatisfied body. She took him into her, feeling heat in the parts of her body he had caressed. He was more than she had expected, but she could not slow her desire to have him. He held her hips high and eased her down. A new and stronger wave arose within her.

"Ah love, now!" he cried out. He let his hips rise, pressing himself into her fully at last. Breathing hard, he pulled her to him, kissed her ear and whispered words she could not understand – except that she did understand.

He was saying what she wanted to say but knew no words. And soon, neither needed words, only the sensation of his hands caressing her body, pressing against her hips, pushing her closer and closer as sensation overtook them.

A long shudder escaped him as he thrust into the depths of her. His motion brought a tightness to her limbs and a concentration of all attention on the place where they joined. Both of them held still, letting their intimate touch imprint on their memory.

He brushed his fingers up her hips, her back to her sides, across the swelling of her breasts and up to her underarms. He lifted her slightly, gazed at her before he brought her mouth close to his for a soft kiss.

Caroline growled, low in her throat, thrust her fingers into his curly hair and kissed him hard. Within her body, his shaft came once more to life, delving again for hot liquid.

"You," he whispered, "are more valuable than all the anthracite in the world."

She smiled down at him, moving her hips to enhance his desire. "I hope you never discover that I am truly Fool's Gold."

He laughed and pulled her closer, running his fingers once more on their path down her eager body.

CHAPTER THIRTY-NINE

Gryf allowed his eyelids to open slightly as Caroline slid from beneath the quilt. He forced himself not to reach for her, but merely watched the satin-soft curves of her nakedness as she walked away from him. On this, their first morning – he hoped it was only the first – she would need to repossess herself, to think through what they had done last night. He would await her verdict in silence.

His body heated as she knelt to pick up something from the floor. Her sweet buttocks rested against her heels. Her breasts swayed when her arms reached out for the object of her attention. Her thighs tightened, and she rose with that graceful, smoothness he had seen her use several times. She slipped into his flannel shirt, buttoned it, and then thrust her foot into the leg of his gabardine pants. Almost rising, he tensed, waiting to see what she planned. By the time she took her boots and stepped out into the waking tent-town, it was too late. She'd taken the only clothes he might wear.

A half-hour later, wrapped in the quilt, he sat in the rocking chair before his reconstructed wood stove. A makeshift clothesline ran from one end of the tent to the other. On it hung his flood ravaged clothes. When she pulled back the tent opening behind him, he knew it was Caroline. He poked a stick into the fire and said, "Close the door. I can't heat the whole valley, and also dry my apparel."

She laughed and closed the tent flap. "You've a very good hand for house cleaning. Already this looks better."

"I ought to be out helping the other men."

"They're doing fine. They saved my papers and I needed some of those papers for this morning."

Turning, he saw that she had removed her boots. She set her pack down nearby. He waited in unbearable tension as she walked softly toward him. "Are you warm enough?" he asked.

She smiled. "You're not usually so oblique."

"Meaning?"

"Yes, last night was wonderful. And yes, I still love you."

The pent-up air gusted out of him. "Thank God!" he roared, reaching for her waist. She came, willing and happy, toward his knees. He let his knees open and pulled her, standing, between them, right to the front of the rocker seat. Her leg brushed his thigh in soft promise.

Laughing down at him, she bent slightly, pulled his head to her breast, and said, "We can start that again soon, but first you must know something."

Resting his head against his own shirt where it disguised her softness, he whispered, "So. You do know what drove Alex."

She hugged him, her reluctance to talk evident in her silence. After several moments, she let her hands fall from his head and shoulders. He sat up. She grabbed up her pack and walked across the room to sit near his blanket chest. "Come look at this." She pulled a set of papers from her pack.

He shrugged out of the quilt and the rocking chair and, stepped toward her, dressed only in his briefs. She glanced at his chest but drew a folded paper from an envelope and handed it to him. He scanned it and remembered it as one she'd brought from Isaac's hidden files. It was written by the man who had petitioned Isaac for help in locating his family. Puzzled, Gryf took it and reread its contents.

"Mr. Wood?"

"Not simply mister. Lord Forest, seeking his sons."

A sharp knife of apprehension jabbed Gryf in the stomach. "No." He shook his head. "This man seeks his family – two sons. Lord Forest had but Alex."

Caroline stood and opened the blanket chest. "I found this when I searched for your metal clippers." She fussed at the edge of the lining paper, drawing out a photo.

He took it from her. As soon as he saw what she'd found, his heart threatened to stop. Then it rushed, thudding in pain against his ribcage. In a worn, browned photo stood his lovely mother, her young face serene, her carriage proud. She offered a cup on a tray to Lord Forest. It was the look on the lord's face that pained his heart. Love, admiration, desire – all that Gryf felt for Caroline was there in that young and hopeful visage. And when Gryf glanced once more at his mother, he saw the cost of those passions. Her white apron thrust forward so slightly another viewer might have thought her inclined to pudginess. But he knew she'd never carried an ounce of fat. And the high, shelving effect of the thrust made it plain – she carried a child.

His hot eyelids closed. "Me," he said. And he knew it for truth. It explained so many things – the hatred his father visited on his mother; and the sea of venom in which the man tried to drown him.

He remembered that moment in the door yard, "Rhodri Williams sold his finest possession for position. God knows I was besotted enough to buy. And now we all shall pay."

his finest possession . . .

Caroline pulled the rocker behind him, wrapped him in the quilt and thrust him back into the chair. He dropped his head against the headrest, and he let her prop his feet upon a box. Except for her loving face, present time appeared to gray as the past rushed in upon him.

424

How could I not have known? Alex and me. Our hair was different. Hair, and mother's darker skin. But size and build, not like Samuel. So, when did Alex begin to hate?

And then he remembered what Alex had asked him just a few days ago: All the way back to the boatman who tried to drown Samuel and me in the Dyfi River.

Was even that a part of these insane things Alex did?

Oh God, give them peace – Isaac, Jesse, Terry, and all the others – back, and back, and back to . . .

Gryf sat up. "Why? Did Alex tell you why?"

She nodded. "He said you robbed him of his future, of his position."

"How could I have done that? Lord Forest treated me like Samuel, like any child of any tenant."

"Who shot your father?"

Her question startled him. "They were out hunting . . ." Of a sudden, the realization flooded in on him. Alex could have lain in wait for an opportunity – Rhodri, his father, beating the undergrowth, scaring the fox out of hiding, unaware of danger . . . Gryf stared at Caroline. "How did you know about the shooting?"

"He said – Alex muttered it twice – 'I should have shot Johanna. Rhodri meant nothing.'"

Gryf covered his face with his hands and collapsed to his rocker. He rocked slowly, remembering that last day when his mother had smoothed dust from Lord Forest's jacket.

He recalled what Samuel had said to him recently about Lord Forest sending them away to keep them safe. Like Alex, his brother had been older – six years old when Gryf was born, twelve when the shooting happened.

He raised his gaze to Caroline's worried face. "What does Samuel know?"

425

She shook her head. "He's not told me. But this morning, he ran to me as I headed back here with the letter. He urged me to give you a message. "If Gryf needs to talk to his brother, tell him I'm rebuilding Freya's barn.""

Gryf reached out and took her hand in his. "What else do you know?"

"Lord Forest disowned Alex after the shooting."

"Alex told you that?"

She nodded. "Yes, and there are other papers hidden in the lining of that trunk."

He glanced at the trunk, afraid of what else his mother might have hidden in there. Instead of investigating, he pulled Caroline into his lap "Anything more?"

"Yes. The By-Gum loan contract is in Alex library, in the shelf left of his desk. His great coat was found in Mrs. Porters's home, in the room where he escaped out the window, wearing the blue fisherman's jacket and the straw hat."

Gryf bowed his head. "Isaac, oh Isaac."

She held him as he cried. Above him, she also let her tears run down her cheeks and into his hair.

All his good friends, his trusted friends . . .

Minutes later, he straightened and touched her forehead with his. "What else do you know?"

She settled her head against his shoulder. "Deirdre says that three men arrived in By-Gum during the night. A fellow named Howard Smith has brought a load of tools to build a smelter. Besides him, my father arrived with the real Lord Forest, Richard Kemp."

Gryf tried to stand up. "Your father is here?"

She held onto the arms of the rocker, effectively keeping him down. She continued talking as if they were not engaged in a tug of war. "Wasn't it a fortuitous circumstance? They met in the train station in Denver and realized they had the same destination."

426

"Alex's body!" Gryf protested.

"Samuel built a coffin last night. Alex is laid out as clean as they could make him."

"But your father . . ."

"And Deirdre is feeding Smith, Lord Forest and Dad, along with the rest of the town in what's left of the school-house kitchen – says she's been keeping them occupied until we awoke and got decent, as she puts it."

Gryf was able to stand with her in his arms. "Give me my clothes so I can meet your father."

"*My* father?"

"I've something important to ask him," he said.

"What would he know?"

"Will he allow you to marry me?"

She gave him an impish smile. "Will Lord Forest want a commoner for a daughter-in-law?"

He felt coldness burn the edges of his love. He set Caroline gently on her feet. "Lord Forest will have nothing to say in the matter."

She turned a somber gaze toward him. "Gryffyth Williams, you will hear him out."

The coldness became a hard thing in his chest. "He left my mother with two sons, an invalid husband and nothing . . ."

"They are letters, bank drafts and a will."

He jerked to attention. "What are you talking about?"

"Last night, while Ellen was fetching the others and more hot water for their baths, I looked at the other papers in the trunk lining. They are from him. He named you his heir. He tried to support all of you, but she never deposited the drafts."

Gryf closed his eyes and leaned into Caroline. "Why? Why?"

"You will only know if you listen to him."

He sighed deeply. Too tired of fear, and too warmed by her concern to fight her, he gave in. "After we bury Alex, he'll have his say, then."

She put her arms around him, a solid support in the maelstrom of his emotions. "I will marry you, Gryf." she said.

He pulled her close, inhaling the sweet smell of her hair and her warm neck. "Thank God I have you," he murmured, kissing her ear and then letting his lips trail up her hairline to her temple.

"There is one thing," she said.

He leaned back, raising an eyebrow as he awaited her condition.

She turned her green eyes up to him, and he noted with pleasure that she jutted out her chin, belligerently.

"I will need a new dress. What with all these explosions, and one disaster after another, I've ruined all three of mine."

His deep rumble of uncontrollable laughter surprised even him. As he swept her into his arms and carried her toward their bed, he realized he was possibly the only man ever to be thankful when asked to finance a new wardrobe.

While unbuttoning his shirt from her body, he whispered, "First, we have to measure you for size."

About the Author

Rae Richen is author of adventures for adults and young
adults, of romantic suspense and of the forthcoming Glyn Jones and
Grandma Willie mystery series. Join Rae Richen as we explore fear and
power, greed and human need in short stories and novels, articles,
interviews and essays.

Using family relationships and the backdrop of historical events, Rae
Richen writes to bring focus to the themes that drive our human
race. The characters in these stories face a confusing world of
hypocrisy with courageous honesty. The humor, friendships, and
caring they bring to these situations help them forge new solutions
to age-old problems.

Learn more about this author at www.raerichen.com or contact her at
rae@raerichen.com .

Thank you all!

To the author and teacher, James N Frey author of *A Long Way to Die, Winter of the Wolves* and other fiction and of *How to Write a Damn Good Novel*. Thanks, James for urging me to choose two characters who must duke it out with each other because they have opposite goals. "Put 'em in a pot and turn up the heat."

Thanks also to Dale Jolly, for his very exciting class at Portland State on geology and the social and historical implications of the physical world in which a character lives.

Dale, I hope you finally were able to study the highly developed cultures of medieval Africa. Maybe you went back after apartheid was demolished. You had me fascinated with the little that you were able to glean before the fearful white government of South Africa shut you down.

Thank you to C.J. Trewartha for his very well-written and clear textbook on geology. Your book was an inspiration to one who wanted to know more and still wants to know.

Thank you to the late Bonnie Bean Graham who discovered and brought me the ancient red book on mining techniques of the late 1800s. Bonnie, you were always thinking of others and on the lookout for what they needed. We all miss you.

Thank you to Trash and Treasures, a resale store in Rockaway Beach, Oregon. In your back room, I discovered the treasure of a poster on coal mining techniques.

Thank you, also, to the collieries and the mining museums of Wales, Canada and Colorado that accept inquisitive visitors and answer their questions politely and patiently.

A note on language:

Welsh is a language in process, just as are all languages that live. And thank goodness Welsh is alive. For instance, when I began learning Welsh, on behalf of a relative who could no longer read, the word most often used for 'Yes' was 'oes' meaning "It is.". In the last many years, I've come to understand that Welsh has no direct equivalent for 'Yes' or 'No'. Questions are answered by using the verb. Ydw means 'I do'. 'Ydich' means you do and so forth. Oes still means 'it is'. A question and answer protocol in Welsh does not call for a simple 'yes'.

In similar change processes, the word 'gwydden', is now an archaic word. In part, that is because the word is very like a verb 'to know'. Gwydden can be an imperfect form of 'we knew'.

In the time of our story, it meant 'forest" or 'woods'. More common now is 'y goedwig' (the forest), 'coedwig' (a forest) or even 'coed' or simply 'fforest'.

There is another word similar to Gwydden, though not the same. It is the name of the county in which the River Dyfi exists, but it is so similar that we won't confuse the issue by more discussion now. You can look it up if curious.

The name form, Gryffyth ap Rhodri ap Withliam (the son or daughter of Rhodri who was the son of William) is not often used now in the United States but may still be in use in some parts of Wales. Gryf's own name would have had many spellings as time changed and as his family moved to new places in the world.

Also, even in his time, Gryf's name might have been written Gryffydd, or Gryffith, or as Griffidd. But English readers would not have known that dd is pronounced th as in think. So, ...

Language change is inevitable, though purists in every country would like for it to be immutable. I remind you that in the United

States 'momentarily' used to mean 'for a moment' but television and radio usage has caused it to become 'in a moment'.

Announcers say they will be back momentarily, but they come back a few hundred advertisements later and hang on for maybe twelve minutes before the next announcement about being back. What's an English speaker supposed to believe?

So, I'll be back momentarily with my next story of love, revenge, suspense and of those who use power over others.

See you in a moment, and for a few exciting hours, at any of the following titles:

Other tales of action and adventure

by Rae Richen

Uncharted Territory – a father-son adventure in the mountains and in learning to accept and love despite the fragility of life. Learn more: https://www.raerichen.com/books

Scapegoat: The Price of Freedom – a teen and his friends struggle with a culture of easy accusation during the McCarthy Anti-Communist era. Learn more: https://www.raerichen.com/books

Scapegoat: The Hounded – after September 11, 2001, a grandfather and grandson work to create safety and freedom for friends falsely accused of treason.
Learn more: https://www.raerichen.com/books

In Concert – A novel of suspense and romance when a famous musician is stalked by a vicious man who wants to own her and her son. Visit https://www.raerichen.com/in-concert and read the first chapter for free.

Frozen Trust – a novel of espionage and romance within the United States during World War II. Visit https://www.raerichen.com/frozen-trust and read the first chapter for free.

Sentinels of Solitude – a novel of suspense and love during a murderous land grab in the lush Willamette Valley of Oregon. Visit www.raerichen.Com/blog for the stories behind the story.

A Fool's Gold , a novel of treachery and romance in the Rocky Mountains

of Colorado during the mining fever of the 1880s. Visit
www.raerichen.com/blog for more information.

And coming soon . . .

Without Trace: A Glyn Jones and Grandma Willie Mystery

When seventeen-year-old Trace Gowen, the drummer in Glyn Jones's band, is kidnapped. Glyn, his Grandma Willie and his friends work to rescue him. They uncover a lot more than kidnapping.

Grandma Willie teaches writing at both the police academy and the nearby Federal prison. Her connections and Glyn's will lead them into a volatile and dangerous mob and threatens all the people they love.

Made in United States
Troutdale, OR
01/20/2024

16988755R00268